This
Fragile
Heart

BOOKS BY KATE HEWITT

A Mother's Goodbye
Secrets We Keep
Not My Daughter
No Time to Say Goodbye
A Hope for Emily
Into the Darkest Day

THE FAR HORIZONS TRILOGY
The Heart Goes On
Her Rebel Heart
This Fragile Heart

KATE HEWITT

This
Fragile
Heart

bookouture

Published by Bookouture in 2020

An imprint of Storyfire Ltd.
Carmelite House
50 Victoria Embankment
London EC4Y 0DZ
www.bookouture.com

ISBN: 978-1-80019-114-3
eBook ISBN: 978-1-80019-113-6

CHAPTER ONE

Boston, 1838

"My mam says you're a thornback, Miss, but I don't know what that is."

"A thornback?" Isobel Moore nearly choked on the word as she returned the slate to Patrick Finnegan, her eight-year-old pupil. He was a bright, cheeky child, and she couldn't tell if he was baiting her or not. It was perfectly possible; he often liked to test the limits of her patience. And today, with autumn closing in and another endless, empty evening ahead of her, Isobel felt as if she had very little patience indeed.

As much as she had come to love teaching the children of Boston's poor at the First School, days like today tried both her patience and her good will. Two of the older boys had scrapped and been sent home with a black eye and a bloody nose each; one of her youngest pupils, sweet Katie Rose, was home ill with what was feared to be dysentery. And her star pupil, Eileen O'Shaugnessy, had told her, at only ten years old, that this would be her last day of school for she was joining her ma and her older sisters sewing piecework in the dark, dank room they called home. Her eyesight, Isobel thought with a grim desolation, would be ruined by the time she was thirty, if not before.

And now Patrick Finnegan was giving her his cheeky grin, his eyes bright as buttons—he *did* know what a thornback was, she was sure of it. Isobel glanced around at the dozen other children in the little school room in Boston's North End, all looking at her with avid but not unkind curiosity, wondering how she was going to respond to the insult, for insult it surely was. No longer even a spinster, at twenty-eight Isobel was worthy of the spikier, more unpleasant appellation of thornback—a woman who was unmarried with absolutely no prospects at all, completely dried up and on the shelf—and even these little children knew it.

"If your mother means that I am not married, then she is correct," Isobel told Patrick, hating how stiff and prim she sounded yet unable to keep herself from it. A thornback indeed! "But it is not a discussion for this classroom, Patrick Finnegan. Check your sums."

Isobel returned to the front of the room, trying to keep her expression serenely unruffled. The barb shouldn't hurt her, she knew. She'd longed ago accepted her fate—or at least she'd tried to. Even so, it still stung, coming from a woman she'd never met who had arrived in this country only a few months ago and yet still had somehow comprehended the utter lack of Isobel's prospects.

Compared to her pupils, Isobel knew she had little to complain about. She was healthy, fed, warmly and well dressed, and able to occupy herself with worthwhile tasks. Yet the thought of returning home to the stuffy confines of her parents' house on Beacon Hill made her spirit wilt. She envisioned the dinner that Cook would have prepared: boiled ham, pigeon pie, and potatoes, followed by Washington cake or gingerbread and cream—all delicious and yet so stodgy and predictable, and accompanied by the equally predictable conversation between her and her parents as they all struggled to cover the awkwardness of having a nearly thirty-year-old daughter, unmarried, destined to live at home for the rest of her life.

It seemed quite incredible to think she'd once been the belle of Boston society—well, nearly—poised to marry an up and coming doctor. Oh, the dreams she'd cherished! She'd envisioned herself as Ian Campbell's wife, had hoped to elevate him into society, to stand proudly by his side... as Caroline Reid—now Campbell—was doing.

It was Caroline whom Ian loved... pretty, vain, spoiled, *silly* Caroline Campbell. At least she had been so when Ian had first fallen in love with her five years ago. Caroline, Isobel acknowledged reluctantly yet fairly, seemed to have grown up a little, matured into a lovely young woman who held her head high in society. When they met socially, Isobel could smile and chat and act for all the world as if her heart hadn't been broken into pieces by the man Caroline called her husband.

Despite his love for Caroline, Ian had behaved like a gentleman back then, and offered to marry Isobel when he'd realized the untenable position he'd put her in. Society had expected it, they'd appeared together so many times; although Isobel had painfully learned later that Ian had seen those pleasant evenings as nothing more than time spent with an affectionate little sister.

Isobel had refused to accept Ian's offer. She hadn't wanted a proposal made of pity, and she wouldn't relegate herself to such an unhappy role as the wife of a man who married out of duty, not love.

For the last five years Isobel had devoted herself to the First School, teaching and organizing the classroom, drawing the pupils—the children she would never have—close to her heart. The other two teachers had left for their own more domestic pursuits: Margaret, the wife of Isobel's brother Henry, had given up teaching when she'd had a child; and Ian Campbell's sister, Eleanor, now married to Margaret's brother, Rupert MacDougall, had headed West, where Rupert had been appointed a U.S. Marshal. Only Isobel had remained, half-wondering if she'd made the wrong choice five years ago, when she'd stood on her pride and told Ian she wouldn't marry him.

Outside the sun was starting to sink behind the battered warehouses and shanties of Boston's notorious North End. Isobel reached for the bell on her desk and rang it. "School dismissed," she called out, and the children began to scramble from behind their desks. Isobel went to the door, watching them head out into the dusky afternoon. Some of them would spend the rest of the afternoon and some of the evening helping their parents with work—assembling matchboxes, sewing piecework, or even hauling crates down at the docks. It made her ache, to think of these bright little souls having to work so hard at such a young age. Sometimes she wondered if she did more harm than good, giving them an education yet not the means to use it.

"I didn't mean it, Miss."

Patrick stood in front of her by the door, a look of earnest repentance on his freckled face. "I don't think you're a thornyback."

"It's thornback, not thornyback, Patrick," Isobel said with both a sigh and a smile. "Although not a word you ever need to use. I'll see you tomorrow." She gave him a quick pat on the head before he skipped off with the others.

Most of the time Isobel could ignore the pangs of longing she felt when she saw couples in society, or the swamping loneliness when she sat against the wall with the other matrons and spinsters at a tea dance or ball, tapping her foot to the music. She reminded herself of how blessed she was, to be intelligent and independent, with a calling as a teacher, surely one almost as high as that of wife or mother. She told herself she would rather have her freedom than a husband or child, although she didn't feel particularly free. She told herself all those things, but in moments such as these, when the day had been thankless and difficult and she'd just been called a thornback by a cheeky child, she didn't believe it. She struggled to keep her spirits from flagging; the temptation to wallow in bitterness and self-pity could become overwhelming, and did her no good at all.

"Ready, Miss?" John Caber, her brother Henry's man, had come into the schoolroom. He stood outside the door every day that she taught, simply as a precaution, for the streets around

North Square were not safe for a woman alone, or sometimes even for a man. John was well over six feet tall, and built like a mountain. He also, Isobel knew, carried a flintlock pistol in the pocket of his greatcoat.

Even with Caber's protection, Isobel knew her parents were not particularly comfortable with having her spending her days with what they saw as the denizens and dregs of Boston. It was only because Margaret had started the school as a pet charity project that she could teach here at all, and feel as if she were doing something worthwhile in the world.

"Yes, John. Thank you." Turning from the empty room, Isobel gathered her mantle and bonnet and headed with Caber into the chilly spring afternoon. The sun was beginning its descent behind the worn brick buildings of the square and already the streets were emptying, a cool breeze from the harbor bringing with it the sharp tang of brine and fish. In the hurrying crowds Isobel caught fragments of the Irish brogue that had become common in the North End, as ship after immigrant ship poured thousands of desperate souls into the city. Not, Isobel reflected, that they'd received a warm welcome; most shops had placards in their windows reading "Irish Need Not Apply".

Lost in her thoughts, with Caber like a dark shadow at her elbow, Isobel almost bumped into the man handing out tracts in front of the Seaman's Bethel.

"Good afternoon, Miss Moore!" Edward Taylor's voice was deep and mellifluous, only one of the reasons his vigorous sermons had dubbed him the finest orator in all of Boston. Yet Taylor was not a man of circumstance or stature; his work was amongst the poorest and roughest here in the North End, where he'd started his seaman's mission ten years ago.

Now he smiled, his eyes stern yet bright under his shock of dark hair, and he thrust a tract at Isobel, who had no choice but to accept the printed pamphlet with surprised grace.

"Adoniram Judson is back in America, after thirty-three years in Burma," he said in that stentorian voice that possessed the power to make Isobel straighten her spine even there on the street corner. "An inspiring man, and a wonderful preacher. He's speaking at the Bowdoin Street Church this Tuesday next. You would consider yourself most blessed to hear of his travails, Miss Moore."

"I'm sure I would." Isobel smiled faintly, the pamphlet still clutched in her gloved fist. "Thank you for availing me of such an opportunity, Father Taylor. Good day to you." If she'd kept her voice brisk to remind him of the distance between their social positions, he did not acknowledge it. He merely smiled, his eyes all too shrewd and knowing under his shaggy brows, and turned to the next passerby, a worn-looking woman in a threadbare shawl and patched dress.

Father Taylor was known to treat all alike, whether it was an Irish mill worker or a lady of some social standing as herself. It gave her only a moment of pique, and even that was softened by her own ashamed acknowledgement of her vanity. After five years of teaching the poorest and humblest of society, she still had pretensions to snobbery, and what for? The children in her school possessed more determination and grit than she did.

She stuffed the pamphlet in her reticule, and urged on by Caber, mounted the carriage.

The carriage rumbled away from the warehouses and tenements huddled by the harbor, past the pavilioned Quincy Market, little more than ten years old and yet already on the fringes of a slum, and finally to the more prosperous Beacon Hill.

Caber helped her from the carriage and Isobel swept into the house on Charles Street she'd always called her home. The elegant foyer was quiet, although Isobel heard a faint rustling from her father's study. She peeked past the half-opened door to see her father frowning down at a pile of papers, his half-moon spectacles perched on the rim of his nose.

Isobel watched him, noticing the worry lines drawn deeply from nose to mouth. She knew the financial crisis known as the Panic last year must have affected her father's business interests, as it had any of the businessmen involved in speculation. More than one of Boston's well-to-do families had suddenly found themselves in desperate straits, selling the family furniture and hiring their children out as governesses or tutors, or worse, living in pitiful dignity dependent on the charity of relatives.

Despite knowing of such people, Isobel realized she had not given more than a flicker of thought for her own family's circumstances. She'd assumed they were different, protected from such risks or dangers. The house on Charles Street was her home, and as much as its comforting confines sometimes seemed like a prison, she could not imagine living anywhere else—or in more reduced circumstances. Surely, with all the other disappointments she'd faced, she would be protected from *that*.

Now, however, as she looked at her father's careworn face, she wondered how badly his business interests had been affected. He certainly hadn't spoken of it, and never would. Neither would she ask. Her father sighed, glanced up, and then caught sight of Isobel. He frowned slightly before his face softened, and he beckoned her in.

"How were your pupils today, my dear?"

Isobel stepped into the private sanctum of her father's study, breathing in the comforting scents of pipe tobacco and polished leather. "As ever, I suppose, Father." She knew her father had, on occasion, wondered at the purpose of educating children who would do no more with their lives than work in the factories or mills, and Isobel didn't always have a clever answer. The answer she felt in her soul, an answer which shamed her a little, was that she was teaching as much for her own sake as her pupils'.

"You're well?" A little crease had appeared between her father's heavy brows, and Isobel knew he was worried about her, just as her mother was. Neither of them liked seeing her unhappy or restless; she was usually better at hiding it from them, but lately it had become more difficult to do so. *Thornback.* She forced a smile and then dropped a quick kiss on her father's forehead. "Of course, Father. A bit fatigued, perhaps, but nothing that cannot be repaired with a night's sleep."

"You must rest before supper, then. I don't want you becoming ill, Isobel." Her father was already worried about the diseases that ran rampant in the city's poorer neighborhoods—dysentery, cholera, typhoid fever. So far Isobel had remained healthy.

"No, indeed, I shall endeavor not to succumb." Smiling, she slipped from the room and headed upstairs, determined to cast off the gloom that had briefly enshrouded her in the quiet solitude of the school.

Once in her bedroom, she tossed her reticule on her bureau, and the pamphlet from Father Taylor fluttered to the floor. Isobel stooped to pick it up, glancing at it with little interest. Although she attended church every Sunday with her parents, she wasn't particularly interested in the fever that had been gripping so much of the country as of late, to hear about mission societies in far-flung places. Still, more out of boredom than any real interest, she scanned the pamphlet's typewritten text. *All Are Invited to Come and Hear of Mr. Judson's Adventurous Journeys and Inspiring Experiences!*

Isobel could hardly imagine being gone from this country for over thirty years, as Adoniram Judson had, or living in such a distant, different place as Burma. She could not even imagine what it looked like! She had certainly never read about it, or seen an illustration. What adventures had Adoniram Judson experienced? What tales might he tell? She placed the pamphlet on her bureau, thinking for a second that she might attend the lecture, and then dismissing it from her mind. It wasn't the sort of thing she ever attended, and she could not imagine she would know anyone there.

Isobel slipped a thin, leather-bound book from underneath a piece of embroidery, and then curled up on the chair as the last rays of sunlight slanted across the floor, and turned to her marked place already deep into the story of *The Runaway Orphan, a Romantic Tale by an Authoress*. Sighing happily, Isobel lost herself in the pages and forgot even to turn up the wick on the oil lamp as the fading sunlight cast longer shadows across the floor.

*

"The fact remains, and will always remain, that ether is a dangerous substance and utterly inappropriate for use in a hospital." James Henderson's voice rang out across the salon, leaving a ripple of speculative murmur in its wake.

Dr. Ian Campbell tensed as he listened to his superior make his blustering pronouncement. Across the room, he saw his wife Caroline stiffen as well, even as she kept smiling. She met his gaze and gave a tiny shake of her head.

After a second's pause, Ian heeded her silent warning, giving a terse nod before he managed a rueful smile even though anger surged through him at Henderson's posturing, and in his own home…! The man's arrogance had no bounds; Ian doubted he would consider, never mind acknowledge, the impropriety of speaking on such a matter in his host's drawing room.

It was an ill-kept secret that Ian had been experimenting with the use of ether as an anesthetic for the last five years. He funded these experiments with his own time and money, and yet still they were disapproved of by the stuffy old guard of Boston's medical community. James Henderson might have been choosing to be deliberately provocative, considering he was currently a guest at the soirée Caroline and Ian were putting on, but Ian suspected that his opinion was no more than what most of the others in the room that night thought, if they had an opinion on the matter at all.

Henderson was continuing to bluster, but interest had thankfully died when Ian had refused to take up the argument. He'd noticed the slyly speculative looks of some of the guests, and he ignored them. Within a few minutes the conversation had moved on to Mr. Alcott's controversial Temple School.

"No corporal punishment—Alcott insists that if anyone's hand is to be slapped, it should be the teacher's," a young woman confided, her hushed tone implying the delicious scandal of it all.

"Ridiculous. The man is a complete charlatan, and a blasphemer as well." Henderson spoke again, his voice raised querulously.

Ian's glance strayed to the ormolu clock on the mantle. He would have to sit through another hour of conversation at the very least. When Caroline had suggested these salons, fashioned after the ones that took place in a libertarian France, as described by the eminent Monsieur Tocqueville who had graced the American shores in the early 1830s, Ian had eagerly agreed.

They had both envisioned impassioned argument and lively debate, the exchange of ideas, or at least the respect of them, like the kind of conversations they had had with Henry and Margaret Moore or Rupert and Eleanor Campbell over many happy suppers. It seemed, however, the scope of conversation and innovation was limited, and too often they encountered guests like Dr. Henderson, determined to pontificate—as well as resist anything that hinted at innovation or reform.

A staid matron dressed in yellow satin, the buttons across her broad bosom threatening to pop open, launched into a lengthy description of her pallid daughter's charms. They'd moved from medicine to education to the never-ending marriage mart. Ian took the opportunity to excuse himself.

He strode out of the overheated room to the balcony overlooking a quiet and peaceful Charles Street. A balmy spring breeze caressed his flushed face and his fingers curled around the wrought iron railing as he fought down the frustration he so often felt in these moments.

A year ago, he never would have been able to afford a house or an address such as this. He and Caroline had been living in rented rooms in the far more middle-class Back Bay. They had, Ian reflected now, been happy there. Happier, perhaps, he acknowledged with a rueful pang, than they were—or at least he was—amidst all this luxury. Their new wealth rested uneasily on Ian, considering he had not earned a penny of it himself. It rested entirely on Caroline's uncle, Sir James Riddell, who had died a year ago, leaving her a small and unexpected fortune.

Five years ago, Riddell had been disgraced in Boston when his name had been linked with that of a counterfeiter, Matthew Dearborn. Ian had been present the night Dearborn died, and had watched the wretched man become engulfed in the flames of a fire Dearborn had started to destroy all evidence—a fire fed by thousands of counterfeit bills he'd been storing in a harborside warehouse.

Ian had been partly responsible for identifying Riddell's role in the crime, and yet as a nobleman, Riddell had escaped the prejudiced hand of the law and had returned to Scotland to live out his days in quiet anonymity. He'd sold his estates and put the money in wiser—and more lawful—investments, so that when he died, he'd left a fairly tidy sum for his only remaining heir: Caroline.

It was hardly a fortune, but it was enough money to buy this house and see them situated comfortably in Boston, allowing them to be part of the city's society, and live, Ian reflected, in the manner to which Caroline had generally been accustomed. He knew he should be grateful, for he had always intended to provide for her in the way she was used to and surely wanted. Yet the fact remained *he* wasn't the one providing for her at all.

"People are beginning to talk." Caroline stood framed by the French doors, her graceful figure swathed in pale blue silk, her blonde hair arranged in artful clusters of curls by each temple. Looking at her, Ian marveled yet again that she was his, and that she loved him. "Ian…"

"I'm sorry to leave the way I did. I couldn't stand another diatribe from Dr. Henderson, and I didn't want to say something I'd regret."

"I know." Caroline joined him on the terrace, resting one hand lightly on his shoulder. "I'm sorry, as well. I had no idea he'd go on like that." She let out a tiny sigh. "Although I suppose it's too much to ask of the man, to express even the most common courtesy. I would advise we not invite him again, but you know he could be useful to your career."

"Indeed." Ian rested his hand over hers and they remained silent for a moment, the cool evening air blowing over them.

"Do you suppose," Caroline asked after a moment, her voice soft, "that ether will be accepted one day? Commonplace, even, for most operations?"

"I pray so." Ian's lips tightened as he thought of Dr. Henderson's swaggering assurance. There was so much ignorance and hostility to fight against, even within the supposedly enlightened medical community. As for outside of it, few people wanted their own bodies and lives to be experimented on with a substance they regarded with suspicion or even fear. Ian could hardly blame them—and yet ether held the possibility, the promise, of so much… surgeries performed without pain, childbirth that was bearable, conditions that doctors now simply shook their head at able to be addressed and even healed. Why could none of them see it?

"I imagine sometimes it must be similar to what the first settlers thought upon coming to these shores," Caroline said with a rueful smile. "Who could imagine that there would be towns and cities built upon such rugged and wild land? Yet they persevered." She squeezed his shoulder. "And you must as well."

Ian lifted her hand to his lips and brushed her fingers in a kiss. "Thank you, my darling. Your support means more to me than that of a pompous old windbag like Dr.—"

"*Ian*." Caroline suppressed a scandalized smile. "Imagine if he heard you."

"He's talking too loudly," he murmured, "to hear anything but his own voice."

She shook her head, her eyes dancing, and Ian smiled and kissed her fingers again, letting his lips linger this time.

"Ian…" His name was a gentle reproof and she withdrew her hand, her expression turning serious. "You know that I want to support your research—"

"And you do," he said, reaching for her hand once more. Laughing a little, Caroline pulled away.

"More than with just words," she persisted. "You know that even after buying this house, there is still a fair bit of my inheritance left—"

Ian stilled, and then straightened as he took a step away from her. "You want to use your inheritance to fund my research?" he asked slowly. He had never considered such a thing; it had been too far out of the realm of desirability for it to have crossed his mind.

"Yes." She smiled, her expression guileless, not seeming to notice how still he'd become, or the tempest he felt gathering within him. "With the money you could take more time away from the hospital and concentrate on your research. Perhaps acceptance will come more quickly if you're able to—"

"No." Ian didn't mean to sound so flat and cold. He saw the shocked hurt flash in Caroline's blue eyes and wished he'd tempered his reply. Yet he knew he could not have kept the instinctive refusal—the *revulsion*—he'd felt spring to his lips from spilling out. To take Riddell's money for the research so precious to him, the research that was entirely his…

"Ian—"

"Listen to me, Caroline." He caught her hands in his and felt how cold they'd become. He chafed them between his own and tried to smile, but it felt more like a grimace. "Caroline, my darling, I could not take that money from you. It was held in trust from you, from your uncle, and it was meant for you to do with as you wish—"

"You know under law it is yours rather than mine," Caroline answered a bit stiffly. She would not be placated with such half-truths, Ian knew. She was too clever and too proud for that.

"I would be a boor to follow that law to the letter," Ian replied. He tried to keep his voice light even though he knew Caroline didn't believe his words. She still looked hurt, a wrinkle marring the pale smoothness of her forehead.

"It's not because it's my money," she said quietly, slipping her hands from his. "I already said I wished to use it to support your research, and it would be my choice to give it for such a purpose. No, it's because it comes from my uncle, isn't it? Sir James. You are still angry about my connection to him."

"Not your connection, of which you cannot help—" Ian protested, knowing even as he said the words that it was not enough for her.

"You still see it as his money, not mine. Not ours." Hurt vibrated in her voice.

Ian said nothing, for he knew he could not deny it. How could he, when a wound that had cut so deeply nearly two decades ago festered still? When Ian had been a mere boy, Sir James had swindled him out of his family farm back on the island of Mull. Bitterness and a desire for revenge had driven Ian for far too long, yet he'd relinquished those vengeful dreams when he'd met and married Caroline, Riddell's niece and ward. She'd helped him forgive, if not quite forget, and that was as far as grace had taken him. Until this moment he'd thought it had been far enough.

"I'm sorry," he said, and then added with quiet but firm decision, "but I cannot countenance taking a penny from that man, even now."

Caroline let out a trembling laugh. "Ian, this house is from that man. This gown—"

Fury burned in his chest that she would throw such things in his face, even though, if he was being sensible, he knew she didn't mean it that way. "Pray do not remind me," he said, his voice low, although he knew their very surroundings acted as a reminder to him every day, even if it was one he did his best to ignore.

She stared at him, her eyes widening with shocked comprehension. "You resent even this?" she whispered. One hand fluttered to the neck of her gown, her fingers touching the lace of her fichu. "Have you been simmering with bitterness all this time, begrudging even the lace on my gown? Why did you not tell me? If it angers you so much—"

"I do not resent anything you wish to do with your inheritance," Ian cut across her words, his tone far too stiff. "It is your money, to do with as you see fit, and I will not stop you from using it as you wish." Even though it cost him to know they were only living in this grand style because of the man he'd hated for so long. He might have let go of that hatred, yet the knowledge still cut him. Deeply.

"And if I wish to use it for your research?" Caroline asked, her eyes flashing, her lips pressed together.

Ian shook his head, the refusal rising up inside him once more, impossible to suppress. "Caroline, the research is… *mine*. I could not bear the thought of Riddell's money being involved in any way. It would ruin all for me."

Caroline let out a soft sound of hurt and Ian tried to reach for her hands again. He hated the thought that he was hurting her, that Riddell could come between them even now, yet he knew he could not—would not—change his mind. Not about this, something that still was so fundamental to him, to his very being.

"Caroline—"

"And I thought *I* was yours." Shaking her head, Caroline slipped from the terrace, leaving Ian alone, and more frustrated and restless than before.

*

"Things are bad, Margaret. I don't like to admit it, but there it is." Henry Moore's mouth tightened, and though she couldn't help but be alarmed by his somber tone, Margaret felt some reassurance in the knowledge that her husband would always be honest with her.

She sat across from him in the drawing room of their Back Bay townhouse, a porcelain teacup suspended halfway to her lips. Her eyebrows rose, her dark eyes bright with questions. "Of course they are. They're bad for everyone," she reminded him, as she felt a rush of tenderness for the man she'd married fifteen years ago now. They'd first crossed paths on a muddy side street in Tobermory, back in Scotland. She'd been furious by the refusal of her brother's tutor to instruct her as well, and so Henry, a sea captain wintering with his aunt, had taken on her education. Chaperoned by his dear aunt, they'd begun a tender and tentative courtship until Henry had left for the sea in the spring, and Margaret had promised to wait for his return.

A year later he'd returned for her as he'd said he would, and they'd wed before settling in Boston. Even after her marriage Margaret had always considered herself independent, and she'd taken on many charity projects over the years, although since the birth of their daughter Charlotte, now four years old, she spent more time in suitably domestic pursuits, although still always looking for ways to improve and reform the city she'd come to love.

"Exactly," Henry told her. "There's no opportunity to be had here, not when we're in these dire straits. Everyone's too frightened, and well they should be. It's been nearly a year since the banks started calling in their loans, and there's no end in sight. I read in the paper only yesterday that over three hundred banks have closed their doors. Rupert was right, you know. All that paper money is the problem." He shook his head, his tea forgotten by his elbow.

Margaret smiled faintly at the mention of her brother, who had been helping their father Sandy MacDougall on the family farm in Prince Edward Island before coming to Boston to work as a clerk in Henry's shipping company and was now a U.S. Marshal out west. Rupert was married to Eleanor Campbell—a match which had brought joy to both the MacDougalls and Campbells as not the first but second union to join the families. Margaret's eldest brother Allan had previously married Eleanor Campbell's older sister Harriet, and they still lived on Prince Edward Island with their family.

Five years ago, when Rupert had exposed a forgery ring along with Ian and Henry, he'd predicted the problems the banks would have as they continued to print paper bills without a thought to the consequence of so much worthless currency released into the market. Now those predictions had come to pass, and they'd affected just about everyone Margaret knew. Still, she said nothing, waiting for Henry to continue.

"So we need to turn elsewhere," he said after a moment, his voice both tense and resolute. "Outside of this country. I've been thinking…" He paused. "I've been thinking I should try to trade with China."

"China!" Margaret returned her teacup to its saucer with an inelegant clatter as she stared at him in surprise. She'd been expecting some sort of change in tactics; her husband had always been an innovative man. But as far away as that…? "Henry, are you serious? You've never traded with China before. It's far too distant, as well as difficult! They won't even accept our traded goods, although of course there is that terrible opium…" She trailed off, her face darkening as she considered what she'd read about the deplorable opium trade both England and the United States had forced on China.

China's Closed Door policy had kept many Western traders from selling their goods, although they were eager to import China's offerings of tea, silk, and spices. Led by the autocratic British East India Company, many traders, Americans included, had begun trafficking in opium, smuggling it into China through third parties despite the nation's imperial decree against the terrible stuff. The result had been profitable for the West and disastrous for the East, who now had thousands of their citizens enslaved in addiction to the sweet poppy.

"It's true," Henry agreed, "it has become more difficult to obtain goods from China, namely because the officials are so suspicious, and rightly so. The opium trade has been disastrous for them, a true blight on our society." He shook his head soberly. "But I believe the time could be ripe for an investment, to bring China's saleable goods to our shores in a way that is fair and profitable to both parties—"

Margaret's gaze narrowed. "And why should the Chinese officials allow you into Canton when they are being so careful?"

"I have connections," Henry replied. "Enough anyway, I believe, to secure a place at harbor. It's a risk, of course, but one that could have a tidy profit, and benefit both sides in the bargain."

Margaret shook her head. "It takes months to travel to China, and with the negotiations and a return trip…" She swallowed dryly, her expression turning bleak. "You'd be gone at least a year." And he hadn't sailed since Charlotte was born, preferring to be close to hearth and home. The thought of being apart for so long made Margaret's insides clench with both sorrow and fear.

Anything could happen on such a long voyage, and she knew Henry was even more aware of the risks than she was.

"At least that," Henry agreed. "I'm sorry, Margaret, but I see no other way."

"Why not trade with Europe?" she protested. "Or the Caribbean?"

Henry sighed. "The profit isn't there any longer, not right now, at any rate. I need to take a risk if I'm going to survive."

Abruptly, Margaret rose from her chair and went to stand by the long windows facing the street. Her back was straight and stiff, her shoulders thrown back. "How bad is it, Henry?" she asked quietly, yet with a thread of steel running through her words. "Really?"

Henry sighed and ran a hand through his now-thinning sandy hair. "Bad enough. Do you remember that dinner we had here, back in '32? Your brother was so full of excitement about this country and all its possibilities. I didn't see it, frankly, but then I've always looked to the water. But Rupert saw the possibilities on land—railroads, canals, cities built where there was nothing more than forest and plain. Do you remember? He spoke of Chicago, an outpost that none of us had ever heard of, and now it's been incorporated as a city, and has chartered a railroad."

"If Rupert was right," Margaret interjected, turning to him and smiling to soften her words, "then perhaps you should follow his advice and invest in this country." Henry was silent, and Margaret's smiled faded, replaced by a frown of concern. "Henry—"

"I did," he told her bleakly, his gaze sliding away from hers, and she felt a sudden, cold stab of fear. She had never seen the look on his face before, so shadowed with regret and self-recrimination. "More than you know. I invested in the railroads and the canals and all that collapsed when the banks became scared and wanted it all back."

"And you never told me?" Margaret couldn't keep the hurt from her voice. She had always believed their marriage was more honest and open than that. She was no fainting flower, to be shielded from life's hardships. She wanted to share them with Henry; she wanted to help shoulder the burden, whatever it was, and she always thought she had. Yet he'd kept this from her—why? And for how long?

"I didn't want to worry you." He held up his hands in a placating gesture. "I know I should have. I know you would have wished to know. In truth I thought my shipping investments and trade could keep us secure, but the Panic has affected—infected—everything." He rose from his chair to stand by her, laying a hand on her shoulder as they both gazed out at the darkening street. "I want to keep you and Charlotte safe, Margaret. Safe and secure and happy. That's all. That's all I've ever wanted."

The earnest look on his face softened her a little, but not enough. Honesty and equality had been the bedrock of their relationship, right from the beginning, when Henry had picked up her battered copy of Boethius. "I have never wanted to be mollycoddled, Henry, you know that—"

"It wasn't just that," Henry cut her off quietly. "It was, I'm ashamed to say, a matter of pride. I didn't want you to know how I'd failed."

"Oh, Henry." Margaret rested her hand over his as she closed her eyes briefly. How could she have had no idea of how troubled he'd been, the cares he'd kept to himself? Her own blindness in this matter shamed her. To think she'd spent the last few months involving herself in nothing more taxing than forming a subscription library for the residents of the South End! "So many people lost money in the Panic," she said quietly. "It's not a failure, not a personal one, at any rate. It happened to the country. To all of us."

He just shrugged, and Margaret watched him, understanding dawning slowly. Travelling all the way to China wasn't just about making money, she realized. It was about her husband proving—to her, to society, to himself, that he could still provide for his family and run his business with success. It was a matter of honor as much as of profit. To argue with him would be pointless as well as hurtful.

"And you intend to go to China yourself, I take it," she asked, turning to look out at the street. "You haven't captained a ship in years, Henry. Since before we had Charlotte."

"Well I know." If there was a shadow of regret in Henry's voice at not having traveled the seas, neither of them acknowledged it. He'd made his choice for the family, and Margaret hoped and even believed that he'd considered the benefit of watching his daughter take her first steps well worth the trade. "But the negotiations with China will be delicate. I can't have someone storming in there, thinking he knows best, not understanding what is at stake or how diplomatic we need to be. I'll need to see to them myself."

"I understand." Margaret nodded her acceptance, trying to remain resolute even as she felt her spirits flag. Not only would Henry be leaving her for a year at the least, but he would be travelling to one of the most unsettled harbors in the world. "You will be careful…"

"Of course." Henry raised her hand to his lips as his eyes crinkled in a wonderfully familiar smile. "I've weathered much in this business over the years, and I've always kept my head as well as my honor."

"I know." Margaret was thankful that Henry had never once considered involving himself in the despicable slave trade; it had been outlawed in Britain some thirty years ago, but had continued on in this country to the present day, even if those in the northern states despised it. She smiled back at him, even though it cost her. "You must do as you see fit, Henry. I will entrust the decision to you."

"Only with your blessing," Henry returned. She raised her eyes to his, saw the worry and strain etched in fine lines on his weathered face and wondered again how she'd not seen it before.

How she'd not realized how much he'd kept from her. Perhaps she'd chosen not to see it, just as Henry had chosen not to tell her. She would not make the same mistake twice. Her husband would have her support now, fully, or at least as fully as she was able to give it.

"Of course you have my blessing," she said softly. "Although I will both fear and pray for you every day that you are gone." She pressed her lips against his hand as Henry drew her to him. "You will have my blessing even so, Henry. Always."

CHAPTER TWO

Prince Edward Island

Harriet MacDougall watched the purple twilight settle over the hills of Prince Edward Island, her home now in Canada for nearly twenty years. From the porch of the farmhouse she shared with her husband Allan and their four children, she could see the fields, now ready for planting, stretching towards the river on one side, the sea on the other. A road made of the island's distinctive reddish dirt twisted through them, disappearing into the hills by the horizon. Smiling, Harriet sat back in her rocking chair and let the cares of the day slip from her weary shoulders.

She heard the creak of the farmhouse door and the familiar squeak of Allan's boots on the weathered porch floor as he joined her outside and settled into the rocking chair next to her. "It's a little brisk out tonight," he remarked.

Harriet gathered her shawl around her shoulders. "Only a bit," she agreed. "No need to build up the fire, I suppose."

Allan chuckled as he reached for his pipe. "Now how did you know I was going to suggest such a thing?"

Harriet slid him a sideways smile. "We've been married an awful long time now, Allan MacDougall. If I don't know what you're going to say before you say it—"

"I think you know it before I even think it," Allan joked.

Harriet smiled again, her gaze moving lovingly over him. Although there were new creases at the corners of his eyes, and deeper grooves from his nose to mouth, his hair was still thick and dark, albeit peppered with gray, and his shoulders were wide and strong. He was, and always would be, the only man she'd ever loved.

In 1819, Allan had left their native Scotland to make his fortune on Prince Edward Island, along with his parents and brother Archie McDougall, all of whom had now passed on. After a couple of years of barely a word from Allan, when Harriet discovered all his letters to her had been stolen by an admirer of hers, Andrew Reid, she made the brave decision to take the long, arduous journey from Mull to Prince Edward Island accompanied by Allan's brother Rupert, who had stayed on in Scotland until the MacDougalls had settled with a homestead of their own. She arrived in Canada to the devastating news that a mail packet from the mainland to the island had sunk, with Allan and his brother Archie on it.

For over a year she'd lived in grief, thinking her beloved was dead. Then, in a meeting surely ordained by Providence, Allan had found her in the Red River Valley out west, hiding in an old shack after the massacre at Seven Oaks. She'd gone west as companion to a widow, hoping to find a new life for herself. She'd found Allan instead, who had been working as a fur trader, and he'd brought her back to Prince Edward Island, where they'd made their lives—and raised their family—ever since.

Rupert MacDougall had eventually left the family homestead, Mingarry Farm, for Boston and then Ohio; Margaret, who had also stayed behind in Scotland with Rupert, never journeyed to Prince Edward Island, for she had met and fallen in love with a Bostonian, Henry Moore, and left her life behind in Mull for a new beginning and married life in Boston. Harriet was glad Allan had decided to stay on the island, and start their family there. All they both had ever wanted was a bit of land to make their own, to love and to tend and then to leave for their children.

The door of the farmhouse opened, and their oldest, Maggie, came out onto the porch. Harriet gazed at her fifteen-year-old daughter with a mixture of fondness and fledgling concern. Just as her Uncle Rupert once had, Harriet knew Maggie was becoming restless with island life. She saw it in the way her daughter never seemed to settle at a chore, although she'd always done her work properly before. She heard it in Maggie's frequent comments about the dullness of living on a farm when her aunt and uncle commanded the best of Boston society. And while Harriet believed she knew her daughter well enough to know she hadn't a care for the shallow charms of high society, she feared Maggie longed to see more of the world than she'd ever get the opportunity to, living on a small farm on the island.

"The mail came today," Maggie said, unnecessarily, for Allan himself had travelled down river to Charlottetown to fetch it. There had been letters from Allan's siblings Margaret and Rupert, as well as one from Harriet's brother Ian, who practiced medicine in Boston. They had read all three letters out at the dinner table, so all the family could be acquainted with everyone's news.

Frowning slightly, Harriet wondered just what Maggie might be getting to now.

"Everyone's well and healthy, thanks be," Allan remarked, drawing long on his pipe. "We have much to be grateful for."

"Indeed so," Harriet murmured. She waited for Maggie to speak, for she could see her daughter's reddish brows—Maggie's hair was the same deep auburn as her own—had drawn together, and her cheeks were flushed with what could only be determination to say her piece, whatever it was.

"You remember Aunt Margaret asked if we might visit her one day," she began, and Harriet gave Allan a quick, searching look. Her husband was frowning; Harriet knew he didn't like to travel. The journey to Boston, now done by steamship, was not overly taxing, but it took time away from the work on the farm that was always needing to be done.

"Margaret says the same in every letter. She could always come here," Allan answered mildly. "She's been here only the once, I think, since we settled in this country, and we've been to Boston three times since her marriage to Henry."

"Why would she come here?" Maggie asked scornfully. "There's nothing to see!"

"Maggie, hush," Harriet admonished, but Allan, ever steady, refused to rise to his daughter's words.

"Sure enough, there are some who think this island is one of Canada's greatest jewels," he replied, his voice still mild. "Plenty of people have written about the beauty of its shores. I think Margaret would do well to leave the city behind for a bit and visit us for a change. She could bring wee Charlotte—we've only met her once, back when she was a bairn."

Harriet smiled at the memory; they'd traveled to Boston for the winter, living with Margaret and Henry soon after Charlotte had been born. It had been a happy time, with Allan's mother Betty in residence, and her brother Ian in the city besides, but the demands of the farm, as ever, had called them back. In truth, Harriet had been as glad as Allan to be back in the land she now thought of her as her home, by her own hearth.

"Well, I think I should be the one to visit her," Maggie said, and now Harriet heard belligerence in her daughter's voice. She glanced at Allan who, while still affable, was shaking his head.

"Not this year, I'm afraid, Maggie, lass. It's planting season and I haven't made any arrangements. By the time we could get away the weather will have turned and I don't fancy a winter journey again."

"You don't have to go," Maggie said. "Nor you, Mama. I could go. By myself."

The ensuing silence felt like a thunderclap as they all gazed at one another—Maggie defiant, Harriet shocked, Allan with a deep frown. "Maggie," Harriet protested, "you are only fifteen. Surely you realize you cannot undertake such a journey by yourself."

"Of course she can't," Allan said, his tone clearly stating that this was the end of the discussion.

Maggie pursed her lips, her hands on her hips. "Won't you even consider the notion? You went all the way to Prince Edward Island from Scotland and then on to Red River by yourself, Mama, when you were just a bit older than me. You told me about it yourself. I've seen nothing of this world, and I want to before I'm too old."

"Maggie, you're not yet sixteen," Harriet murmured.

"And how old would I have to be? I warrant there's no age either of you'd be willing to let me go."

"Not as a young woman alone, no," Allan stated, and Maggie turned to Harriet, tears filling her eyes.

"*Please.* We could find a chaperone for the steamship journey. Aunt Margaret will be alone now that Uncle Henry is going to sea, and I could be company for her. I'd stay through the winter and come back to help next spring. There's not much work to do over the winter, and George can help. Anna's big enough to do some of my chores. Please…"

Harriet sat speechless, amazed at the urgency and desperation with which her daughter pleaded. She'd known Maggie was restless, but this amount of hunger, of restlessness? She hadn't seen it. She hadn't wanted to.

"No," Allan said again, flatly, "and that's final." He rose from his chair and walked inside, slamming the door behind him in a way he never did. In the ensuing silence Harriet could only stare helplessly at her daughter.

"Why does he have to be so unyielding?" Maggie cried, and Harriet shook her head.

"Do not speak of your father that way. If he is firm, it is because he knows the dangers. You do not." Maggie scowled and Harriet reached out a hand to her that her daughter shook off. "Why do you want to go so very much, *cridhe*?" she asked gently. "I know farm life is not always an adventure, but come summer there will be a few dances and parties—perhaps you could stay a week or two with the McPhees…" They had two girls of similar age to Maggie, and Harriet knew how they liked to chatter and dance together whenever the farming families gathered.

"I don't want to stay with the *McPhees*," Maggie said in a tone of disgust, and Harriet did her best to hide the needleprick of hurt she felt. Letting her daughter go visiting for a week would have been a sacrifice, as Maggie helped her greatly with both the children and never-ending housework, but she could hardly expect a fifteen-year-old, desperate to know more of life, to understand that.

"I'm sorry, Maggie, but it really is not a credible idea. You're far too young, and in any case, if your father says no, then there is little I can do." Harriet spoke severely although not without sympathy; she empathized with her daughter's feelings, but she knew she could not encourage them.

"You could speak with him." Maggie sat down in the chair her father had vacated, her fingers pleating her apron, her expression managing to look both pleading and defiant. "I know you and Pa are happy here, but does that mean I must be? So many in our family sought their own fortunes—Pa did himself! Why can't I?"

Harriet stared helplessly at her daughter, knowing that although it seemed like a reasonable-enough request, Maggie was only a young girl. It was true Allan had struggled against his father's ruling over his own life in much the same way as Maggie was now, all those years ago. Although she doubted he could see it, Allan now possessed a daughter who had a mind of her own, just as he'd had. He'd protested the way Sandy MacDougall had sought to arrange his son's life with Allan having no say in the matter, and yet now Allan seemed poised to be almost as unyielding with Maggie as his father had been with him.

After a moment, she reached over and patted her daughter's hand. "I know you long for adventure. Heaven knows both your father and I did, once upon a time. I'll speak to him, Maggie, if only so he can see how like him you are!" She smiled, and was gratified by her daughter's small smile back. "Although I warn you, it may well come to nothing."

Maggie's face shone as she enveloped Harriet in a quick, tight hug. "Thank you, Mama!"

"It may come to nothing," Harriet repeated, uselessly, for Maggie was already skipping indoors, as good as if she'd promised her a trip to the moon, never mind Boston.

*

Boston

"We have some news."

Isobel looked up from the gingerbread and cream she'd been pushing around her plate, noting Margaret's determined look, as well as her brother Henry's more resigned one. They'd come to supper with her and her parents as they often did, and the meal had passed pleasantly enough, although Isobel hadn't been able to help but notice how strained her father still seemed. And now Henry as well? There was a certain bleakness in her brother's gaze that made her stomach turn over.

"News?" Isobel's mother Arabella looked between Margaret and Henry, her eyebrows raised in speculation, a small smile curving her mouth. "Happy news?"

"No, Mamma-in-law, not that kind of news," Margaret answered with a slightly forced laugh. Isobel knew Charlotte had been an unexpected blessing after many years of childlessness, and no more had followed. Her mother's face fell.

"I'm sorry, I was hoping…"

"Of course," Margaret murmured, looking at her plate. Her gingerbread, Isobel noticed, had not been touched either, and she did not think it was due to the most capable hand of the cook. What could be bothering her brother and his wife?

"It is my news, really," Henry interjected with a smile as forced as Margaret's laugh. "I have decided to captain the *Charlotte Rose* myself this spring. I shall be sailing to China."

"China…!" The word practically exploded from Isobel's father. "Are you serious?"

"It is so far away, Henry," Arabella Moore protested, one hand fluttering to her throat. "So dangerous…"

"Any journey is dangerous, Mother," Henry returned with a smile. Isobel stared at him in surprise. She knew nothing of China; she did not even think she could place it on a map. What little she knew had been drawn from the occasional reference to it in one of her fashionable novels, or an article in the newspapers that she rarely read—nothing to form a real opinion other than that it was far away, across a vast ocean.

"Why are you going such a distance?" she asked. "What is there?"

Henry turned to her with a quick smile. "All manner of things, I'm sure! It is a large country, and I've heard the landscape is quite varied."

"Yes, of course," Isobel murmured, flushing. She hadn't meant to sound like quite such a ninny.

"But if you are asking what there is for *me*," Henry continued, "then there are many things of interest to purchase. There is great demand here for Chinese goods—their silk and other cloth is unparalleled for quality, and of course there is the tea you drink."

His smile widened as he nodded towards her cup. "It all comes from China."

"I—I knew that, of course," Isobel stammered, although she'd known it without really reflecting on it at any great length.

"And what will you trade to them?" Stephen asked practically. "The Chinese do not seem to want anything we offer."

"They do not need it, it is true," Henry agreed. "With such a large country, they can produce most of what they require themselves. I will have to purchase everything with coin—it is the only way these days."

"An expensive venture," Stephen remarked, and Henry inclined his head in acknowledgement.

"But with the potential for more profit." He glanced at his mother, who had begun to look disapproving at all the talk of money. "But that is enough discussion about business for one evening, perhaps."

"What about you, Margaret?" Isobel asked. "You will be on your own for so long. Will you mind terribly?"

"I shall manage," Margaret answered, with a brave tilt to her chin. "I always have, and I have much to occupy me. I'm sure I will look forward to all of Henry's tales when he returns—he will have been to ever so many interesting places. I confess, I cannot wait to hear all about them."

Isobel saw Henry give his wife a grateful look, which she returned with a smile. Margaret's comment, so determinedly given, made Isobel suddenly think of the pamphlet still up on her bureau. "I was considering attending a lecture by Mr. Adoniram Judson at the Bowdoin Street Church next week," she told Margaret, although she hadn't been, not really. "Perhaps you would like to accompany me? He is speaking about his work in Burma—it looks very enlightening, and perhaps it would give you some idea of the lands to which Henry will be travelling. At least… lands close to them?" She glanced inquiringly at Henry, realizing she had no idea whether Burma was close to China or not.

"There is at least a thousand miles between them," Henry answered with a laugh, "but I'm sure the conversation will be of great interest, at any rate."

"I didn't know you availed yourself of such opportunities, Isobel," Margaret said, making her blush again, for of course she didn't. "I would be delighted to attend."

"I'm so glad," she murmured. She realized she was; although she hadn't seriously considered going to such an event, now she knew she wanted to. It would be inspiring to listen to someone who had made more of their life than she had, she hoped.

*

"I'm going to Hartford again."

Ian saw Caroline's back stiffen as she met his gaze in the mirror above her dressing room table, drawing her brush through the long, dark blonde hair that fell over her shoulders in a tumbled array. "So soon?"

"It is important."

"I know."

He heard hurt as well as accusation in her voice, and inwardly he sighed. They had not spoken of using Riddell money for his research since the night of the salon, and Ian had not wished to. Even so, he had sensed a tension that had sprung up between him and his wife and he disliked it exceedingly. Their relationship had always been tumultuous; they both possessed tempers and Ian would not have wished it another way. This chilly silence, however, was something else entirely.

"Do you mind my travels?" he asked, and she set the brush down on the table.

"You know I do not. My disquiet is not with your travel, Ian, although heaven knows you have gone up and down this country more days and weeks than I care to remember." She pressed her lips together as if she did not want to speak more on the subject, but Ian knew what she was implying. They had been married these five years without Caroline quickening once; she blamed his travels, but he wondered if it was simply a way to keep from blaming herself. He wished to blame no one, and yet he knew he still needed to grasp the nettle in this particular conversation.

"You are vexed about the money," he said heavily. "And that I will not take it."

"I am not vexed," Caroline said sharply. "I am hurt. There is a difference."

"It is not a reflection of my feelings for you," Ian insisted, his voice rising. "You must know that."

"It is a reflection of how you see our marriage," Caroline returned steadily. "Our partnership." She met his gaze in the mirror once more, her own resolute. "I have always supported you, Ian, because I love you and I believe in what you are doing. I have always wanted to stand by your side and aid you in whatever way I can. But the way you have spoken. The way you feel…" She shook her head, her expression shadowed with a deeper hurt than Ian cared to consider. "I fear I am nothing more than an accessory to you, like a bauble to admire and then put back on the shelf."

"Caroline, that is a nonsense!" he could not keep from protesting, his tone turning vehement. "You are taking this all out of proportion. It is the money—that is all." He walked over to her, dropping his hands onto her shoulders and feeling grieved when they stiffened. "I love you. I'll always love you."

"'I could not love thee, dear, so much, lov'd I not Honor more,'" she quoted sadly. "I never agreed with Lovelace. I find I do not, even now."

The despondency in her tone tore at him. Not knowing how to make amends, Ian took her heavy silver hairbrush and drew it through the long, golden hair he loved. "Do you remember when I used to brush your hair every evening?" he asked softly.

"Yes—I adored it."

"As did I." He drew the brush down her hair again, enjoying the way it gleamed in the candlelight. "I don't remember when I stopped."

Caroline met his gaze in the mirror once more. "It was some time ago."

Ian absorbed her quiet censure, trying not to flinch. "I suppose it was."

He tried to draw the brush down again, but she twitched away from him and then rose from her chair. "When do you leave?" she asked as she reached for her nightcap.

Ian sighed and set the brush back on the table. "I thought I would take the coach on Thursday."

She nodded, climbing into bed, and before Ian could say anything more she had blown out the candle, leaving them in darkness and silence.

CHAPTER THREE

Prince Edward Island

The fire cast flickering shadows over the hearth as Allan MacDougall stretched his stocking feet towards its warmth. The children were all settled in bed, although Harriet doubted that Maggie had fallen asleep yet. Harriet sat across from him in the rocking chair his mother had brought over from Scotland, her face as placidly composed as she could make it and her eyes on the pile of darning in her lap. Still, Harriet could tell Allan wasn't fooled.

"I know what you're thinking, *mo leannan*," he said with a little laugh. "You want me to say yes to Maggie."

A smile curved Harriet's mouth as she raised her gaze to Allan. "I can never hide a thought from you."

"I'm glad of it."

"It isn't that I want her to go—at least, only if you think it wise."

"If I think it wise!" He shook his head. "I've already given my opinion on the subject. I don't think it wise at all. A lass of fifteen? But I warrant your opinion is a wee bit different."

"Not that different," Harriet protested as she drew her needle through the cloth. "If truth be told, I'd like nothing better than to see Maggie settled with a husband of her own in the homestead next to ours; same as you would, I reckon."

"In time," Allan answered, and Harriet suppressed a smile.

"Aye, in time. I'm not wanting to see her settled too soon, Allan MacDougall. She is only sixteen come summer."

"My thoughts exactly." Allan raised his eyebrows. "So it seems we're agreed on the subject, then? And no more need for discussion?"

"Perhaps only a bit more," Harriet teased, although she knew she needed to choose her words carefully. "We might be agreed, Allan, as to what we want for Maggie, but there's the question of what she wants herself."

"And at all of fifteen years old she'll be knowing that?"

"Starting to," Harriet returned. "As you did, I warrant. But more than that, she needs to discover it for herself. Heaven knows I'd like my children to be happy where they are, tending the land and finding someone to love. But I also know how far love can take us—whether it's to Boston… or Red River."

Allan frowned as he gazed into the fire. Harriet didn't speak, knowing he needed to reflect on her words. He had been in Maggie's position, chafing against his father's firm hand and longing to make more of his life. In an act of both defiance and rebellion he'd left his father's farm to set out on his own, and made his way as a fur trapper, paddling his canoe down the many rivers of Upper Canada, all the way to the Red River in Rupert's Land where they had been reunited, and had returned to the family homestead on Prince Edward Island.

"It's not the same," Allan said at last, still frowning.

Harriet completed a stitch before answering. She knew her husband well enough to know she would have to handle this conversation with both gentleness and wisdom. "How is it different?"

"She's a lass, for one thing," Allan answered. "I'll warrant you wouldn't have even thought of going to Red River on your own."

"You know very well I didn't," Harriet replied with a smile. "I was the companion for Katherine Donald, because both of us knew we couldn't travel as a woman alone. However," she continued before Allan could interrupt, claiming his point proved, "Maggie isn't proposing to travel to the wilderness like you or I did, and neither will she be alone. She'll be a companion to her aunt and namesake, just as I was a companion to Katherine." Harriet paused, letting Allan reluctantly digest and accept this, before finishing, "If you are concerned about her ship journey, I am sure we can arrange a chaperone. Someone from Charlottetown is likely to be making such a voyage, and it is done so quickly now—a matter of a few days. We can take her to Charlottetown, and Margaret can meet the ship in Boston. It would all be perfectly safe and respectable."

Allan scowled at her, but Harriet could tell it was more for show, and perhaps pride, than anything else. "For someone who'd like to see her settled in the homestead next to ours, you've spent a fair amount of time considering how our Maggie can get herself to Boston," he observed wryly.

"I want to see her happy," Harriet said simply. "And I hope and pray that if she satisfies that urge for adventure that all young people seem to have, she'll return to us wanting to settle here of her own choice." She spoke gently, knowing Allan would take her point. He could force Maggie to stay, but he couldn't make her like it. In the end, such a bending of her will would surely lead to discontent and resentment, just as it had with Allan and his father... and she hoped he realized that.

Allan was silent for a long moment, staring into the fire, his brow furrowed. The only sound was the settling of logs in the grate, and a few embers scattered across the worn hearth before graying into ash.

"And what she will she do, all that time in Boston?" he asked finally, still sounding reluctant.

"I'm sure Margaret can think up all manner of useful endeavors and amusements for her. You know how she involves herself in charitable works—and of course there is Charlotte to think of. Maggie is adept at managing little ones, much to her credit."

"You'd miss her too much," Allan said, and Harriet nodded.

"Aye, I would. She's been a great help to me, and even better companion." How many afternoons had she whiled away laughing with Maggie as they'd done the washing or darning, the hours seeming to fly as they'd chatted and teased? "But if I'm willing to let her go," Harriet told her husband gently, "then perhaps you could be, as well?"

Another silence passed between them; from one of the bedrooms Harriet heard a creak, and she wondered if Maggie were still awake, straining to hear what they were saying. Since Harriet had made her promise to speak to Allan a week ago, Maggie had given her any number of imploring, questioning looks that Harriet had replied to with a shake of her head. She'd wanted to pick her moment, and she hoped now she had.

"I suppose there's no harm in writing Margaret," Allan finally said with a sigh.

Harriet resumed her sewing, completing several stitches before she spoke. "I'll compose a letter on the morrow."

Allan nodded gruffly, his face still settled into a frown. Harriet knew how hard this was for him. He had lost too many family members already; his brother Archie on the mail packet while in the prime of life, and his mother Betty here on the island, just last summer, after spending several years in Boston. Rupert was far away, serving as a marshal in the western territories of the United States, and with Margaret in Boston, Allan was the only MacDougall left on Prince Edward Island.

He looked up, and Harriet was glad to see a small smile lighten his features. "Maggie, *cridhe*," he called, "I know you're listening."

Sheepishly, Maggie peeked her head out of the back bedroom. "Thank you, Pa," she said, and Harriet saw how her eyes sparkled like stars. Allan shook a finger at her even as he smiled.

"It's just a letter, mind," he warned. "That's all."

Maggie nodded quickly, but from the high flush on her cheeks Harriet knew she was imagining herself in Boston already.

*

The church hall was buzzing with conversation as Isobel took her program and followed Margaret to the front row to hear Adoniram Judson speak.

"I've heard he speaks very quietly," Margaret explained as she settled herself in a chair, arranging her wide skirts on either side of her. "The poor man's voice has given out, both from speaking so much and all the illness he's suffered over the years, in climates he's not used to. I am so looking forward to hearing what he has to say."

Isobel sat beside Margaret and glanced at the program detailing some of Mr. Judson's experiences abroad—living in a zayat, imprisoned for nearly two years on a trumped-up account of spying for the British, and travelling all over the country, in difficult conditions and conveyances. It all sounded terribly dangerous, but also exciting—far more exciting than anything she'd ever experienced or likely would. Simply travelling on a ship across the sea felt incredible to her, and impossible to imagine. Yet Henry was leaving in only a few weeks to do that very thing.

"What a courageous man he must be," Margaret remarked. "His first wife died of smallpox, you know, as soon as he was released from prison about ten years ago. Terribly sad." Her eyes clouded as she gave a little shake of her head.

"What of Henry, Margaret?" Isobel asked. "Are you very worried?"

Margaret pursed her lips for a moment before replying. "I am trying not to be. Henry has travelled half the world over. I suppose it is natural for him to want to travel the other half." She tried to smile and almost managed it.

"Did you ever want to go with him?' Isobel asked suddenly, thinking of the Judsons travelling together, and Margaret looked at her in rueful surprise.

"Go with him! On a merchant ship? I believe myself adventurous, Isobel, but I confess not quite that much." She cocked her head, her gaze sweeping thoughtfully over her. "What made you consider such a question? It hardly seems like you."

"I don't know." Isobel blushed. She knew it had been an absurd idea, and yet it rankled that Margaret had judged her in such a way, incapable even of thinking such a thing. "I suppose I asked because Mr. Judson's wife accompanied him all that way—"

"Yes, that is true," Margaret acknowledged. "Although I don't envy her! From what I have read of the first Mrs. Judson, she had an incredibly difficult lot in life, often alone and in ill health, with small children to care for and no family nearby."

"I suppose," Isobel said, for she could hardly say anything else, and yet she wondered if it were truly so difficult, why they went at all. Was it because of conviction of belief or a thirst for adventure or both?

"Are you wishing for adventure yourself?" Margaret guessed shrewdly. "The First School has lost some of its appeal, perhaps, day after day? Anything can become drudgery, with time."

"I do enjoy teaching," Isobel returned quickly. "It's only…" She paused, not wanting to elaborate on what made her feel so restless. *It's only I don't have a husband and I never will, and sometimes I feel so lonely that I want to scream—or weep. When a pupil brushes my hand it makes me ache for my own children. My own home. My own life…*

"I think I understand," Margaret said quietly. "Everyone must experience disappointed hopes in a lifetime, but I fear yours have tried you sorely."

Isobel made a pretense of studying her program so Margaret wouldn't see the expression on her face, which she feared would confirm what her sister-in-law had just remarked on so astutely. "I would like to travel," she said rather inanely, for she did not know if she would like to travel particularly, and in any case it encompassed so much less than what she'd been thinking and Margaret had been referring to.

"Perhaps to Europe," Margaret answered with a smile. "On a Grand Tour, with all the usual comforts and luxuries. That is how I would do it!"

"Do you think I could not manage, as a missionary's wife?" Isobel asked, a little stung.

"Would you even want to be such a thing?" Margaret asked, eyebrows raised. "I did not think you had the necessary zeal, for a start."

She didn't, Isobel knew, but she still resisted the idea that she might not be capable of it. "From what I have read, the missionaries involve themselves in many good works, including starting schools, often especially for girls."

"A very worthy enterprise, to be sure."

"And one I am perfectly capable of," Isobel returned with some asperity. "As I have been doing just the same for these last five years."

"I never meant to imply you were not strong enough, only that you would not wish to experience such hardship and deprivation, travelling to places without the comforts you are accustomed to." Margaret touched her sleeve in a placating gesture. "Mr. Judson is now a widower, with seven children to feed, and I shudder to think of such difficulty. But we shall hear of such things from the man himself—look, he has arrived!"

Isobel turned to see that Dr. Sharp had ascended the pulpit to introduce Adoniram Judson. The crowd fell to a hush. Isobel listened to Dr. Sharp with only half an ear; her mind was still mulling over their conversation. Of course she didn't want to be a missionary's wife. The idea was utterly ludicrous. She didn't even know any missionaries, and in any case, she did not particularly wish to experience the hardships Margaret had spoken of—an arduous and often dangerous sea journey, and then a life in a place that would be entirely unfamiliar to her, far from family, most likely never to see them again, and all the while she would be doing the same enterprise she was involved in here! No, of course she didn't want that.

She turned back to the pulpit as Mr. Judson began to speak, his voice little more than a low rasp. She tried to suppress her expression of shock at his awkward manner of speech and husky whisper; Margaret had already told her that a pulmonary condition kept him from speaking at a normal volume, and his many years speaking a foreign tongue made English awkward to him. He had an interpreter to "translate", repeating his utterances in a booming voice to the crowd at large, and the effect was both disconcerting and strangely inspiring.

Mr. Judson was an unprepossessing figure of about fifty years of age, although he looked much older, and in exceedingly delicate heath. Despite these detractions, there could be no denying or dimming the passion for his work that shone in his eyes, and the affection and even love with which he spoke for his adopted land and its people.

"Through the mercy of God I am permitted to stand before you this evening, a pensioner of your bounty," Adoniram's aide intoned. "I desire to thank you for all your sympathy and aid, and I pray God's blessing to rest upon you… all that has been done in Burma has been by the churches, through the feeble and unworthy instrumentality of myself and my brethren…"

As he spoke of his experiences in Burma, and all that he had accomplished there—the zayat he'd built with his own hands to meet with the Burmese people; the school he had started, and the ten years he'd spent studying the language, nearly ruining his eyesight in the process—Isobel felt herself caught up in the altruistic spirit, inspired by both his humble manner and his impressive deeds.

To give of oneself so utterly, to work so unfailingly for others… and to experience so much! His description of the lands she'd never

seen and could barely envision still captured her imagination...
mist-shrouded hills, skies the color of a rose, beaches of pearly
sand... she could both picture it completely and not at all, and
yet it still fired her blood. To *live*, to truly live!

For a fierce moment, Isobel envied her brother and Adoniram Judson and all the men—and some women—who had
adventured far beyond Boston and her own limited experience.
They had seen and done things she never would. They could
make their own choices, be captains of their own souls. The
romance of it was better than anything she'd read in one of
her silly novels.

The crowd began to applaud, and with a ripple of surprise
Isobel realized Mr. Judson's address was over, and she'd only heard
half of it, yet that had been more than enough to make her feel
filled with purpose—and yet for what?

"That really was quite stirring," Margaret said as she gathered
her gloves and reticule. "The poor man has been beaten down
by this life, yet he is still determined to serve and improve all he
turns his hand to. May we all have his fortitude."

"Quite so," Isobel murmured. She felt as if she were half in a
daze, dreaming of vague yet wonderful places, courageous and
compassionate deeds, and she wanted to hold onto the wondrous
feeling that had buoyed her soul for a few lovely moments.

"Pamphlet, Miss?"

Startled, Isobel took the paper from one of the church volun-
teers. She read the large, black type: *Support Missions*. Instinctively
she reached for her reticule, where she had a few coins, only to
check herself at the next line: *Give your Time, Talent, and Treasure:
Become A Missionary Yourself.*

A strange, shivery sensation passed over her, making her heart
leap within her chest in a most peculiar way.

"The man truly is a saint," Margaret murmured. "They do call
him the Saint of Burma, you know." She glanced at Isobel, and

then touched her sleeve. "My dear, are you feeling well? You've gone quite pale."

Isobel let out a laugh as she reached for a few coins and dropped them into the waiting basket. The pamphlet she slipped into her reticule, determined to dismiss it from her mind. "Yes, of course," she told Margaret. "As you said, these rooms get so overheated."

Yet as they moved out into the cool night air, the crowds dispersing, the queer, shivery feeling did not leave Isobel. She reached into her reticule to touch the hidden pamphlet, and wondered, with a thrill of incredulity, if there might be a way to escape her life in Boston after all.

*

Hartford, Connecticut

Ian Campbell was used to the bumpy rumble of the stagecoach from Boston to Hartford. He had travelled it over a dozen times in the last few years in his continuing attempt to experiment with ether and its use as an anesthetic. Usually he was filled with a blazing excitement as he made the journey, his optimism for a future of medical innovation and pain-free procedures keeping his spirits high. Today that anticipation was tempered by the cool distance he had felt between himself and Caroline.

In the five years since he had wed Caroline, they'd certainly argued. They both possessed passionate tempers, and Ian privately thought they both enjoyed, to a certain measure, the blazing rows that often ended rather delightfully with Caroline throwing herself into his arms and him kissing her thoroughly.

This time it was different. Caroline was different, and although she remained dutiful and attentive, Ian could feel the difference, and had done ever since the wretched salon they'd hosted, as well as the confrontation he'd had with her later, that had made him ache with sadness at how resigned she'd seemed.

On several occasions he'd caught Caroline gazing at him, her eyes shadowed with what he feared was disappointment. By refusing to use the inheritance Caroline had received from her uncle to fund his experiments with ether, Ian knew he had disappointed, and even worse, hurt his wife. He saw it in her eyes, and he felt it in the silent chasm that had opened up between them—a chasm he did not know how to bridge. Not without relinquishing his position, and he wasn't willing to do that.

Restlessly he shifted in the uncomfortable coach seat. Across the coach an elderly matron gave him a sternly disapproving look. A tabby cat crouched in a covered basket at her feet, and it yowled as if agreeing with its mistress. Ian ducked his head in apology.

He did not know how to make amends with Caroline. He did not know if he could. The thought of accepting Sir James Riddell's money for his own purposes made his stomach churn and his body burn with a righteous anger he'd thought he'd surrendered long ago. It was nearly twenty years since Riddell had cheated Ian of his family farm back on the Isle of Mull, and as an adult Ian could now see his own foolish part in the sorry tale. He'd been proud and naive and worse, careless, but Riddell had taken advantage of the fifteen-year-old boy he'd been, so desperate to prove himself to his family, and especially to his father, that he'd signed a contract without reading all the terms. He had signed away his family's farm and legacy for a fraction of its value—and Riddell had set him up to do so.

How could he forgive that? How could he forget it? He couldn't take Riddell's money, even though he was fair enough to suppose it was reasonable for Caroline to expect him to use the funds she had inherited to any purpose that bettered their situation. He'd agreed to the purchase of a townhouse in a well-to-do neighborhood of Boston, and he was happy for Caroline to use the money for gowns and fripperies and whatever else she liked, but he himself would not touch it, not for that which mattered to him so deeply.

The suggestion alone had set a new fury pulsing through him, followed by a deep, wounding regret. *And I thought I was yours.* Caroline's sorrowful voice echoed through his mind and heart. He wished she could understand. He even wished he could feel differently, and in so doing end this coldness between them. Yet he knew he couldn't, and he doubted he ever would. Caroline would simply have to become accustomed.

His concerns about Caroline and her inheritance were momentarily and necessarily pushed aside when Ian arrived in Hartford. He hired a hansom to take him to Horace Wells' dental practice, already anticipating the rousing discussions they would have, the experiments they might perform. He had been collaborating with Wells for several years, and they had progressed from using the ether on small animals to using it on themselves, with undeniable success. Ian had performed a minor surgery on Wells' arm while the man had been under the influence of ether, and Wells claimed he hadn't felt a thing! They'd progressed to more invasive procedures, and the possibilities it opened up for surgeries were breathtaking. For a surgeon, to not have to be as quick as he possibly could, to have the unimaginable luxury of taking his time…

The goal, of course, was for ether to be accepted by the medical community at large, and used regularly. Unfortunately, based on the loud opinions of some of Ian's older colleagues, he bleakly wondered how, or even *if*, it would ever come to pass.

Wells was in a fever of excitement as Ian arrived. "Take your coat off, man, and come right into the examining room," he bid Ian, shoving aside stacks of dusty books and piles of papers. Ian stepped gingerly amid the detritus, surprised and a bit alarmed by the way Wells' house had descended into dust and dirt in the months since he had last been there. Admittedly, as a single man, Wells had never been the tidiest of gentlemen, yet Ian recalled that he had still employed a rather dour woman to do the scouring and cooking several times a week. If the state of the sitting room was anything to go by, she had not been in attendance for some time.

In just his shirtsleeves, Ian came into the examining room. It, at least, was in a better state than the sitting room, although he noticed a crumb-scattered plate and a dirty glass pushed to the side.

When had he become so fastidious, Ian wondered, even as he acknowledged that the state of Wells' house did not alarm him as much as the feverish glitter in the man's eyes. Together they were most unsettling, but perhaps Wells was simply excited by the possibilities ether presented, just as Ian was.

"I've been experimenting on myself, of course," Wells began, and Ian's eyebrows rose.

"Have you? Without an assistant? I thought we had agreed—"

"I had no choice. You have been kept busy with your own affairs in Boston."

Ian did not know if he was imagining the slight note of scornful accusation in his colleague's voice. "I have a profession to maintain," he said stiffly. "As do you." He glanced once more around the room. "Have you seen many patients?"

Wells shrugged impatiently. "Why should I? There are more important things to attend to."

"I agree the research is paramount," Ian said after a moment. He felt a deep and growing unease at the state of his colleague. He had always found Wells a bit reckless; it was what had given the man the boldness to start his experiments with ether. "But, Wells, man, we both have professional obligations we cannot ignore. Surely you see that."

"Well, we can certainly make use of your professional status," Wells interrupted, his tone turning both sharp and wheedling.

Ian raised his eyebrows. "Indeed?"

"It's time you earned your place at the table," Wells continued, and Ian stiffened in affront. Surely he had earned that already, and more. He was as committed to the research as Wells was. "The only way for the use of ether to be accepted by the medical community is to perform an experiment in public," Wells stated, his face flushed, his eyes still possessing that disturbing glitter. "And what better place than the operating theatre of the Massachusetts General Hospital?"

Ian stared, excitement and trepidation warring within him. He agreed with Wells in principle, of course, but the reality was that attempting to arrange such an experiment could cost him his position—and thus his livelihood. Then he really would have no choice but to rely on Riddell's money.

Wells narrowed his eyes. "You're not frightened, are you, Campbell?" he asked softly. "Not afraid to put the full weight of your position—your reputation—behind these experiments as I have?"

"Of course not," Ian said, knowing he was being drawn by the most obvious and base of methods, yet unable to respond in any other way. He straightened, his expression cool. "It won't be easy, as you must already know. Many of the doctors and surgeons I work with do not see as I do on this matter."

"Surely they might agree to a single experiment. All it would take is one success for people to change their minds."

Ian thought it might take more than that, but the point was not worth arguing, he knew. "I shall see what I can do," he said. "I will make inquiries, at any rate."

"Good." Wells was already rolling up his sleeve. "Now let us get down to business. I want you to put me under the ether, and operate on my arm."

"We've done this before—" Ian protested.

"This time you're to only give me enough for my eyelids to flutter. We'll see how low the dosage can go. That will give those fussy surgeons in Boston something to think about."

CHAPTER FOUR

Prince Edward Island

"Has there been a letter yet?"

Harriet laughed and shook her head, rolling her eyes at Maggie's eager expression. "Maggie, *cridhe*, I doubt your aunt will have even received our letter yet! It takes a week or more, and then another week to reply. And that's only if she sets pen to paper the moment she reads it."

Smiling, she opened the letter she'd received from Eleanor. Letters from the Ohio Territory could take far longer than ones from Boston, sometimes many months, and when news came it was always precious, if out of date.

Maggie sighed and flung herself into a chair at the table where Anna had been sorting buttons. She picked up a bright red one and rolled it between her fingers restlessly. "What is the news from Aunt Eleanor?" she asked, her tone indifferent. It was Boston her daughter cared about, Harriet knew.

"She and Uncle Rupert are well," Harriet said after a pause as she scanned the lines. "Alexander is already three!" She looked up, shaking her head as sorrow sent its familiar pang through. "We have never even met the little lad. And there is another on the way... born in the early summer, God willing. Not long now."

"It's been over a week since you wrote," Maggie said as she tossed the button back into the box. "Surely a letter will come soon?"

"Perhaps, but we can hardly be up and down to Charlottetown three times a week to fetch it! Patience, Maggie. The letter will come when it comes."

"And if she agrees?" Maggie twisted around in her chair, her dark eyes reminding Harriet so much of Margaret's. "There are steamers leaving Charlottetown for Boston once a week—"

"Are there?" Harriet asked, amused. "And where have you been learning such knowledge?"

"It's in the *Prince Edward Island Advertiser*. Papa brings it back when he goes into town."

"I see," Harriet said. Her daughter really was eager to be on her way.

"What will Boston be like?" Anna asked, looking up from her buttons. "Is it very big?"

"Bigger than this," Maggie returned. "Bigger than Charlottetown."

"You went there when you were little more than a bairn," Harriet reminded Anna. "Although I'm not surprised you don't remember. Yes, Boston is bigger, although I think Charlottetown is prettier." She gave Maggie a teasing look her daughter ignored. It was clear she would not have a word said against the city she'd decided to adopt as her own, even before she'd travelled there.

"But what will you do in Boston?" Anna asked, sounding dubious, and Maggie's face lighted up with expectant pleasure.

"All manner of things! Dances and plays and balls…"

"I'm not quite sure you'll be doing all that, my love," Harriet interjected hastily. "Your aunt lives a fairly quiet life, and will do so especially when Uncle Henry is gone, and there's also little Charlotte to think of."

"Oh, but surely we'll go out!" Maggie exclaimed, her face falling a little bit at Harriet's words.

"Aye, a bit, of course. And there's also Uncle Ian to think of—you know your Aunt Caroline is quite a sociable woman.

Perhaps she'll take you under her wing." Although those might have been rash words, Harriet acknowledged; she was not as close with Ian and his wife as she was with Margaret and Henry. Even though they'd reconciled long ago over Ian's part in the loss of Achlic, their relationship had never been quite the same. As for his wife, little Caroline Reid… Harriet had never been able to shake the image of the spoiled and petulant eight-year-old she'd once taught pianoforte back on Mull, even though Caroline was now a lovely, gracious young woman of twenty-three.

"Would they?" Maggie asked eagerly. "Aunt Caroline was always so fashionable when we saw her…"

"Yes, well, we shall see. We haven't even received a reply, so there's no point counting our chickens quite yet."

"I'll have to learn to waltz," Maggie said dreamily. "Mama, will you teach me?"

"Waltz!" Harriet laughed, amazed at the extent of her daughter's dreams. "I never learned the waltz, Maggie. You'll have to ask your father—he's the one who had dancing lessons!" She'd had a far humbler childhood as the daughter of a farmer; Allan had been the tacksman's son, with a mother who'd had a season in Edinburgh.

"What's this about dancing?" Allan asked with a grin as he came in for the noonday meal, George and little Archie trailing behind.

"Mama says you learned to waltz," Maggie said.

"Aye, and so I did!"

Harriet let out a little shriek of surprise as Allan took her by the waist and began to waltz her around the room.

"I have a frying pan in my hand," she exclaimed, laughing, while George and Archie shouted and danced around them in excitement.

"So you do, my love, so you do." Allan plucked the frying pan from her hand and put it back on top of the cast iron stove that had been a recent and useful addition to the house.

"Dance with me, Papa," Anna exclaimed, scrambling out of her chair, and gallantly Allan took a turn around the room with her before turning to Maggie with an expectant smile. "Shall you learn the way of it, lass?"

Hesitantly Maggie took his hand, and Harriet's heart filled with both thankfulness and sorrow as she watched Allan gently lead their daughter around the room. How sweet these moments were, and how fleeting! In a few weeks Maggie might be gone, and once she went, who knew if she would ever come back? Harriet thought of Eleanor... of Ian... of Margaret and Rupert. They had all left to find their callings... and they'd never returned.

Would Maggie be the same?

*

Boston

Margaret shivered in the brisk spring breeze as she stood on one of the quays of Boston Harbor, her young daughter Charlotte's arms wrapped around her waist. The sky was full of the bristling masts of the harbor's many ships, and the air echoed with the raucous cries of gulls as well as the shouts of sailors and the creaking of pulleys and ropes as crates were heaved to and fro, a world in motion, and one to be transported.

They were here to say a final goodbye to Henry—one that had come too soon for Margaret when his arrangements to sail for China had developed apace. She was still trying to make peace with the fact he would be once again taking a long, dangerous journey across the world. She watched fearfully as gusts of wind snapped the sails of the *Charlotte Rose* back and forth. Henry had named his clipper ship after their daughter; the ship's name would serve as a heartening reminder of family, of home, as he sailed. But what, Margaret thought, of her and Charlotte, waiting at home, missing him, as the months became a year, and a year might become more?

Margaret had had several weeks to resign herself to Henry's journey, yet she feared she had not been entirely successful. As much as she wished to put a brave face on it for her husband's sake, she'd spent many nights staring wide-eyed at the ceiling as she considered the many things that could go wrong on such a voyage... Storms, disease, even pirates. And what if tension flared in Canton, over the miserable opium trade? Margaret had read in the newspaper only that week of possible discussions of a blockade, to keep the British and American ships from unloading the opium they continued to smuggle into a country that didn't want it.

A few evenings ago they'd had a farewell dinner at Henry's parents' house, everyone trying to keep their spirits up for Henry and Margaret's sakes. Isobel had been the only one who had seemed genuinely excited for Henry's journey, peppering him with questions about the sea voyage and what he thought China would be like.

"I don't know, I haven't been before," Henry had answered with a laugh. "But since you seem so interested, I will lend you my book *Journey to the Far Seas*. It has some illuminating descriptions." To Margaret's surprise, Isobel had been pleased by the idea, and had even suggested she come to fetch the book the next day. Her sister-in-law had become uncommonly taken with the idea of travelling since they'd listened to Mr. Judson a few weeks ago. Margaret hoped she did not get too many impossible ideas in her head.

Just as she hoped Henry would be safe on the *Charlotte Rose;* clipper ships were known to be sleek and fast, and they were well-suited to carrying tea and spices from China as they were smaller—and faster, thanks to their many sails. Flimsier, too, though, Margaret feared. She could scarcely suppress a shudder at the thought of Henry battling the China Seas, known to be some of the roughest in the world, in such a light craft. She turned to Henry with a smile, determined for him not to see how afraid she was. She'd been brave these last few weeks; she could be brave a few minutes longer.

"I shall miss you." Henry's expression was tender as he gazed down at her. She knew he was staying strong for them all, just as she was. "I shall write to you as often as I can."

Margaret nodded, not trusting herself to speak. She didn't want to point out that letters would take months to arrive, or even longer, for he would have to find someone heading towards Boston at one of the ports where he put in. His promise to write provided little comfort, but she knew he meant it as such.

"And I shall think of you every day," she finally answered, her voice choking only a little. "And pray for you." Pray for the safety of his ship and his men, his very life. The dangers and threats of an ocean crossing, never mind what reception might await him in China, made her throat close and she blinked rapidly.

"Ah, Margaret." Henry drew her into his arms, Charlotte still pressed to her side. "I know this is not easy for you."

Margaret pressed her face against the scratchy wool of his coat, her eyes closed against the hot onslaught of tears. She did not want to cry at this most precious of farewells, and with Charlotte present, as well. She wished she'd been able to convince Henry of her good cheer, but he knew her too well.

Finally, she drew in a deep breath and pulled away from him. "Go safely," she said, and this time her voice sounded sure and strong. "I trust you to God."

Henry stroked her cheek. "And you go safely as well, my love," he said, softly enough that only she could hear. "I love you more than you could ever know."

"Papa." Charlotte yanked on the bottom of Henry's coat, her lower lip pushed out as she gazed up at her father. "Aren't you going to hug me, as well?"

"Of course I am, my poppet," Henry said, his voice as jolly as ever, for their daughter's sake. He scooped Charlotte up into his arms, and Margaret smiled to see Charlotte loop her little arms around his neck and press her cheek to his.

"You will write me too, Papa?" Charlotte asked.

"Of course."

"And think of me every day?" She leaned back to look seriously into her father's face. Margaret saw the gleam of emotion in Henry's eyes but his smile was just as wide as it had ever been. "Every moment of every day. How could I not, when I am traveling on you, after all?"

"Papa!" Charlotte squealed in delighted protest. She never tired of the proud thrill of having a ship named after her.

Slowly Henry set down Charlotte and looked into Margaret's eyes. His, she saw, were shadowed with worry, despite his cheerful tone with Charlotte. Was it the same fear she felt for his wellbeing, or was he simply worried for hers? She had a terrible, creeping feeling that Henry was not being completely honest with her about the dangers of travel to China. The rough seas, the awful opium trade, the hostile Chinese government—what if there was even more to fear, that he hadn't told her?

Charlotte tugged at the hem of Henry's frock coat. "How long will you be gone, Papa?"

Henry exchanged a quick, guarded look with Margaret; once again, it took all her strength to keep her face as bland as she could. Henry already knew her opinion on the subject; a year was an incalculable amount of time to a child. Charlotte might not even remember him when he returned. *If* he returned.

"I shall bring you a present next Christmas," Henry finally said.

"Christmas!" Charlotte exclaimed in surprise and disappointment. "That's ever so long away."

And more than she even knew, Margaret thought sadly, for Henry did not mean this Christmas, but the one next year. Forever, especially to a four-year-old girl.

"Never mind, Charlotte," she said with brisk cheer, drawing her daughter close in reassurance. "We'll have fun plotting Papa's journey on the big map in his study. You know the one I mean, don't you? And the time will go by quickly enough, I promise you."

Charlotte frowned, still trying to comprehend such a large amount of time. Margaret squeezed her shoulder. "Say goodbye now, sweeting."

Charlotte dutifully stepped forward. "Goodbye, Papa."

"Goodbye, my precious girl." Henry enveloped his daughter in another great big bear hug before turning to his wife. "Margaret…"

"Godspeed," Margaret said, blinking hard. "You are in my thoughts, always."

Mindless of the sailors and stevedores working the docks, Henry swept his wife into his arms and kissed her soundly on the mouth.

"*Henry!*" Margaret tried—and failed—to sound scandalized. She needed that kiss to sustain her for many long, lonely months to come.

With one hand pressed to her lips, her other holding tightly onto Charlotte, she watched Henry board the *Charlotte Rose*. As the bell rung signaling the ship's departure, the *Charlotte Rose* pushed off from the dock, and Margaret felt a piece of her heart die within her. He had gone.

She and Charlotte were both quiet on the carriage ride back to their home in Back Bay. Charlotte rested her head against her mother's shoulder, as if to absorb the pain Margaret felt coursing through her. She stroked her daughter's soft cheek, grateful for her company at least in the long months ahead, knowing she would need to be strong for Charlotte's sake, as well as her own and Henry's. She did not want him worrying about her when he would have so many other cares to occupy his mind.

Back at the house, Margaret listlessly sifted through the morning post that had been left in the hall as she waited for their maid to bring tea. "A letter from Prince Edward Island," she said aloud, her heart skipping a bit faster in alarm. Her sister-in-law Harriet wrote her regularly, once a month when possible, with all the family's news, but since she'd only received a letter from her a week ago, Margaret was surprised to find another sent so quickly after. She prayed it did not bring ill news.

"What is it, Mama?" Charlotte asked as she went into the drawing room and sat down. Charlotte perched next to her on the settee.

"It's from your aunt…" Margaret scanned the letter, her frown of concern quickly turning into a smile first of relief, and then of excitement. "She's asking if your cousin Maggie can come to stay for a while, perhaps even until Papa returns. What a lovely idea! She'll keep us company, won't she?" She smiled at her daughter, the pain in her heart lightening just a little. Company, at this moment, would be most welcome. She didn't know her niece Maggie particularly well; she'd only been ten or so when they'd come to Boston for the winter, and now she would be a young woman. Company indeed, Margaret thought as she put her arm around her daughter. She would be glad for it.

*

Isobel stood in front of the bow-fronted building that housed the offices of the American Board of Commissioners for Foreign Missions and tried to summon the courage to enter. Last week she'd written the board rather recklessly, after another interminable evening sitting alone at a recitation, trying not to notice as a gaggle of young girls, barely out of the schoolroom, whispered about her. Calling her a thornback, perhaps? A dried-up old maid? A bluestocking? She tried not to mind, and yet she did. She did unbearably.

She'd come home and that very evening penned a letter to the Board, asking if she could call on them at their earliest convenience. She'd sent it in the morning's post before she could talk herself out of it. It would come to nothing, she told herself—until she'd received the note from the Board's General Secretary, Mr. Rufus Anderson, yesterday morning, saying he would be happy for her to call at his offices at four o'clock today, after she finished her day of teaching at the First School.

It was now three minutes before that hour, and Isobel felt an alarming flutter of nerves in her middle; her lunch sat queasily in her stomach. Drawing a deep breath, she squared her shoulders, her fingers tightening around the bone handle of her reticule, and marched up the steps to the building.

Her knock was answered after a minute or two by a harried-looking young man with ink-stained fingers and a crooked cravat. Isobel eyed him with some trepidation, as well as an innate disapproval. "I have an appointment with Mr. Anderson?" she said, her tone turning a bit more imperious than she would have liked because of her nerves. She always became more stiff and formal when she felt anxious or uncertain.

"Of course, you must be Miss Moore. Won't you come in?" He stepped aside, and Isobel sailed into an unprepossessing front room with piles of books and pamphlets covering most of the chairs and the table. She looked around in dismay, half-wanting to back out already, but it was too late.

Mr. Anderson opened the door to his private study and beckoned her in. "Miss Moore, I'm delighted to welcome you. Please do come in." He gestured to the clerk. "Mr. Smith, fetch us some tea, would you, please."

Gingerly Isobel made her way past the stacks of books into a far more comfortable room. Mr. Anderson gestured for her to sit down and he returned to the other side of the desk, steepling his fingers under his chin. "I was very pleased to receive your letter," he said, smiling, his eyes twinkling behind his spectacles. "And indeed, pleased to hear of your family's interest in missions. It is most gratifying to have such a fine family of this city take an interest in our endeavors."

"I see," Isobel said, although she didn't, not really. She shifted in her seat, frowning in uneasy confusion. "My family's interest… but I wrote to you on my own behalf, Mr. Anderson, not that of my family."

Anderson shrugged this aside. "Forgive my presumption, but naturally I assumed your interest in missions is your family's interest, Miss Moore. Perhaps I should tell you of some of our more pressing needs, and then you might relate these to your father?" He raised his eyebrows expectantly, already drawing a sheet of paper, no doubt detailing those many needs, towards him.

Isobel's face warmed and her hands were slippery inside her thin gloves. "I am afraid, Mr. Anderson, that you may have been mistaken in your assumptions. Perhaps I should have been clearer in my letter to you. If so, I do apologize."

Anderson gave a little shake of his head. He was still smiling, but a furrow had appeared between his eyebrows. "I'm afraid I don't understand, Miss Moore."

This was not, Isobel thought with some panic, going at all how she'd anticipated. Not that she'd even dared imagine the particulars. Her letter had been a moment's madness, and she'd decided to act upon its receipt because—oh, because she didn't know what else to do! This morning she'd seen a streak of gray in her hair and been appalled. She felt as if the very grave were creeping up on her, clutching her by the throat, and she had to *do* something. Anything… even this. She drew a shaky breath. "The truth is, sir, that my family is not even aware of this visit."

Anderson sat forward, his smile fading as the furrow deepened. "Oh?" He sounded puzzled, and already faintly disapproving. "I'm afraid then I'm not clear on why you have visited here, Miss Moore."

Just then Mr. Smith, the clerk with the ink-stained fingers, knocked on the door, and Isobel was given a few moments to compose herself as he bustled in with the tea things. Mr. Anderson's tone, she thought, had sounded quite a bit cooler when she'd admitted her family didn't know she was here. But he'd surely authorized the printing of those pamphlets. Why shouldn't she take him up on the challenge he'd issued? Why shouldn't he be pleased by it?

Bolstered by this thought as well as a much-needed sip of tea, Isobel felt emboldened enough to speak plainly. "I'm here, Mr. Anderson, because I am interested in missions for myself. That is, to become a missionary."

Anderson did not speak for a moment, and Isobel took another sip of tea, burning her tongue. She felt as if she'd said something ridiculous; she felt ridiculous in herself. Was she not missionary material? Was the notion so completely absurd? Margaret had looked at her askance at the mere possibility; why should this man do any less? She would do the same; she felt as if she were playing a role or trying on a dress. This wasn't *her*.

And yet…why not? What about her was so objectionable? She lifted her chin, giving Mr. Anderson a faint, cool smile as she waited for his reply. She realized she'd envisioned, in a vague sort of way, for him to fall over in delight at her announcement, to proclaim how grateful he was to have a woman such as herself willing to brave the mission field. Clearly she had been reading too many romantic novels.

"I see," he finally said, and his voice sounded regretful. "I'm afraid I did misunderstand your intent, Miss Moore. I assumed you had requested an appointment to discuss a donation on behalf of your family."

"I see." Mortified, Isobel looked down. He hadn't understood her purpose at *all*. "Of course, my family—my father would be delighted—"

"No, no, it is my own mistake." He waved her stammering protestations aside, offering a rueful smile. "I made a wishful presumption. However…" His expression softened slightly as he continued, "I'm afraid, Miss Moore, that we no longer accept unmarried women into the mission field."

She bit her lip. "But I read about Miss Stockton travelling to the Hawaiian Islands…"

"Yes, yes, that is true." He nodded, but the gesture was one of regretful dismissal. "However, that was many years ago now, and since then, based on some unfortunate experiences women have had in the field, we have chosen only to allow married couples to embark on what surely is an arduous, painful, and often fatal journey." He regarded her rather sternly, as if he suspected her of wanting to be a missionary out of boredom rather than zeal. And really, Isobel thought miserably, wasn't that at least partially the truth? Maybe even mostly. She knew her zeal was sadly lacking, and yet she did want to do something meaningful. Something important. *Something somewhere else*. She felt her face flush yet again and she stared down at her lap.

"I… I see." Taking a deep breath, she placed her cup and saucer back on the table with a rather unsteady clatter. "I'm afraid I didn't realize how things had changed. I'm sorry to have wasted your time."

"There is no need to apologize, of course. We do, however," Anderson said after a pause, "maintain a list of missionary-minded young women who are educated, pious, and of good health, for marriage purposes."

Isobel stared at him blankly. "Marriage purposes?"

"Many young men who wish to enter the mission field are unmarried," Anderson explained. "And they wish to find a suitable life partner to accompany them on missions. We maintain a list for such men, to aid them in seeking a wife. Perhaps you would like to include yourself? Naturally I would need a reference from your own minister."

"A reference..." she repeated, her mind spinning. She could feel her face redden further and she pleated her fingers together in her lap, nervous and unaccountably embarrassed. Humiliated, even. To put her name on such a list! It was galling indeed. She was annoyed that Mr. Anderson had mentioned it at all, especially to a woman of her position and standing in society, and yet...

Thornback. Spinster. Bluestocking. Wife? Could she possibly be considering such a thing, even for a moment? It seemed ludicrous, pathetic, the actions of a desperate woman indeed. She would not do it, of course. Imagine the gossip! Isobel cleared her throat. "Well, that is a rather different proposition than I was anticipating, Mr. Anderson. I'm not sure I can give you an answer today regarding such a serious consideration, and I must confess one that has taken me quite aback. It is true I am unmarried, but I never..." She trailed off, unable to finish that sentence.

"No, of course not, I understand completely," Anderson said quickly, clearly sensitive to her embarrassment. "I mentioned it only because you seemed so disappointed not to be able to enter the mission field, and it is an alternative, should you wish to consider it in due course."

Isobel forced herself to meet his compassionate and far too knowing gaze. Did he see the gray in her hair? Did he realize how little adventure or even hope life had afforded her? He surely must guess her age, and realize how few prospects she had. "Yes," she said, lifting her chin even as her face flamed. "I...I suppose I might consider it."

CHAPTER FIVE

Boston

Isobel tapped her slippered foot in tempo with the lively waltz that was playing as she sat on the periphery of the ballroom—on the periphery of a life that no longer fit, that somehow was no longer hers. It was as if she were staring through a looking glass as the couples waltzed, the women's bright skirts brushing by in a swirl of silk. She would not be asked to dance; it would not even be considered, and she had not so much as brought her dance card. Even if she were asked, Isobel knew she would not accept. To receive such obvious pity would be humiliating in the extreme.

She glanced at Elizabeth Ascott, the seventeen-year-old girl sitting next to her. Elizabeth watched the waltzing with forlorn eyes, her empty dance card dangling from one wrist. Isobel felt a stab of pity for the girl; in her younger years, Isobel at least had never had to deal with the disappointment of an unfilled dance card. She had always been in demand, until Ian Campbell had married Caroline Reid and overnight Isobel had become unwanted—a spinster, and in this case, merely a chaperone, for the girl's mother had asked Isobel to keep an eye on her. Isobel had agreed, as she had many times over the years, for at least it gave some purpose to these tiresome events she only attended for her parents' sake, as well as her own pride. To refuse to attend would be even more humiliating than sitting on the side for the whole evening.

"They are doing a reel next," she told Elizabeth with bracing cheer. "I am sure you will be asked to dance."

Elizabeth gave a small, unhappy smile and looked away without replying. Isobel was used to such reactions to her attempts at encouragement; she thought sometimes these young ladies believed spinsterhood to be catching. And perhaps it was, for the reel started and Elizabeth remained where she was.

"Shall I fetch us some punch?" Isobel suggested, in a vain hope to lift the girl's spirits, and Elizabeth just shrugged. She was only seventeen or so, Isobel knew. She had plenty of time to wait and hope, and yet she knew how insufferable such waiting could be. "I shall return shortly," she promised, and she made her way to the table of refreshments at one end of the drawing room that had been cleared of furniture for dancing. The windows were open to the warm spring air, and people gathered in clusters around the room while the reel started its lively tune. It had been years since Isobel had danced, and yet she still couldn't keep from humming under her breath as her feet twitched to take to the floor.

"Good evening, Isobel. I trust you're well?"

She'd just reached the table of refreshments when she turned in surprise to see Ian smiling at her. They had met often enough in society, of course, and their conversations, while formal, were pleasant enough. Five years, Isobel knew, was a long time. At least it was meant to be.

"Very well, thank you." She gave him a stiff smile as she took a cup of punch. "As you are, I hope? And Caroline?"

A shadow flickered in Ian's eyes, making Isobel wonder, but he nodded. "Yes, thank you."

And that, she supposed, would be the extent of their conversation. He wouldn't tell her about his work in the hospital, not that she would have ever inquired, and she certainly would not mention her visit to the American Board of Commissioners for Foreign Missions last week, or that dreaded list she was still thinking of putting her name on. The very idea of it caused her face to flush in embarrassment. She would write Mr. Anderson tomorrow and tell him she had no intention of considering it. Of course she would.

"Your teaching work fares well?" Ian asked, doing his valiant best to keep the conversation afloat. "I find it so admirable."

"It fares well enough. And I do not know that you should find it particularly admirable, for I confess my desire to do it is almost entirely selfish."

Ian looked surprised by Isobel's words, as well as her slightly waspish tone. Normally she wouldn't have said such a thing, but some restless contrariness inside had forced the remark. "Selfish?" he repeated. "How so?"

Isobel shrugged. "I have nothing else to do but read, sew, or play the pianoforte. A life lived for amusement only is hardly one at all." She had tried to sound matter-of-fact rather than bitter, and feared she hadn't succeeded.

"Yet there are many who do exactly that, and without it pricking their conscience in the least. Surely that is admirable in itself."

"You are very forgiving," Isobel returned tartly, and Ian gave her a wry smile, shadowed by sorrow.

"As you have been."

Was he referring to his behavior five years ago? They had never mentioned it in all that time, and the sudden reference discomfited her in the extreme—and made her reckless. "I am considering something," she said abruptly. "Something I never thought I would."

Ian's eyes glinted with interest. "I am intrigued."

"It will no doubt be looked upon by all of society as a madness caused by desperation," she continued, growing more reckless by the second, "and yet I find I do not much care."

"Then I am glad," Ian returned. "For to be constrained by society's narrow expectations is stifling indeed."

"Have you felt such a thing?" Isobel asked in disbelief, and Ian inclined his head.

"I have, with the medical experiments I wish to conduct. But I know you do not wish to discuss such unpleasant things."

Had she said so once? Isobel knew she must have. "I do wish it," she told him now. "I had heard something of it, but I confess I did not follow it closely."

"An entirely sensible response, and one many people share," he replied with a small smile, although his eyes looked strained. "It has to do with the use of ether in surgery—very tedious stuff, I assure you. But tell me, what act of madness are you considering? For I dearly wish to know."

"Oh…" Isobel looked away, unwilling to tell him about the missions board, the list. To marry a missionary, a man who was looking for a wife of manners and piety. *That* sounded tedious, surely. "It will come to nothing, I'm sure."

Briefly Ian laid a hand on her sleeve, startling Isobel so much she nearly spilled her cup of punch. "I hope it does not, for whatever it is, when you speak of it I see a spark in your eye and a spring to your step that I have not seen for some time. It would be good to see it again, Isobel, for both our sakes. I have followed my own dream, though it has had its risks and costs, some of which grieve me sorely." She looked at him in surprise, but he shook his head, not willing to speak of it. "And yet still I would follow it, as far as I could. You must follow yours."

The reel had ended, and with a parting smile for Ian, Isobel returned to her glum charge with two cups of punch. As she resumed her seat on the side of the room, the dreaded wallflower, she considered Ian's words.

Follow your dream. Was this hers? Could it be?

Isobel took a sip of cool punch as she considered the matter again, and this time with more intent than she had ever felt before. Her dream, she knew, was not just to marry, as much as she wished for that, but to travel, to learn, to experience life in a way she hadn't yet. She wanted to live for a greater purpose than sitting on the side of a ballroom, and while teaching at the school addressed that to a degree, it was not enough.

Would marriage to a missionary, a life lived somewhere far away, in tireless service to others, satisfy her? Briefly Isobel closed her eyes, imagining the list Mr. Anderson had mentioned, of prospective wives for missionary-minded men. What kind of women would be on that list? Pious, well-mannered, God-fearing. They sounded so *dull*, and yet Isobel knew that was unfair. Yet how did one go about actually marrying such a man? Could such a practical arrangement lead one day to affection and even love? She could scarcely imagine it, yet she had spent a good amount of time in the last week attempting to do so. There was one certainty: it could be a way out of this constrained life; the answer to her barely-formed dreams of seeing the world, and doing something with purpose in the bargain.

Of course she'd left the office of the Board of Commissioners for Foreign Missions in a huff of indignant denial; she was surely not yet in such a sorry state as to put her name on a *list* of women for men to pick and choose the candidates as they so wished! The idea was preposterous, as she'd kept telling herself.

Yet even so, in her loneliest moments Isobel was forced to concede the idea held some merit. She still wanted a husband, perhaps even children. A *life*. And if she had to go to such dire extremes to get those things, well, what of it?

At least, Isobel told herself, she would have some choice. She did not have to marry anyone she did not like. Just as the man could refuse, so could she. She would have some power, more perhaps than she'd yet known. And yet the awkwardness of discussing marriage with such a man, of going over her attributes as if she were a cow to be sold at market…

Well, Isobel reminded herself, was it any different than what happened in a ballroom such as this, or a proud papa's study the next day? A woman's future was all a matter of barter and trade.

"Good evening, Isobel. What a lovely gown. I don't believe you've worn it before, have you?"

Isobel turned to see Patience Fairley smiling sweetly at her. She recognized the supposed compliment for the barb it truly was; Patience had not seen this gown before because Isobel had had no occasion to wear it. Most women, even among the highest circle of Boston society, would wear a gown more than once in a season.

"It is lovely, is it not?" Isobel agreed, keeping her voice and manner pleasant by sheer force of will. Patience was her own age, and had married a decade ago. She had long since cultivated the smug satisfaction of the successful matron, with four young children and a husband who, with the passage of years, had become florid and corpulent. Still, Patience basked in how much she had in comparison to Isobel.

"Are you still teaching at that school?" Patience asked, in a tone that suggested that it would be rather dreadful if she were.

"Yes, as a matter of fact," Isobel said, and saw Patience's expression soften into pity—the most painful of all sentiments to bear.

"I suppose it keeps you occupied," she stated almost mournfully, and Isobel gritted her teeth.

"Indeed it does, as do all good works. But as it happens, I shall be leaving the school shortly." The words shocked Isobel even as they came out of her mouth, and she watched in dazed satisfaction as Patience's complacent expression faltered, and her eyes narrowed.

"Is that so? And for what reason, pray?"

Isobel smiled mysteriously. "I'm afraid I am not yet at liberty to say. But you shall hear of it soon enough, I daresay."

Patience frowned, as if she doubted Isobel yet could not say so, and so she said nothing.

And the truth was Isobel was lying, or nearly. What had made her say such a thing? She had no intention of leaving the school.

Unless…

Unless she married. Unless she put her name on that list.

"Please do excuse me," Isobel murmured. "I think Elizabeth and I would like to take some air." She glanced at Elizabeth, who nodded dolefully, and with a murmured farewell they walked across the room, to the set of windows open to the evening air.

"Are you leaving the school?" Elizabeth asked without much interest, and Isobel gave her a mysterious smile.

"Indeed I am," she replied as certainty hardened within her. She was not going to spend the rest of her life like this, restless and waiting. She was going to put her name on that list.

CHAPTER SIX

Boston

The drawing room windows were open to the fragrant June air as Isobel's father Stephen sipped his port, his slippered feet stretched out in front of him and *The Boston Post* folded and waiting on a table beside him.

Her mother sat across from him absorbed in her embroidery hoop; Isobel made up the third point of this domestic triangle, seated in an armchair with a book forgotten in her lap. It had become the custom when there were no outside engagements for the three of them to spend a quiet evening at home in various pursuits, whether reading or embroidery or, for her father, a leisurely perusal of the paper.

Yet tonight Isobel could barely concentrate on her book, a slim volume of poetry by Wordsworth, because she had decided that she would tell her parents of her plan to be added to Rufus Anderson's list. The very thought of the conversation that would follow set her heart to thudding and made her palms slick. She was not so naive to think her parents would approve of her decision, or let her do it without protest. Perhaps they would forbid her entirely. They would not, she suspected, altogether approve of her being married to a missionary, or of the life that awaited her in some strange and possibly hostile land, where she would most likely be doomed to live out her days in difficulty and grief, to bury her children as they sickened from some dreadful, foreign disease…

What really, then, was she thinking? Working over every argument they might have in her mind shook her, for even she saw reason in it. Why, truly, did she wish to do such a reckless and dangerous thing? Terror clutched at her, but she pushed it away, determined to see this through. Anything, even danger or grief, was better than this wasting of her days, the very last of her youth, here in Boston.

"Isobel," her mother murmured reprovingly. "You are fidgeting. It is not ladylike."

Isobel flushed. There was no greater sin in her mother's eyes. "I'm sorry," she murmured. She stared blindly down at her book. "I have quite a lot on my mind," she continued, her words coming out in no more than a whisper.

Arabella raised her eyebrows. "I did not realize you were so preoccupied." She completed several neat stitches before raising her gaze to Isobel once more. "That school takes too much of your time. I have always thought so. Perhaps it is time to consider other pursuits."

Isobel knew her mother didn't like her spending so much time at the First School. A bit of charity met with approbation, but six hours a day, in her mother's mind, smacked of being a bluestocking or worse, a reformer.

"It is not the school that preoccupies me," she said. "But it is just as well you have mentioned a change of pursuits." Both her parents must have heard some of the strained stridency in her tone for her mother simply waited, her embroidery forgotten, her lips slightly parted, and her father looked up from the paper he'd only just started to peruse, rustling its pages as a signal that he was not entirely pleased by this interruption. Isobel took a deep breath. "I have made a decision regarding the rest of my life."

Her mother's eyebrows arched once more. "There is no need to be melodramatic, surely."

Her father tried for a smile as he laid his paper down on his lap. "What is this all about, sweetheart?"

His manner was gentle; her father had always had time and patience for her, and Isobel had appreciated his affection. Yet despite his kind words, Isobel felt almost dizzy with nerves. She took another breath. "A few weeks ago I spoke to Mr. Anderson of the American Board of Commissioners for Foreign Missions—"

"Missions," her mother interjected, her tone faintly scandalized. "Whatever for?" Isobel hesitated and her mother continued in a voice of blatant incredulity, "You cannot possibly be considering becoming a missionary."

"No," Isobel replied evenly, "I am not. Single women are not allowed to become missionaries."

"And rightly so," her father said. "It is a far too dangerous for a gently-bred lady. It's all and good for the work to be done, of course, but hardly by a woman on her own."

"Missionaries," Isobel continued, staring straight ahead, her hands clenched around the book in her lap, "need to be married. They are allowed to accompany their husbands to the mission field, which is entirely appropriate and respectable, I'm sure you'll agree." This was met with a profound silence.

"I cannot," her mother finally said quietly, "conceive what you are thinking to suggest." She sounded genuinely mystified, which made it all the more difficult for Isobel to explain just what her intention was.

"Mr. Anderson told me of a… a list." Her knuckles had turned white as she continued to clutch the book in her lap tightly. "A list of… of suitable women, women who might wish to…" She stopped, took another breath. "Who might wish to marry a missionary," she finished, her voice dropping to an apologetic whisper. The silence that followed this information was, Isobel thought numbly, quite deafening. It rang in her ears.

"Izzy," her father said, using her pet name in a way he hadn't for years, "I confess I am confused. What could such a list possibly have to do with you?"

"I can quite see where this is going," her mother informed him frostily. She shook her head slowly, her cool gaze trained on Isobel. "Our daughter is imagining she will put her name on this list."

Her father stared at Isobel in mute appeal, clearly expecting her to deny such an absurd allegation. Isobel forced herself to let go of her book and she smoothed her skirt before folding her clammy hands in her lap. Despite all her fears and reservations, she still felt determined to forge ahead… whatever it might cost her. "It is true, Father. I do wish to put my name on Mr. Anderson's list. It is a perfectly respectable, and even admirable, thing to do, especially for a woman in my position."

"It is not," her mother countered, her tone fierce. "A list! Of spinsters, dangling after men to marry! You cannot think to include yourself in such a number."

"I am a spinster, Mother," Isobel reminded her steadily. "A thornback, even—"

"What a ridiculous word—"

"I shall be thirty years old next year. *Thirty*."

"You have no idea what sort of men would go fishing for a wife in such a way," her mother countered. "They could be the lowest, basest of creatures! And to marry a man you barely know—"

"I would come to know him," Isobel answered. "In time. And we are talking of missionaries, Mother, men who are giving their lives to serve others and God. Hardly the lowest or basest of creatures. Indeed, quite the opposite."

"Still—a stranger. A man with possibly no connections, no social standing at all."

"I no longer care," Isobel said, "for social standing."

Arabella sat back in her chair, her eyes locked onto her daughter, her embroidery hoop discarded. "I cannot believe you could seriously entertain such an insulting idea. And if some man selects your name from the list? What then?"

"Then we would meet," Isobel said hesitantly. In truth she did not know exactly how it would play out; Mr. Anderson had not told her such details. Would there be some sort of courtship, an opportunity to decide if they suited? She hoped so, yet she knew she could not be sure. "We would discuss... arrangements—"

"Like a cow gone to market, sold to the highest bidder?"

"Arabella," her father protested, although he still looked winded by Isobel's unexpected announcement.

"Should I not say it as it is?" her mother challenged. "Our daughter actually thinks to offer herself in such a fashion!"

"Is it so different from what would happen in a drawing room?" Isobel countered. Even though she had thought previously as her mother did, she now found herself a staunch defender of Mr. Anderson and his list. "It's sensible, Mother, really—"

Mrs. Moore shook her head, the movement alarmingly final. "No," she said flatly. "I cannot believe you considered it for a moment! A missionary's wife." She shook her head again. "No."

"To be a missionary is a high calling," her father said mildly. He looked at his daughter, clearly troubled, although Isobel was glad to see he did not object as vociferously as her mother had. She supposed she should not be too surprised, as Arabella had been born to wealth, but Stephen was a self-made man. Her mother had more pretensions to snobbery than her father ever would.

"And to be a missionary's *wife*," Arabella returned, "is to be subjected to all sorts of rude deprivations, to have your children succumb to disease, to be away from your family for all your days, and then die alone in a foreign and hostile land!"

Isobel blinked in shock at the emotion in her mother's voice. She had thought all the same things herself, and yet she had not considered that her mother might feel them too, for her sake.

And yet Isobel was still determined.

"Arabella..." her father murmured. "If she wishes it..."

"I will not allow it. Your father will not allow it."

He turned to Isobel with a frown. "This is unexpected, to say the least, Isobel. I did not know you had such a desire to go into the mission field."

"I admit, it is recent," Isobel answered. "But it is indeed respectable. Mr. Judson's wife was a Hasseltine, a well-to-do family from Bradford." She had read as much, at any rate. "And she spent her days in Burma, accompanying her husband." And burying three children and dying of smallpox, but she would not think of that now. "The list is maintained by the American Board of Commissioners for Foreign Missions, a most worthy organization. How can you truly object?"

Her father rubbed a hand over his face. "It is not," he said after a moment, "what we ever envisioned for you."

"What did you envision…?" Isobel asked, her voice trembling with emotion. "To live with you all of my days? To watch as friend after friend marries and has children while I wait alone, an object of pity and even scorn?"

"It is not so," he tried. "You have many pleasant and worthwhile occupations—"

"They are simply ways to pass the time," Isobel told him flatly. "I want more for my life, whatever left God has granted me…"

"And more is this… this *plan* of yours?" her mother demanded. "Isobel, you are not thinking clearly. You are not considering all you would be sacrificing, all you would endure! And to be the wife of a stranger, a man who might be hard or harsh, who might abuse you—"

"I hope I have more discernment than that in choosing a husband," Isobel told her, trying to smile and not quite managing it.

"You are not showing such discernment by presenting such a plan to us in the first place," her mother returned quietly. "I am truly at a loss."

Isobel turned to her father, knowing her fate lay in his hands. He stared at her sorrowfully for a long moment and then slowly shook his head. "I am sorry, Isobel. I appreciate that the lot God has granted you in this life holds its own tribulations, but I cannot countenance such a plan as this, for your sake as well as ours."

Isobel's hands clenched into fists in her lap as disappointment roiled through her. She had thought he would agree, despite her mother's protests. She had hoped he understood her life was her own… except it seemed it wasn't. "I am of an age—" she began, and her father shook his head.

"You are a member of my household," he stated flatly. "And if you draw me thus, I must speak more plainly." His face settled into a frown. "I tell you, Isobel, I forbid it."

*

Prince Edward Island

The wind blowing off Charlottetown's harbor was chilly, even though it was already early June, and the island was leafy and green. Harriet tucked Maggie's shawl more firmly around her, and smiled ruefully as her daughter jerked away, impatient to be on her journey.

"Don't fuss, Mama."

"I just want you to be warm—"

"I'm fine," Maggie said firmly. And with her flushed cheeks and shining eyes, she looked more than fine. She looked, Harriet thought with a sorrowful pang she couldn't quite suppress, like she was embarking on the adventure of a lifetime—and was more than ready to do so.

"Let your mother fuss," Allan said gruffly. He'd been in a bit of a temper all morning, and Harriet knew it was because he didn't like the thought of letting his oldest child leave the nest. Yet he'd given his reluctant blessing for Maggie to sail to Boston and reside with his sister Margaret while her husband was away on a merchant voyage to China... however long that might be.

Now the day was here, Harriet was fighting her own fears and even regrets. Boston was so far away... and not only that, it was full of so many enticements for a country lass like their Maggie. More worrying than Maggie going at all was the fear that she might never come back. Who knew whom she might meet, what she might experience, in such a fine city? Any matter of opportunities might entice her away... forever. A tear sprung to Harriet's eye at the thought.

Just then Maggie's chaperone, Mrs. Annabel Dunston, bustled up to them, her wide skirts brushing both Harriet and Allan. With her gigot sleeves and her hair dressed in elaborate braids looped over her ears, Mrs. Dunston looked, Harriet thought rather sourly, like a fashion plate. She'd been visiting her sister in Charlottetown, but had already made it quite clear that she much preferred Boston society to the rustics of Prince Edward Island. Harriet would have preferred someone who was in less danger of turning her daughter's head to accompany Maggie on the ship journey, but there had been few choices and her views on the island aside, Mrs. Dunston was eminently suitable. Harriet just hoped she wouldn't influence Maggie to disdain her island home too much.

"Well then, my dear! Are you quite ready?" Mrs. Dunston eyed Maggie's homespun dress, old-fashioned shawl, and sensible boots rather beadily. Harriet noticed she had eschewed a shawl for a lace pelerine over her gown, quite the latest fashion. Harriet had seen one only in a copy of *Godey's Lady's Book* that occasionally found its way to the island.

"Yes, I'm more than ready," Maggie exclaimed, and Mrs. Dunston narrowed her eyes slightly at her charge's obvious high spirits.

"Very well. You may say your farewells and then we shall board." She turned only slightly away for this important moment, making Harriet feel a stirring of resentment towards the woman. Harriet knew Maggie would not want embraces and tears with the fashionable Mrs. Dunston hovering nearby.

"Well then, *cridhe*," Allan said, stepping forward. "You take care."

"I will, Pa."

Unmindful of the chaperone standing so close, Allan enfolded his daughter in his arms. After a second's resistance Maggie hugged him fiercely back, and Harriet was glad. "Write every week and mind your aunt Margaret," he told her, stepping back.

"I will."

Allan nodded at Harriet, and she stepped forward, cupping Maggie's cheek as Anna, Archie, and George all clustered around. Her daughter's skin still felt as soft as when she'd been but a babe. "I love you, Maggie." She held back the tears, as a wave of sadness swept over her.

Maggie flushed, her eyes darting to Mrs. Dunston, who was now tapping her foot in thinly-disguised Impatience. "Mama—"

"I just want you to remember it," Harriet said firmly. "I know you're bursting with excitement now, but in a week or two or a month, whatever it is, you might be feeling homesick and I want you to have something to hold onto." Quickly she pressed a card into Maggie's hand.

"I can't—" Maggie protested in surprise, for the card contained a precious pair of silhouettes of Harriet and Allan, cut when they'd travelled to Boston five years ago.

"Yes, you can," Harriet said. "I want you to have something to remember us by."

Maggie's eyes brightened now not with excitement, but with emotion and perhaps even tears. Their daughter had always been so caring and so close to them that now Harriet knew deep down

Maggie wouldn't have taken this decision lightly. It was a small salve through this goodbye.

"Thank you, Mama," Maggie whispered, and heedless of Mrs. Dunston, Harriet pulled her daughter to her in a tight hug. The other children made their goodbyes, promising to write and asking Maggie to send them trinkets, and then Mrs. Dunston was leading Maggie up the gangplank, and then onto the steamer, with its wide decks and tall, strange-looking stacks. Allan reached for Harriet's arm. "We should go back," he said. "The farm won't wait for us all day."

"I know." Harriet fished for the handkerchief in her pocket and tried to surreptitiously dab the tears from her eyes. Allan, of course, noticed.

"Harriet, *cridhe*," he said gently. "Why these tears? You were the one who wanted her to go so badly."

"I know," Harriet sniffed, giving him a watery smile. "But that doesn't mean I can't feel a little sadness that she is going."

Allan pulled her towards him, resting his chin on her head for a moment. "She'll be all right," he told her. "She'll find her way back, you'll see. It might take time, but in the end she'll come home."

Harriet nodded, wanting to believe it, yet she couldn't help but feel that Allan was trying to convince himself as much as he was her.

CHAPTER SEVEN

Ian straightened his frock coat and cravat before knocking on the door of the office of the Chief of Surgery, John Collins Warren. Warren had granted him an audience when Ian had written him a note, asking to discuss "matters of consequence in regard to the new science of anesthesia," but Ian was under no illusions about his time with the renowned and revered doctor. He would have ten minutes to make his case, maybe less, and most of it would no doubt be spent with Warren frowning and tapping his foot.

"Enter."

Ian opened the door and slipped inside. Warren sat behind his desk, papers spread out in front of him. He did not rise as Ian came to stand before him, and for a few moments Ian simply stood there, ignored by the man before he'd even begun.

"Campbell," he finally acknowledged, his tone neutral as he looked up and appraised him coolly. "You wished to discuss some matter with me, I believe?"

"Yes, sir. The subject of anesthesia—"

"I assume you are speaking of the use of nitrous oxide to dull pain," Warren interjected dryly.

"Dr. Holmes himself suggested the word," Ian countered, trying to keep his voice mild. Oliver Wendell Holmes had coined the term only recently, but Warren would not necessarily applaud a man who was known as a reformer.

Warren waved his hand in impatient dismissal. "Never mind Holmes. Continue."

"I have taken an interest in the matter myself," Ian resumed. "With a certain gentleman, a dentist, Mr. Wells—"

"I know," Warren interjected dryly, "of your rather frequent visits to Hartford."

Ian flushed. Dr. Warren did not sound precisely disapproving, but there was no hint of approbation in his tone either. Ian had not realized the Chief of Surgery was so aware of his movements, although he'd known that Warren was aware of his interest. "The time I've taken has been my own, sir, funded entirely by—"

"I am not interested in explanations or excuses," Warren said shortly. "What is it you wish to suggest to me, Dr. Campbell, as a doctor of this hospital?"

Ian swallowed. "My colleague, Mr. Wells, would like to demonstrate the use of ether in a formal setting," he said. In his nervousness, his voice, he thought, sounded too loud, almost brash. "Preferably in the Bulfinch Operating Theatre."

His words seemed to echo in the sudden frosty stillness of the room. Ian could feel his heart thumping hard under his shirt. Had he just jeopardized his position? Lost it, even? If so, then he would be dependent on his wife's inheritance… and the fortune of James Riddell, although that mattered less to him in this moment than Warren's response.

"You have been a doctor here for how long?" Warren asked after a moment. "Five years, at least, I believe?"

"Seven." Ian swallowed. He tried not to fidget like a schoolboy under Warren's narrowed gaze.

"Not as long as all that, then," Warren mused. "I have been here, you know, since the doors of this institution opened in 1821. Nearly twenty years."

"Your accomplishments are well known and admired, sir," Ian said, hoping he did not sound sycophantic. He spoke the truth; John Collins Warren had helped to found the hospital; had established the *New England Journal of Medicine and Surgery*, and had also served as Dean of Harvard Medical School. His surgical skills were unparalleled, his reputation exceedingly high.

Warren smiled wryly. "Thank you, Campbell, but such flattery is not necessary."

Ian flushed again. He wished he had not risen to Wells' juvenile challenge, accusing him of cowardice if he did not put forward the suggestion to his superiors. To think he might have just jeopardized his entire future by putting forth such a bold suggestion…

"I am willing," Warren said abruptly, "to consider it."

Ian blinked. "You… you are?"

"Do not sound so incredulous. I did not, you will appreciate, say that I thought this idea would have a successful outcome. But the aim of medicine is to heal, and innovation is a necessary part of the discipline."

"Indeed, sir," Ian said quickly. His mind reeled with the implication of Warren's words. He realized he had never truly expected the Chief of Surgery to consider allowing Wells, an unheard-of dentist, to experiment with a questionable substance in the revered Bulfinch Theatre. He had never thought for a moment that the operation would go forward, and that he might be a part of it. His hope soared, and he had an urge to laugh out loud with the sheer, incredulous joy of it.

"In fact," Warren continued, his tone turning censorious, "I have every belief that it will be a dismal failure. The idea that any substance could completely numb the human body to excruciating pain—it boggles the mind."

"That it does, sir," Ian agreed, and Warren favored him with the faintest flicker of a smile.

"And it is that possibility that makes me agree to your preposterous suggestion," Warren finished. "Write me a formal proposal, Campbell, and I will put my stamp upon it."

"Yes, sir."

Warren nodded his dismissal. "It will not be I who is the fool when this all turns out to be a humbug," he said warningly, and Ian swallowed.

No, he would be the fool.

Still, Warren's warning could not diminish his ebullient mood as he returned home that night, hurrying through the public garden that had been recently made out of Boston Common, with a lovely pond as well. It was a point of pride with the city that it was the country's first public park, but Ian barely noticed the trees in blossom over the pathway that bisected the green space. His mind was entirely on his intention to send a letter to Wells in the next day's post.

He whistled as he hurried up the steps of his home, throwing off his hat and cloak with abandon before coming into the drawing room and sweeping a bemused Caroline into his arms.

"What is the meaning of this!" she exclaimed, laughing, after Ian had kissed her soundly.

"Mr. Warren, the Chief of Surgery, has agreed to allow us to perform a surgery with the use of ether—and in the Bulfinch Theatre, no less!"

Caroline drew back a little from him, a slight frown puckering her brow. "Us?" she repeated, a strange note of hope in her voice.

"Wells and me, I mean, of course," Ian clarified, and Caroline slipped from his arms.

"Odd," she said, her hand to her throat, "I know it is ridiculous, but for a moment I thought you meant you and… and me."

Ian stared at her in bewilderment. "Surely you could not think… the Bulfinch Theatre…" he protested helplessly.

"Of course I did not think I would be present," Caroline replied, her voice sharpening. "I am not quite so deluded as that, I assure you. But I did think, for a moment at least, that the successes in your research were mine also, as your wife. That you wished to share them with me." Her voice trembled and she turned away. "How foolish of me. I should have realized."

This was about Riddell's money, Ian thought with a pang of both irritation and guilt. Again. Caroline could not let go of the fact that he refused to use it and in consequence she saw everything to do with his research as a slight, a fact that both grieved and frustrated him. He wanted her to share in his joy, but she refused to.

"The success belongs to both of us, Caroline," Ian said. "Of course it does. No matter what funds I use, I know how you have supported me throughout, and I greatly appreciate—"

"I am afraid I disagree," Caroline interjected. She turned back to face him, her lovely face pale, her eyes wide and sad. "You have never shared your research with me. You have never really wanted to."

He let out an annoyed huff of breath. Was this about more than the money, then? Why had she never said? It seemed as if the tension between them was developing nuances that had not existed a month or even a week ago. "If you mean, do I keep you informed of all the particulars, then, as a woman—"

"Don't tell me that as a woman I could not countenance it!" Her eyes flashed a warning. "I think you know I am made of stronger stuff than that, no matter how silly and foolish I was as a young girl." She took a deep breath and shook her head. "In any case, it is not even the particulars I am concerned about. I have read about the research into ether, Ian, and I suspect I know more than you even realize. But this is something different, something deeper, and I fear it is something you will never understand, and that makes it all the harder. In our marriage, in your research, I thought—I hoped we would be… partners, of a sort. At least in heart and mind. But ever since I offered my inheritance you have withdrawn from me with both, and I wonder if I ever truly had them. The loss, as well as that fear, grieve me sorely." She tried to smile, her lips trembling. "Which, in turn I fear, only annoys you more."

Ian stared at her, wishing he could offer words of comfort, yet not knowing what they would be. He knew she was, at least in part, correct in her suspicions. He had drawn away from her rather than face another battle about Riddell's money. He had convinced himself she had been the one to turn cool, but he knew he had, as well. It had been foolish of him to think she wouldn't notice—or care.

As for her observations about heart and mind… he did consider Caroline his partner in both. Didn't he? Ian searched his memory as well as his heart as he tried to consider the question fairly. It was true he had not involved her in all the particulars of his research, although he'd certainly told her the most salient points, and been gratified by her interest. But had he kept something back, and if so, why? Was there some prideful part of him that wanted this research to be his and his alone? Was it some sort of matter of honor to keep a part of himself separate from the woman he loved? He disliked the thought, and yet he saw some truth in it… and he knew his wife did, as well.

"Caroline, if I have kept some part of myself—" he began, unsure what he wanted to say, but she shook her head.

"Let us not speak of it," she murmured. "I do not think I can bear to hear your excuses."

"That's not fair—" he began, and Caroline whirled on him.

"What, then, were you going to say?" she challenged. "You kept some part of yourself from me because you did not realize I wanted it? You did not share your life and heart with me because such a notion did not occur to you?" Ian stayed silent, and Caroline lifted her chin, her eyes bright with tears. "Either those are excuses, and I have no wish to hear them, or they are the truth, and that would hurt me just as much. In truth, I do not know which would be worse." Without another word, and with Ian still unable to make a reply, she brushed past him into the hall.

*

"Isobel!"

Margaret sailed into the drawing room with her usual graceful flourish, kissing her sister-in-law on both cheeks before gesturing for her to sit in one of the chintz-covered chairs by the fireplace. "I've asked Ella to bring tea," she said, sitting across from Isobel and arranging her green and gold striped skirts around her. "I'm so pleased for your visit."

As usual, Margaret looked lovely and vibrant in the latest fashion, her gigot sleeves flaring to the elbow and then tight to the wrist. Her hair was arranged in a sleek chignon, with clusters of curls dancing at her brow. She smiled merrily. "I have had such pleasant news. My niece, Margaret MacDougall—Maggie, as she's called—will be coming to stay with me while Henry is away. She is to arrive at the end of the week."

"Mother told me your news," Isobel murmured. "It is indeed pleasant for you to have company at this trying time. Have you heard from Henry?"

Margaret shook her head. "Not yet, but I would hardly expect to. It has only been a month, after all, and he will only have just reached Trinidad, where he is to put into port before heading on to the Cape of Good Hope."

Her sister-in-law spoke matter-of-factly, but Isobel noted how quick her speech, how fluttering her hands. She'd learned from her recent reading that rounding the Cape of Good Hope, on the southernmost tip of Africa, was considered to be one of the most dangerous parts of the sea voyage, with strong winds and currents that many sailors feared.

"I trust you will have news soon," she murmured, and Margaret cocked her head, her eyes brightening with speculation.

"Indeed, in another few weeks perhaps. Pray forgive me if I am speaking out of turn, but dear Isobel, you do look a little peaked. Has something happened to concern you?"

"It is astute of you to notice, for indeed something has happened," Isobel answered, doing her best to steady her nerves. She had always found Margaret, with her assured airs and easy graces, to be more than a bit intimidating, and now more than ever, when she thought of what she intended to discuss. "Or rather, something has not happened, I suppose."

"You leave me quite confused," Margaret answered with a little laugh. "What can it be?"

Isobel hesitated, trying to frame her reply. It had been a week since her father had forbidden her to put her name on Mr. Anderson's list. She had attempted to talk to him again, and he had been quite severe with her. Her mother she had not dared speak to at all, for her stony expression was far too forbidding.

Both of her parents, Isobel had mused with quiet desolation, had seemed to become even more determined for her not to marry a missionary, or at least put her name on the list of women who were willing to do so. And just as they had deepened their convictions, so had Isobel. There was nothing for her in Boston but more of the same—teaching and living with her parents, waiting out her days. The older she became the drearier such a life would seem. She *had* to find a way to escape.

She had to put her name on that list—and so she had come here.

"Isobel?" Margaret prompted, frowning a little, but before Isobel could reply the maid bustled quietly in with the tea tray. The next few moments were taken up with pouring, giving Isobel enough time to gather her courage to tell Margaret of her plan. Her sister-in-law was her last hope; Margaret, with her confidence and determination, just might prevail where she had not succeeded.

"I know you can appreciate, Margaret, for you have said so before, that my lot these last years has not been an easy one."

Margaret's expression sobered and she set her teacup down. "The life of an unmarried woman is never easy," she agreed quietly, "although I would think the First School would afford you some pleasure as well as purpose. I know as of late it has felt more taxing, but surely that will pass?"

"It does give me both pleasure and purpose," Isobel assured her. Margaret had started the school, and though with Charlotte's birth she had too many cares to continue in her role, Isobel knew the cause was still dear to Margaret's heart—more dear, perhaps, than it was to her own. "But I confess, I do not relish a continued life of teaching and living at my parents' home."

Margaret considered the matter for a moment. "Perhaps there are more options available to you than you might realize," she said finally. "Women are able to accomplish far more now than they used to. Why, look at Elizabeth Palmer Peabody—she helped to start the Temple School with Mr. Alcott, and it has been a great success."

"I am not Elizabeth Peabody," Isobel said with an attempt at a smile. Although she had never met Miss Peabody, she was well acquainted with the woman's sometimes shocking exploits. The Temple School was considered liberal enough to have become somewhat ridiculous, and the Peabodys were caught up in the recent fashion of Transcendentalism, which Isobel's far more conservative parents would never condone. As much as she wished for adventure, she knew she was not that much of a 'free thinker', as the Peabodys claimed to be.

"Still," Margaret continued, ever the reformer, "She runs a salon out of her living room and Dr. Channing himself reads the paper there, and lawyers and professors discuss—"

"I have no wish or talent to start a salon," Isobel interjected flatly. "The First School's more modest aims are more to my liking."

Margaret pursed her lips. "Yet you do not wish to continue?"

Isobel suppressed a sigh. This conversation was not going as she had hoped or planned. She knew Margaret possessed more intellectual curiosity than she did; her sister-in-law sometimes socialized with the less radical of the Transcendentalists, and enjoyed discussing a variety of topics from poetry to politics. Meanwhile, Isobel acknowledged grimly, she simply wanted to leave Boston—and marry. "It is not that I wish to stop teaching," she finally said, "but that I wish for more."

Margaret wrinkled her brow in confusion. "What sort of 'more' do you refer to?"

Why, Isobel wondered, was it so hard for her family to understand? Were they simply so cushioned from the reality of a life of loneliness, the endless, terrible ache of it, when a mere brush of a hand could make her catch her breath with longing? Could no one understand how she felt? She took a deep breath. "There is a list," she began, and Margaret leaned forward, curiosity sparking in her eyes.

"Go on."

Quickly, her face flushing with a humiliation she could not help but continue to feel, Isobel told her of Mr. Anderson's list and both her ambition and difficulty to be named on it.

"You wish to marry a missionary?" Margaret said, her tone incredulous. "Isobel, you might live in the rudest sort of place! In a... in a grass hut, even!"

Isobel gazed at her sister-in-law levelly. "I might. Would that be such a terrible thing?"

"Of course it is not for me to pronounce such judgments, and yet..." Margaret shook her head in stupefaction. "You would be willing to forsake the comforts of known society for such a life?" She sounded half-horrified, half-fascinated.

"Yes." In truth Isobel had not attempted to envision her life as a missionary's wife too closely. She could certainly not see herself in a grass hut, but if she was, then so be it. At least she would not be alone, and she supposed there could be worse places. But hopefully it would not come to that. In any case, she would have time to consider such things later, when she'd actually agreed to marry a missionary. When she'd found a man who possessed gentleness and humor, someone she could like and admire—and that still seemed like a distant day indeed. Getting her name on that list—finally having *hope*—was the extent of her ambition at this point.

"But if your father forbids it…" Margaret began slowly, trailing off as she looked helplessly at Isobel. "I do not know what it is you think I could do…"

"I seem to remember," Isobel stated quietly, "that you went against your own father's wishes, once upon a time."

Margaret blushed and looked away, a small smile playing about her mouth as she no doubt remembered those heady days of romance. Although it was before Isobel had even met her, she recalled the story of her brother Henry and Margaret's courtship well enough. Margaret's father had refused to allow Margaret to be included in her brother Rupert's tutorials back in Scotland, and when she had met Henry, without her father's knowledge or approval, Henry took on a role as tutor and she pursued her own education, eventually marrying him.

"So I did," Margaret said slowly, "and I've never had any cause to regret it. But even so, Isobel, I'm afraid I don't see what that has to do with your present situation. If your father has made his decision, I'm not sure he will listen to any appeal you might hope me to make."

"Won't he?" Isobel challenged. "He has always held you in high regard, and you can be very persuasive when you wish to be, Margaret. You could convince him that it is worthwhile for me to pursue this course. I know you could. And as you sympathize with my situation, I would hope you could see the need for such intervention. I don't want to live the rest of my life like this, Margaret. I won't."

Margaret didn't answer for several moments. Isobel's heart seemed to still and then beat harder in expectation of her answer; she knew she needed Margaret's powers of persuasion to help her be named on Mr. Anderson's list.

Finally, Margaret looked up, her gaze terribly serious. "Are you sure, truly sure, this is what you want, Isobel? For the rest of your life? No matter what hardship or even tragedy might come your way?"

Isobel swallowed hard and nodded. "*Yes.*"

"Then I shall do it." Margaret nodded decisively. "Although your father's wrath may come upon my head!"

"He's always had a fondness for you, Margaret."

"I fear it shall be tested severely," Margaret warned, but she was smiling. "And who knows, perhaps we shall see you married yet, to a man of your own choosing—if I have anything to do with it!"

*

Near Cape of Good Hope, Africa

Dearest Margaret, I know full well this letter will not reach you for many months, perhaps when I have already, God willing, arrived in Canton. Yet still I write, for writing to you helps me to imagine you sitting in your favorite chair, reading my letter with a faint smile on your lips…

"Captain?"

Henry Moore looked up from the letter he'd been composing to see his first mate standing to attention in the doorway of his small cabin.

"Yes, Mr. Martin?"

"There is some black cloud boiling on the horizon, sir. We need to make ready for a storm, I should think."

Henry nodded briskly, suppressing the queasy churning in his stomach at the prospect ahead of them. He'd never been too afraid of a storm before, but then he'd never had so much to lose. They had only just rounded the Cape of Good Hope a few days ago, the most treacherous place for storms, and many a clipper had foundered or sunk when buffeted by the severe waves and wind. He was grateful they had come through safely, and yet he knew this area of the Indian Ocean was known for its storms as well as its endless, empty waters. "Thank you for informing me, Mr. Martin. I shall be on deck shortly."

The first mate nodded and left, clicking the door shut behind him. Henry put his letter to Margaret in a leather portfolio to finish later. It was his second letter to her, although he did not know when he would find a way to send it. He'd been able to send one back when they'd put into port at Trinidad, although he knew not when she would receive it. Still, it made her seem closer, to write to her, to imagine her reading his words—Charlotte on her lap, tea on the table. Such a cozy scene, and one that felt impossibly far away at present. Rising, he put on his coat and reached for his spyglass before ascending to the deck.

Outside the air was still and drowsy, the sky a brilliant blue, the sea flat and shimmering. They had left Trinidad two weeks ago, having gone through the dangerous doldrums, where the north and south trade winds collided at the Earth's equator, creating a dangerous calm that could take weeks to get through. Thanks to Providence, they had gone through quite speedily, and had rounded the Cape of Good Hope without too much difficulty, before now facing the endless expanse of the South Seas.

Putting his spyglass to his eye, Henry could see what his first mate referred to—clouds that now were no more than a dark smudge on the horizon, yet within hours could be a full-blown storm right above their heads. It was impossible to predict how fast such a thing could travel, especially in these dangerous waters.

He lowered the spyglass. "Let us return to my quarters," he told his first mate. "And bring Mr. Ellison."

Just a few minutes later Henry stood poring over a map of the Indian Ocean with Mr. Martin and Mr. Ellison, the ship's navigator, at his side. All three men were silent, their faces grave as they studied the parchment below them. Their journey was almost half over, the most dangerous part of it completed, and yet they all knew that the storms and fierce winds known as the Roaring Forties still presented grave dangers.

"Can we outrun it, do you think, Mr. Martin?" Henry asked his first mate. Since clipper ships were so fast, often keeping ahead of the storm was the wisest course of action, speeding towards the horizon with all haste.

The first mate lifted his gaze from the map. "I don't rightly know, sir. These storms can boil up something fast, and if we're caught with our sails—"

Henry nodded, knowing no more needed to be said. To be caught in a tropical gale in full sail could mean devastating damage to the sails, rigging, or mast... and leave the ship dead in the water, miles from anywhere. It was as good as a death sentence for the entire crew.

"Mr. Ellison, is there an island nearby where we could shelter?"

On the map the area of the ocean they were sailing through was a depressingly empty square of blue. As they had traveled further from the Cape, they'd left behind the islands that hugged the southeast coast of Africa, and they were still weeks away from the cluster of islands that made up Indonesia.

"Not with a known harbor or cove," Mr. Ellison said after a pause. "As you know, sir, there is little land in this part of the ocean."

"I do know it." Henry gazed grimly down at the map. "Then, gentlemen," he said as bracingly as he could, "we shall have to attempt to outrun the storm. The *Charlotte Rose* is one of the fastest tea clippers out of Boston. Let us put her to good use today."

Nodding, the men returned to the deck to begin issuing orders. Henry rolled up the map and stared out the porthole at the stretch of blue sky he could see. Already the dark smudge on the horizon was widening, and the wind was picking up, ruffling the surface of the sea. The *Charlotte Rose* would, Henry acknowledged grimly, have to race for her life... as well as his and his crew's.

Two hours later the winds were already screaming down on them and waves had begun to crest over the deck as the men battled valiantly on board to save both their lives and the ship, doing best to make sure neither the rudder nor mast was damaged. They had not been able to outrun the storm, and Henry feared worse was to come. He sluiced water from his face, squinting through the wind and rain as the timbers of the boat creaked ominously. Men scrambled to safety as a wave crashed over the deck, washing away anything that wasn't fastened securely. Henry clung to the wheel, attempting to keep the ship on an even keel as the winds and waves rocked the craft mercilessly, threatening to destroy it completely.

Was this to be the end? As the *Charlotte Rose* shuddered beneath the onslaught of nature's fury, Henry knew he did not want to die like this, so... so far from home, in a strange and endless sea, with neither Margaret nor Charlotte ever even knowing what had become of him. He pictured their faces, the sorrow and worry he'd seen in his wife's eyes as he'd left. Dear heaven, but she'd feared this, and she'd been right to! He could not let it end here, not for him, not for any of them.

Henry's fingers clung to the wheel as he shouted to his first mate, but his words were torn away from his throat on the wind and in frustration he drew a breath to call again—only to be silenced by the slam of something into the side of his head.

Stars burst into his vision as he desperately tried to blink the tempestuous world back into focus, only to stumble and then slump to the deck, unconscious.

CHAPTER EIGHT

Boston

Maggie MacDougall stood on the deck of the ship that had taken her all the way from provincial Prince Edward Island to the grand harbor of Boston itself. The city lay before her, shining under a late June sun, the tall, proud point of the Boston Light seeming to watch over the many ships in the busy port, bidding them welcome.

"Tie your bonnet strings," Mrs. Dunston, her dragon-like chaperone, chided. "Or it shall sail clear off into the water."

"I'm sorry, Mrs. Dunston." Meekly, Maggie tied the ribbons, although a good part of her wanted to tear off the restricting item, toss it to the wind, and whoop for joy.

She was here. Here at last. The journey from Prince Edward Island had only taken a few days, but they'd seemed interminable to Maggie, especially under Mrs. Dunston's beady eye. She'd had to endure several extended lectures on Boston society and expected behavior, and Maggie quickly gathered that her country ways and best Sunday dress were not up to city standards—or at least those of the likes of Mrs. Dunston.

Yet even the worry that she might embarrass her aunt Margaret or seem like a country bumpkin to most sophisticated Bostonians could do little to dim Maggie's enthusiasm now. After living for fifteen years having not travelled much more than a mile from her home—except for two voyages to Boston when she'd been but a child—she was finally having a grand adventure, all on her own. The thought made her spirit fizz and her hopes soar as they docked in the harbor and the gangplank was lowered. As they made their way onto the wharf, Maggie could not keep a huge, unladylike grin from spreading over her face, much to Mrs. Dunston's clucking disapproval.

Her Aunt Margaret was waiting for her, and recognized her right away. "Maggie!" she called, moving quickly towards Maggie, her face wreathed in smiles, her arms outstretched.

"Hello, Aunt Margaret." Quite suddenly, despite her earlier exuberance, Maggie felt shy.

Her aunt clearly did not, and she embraced her warmly. "You've grown so since I last saw you! But I shall always remember your fiery hair. Just like your mother's." Her hands on her shoulders, Margaret drew back to give Maggie a thorough, smiling inspection.

Maggie tried not to squirm under her elegant aunt's scrutiny. She was far more conscious of her worn dress—the hem had been turned down twice—and her simple ways next to Margaret than when she'd been with the fussy Mrs. Dunston. Margaret might have come from Scotland the same as her mother, but she spoke and looked like an American now, and an elegant one at that.

Her aunt's dress was of the latest fashion, in cheerful sprigged cotton with wide gigot sleeves, full not from shoulder to elbow, but rather elbow to wrist as was the very latest style, and a bodice that came to a sharp point at her slender waist. Maggie had seen such dresses in the *Godey's Lady's Book*, but never in person. Even Mrs. Dunston had not dressed so stylishly.

No matter her gown, Margaret, Maggie thought, was very beautiful. Her dark, gleaming hair was dressed simply, unlike Mrs. Dunston's elaborate curls and swirls, and somehow the severe look suited the strong lines of her face, drawing attention to her large, dark eyes. She possessed no simpering, girlish charms or fussy matronly airs; she was a woman in command of herself, and happy to be so.

All of it together made Maggie feel awkward and even slovenly in her homespun dress, her bright red hair scraped back into a simple bun, an old shawl thrown about her shoulders. She hadn't been bothered by such things on the steamship, when Mrs. Dunston had been by far the fussiest and most fashionable person aboard. Now, however, standing next to her elegant aunt, Maggie felt unsure of herself and the adventure she was so determined to have. For a second—though no more—she almost wanted to go home.

"I'm pleased to make your acquaintance again," she said to her aunt, bobbing a little half-curtsey, and Margaret looked startled before letting out a rich chuckle and drawing Maggie to her once more.

"Oh, my dear! You needn't stand on formality with me. Why, your mother and I lived in the same house for many years, and we were as close as sisters. It grieves my heart that we don't see each other now. To think it has been four years or more!" Her smile turned a bit sad for a moment, but then she shook her head and brightened once more. "But never mind! I am so pleased to have you with me now." Slipping her arm through Maggie's, she turned to Mrs. Dunston who was descending upon them like a ship in full sail, her expression bordering on disapproval, although for what Maggie didn't know. She'd surely conducted herself appropriately on board ship. "Thank you so much for taking care of dear Maggie. You have been quite a godsend."

Privately Maggie thought she wouldn't go so far as to call Mrs. Dunston that, but she said nothing as the two women exchanged pleasantries before parting company, Mrs. Dunston seeming appeased by Margaret's obvious high station in life. The old dragon might have disapproved of her, but clearly her sophisticated aunt had the snobby woman's admiration.

"Now we must get you home," Margaret said as she led her to a shining black barouche with two bay horses at its front. "You must be exhausted."

"Oh, I feel well enough, Aunt Margaret," Maggie said earnestly. Her aunt had, at least in this moment, put her insecurities to rest, and once more Maggie was determined to enjoy every last drop of this adventure.

The ride from the harbor back to Margaret's elegant townhouse was an adventure in itself. Maggie had never seen so many buildings so close together, from a splendid, grand open marketplace to an imposing, brick-fronted church. Margaret cheerfully pointed out all the sights. And then there were the people! First, as they left the harbor, she saw immigrants in all manner of dress, even humbler and plainer than she was. The further they drove on, the more elegant the neighborhood and its residents became, and Maggie saw smart-looking businessmen in top hats and frock coats, and elegant ladies with wide skirts and parasols, everyone seeming busy and important.

"Do you remember much of Boston from your last visit?" Margaret asked.

Maggie turned away from the sights with some reluctance. "A bit, but it feels new this time," she answered. "I was only ten years old back then and everything was such a flurry. I hardly remember Uncle Rupert and Aunt Eleanor, or even Uncle Ian and Aunt Caroline."

"Yes, I suppose it was a lot for such a young girl to remember," Margaret agreed with a smile. "Well, Rupert and Eleanor might be far away in the Western Territories now, but your Uncle Ian still lives in the city. I shall be sure to have him and his lovely wife Caroline for a dinner party."

A dinner party! It sounded so grownup and sophisticated, Maggie thought, even as she realized her Sunday dress would probably not do for such an affair. She wished there had been time and money for some new dresses to be made up before she had left the island, yet she knew in reality there had not been either. She could not begrudge her mother or father for the lack, when they had given so much to make sure she could go.

The coachman helped Margaret and Maggie both down from the landau, and Maggie followed her aunt into a spacious townhouse with an impressive set of front steps and a shiny black door. Her eyes widened as she took in the elegant foyer and sweeping staircase. She'd never seen anything half so grand. A maid took Margaret's mantlet and reticule, and clumsily Maggie gave the smartly dressed servant her worn shawl.

Her aunt, she saw, had slit open a letter that had been lying on a silver tray and was now reading it with a little smile on her face. "Excellent," she said and turned to Maggie. "My sister-in-law, Isobel, will join us for dinner tonight. But as for now, you must be truly fatigued, my dear. Why don't you rest?"

Maggie nodded, for although part of her wanted to explore every inch of the house and even the city, the excitement of arriving was taking its toll and she felt quite tired. The maid showed her to her room, and she gazed in wonder at the silk bed hangings and Turkish carpet, a small city garden visible from the large bay window. The sight of that little scrap of land, pretty as it was, suddenly made her feel homesick, for in her mind's eye she could so easily see the rolling green fields and reddish roads of Prince Edward Island. Her home. She could picture Anna and Archie and George all gathered round the table, her mother at the new stove she was so proud of, her father coming into their cabin with Patches trotting behind him. She'd disdained the smallness of it all, but part of her longed for it now.

Swallowing down her homesickness, Maggie turned from the window, shed her shoes, and lay down on the bed, its counterpane as soft as a cloud. She was asleep within minutes.

*

That evening, having brushed down her Sunday dress and added a fresh lace collar, Maggie headed downstairs to the drawing room to join her aunt, where they were to meet her aunt's sister-in-law, a true Bostonian. Anticipation fluttered in her middle, along with a few nerves. Isobel Moore might look down her nose at someone like her, and Maggie was worried she'd have nothing intelligent or interesting to say to either Isobel Moore or her aunt.

Margaret smiled at her as she came into the room. "Maggie, my dear. Did you have a good rest? Charlotte has been so eager to meet you." She summoned the little girl, already in her nightgown and dressing gown, her hair in dark blond braids. "Charlotte, do you remember Maggie? You may say 'how do you do?'"

Charlotte gave an adorable little curtsey that made Maggie smile. "How do you do?"

"How do *you* do?" she replied, and Charlotte grinned. Maggie let out a little laugh. She'd been longing to get away from the responsibilities of caring for her three younger siblings, but looking at Charlotte she realized she missed them.

A nursery maid took Charlotte up to bed shortly after, and Margaret nodded towards the window. "I see Isobel coming up the path."

A few minutes later a tall, slender woman with dark hair and clear, porcelain skin came into the drawing room. "Isobel!" Margaret rose from her seat and embraced her, while Maggie watched nervously, smoothing her hands along the sides of her skirt.

"I have news," Margaret said, drawing Isobel forward. "But first you must meet my dear niece, Maggie MacDougall."

"News?" Isobel repeated a bit sharply, and as she turned to greet her Maggie saw there were faint crows' feet on either side of her eyes and lines of strain marking her forehead. "Pleased to meet you, I'm sure."

"And you, ma'am." Before she could think better of it, Maggie bobbed a curtsey.

Isobel arched a dark eyebrow, shooting Margaret a curious, amused glance. Maggie felt her face heat. She'd been acting like Charlotte rather than the grown woman she wanted to be.

"Maggie is very excited to be here," Margaret said, her lips twitching in a smile, and Maggie kept her chin up and a smile on her reddened face with effort. She was so obviously a country bumpkin to women such as these, and she knew there was no way to hide it. Even if her dress were as fine as her Aunt Margaret's or Isobel Moore's, she'd still be awkward and clumsy, no more than a girl fresh from the farm, and everyone would be able to tell.

"I'm sure she is," Isobel said smoothly. She turned back to Maggie with a distracted smile that didn't quite meet her eyes. "I hope you enjoy the delights of the city, Miss MacDougall." Maggie opened her mouth to reply, but Isobel had already turned back to Margaret.

"And now, Margaret, you said you had news? Pray do not keep me in suspense."

"I shan't," Margaret said with a little laugh. With a whirl of her skirts she turned towards a table and rang a little silver bell. "But first I must call for champagne! For your father, Isobel, has agreed."

*

Isobel reached for the back of a chair for support as Margaret's news, so ebulliently given, ricocheted through her. Her father had agreed? She realized, despite the desperation with which she'd asked Margaret to intercede, she'd not expected an answer such as this.

"Agreed…" she repeated faintly, and Margaret laughed and shook her head.

"Isobel, you look as if you might faint! In truth, I expected you to greet such news with a good bit more cheer."

Isobel tried to smile, but she still felt dazed, as well as strangely uncertain. This was very good news indeed, and yet some odd part of her felt appalled. She couldn't back out now, at least not without being humiliated by her about-face. "I am just so surprised," she said. "I did not expect him to relent. I had resigned myself to staying here."

"Yet you seemed so sure the last time we spoke!" Margaret exclaimed. "Are you having second thoughts?"

Isobel didn't speak for a moment, as she tried to order her scattered thoughts. Was she reconsidering her decision? No, she realized, she was not. Despite that moment of panicky dread, she still wished to go forward with her plan. "No," she finally said. "No, I am not. I'm just surprised. Very surprised."

One of the maids opened the door and gave a brief curtsey. "Ma'am?"

"Champagne please, Ella. And three glasses." While Isobel still reeled, Margaret turned to her niece with a merry smile. "You may have a taste, Maggie, but that's all. Your mother wouldn't like it otherwise, I'm sure!"

"Thank you, Aunt Margaret."

Isobel would have preferred not to have this conversation in front of this young chit of a girl, but she had questions to ask, and she could not wait for answers. "But Margaret," she said, "if it… if it all comes to pass, what shall become of the school?"

"You need not concern yourself with that," Margaret said airily, and Isobel shook her head, insistent now. She had not considered the school overmuch since she had decided to put her name on that list, but now it suddenly felt like a matter of the utmost importance.

"But I must. I confess the teaching has tried me at times, but that school has been my life for years, Margaret. I will not see it come to naught for the sake of my own folly."

Margaret pursed her lips. "You think this folly?"

Isobel glanced at Maggie, so obviously curious as to what they were talking about. "I do not know," she admitted. "But I am still convinced of it." She bit her lip and looked away.

"I'm sure a teacher can be found," Margaret said. "We have found one before. Perhaps Caroline…" she paused and Isobel did her best not to blush. Of course she could speak of Caroline without feeling pain, yet she still resisted the idea of her in the school that had become so close to her heart.

Before she could think or guard her speech, Maggie burst forth with what, to her, seemed a marvelous and obvious idea.

"What school are you talking about?" Maggie asked, her voice both brash and hesitant. "Is it the one you started, Aunt Margaret?"

"Indeed it is, Maggie. Isobel has been teaching there for some years, but she is hopeful of quitting the country soon." She gave Isobel a fleeting smile. "We shall have to find another teacher when she does, but I daresay I could step in if need be, at least for a little while." She glanced at Maggie. "Or you could help? Your mother has told me how much you like to read."

"Oh!" Maggie looked both pleased and nervous. "I do enjoy reading…"

"We shall see when the time comes," Margaret said, with another glance at Isobel. "Nothing has to come pass as of yet."

No, Isobel thought, and perhaps nothing would. Putting her name on Mr. Anderson's list did not guarantee her a husband, or even the passing interest of a man. A terrible thought occurred to her—that it would be worse to put her name on that list and not to be chosen by any mission-minded man, than to have never done it at all.

*

The South Seas

Henry blinked the world back into focus, like a swimmer coming up to the surface of the sea. His head ached abominably, and his mouth was as dry as a desert. Coughing, he struggled to sit up only to have his vision swim as he was dragged back under again.

"Captain," he heard his first mate, Mr. Martin, call, as if from a long way off. "The captain is awake!"

With effort Henry opened his eyes and saw the anxious face of his first mate gazing down at him. He was in his own quarters, he realized, in his own bed. The ship, then, had survived the storm. But had his crew? "Mr. Martin." His voice was no more than a croak. "Have we sustained any casualties?"

"No, sir. That is… no persons."

Henry closed his eyes in relief, even as he realized Mr. Martin's hesitant answer meant there had to be other injuries to sailors or vessel. "Water, please," he said in little more than a whisper, and those few precious sips relieved his parched throat. He put one hand to his head and felt a bulky bandage covering his left temple. "What happened?" he asked.

"You were hit by a falling piece of timber, sir." Mr. Martin paused. "The mast nearly cracked in half."

Henry fumbled to put the cup back on the table as he sank back onto the pillows, his eyes fluttering closed. "And the state of the *Charlotte Rose*?"

Mr. Martin paused before replying, "Not good, sir, I'm afraid."

Henry struggled to a seated position even though it made his head swim and his stomach revolt. He suppressed the urge to retch and forced himself to give Martin a direct look even though it made his head pulse with pain. "Give me the particulars."

"The mast is cracked, sir, as I said, and the main sail is in tatters. Others are damaged, as well, and two of the crew have broken arms, several have been coshed in the head as you have. They'll be all right, but we won't be able to make repairs until we put into port."

"In port," he repeated. His head throbbed even worse and he closed his eyes briefly. They were in nearly the most desolate stretch of ocean on earth. Putting into port anywhere was unlikely, perhaps impossible. He thought of the water he'd just drunk. "How are we for supplies?"

"We have water for ten days, more if we ration it carefully, or of course if it rains."

Ten days. Dead in the water on this endless stretch of blue, drifting uselessly. It was not enough. It was practically nothing. Exhausted, Henry leaned back against the bolster and closed his eyes again. He could taste bile in the back of his throat, and he fought the urge to heave. "Begin rations," he finally said. "And let us pray that God sees fit to send us a ship to come to our aid." For surely, another ship was their only hope in such dire circumstances. They needed a savior.

When Henry made his way to the deck the next morning, he saw the storm that had devastated the ship had given way to a hazy, languid calm. The sky and sea shimmered in the heat, the horizon flat and endless, without any sign at all of life. Henry tried to keep his attitude cheerful and efficient as always, but his own injuries and the fear that twisted inside him made it difficult. He saw his men's tense faces, knew that none of them wished to die of thirst. It was every sailor's fear, worse than being lost overboard in a storm, or wasting away from one of the many diseases that could be caught in distant lands: a terrible, endless agony until death seemed like a mercy.

After an hour of supervising his men's work on the ship, doing what little repairs they could, Henry retreated to his cabin once more. He sank onto his bed, his aching head in his hands as realization echoed emptily through him. They could all very well die. They most likely would.

What could he do? There was no way to repair the ship, not enough to sail on, even if there was a wind, which there wasn't. He could send some men out in a dinghy to look for land, but it would be a fool's errand, and one that would most likely result in death.

He rose from his bed and paced the small confines of his cabin, filled with a restless anger at the futility of his situation. He thought of Margaret's fear for his safety when he'd insisted on this trip to China, and everything in him cried out for both her forgiveness and her comfort. To feel her arms around him one more time, her sweet breath fanning his cheek, her light laughter in his ear…

He would not give up. Not now, not ever. Straightening, he unrolled the map and placed it flat on the table, scanning this section of ocean as if a new land mass would magically appear. His distant gaze fell on the leather portfolio, now water-stained and worse for wear, and with trembling fingers he withdrew the letter he'd been writing to Margaret before the storm had hit.

Margaret, dear Margaret… She would never get this letter, he thought. Never even know what happened to him or his ship. She would only be able to guess, and she might always wonder…

Swallowing hard, he shook his head and returned his resolute gaze to the map before him. There had to be some solution. Some way forward. He just had to find it.

*

Boston

"Ian, what is it that's troubling you?"

Ian looked up from his mostly untouched meal to smile ruefully at his wife. Caroline gazed at him, a frown between her fine brows. The tension that had pulsed between them since that first heated exchange in the salon had abated somewhat in the last few weeks, as Ian had not made any return journeys to Hartford, and they'd had the delights of the summer social season to enjoy. Now he saw that Caroline's concerned glance was still a little shadowed, and he knew the tension remained, unspoken yet still present. "I apologize. I'm not very good company tonight."

"You are brooding," she told him. She neatly forked a sliver of lamb and gave him a look of both reproof and concern. "What is wrong?"

He sighed, not wanting to trouble Caroline with his worries, but also reluctant to alienate her further by refusing to discuss his work. The last few weeks they had called a silent truce, not speaking of his research with Mr. Wells after their argument on the matter, but now Ian felt it come to the fore yet again.

"Ian?" she prompted now. "Will you tell me? Is it… is it your research?"

He heard a trembling thread of uncertainty in her voice and guilt and regret both assailed him once more. He couldn't stand this distance between them, and keeping his concerns from her would surely only make it worse. Trying to smile, he met her troubled gaze. "Of course, my dear. I'm only thinking of the surgery Mr. Wells is to perform next month, in the Bulfinch Theatre. It is so important that it is successful."

She cocked her head, her thoughtful gaze sweeping over him. "So what is your concern? You think it won't be?"

Ian shrugged. "It is not that I believe it will fail, only that there is simply so much depending on it. If it does not go well, the work shall be set back indefinitely, perhaps forever. We will surely not be afforded another opportunity such as this." He smiled wryly. "And I will be a laughing stock, to say the least." If he and Mr. Wells suffered a public failure and humiliation in the hospital's operating theatre, no one would ever take ether, or even him, seriously again. Both his research and his career were under threat and the prospect had occupied his thoughts far too much already.

Caroline took a sip of her wine, her fine eyebrows drawn together. "But there is no reason to think it will fail, is there? Your experiments in Hartford have been overwhelmingly successful.

You have told me so yourself. You operated on Mr. Wells' arm and he didn't feel a thing, even though he needed stitches!"

"So I did," Ian agreed with a smile. He felt a welcome surge of love and admiration for his wife. Despite their disagreement over the use of Riddell's money, she still supported and believed in him, and he'd been glad to share with her his successes as well as his setback. In the aftershocks of their argument he'd begun to doubt that, but now her confidence was a much-needed balm. He also knew her determination now to remain even-tempered and solicitous was an effort to restore harmony to their marriage, and one he greatly appreciated. He intended to make just as much effort.

"And yet you are worried," Caroline stated, and after a pause he gave a brief nod.

"I… I fear Mr. Wells has not quite been himself the last few times I visited."

"Not himself? Do you mean he is unwell?"

"I do not know if I would say he is unwell," Ian replied slowly. "But he has seemed… frantic."

"Frantic? Do you mean he's concerned about the surgery, as you are?"

"Yes, of course—" He stopped abruptly, not wishing to go into what he believed could be the sordid particulars of his colleague's condition. He didn't want to believe it, and yet…

"I fear you are not being honest with me," Caroline said, "or perhaps even with yourself, Ian. There is no shame in being ill, yet you are looking as if you are ashamed on Mr. Wells' account."

Ian forced a small smile. "You know me too well, my love. It is true, I am worried and even ashamed on Mr. Wells' behalf, for I fear his ill health is indeed shameful."

"Shameful?" Caroline looked both confused and shocked. "How?"

Ian hesitated, not wishing to speak of so indelicate a subject, and yet—wasn't this what Caroline wanted? Wasn't it what she'd complained he wasn't doing? He took a deep breath. "The truth is, when we were last together, he was forgetful and disorganized, and his hands trembled."

"What," Caroline asked, frowning, "is the shame in that?"

"None, if you take each symptom by itself. But as a whole…" He trailed off, shaking his head, and Caroline simply waited. "They are all symptoms of addiction to ether," Ian confessed quietly. "The substance we have been using for our operations. The substance which Mr. Wells has been using on himself, even when I have not been present."

"Addiction…" Caroline paled, and Ian regretted mentioning such a thing. It was surely no topic for conversation with a lady over the dinner table, or even at all, no matter what kind of honesty Caroline wished for them to have with one another.

"I'm sorry, Caroline. I should not have spoken of it."

"Nonsense, Ian. I may be a gentlewoman, but I am no wilting lily! It is simply a terrible thing to consider." She paused, frowning in thought. "I had no idea it was something to which you could become addicted, but of course it must be."

"Sadly, yes. It is a powerful drug, and when used for ill—" He toyed with the food on his plate. "Even the medical students I studied with sometimes indulged in it. 'Ether frolics', they called it."

Caroline stared at him in surprise. "But I thought it rendered you unconscious!"

"When the proper dose is administered," Ian explained. "But if you inhale just a little, it makes you feel… well, inebriated, I suppose. Or similar. I never tried the stuff myself, nor had any wish to."

"And you think Mr. Wells is using the stuff for this purpose? To feel so?" Caroline spoke matter-of-factly, and Ian could not help but admire her practicality in the light of such a dreadful discussion. His wife was no wilting lily, indeed.

"I could not say for certain, but he was certainly not the man I first met all those years ago, the last time I saw him," he told her heavily. "Besides his hands trembling, he seemed almost… wild. As if he were not in control of his emotions, or even his faculties. I felt as if a single word might set him off."

"And you think this is because of the ether?"

"The ether, yes, but also the nature of addiction. An addict will experience withdrawal symptoms if he does not have the stuff regularly, whatever substance he is using, and that is what I fear was happening to Mr. Wells when I visited."

Caroline shook her head slowly. "How very dreadful."

"Indeed. I should not have mentioned it."

Caroline's eyes were bright, her smile sure as she shook her head. "And yet I am glad you did! I want you to share your concerns with me, Ian." Her face softened for a moment before determination hardened her features. "But if Mr. Wells is addicted to this substance as you suspect, he surely cannot be trusted to perform the operation. It would undoubtedly be a disaster for you both, as well as the progress you hope to make."

"Yet it is the culmination of his life's work." Even though he had to agree with his wife, Ian could not imagine Wells stepping aside for any reason. He would not be forced, and Ian did not think he could make him do it.

"And yours as well," Caroline reminded him. "If Mr. Wells cannot perform the surgery, then surely the solution is obvious." She smiled at him, her eyes shining with certainty and purpose. "You must do it yourself."

CHAPTER NINE

Prince Edward Island

High summer was always one of the busiest times in a farmer's life, and this summer was no exception for the MacDougalls. Harriet found she missed Maggie's help with the household chores and the management of the kitchen garden, but even more so she longed for her daughter's sunny presence and cheerful chatter. Her twelve-year-old son George worked in the fields with Allan, and quiet, serious seven-year-old Anna did her small bit to help Harriet, often minding five-year-old Archie—but Harriet knew her children missed Maggie as well. They had never been apart before.

One afternoon, a fortnight after Maggie had left on the ship, Harriet stood out on the front porch, one hand raised to shield her eyes from the glare of the noonday sun. She could see Allan in the potato field, bent over the tender new plants as he and George weeded. There was so much work to be done, Harriet thought with a sigh, with the weeding and watering, the care of the animals, the ceaseless toil for both the land and the living. Allan was only forty-five years old but from a distance she saw how tired he looked stooped over in the field, how *old*, and the realization gave her a little pang of sorrow—and worry. How quickly the years slipped away, and yet surely God would grant them many more together.

"Mama?" Anna stood in the kitchen doorway. "The raspberry jam is ready to be set."

"Good lass." Harriet turned away from the sight of the fields, and her husband still stooped over. She pushed aside the worry and sorrow as she smiled at her daughter. There was work to be done.

Yet that evening, after the children had gone to bed and she and Allan sat in their usual chairs with the night falling softly all around, Harriet felt the worry pick at her again. Allan's dark hair was liberally streaked with gray, and a life out of doors had given him deep creases by his eyes and from his nose to his mouth. He squinted in the light of the oil lamp as he bent his head to the bridle he was mending, and Harriet felt a twist of anxiety inside. She didn't realize she had made a sound, for Allan glanced up, the creases by his eyes deepening as he smiled at her.

"Now what was that sigh for, *mo leannan*?"

"I didn't mean to," Harriet admitted. "It's only there is so much work to be done."

Allan lifted one powerful shoulder in a shrug. "No more than there ever is this time of year. Summer is always busy."

"I'm not the lass I once was," Harriet said, trying to sound rueful, and Allan frowned.

"I should have considered, with Maggie gone, that more work would fall to you. We can hire a girl if you like, to come in some days—"

"No, no," Harriet said quickly. "There's no need for that."

"Are you certain?"

"Yes, I'm certain." She paused, threading her needle carefully before she spoke again. "If we were to hire anyone, I think a man to help you with the harvest would be best."

"A man? I'm not in need of any help. I've got George, after all."

Harriet glanced up from her darning. "It's a good deal of work for just one man and a boy," she said. "George is only twelve, after all. You've hired men before—"

"For a season," Allan allowed. "When I was tending my father's land as well as our own. But there's no need of that since we sold his acreage."

They'd sold Mingarry Farm several years ago, and invested the money in their own property. It had been a hard decision, but the right one, and yet still Harriet worried. It was true there was not as much work as there had been when Allan had been managing the work of two farms, but there was still a great deal for one man and his young son. "Even so," she murmured.

"What are you about, Harriet?" Allan asked mildly enough, although she recognized that thread of steel in his voice. "What's got you in such a fash about how much I'm working?"

"Neither of us are getting any younger, Allan."

"You think I'm too old for this?" he demanded, and she couldn't tell if he was angry or amused. Knowing Allan, probably both.

"No," Harriet answered, trying to keep her voice steady, "but I know your father worked himself to death on this land and I don't want to see the same happen to you. I love you too much for that, Allan MacDougall."

Allan smiled, his eyes crinkling. "My father was far older than I am when he breathed his last. And in truth he died the way any farmer or man for that matter would hope to—strong until the very end." He leaned forward and covered Harriet's hand with his own work-roughened one. "I know having Maggie leave us has cost you, whether you'll admit it or not. And I feel my years more keenly when I see what a grown-up young woman our Maggie is. But I don't need a man to help me now, and hiring one won't keep me alive any longer than Providence allows." He gave her a rueful smile. "God surely ordains all our days, my love. I trusted that when I sailed away from you all those years ago, and I trust it now."

Tears pricked Harriet's eyes and she nodded, her throat too tight and her heart too full to manage words. "Aye," she said. "I trust it as well."

*

Boston

It had been an entire fortnight since Isobel had written to Mr. Anderson of the Commissioners for Foreign Missions to say she wished to add her name to the list of women, and she had not had a single reply, a fact that filled her with both relief and irritation. She realized she had been foolish to think that a suitable candidate for husband would present himself immediately, and yet placing her name on that list had felt so monumental a decision that it was dispiriting not to have an immediate response.

And, in her most private and pained moments, Isobel wondered if a candidate would choose her at all. The thought of the humiliation she would experience if it were ever to be made known that she'd put her name on such a list and *not* been chosen made her insides writhe in an agony of anticipated embarrassment.

It was July, and the weather was drowsy and hot. The children in school were irritable; Isobel was irritable herself, longing for something more and yet still not knowing if she would ever take possession of it. She refused the social engagements her parents tried to coax her to attend, yet sitting at home with a piece of embroidery or another novel was hardly more amusing. Her life had become one of waiting, and for something that might never happen.

After two weeks she started to think nothing would ever happen. She would turn twenty-nine years old in a few weeks; what man would choose such a spinster, especially if he wanted children? She would be a poor choice, indeed, and there might be all manner of eligible, pretty young women on Mr. Anderson's list—women with more zeal for the work than she could ever hope to have.

It was a balmy afternoon in early July when she returned home to find a letter addressed to her on the silver salver by the front door, the writing spiky and familiar from her last correspondence with him. Her heart bumped in her chest and she tore it open, heedless of how she crumpled the paper. Quickly she scanned the lines and her heart stopped bumping and seemed to freeze instead. Mr. Anderson had a possible candidate in mind and wished to see her at her earliest convenience—preferably tomorrow.

At four o'clock the next afternoon Isobel presented herself to the office where she'd had that first wretched interview. She'd spent a sleepless night pacing her room and wondering what sort of man Mr. Anderson had in mind. She was caught between a thrill of excitement and one of terror; what if he wasn't suitable? What if he was? What if he didn't like her? Would he be there at the office, or would Mr. Anderson arrange a meeting? She had no idea how any of it worked, and it left her even more agitated.

She had not said anything of it to either of her parents; since her father had agreed they had both been resigned to but cool about the matter, and the three of them had agreed, without any discussion, to not speak of it unless they had to. Isobel decided that there was no need to alarm her parents with only a possibility; indeed, the matter—and the man—might come to nothing. She would hear what Mr. Anderson had to say first.

As she entered the little office which was just as disordered as before, she knew she seemed haughty, her only defense against the terrible embarrassment she was afraid this interview would make her feel. She spoke coolly to Mr. Anderson's clerk and declined his offer of tea. When Mr. Anderson came to the door, Isobel swept past him, her head held high.

"Miss Moore," he said as he closed the door behind him. "Thank you for attending me so quickly."

She nodded regally, her throat too tight to form words. She knew her behavior bordered on rudeness, but she realized, to her own shame, that she would rather Mr. Anderson think her rude than pitiable. She longed to hear what he was going to say, and yet she was terrified as well. She did not even know what she wanted him to say—what sort of man she might reasonably hope for.

"A situation has arisen," Mr. Anderson said, folding his hands on his desk and looking at her over the rim of his spectacles.

"Indeed?"

"There is a young man, a God-fearing, studious and earnest young man." She nodded even as her heart fluttered with both excitement and trepidation. He was talking about her potential *husband*. "He wishes to take a wife."

She swallowed dryly. "I see."

Mr. Anderson straightened his cravat, suddenly seeming hesitant, almost nervous. "Generally, in these situations, we simply make an introduction. There is a period of courtship of at least two months, and then, God willing, a marriage. After a couple has been married some time, preferably at least for a month, an appointment is made in the missionary field."

Isobel nodded, relieved by such a sensible approach, and yet aware that this must not be the case for her, based on his look of uncertainty. "Is that not the case in this instance, Mr. Anderson?" she asked.

He seemed almost relieved that she grasped the particulars so quickly. "Indeed it is not, Miss Moore. For you see, this young man is already in the mission field. He left three years ago, before we made the provision that all missionaries must be married."

"I see," Isobel said after a moment, even though she did not. How could she marry a man who was already abroad? She would not be able to meet him, talk to him, or be able to discern whether they were remotely compatible, and she could hardly travel all the way to she knew not where, without knowing such essential facts.

"When he first wrote last year," Mr. Anderson continued, "I suggested that he return to this country and find himself a wife. But the fact of the matter is he is reluctant to leave his important work, and travel takes so much time. He would be gone for more than a year, to the detriment of the good work he is doing abroad. Considering your own situation, it seemed perhaps a solution could be found."

Isobel blinked, trying to make sense of his words. *Considering your own situation*. He must mean, she realized with an icy ripple of humiliation, her age. She was too old to wait around to see if this nameless man and she would suit. She would have to take a most appalling gamble.

"What is it exactly," she asked, her voice hardly more than a whisper, "that you suggest?"

"You could travel to where he is," Mr. Anderson stated, a slight note of apology in his voice. "As it happens, another missionary's wife is making the journey, as she had to return to America to see to her children's schooling. She could accompany you, so you would be suitably chaperoned."

One hand flew to Isobel's throat as if of its own accord. "Travel on my own?" She had never considered such a thing. "And what would happen once I was there, Mr. Anderson? I confess, I had always imagined I would have the opportunity to meet the man I was going to marry, before I embarked on such an arduous journey!" She spoke sharply, as if she were rebuking him, but Mr. Anderson remained calm, a courteous smile still on his face. Isobel stared at him, her heart starting to beat rather wildly. This really was most unexpected. Most alarming. *Most exciting*. "Really, I must say, this all seems quite out of the ordinary."

"Indeed it is, Miss Moore."

"Are there—are there no other gentlemen, missionaries, who might wish to arrange an introduction? Who are in this country?" One hand fluttered again at her throat as she fought to keep herself from flushing bright red from the humiliation of the question. She failed.

"I am afraid no other gentlemen have… expressed an interest," Mr. Anderson answered delicately.

"I see." And she did see, all too well. She had no idea how many women had put their name on that wretched list, but clearly hers was at the bottom of it. An almost thirty-year-old spinster, one who had expressed no interest in missions, only in marriage. Someone who must smack of desperation to the pious young men perusing the names. Tears stung Isobel's eyes and she blinked them back rapidly. "Where is the gentleman in question?" she asked when she'd composed herself sufficiently to sound brisk once more.

"He is presently in Burma," Mr. Anderson said, and Isobel could not think to reply. *Burma?* That distant land Adoniram Judson had spoken of so warmly, with such affection… and yet so far! She tried to imagine it and could only come up with vague images of white sand beaches, dense jungle, cloudless skies. Such descriptions had been in one of the travel books she'd read of Henry's, but it seemed impossible now that she might consider actually travelling to such a place. Quite, quite impossible.

"And this man's name?" she finally asked in a whisper.

"Mr. George Jamison."

"A Scot?"

"Of Scottish ancestry, yes, but he was born in America. His family is from Philadelphia, and he studied theology at Yale. He is thirty years old."

"I see." *George Jamison.* The name echoed in her head, meaningless and yet incredible. Perhaps the name of her future husband. *Isobel Jamison*, she thought, and felt a strange, shivery sort of thrill, even now, when she did not know what manner of man he was at all.

"As for your arrival, of course you would need to marry Mr. Jamison as soon as possible. It is quite unsuitable for you to remain in that country as an unmarried woman. Quite impossible."

Isobel stared at him in shock. "But… but what if we don't suit?" She realized she was clutching the wooden arm rests of her chair so hard her knuckles were white, and she released them, sitting back as she tried unsuccessfully to relax.

"That would be exceedingly difficult," Mr. Anderson answered after a moment. "Burma is no place for an unmarried lady. You could return on another ship, of course, but it might be months before you could find a suitable passage. In any case," he continued with a gentle smile, "that does not seem to be a desirable outcome for either you or Mr. Jamison."

"No," Isobel agreed faintly. Return to Boston unwed after travelling all that way and back? She would rather remain in Burma and cast her lot with George Jamison, whoever he might be.

"He has written a letter," Mr. Anderson offered carefully. "He entrusted it to me, when I suggested that I select one of the young ladies from our list. If you read it, you might feel as if you know him a bit more."

A letter. A single letter, and yet it might promise so much. Already she longed to read it. "Yes," Isobel said. "I suppose that is true."

"And if you decide you wish to pursue this course of action," Mr. Anderson continued, "we will make preparations for you to sail to India, and then on to Burma, as soon as possible."

India. Burma. Isobel felt the room spin dizzily around her and she blinked, willed the world to right itself. She could not faint in Mr. Anderson's office. He handed her a single sheet of paper, folded and sealed with wax, which she took with shaking fingers. "And when would you expect me to sail?"

"A ship leaves Boston for Calcutta next week," he told her, and the world spun again. "I would hope to see you on it."

*

The South Seas

"Captain!"

Henry walked as briskly as he could over to his navigator, Mr. Ellison, who had had his spyglass trained on the flat, unending line of the horizon. They had been dead in the water for six days, and the men were down to half-rations. Skin was blistered and peeling, tongues swollen and dry. The heat had not relented, and the air remained unbearably still.

Even worse, the men had become irritable in their fear; more than one fight had flared up between his crew, ending with several broken noses, and any numbers of bumps, bruises, and cuts. Henry had known he needed to maintain discipline in order for there not to be a mutiny, but he was most reluctant to enact the kinds of punishments that were still prevalent on U.S. Navy ships—flogging or caning, or the far worse keelhauling, which could end in a man's death by drowning as he was dragged in the water underneath the ship.

Instead Henry had chosen to limit the men's ration of rum, and give them a stern talking to, along with what he hoped was some encouragement.

"We must keep our spirits up, or we will never continue in the strength we need," he told them, and had been met with some surly stares, and worse, too many despairing gazes.

"What is it, Mr. Ellison?" he asked now, as he joined his navigator at the bow of the ship.

"I believe I see something, sir."

Hope leapt in his chest, although he tempered it with caution. Ellison had not said another ship. "Permit me?" Henry asked, holding his hand out, and the navigator handed him the instrument.

It took him a moment to find it, but then he saw a faint black smudge on the horizon. A ship or a cloud? It was impossible to say, and yet Henry hoped, for another ship was surely their only hope of salvation. "Continue to observe," Henry said briskly, "and inform me of any movements."

With an encouraging smile for the crew who had gathered around, he returned to his quarters and the letter he'd been writing to Margaret, the last letter, perhaps, that he might ever write. He had no idea if she would ever even see it, and thought it more than likely she wouldn't, but writing to her made him feel as if she were closer, and he needed that now. Swallowing past the tightness in his throat, he dipped his quill in the inkpot and began to write.

> *We have food enough but water only for two more days, a few more if we are sparing. I pray that we might yet be rescued from this calamity, but my heart fails within me, my dearest, without you near me to bolster my spirits. I think of how I left you on the quay, with tears in your eyes, and I remember you at our first meeting, so put out by your father's refusal to allow you to study! I have never been so thankful for Boethius in my life, for I can't imagine what my own would have been if I had not picked up that battered book and made your precious acquaintance. I think of that moment now, and so many others, and long only to know them again. Even the most mundane or trivial of conversations with you would thrill and inspire me now, and I hold onto each one we have shared, praying that we will have many more and yet fearing, my dear love, that we will not …*

Sighing, Henry laid the quill down and pushed the inkpot away. He wanted his last words—if they were indeed his last words—to Margaret to be ones of love and encouragement, not fear and desperation, yet he did not think he was capable of it now. Anxiety gnawed at his gut and he raked a hand through his stiff, salt-encrusted hair. How could it end like this, for him, for Margaret? They had perhaps two days of water rations left, maybe three. Perhaps if it rained… but the skies had been utterly cloudless.

"Captain!" Henry turned to see his first mate at the door.

"Mr. Martin?"

"It is a ship, sir, it is a ship!"

Hope rose buoyant inside him as Henry rose from the table and hurried to the deck. It was early evening, the stars just coming out in a violet sky, the air still heavy and warm. Mr. Ellison wordlessly handed him the spyglass and he stared at the now-visible form of a ship, hardly daring to believe, and yet… what kind of ship was it? And from what country?

He hesitated, knowing that in these distant waters a ship could just as easily be foe as friend, from a country he did not count as a friend, or worse, pirates. Yet what choice did he have? Already they had been adrift for too long. This might be their only chance.

He nodded towards his first mate, his heart thudding hard in his chest. "Fire the first rocket."

"Are you sure, sir?" the first mate asked, looking nervous, scared enough to question his captain's order. Even so, Henry did not blame him.

"We must take our chances," Henry answered, "for we have no others." He nodded again. "Fire the rocket, Mr. Dennison."

He watched as the sailors set the distress signal to light and it rose into the twilit sky, showering sparks high into the air.

"We'll fire another in an hour," Henry said. "God willing, we will be seen, and by a friend."

The night passed slowly; under a silvery sickle moon, it appeared the ship on the horizon was moving closer, but there was no acknowledgement of the three rockets they'd sent up into the sky. Anxiety twisted Henry's insides. What manner of ship could it be? Why had it not responded? In the darkness it was impossible to tell its intent.

When dawn broke, shreds of silvery mist lay low over the water, the air heavy and damp. Every man stood on deck, straining through the fog to see if the ship had come closer in the night, or sailed past them forever.

Then it appeared through the shreds of mist now evaporating in the rising sun, slipping silently through the water like a ghost ship. Ragged cheers rose from his crew and then were fell silent as the ship came closer. There could be no mistaking its red sails and brightly painted hull. The ship that now approached them was a Chinese war junk, and almost certainly an enemy.

CHAPTER TEN

Boston

Maggie sat on the nursery floor, constructing a tower of wooden blocks with Charlotte. She enjoyed playing with her little cousin, and in truth she found the nursery a far safer and more comforting place than the world of Boston society which Margaret was determined to show her, and that she'd been so excited to experience, yet had found, upon encountering it, that she did not like nearly as much as she'd hoped.

The uncertainty she'd experienced on the docks, when her aunt had seemed so impossibly sophisticated, had reared its head again when Margaret had suggested she have some dresses made up for her. When Maggie had protested the expense, she'd said gently, "Maggie, my dear. You cannot appear in society in a homespun dress and worn work boots."

Maggie had flushed and hung her head, and with a soft, sympathetic laugh, Margaret had quickly embraced her. "Do not be so cast down, my dear. I was once like you, my dear. I came to this country having been no farther than Oban, back in Scotland. I was quite overwhelmed, and in truth I don't think Henry's parents were too taken with me, at least at first."

"But you seem so elegant now," Maggie had protested, her voice muffled against Margaret's shoulder.

"And so will you! I want you to enjoy yourself, Maggie, new dresses included. Isn't that why you came? To have an adventure and experience something new?"

Wordlessly Maggie had nodded. Yet just two weeks after her arrival, here she was hiding in the nursery. She'd been to several dinners and parties, and she'd been hopelessly tongue-tied the entire time, while the other guests had regarded her with either amusement or pity. She'd wished only to be far away—even back in the familiar fields of home, sitting on the porch shelling peas or playing with little Archie. Just the thought of such mundane pastimes that had once filled her with frustration and boredom brought a sweet ache of homesickness. Oh, to be home!

Margaret had continued to cajole and coax her to come out, but Maggie had begun to think of any number of excuses to stay in. She had a headache; she didn't know how to dance—her father's waltzing lessons aside; she was tired. After a while, Margaret had let her be, to both Maggie's relief and misery. She did not know if it was worse, to be willfully forgotten, or to have continued to endure all the events on which she'd once pinned so many naïve hopes. The sudden clatter of the tower of blocks toppling to the floor jerked Maggie out of her own thoughts.

"I'm bored," Charlotte complained, her pretty little face turned into a childish pout. "Can't we do something else, Maggie? Building towers is for babies."

"Is it now?" Maggie said, amused. "Well, then, how about we play school? You shall be going to school one day, won't you?" Charlotte shrugged, and Maggie wondered if her aunt would send the girl to one of the new 'kindergartens' she'd told her were starting in the city, or have her educated by a governess at home. Margaret was a reformer, but she still adhered to many of society's conventions. "In any case, you will need to know your letters and numbers. Why don't we make a start?" Charlotte looked dubious, and Maggie chucked her under the chin. "It will be fun, I promise. Your cousin Archie knows his letters and numbers already."

"Does he?" Charlotte had been quite curious about the cousin she'd only met as a baby, and who was but a year older than her.

"Yes, and so shall you." Smiling, Maggie fetched a slate and chalk and began to write Charlotte's name on it.

Charlotte loved seeing her name on the slate, and after just a few minutes she was recognizing the letters and numbers Maggie wrote. They played happily for a little while, with Charlotte telling Maggie what words to write, when footsteps sounded, followed by the creak of the door.

Maggie looked up, smiling awkwardly as Margaret appeared, elegant as always. She scrambled from the floor, aware that her hair had half-fallen down and there was dust on the skirt of her dress.

"Well, here you both are," Margaret said with a twitch to her lips. "As I thought you'd be. You are spoiling Charlotte with all the attention, Maggie, but I cannot be sorry." Charlotte rushed towards her mother, and Margaret clasped her to her before the little girl squirmed away and ran to retrieve the slate Maggie still held.

"Look what we've been doing, Mama," she exclaimed, and thrust the slate towards Margaret.

"Just a bit of fun," Maggie said quickly, and Margaret glanced down at the slate.

"Why you've been learning your letters, Charlotte," she said in surprise, and lowered the slate to give Maggie a rather considering look. "I just came up here to tell you the gloves and bonnets we were waiting upon have arrived. I thought you could try them on."

Maggie nodded rather dumbly, and, her glance still considering although she said nothing, Margaret glanced again at the slate.

The bonnet was beautiful, of green silk with feather dyed to match, and surely the most gorgeous thing Maggie had ever worn—even nicer than the simple but elegant gowns Margaret had had made up, which she'd worn on her few evenings out. And yet, looking at her reflection in the mirror, Maggie felt like a fraud. She could put on all manner of silks and satins, frocks and fripperies, but she was still a farm girl at heart.

Margaret knocked on her bedroom door as she was studying herself, smiling as she came in. "How lovely you look, Maggie! The green quite suits you, especially with your hair. It is positively Titian."

Maggie didn't know what Titian meant, and so she just mumbled a reply as she removed the bonnet and put it back in its box.

"You like it?" Margaret asked gently, and Maggie blushed as she answered.

"Oh, yes. Of course. It's the loveliest thing I've ever seen. Thank you, Aunt Margaret—'

"You have already thanked me for your wardrobe, Maggie. There is no need to do it again." Margaret put the lid on the box as she gave her a small, understanding smile. "You have not been as pleased with your clothes as I had hoped."

"Oh, but I am—" Maggie insisted, flushing all the more. She hated the thought that she seemed ungrateful.

"Forgive me, it sounded as if I were scolding you, and indeed I was not. I have not been able to help but notice, Maggie, that the amusements and entertainments you have attended with me have not accomplished their purpose at all. You have seemed quite…" She paused, her brow furrowing. "Uncomfortable. Unhappy, even." Maggie fidgeted, too miserable to reply, and Margaret raised her eyebrows. "Has that not been the case?"

"I suppose it has," Maggie admitted reluctantly. "I'm sorry, Aunt Margaret. You've been so kind and generous, and I know I must seem ungrateful." She struggled against sudden tears as she made herself ask, "Are you going to send me back?"

"Send you back?" Margaret repeated in surprise, before she gave a quick shake of her head. "Oh Maggie, no, of course not! Why would I do such a thing? You are not here on sufferance, you know. I have quite enjoyed having your company, but I do not wish to make you miserable. Perhaps you wish to go home?"

Maggie hesitated, for part of her yearned for such a thing, and yet even so she did not want to leave Boston, humiliated and defeated by her own inability to adjust. "I am homesick," she admitted, "but I don't wish to leave. It's just… I'm not… I don't like dances and things like that. I thought I would, so much, but I just feel a fool."

"You do not look a fool," Margaret said gently. "You look like a lovely young lady, if a trifle shy, which is no bad thing."

Maggie shrugged helplessly. "It's not me—that world. I thought it could be, I wanted it to be, but… I just feel as if I'm pretending. I'd rather stay home and read a book, or play with Charlotte."

"Yes, you're very good with Charlotte. Harriet had written to me, about your way with little ones." Margaret was silent for a moment, seeming to brood, and Maggie waited, uncertain what her aunt was thinking, or what she might suggest. "Do you remember," she finally asked, "when I suggested you could help with the First School?"

"You mean teaching?" Maggie asked uncertainly. Playing about with Charlotte's slate was one thing, being a proper teacher quite another.

"Yes, teaching. Isobel—it looks likely that she might go abroad, although nothing is certain yet. It is all happening much sooner than we expected, and I cannot imagine how to find another teacher at such short notice. I wouldn't expect you to teach every day, of course, and I'd come with you, at least at the start. I wouldn't mind being back in the classroom, for a little while at least. We close the school next week for the month of August, mainly because the hot weather breeds so much illness, so you could start in September. If you think you'd enjoy it…"

"I'd love it," Maggie said honestly. Even though her aunt had suggested it earlier, she'd assumed it had been nothing more than an idle thought, even a tease. She hadn't considered it seriously for a moment, and yet she thrilled to the possibility now. She'd so much rather be in a schoolroom, with pupils whose experience was closer to her own, than feeling stiff and awkward in the drawing rooms of Boston's best. "But I don't know how good I'll be," she warned her aunt. "I've never taught before." Which was surely obvious, and yet she felt she had to say it.

"I'm sure you will be more than capable, Maggie. I am quite certain you shall more than rise to the occasion." Margaret let out a little sigh as she smiled wryly. "I did want you to enjoy yourself here, my dear—"

"I will enjoy myself," Maggie insisted. Much more than drinking tea or dancing. "And there will still be time to see the sights and meet people, won't there?" she asked, even if she dreaded the thought. "Especially if the school is closed for August."

"Yes, of course there will," Margaret answered. She gave Maggie a knowing look. "Perhaps we could have a tour of the city, rather than one of its drawing rooms? I imagine you'd much prefer those sights."

"I would, Aunt Margaret," Maggie said feelingly, and her aunt laughed.

"Then it shall be done."

*

Isobel closed the lid of her trunk, her hands shaking. She took a deep breath and smoothed down the front of her dress, trying for calm. She was packed, ready to leave for Calcutta, and then on to Burma, on the morning's tide. This evening would be her farewell dinner, with her parents as well as Margaret, her niece Maggie, and the Campbells. She could hardly believe it had all happened so quickly… a week ago she had not even known of Mr. Jamison's existence!

Drawing a shaky breath, she turned away from her trunk, pacing her room with restless agitation. She had not, she acknowledged, had a moment's peace since she'd written to Mr. Anderson and accepted George Jamison's proposal by proxy, flitting from wild excitement to deep and abiding terror at the huge step she was about to take.

She'd left Mr. Anderson's with George Jamison's letter clutched in her hand, and so much excitement and hope fluttering in her breast. What manner of man he would be? What would he tell her of himself?

It had felt an age but had only been half an hour, before she'd been seated in the smaller parlor in the back of the house, the windows open to the summery air, and broken the seal on the letter that might decide her fate.

As she'd unfolded the stiff pages, she'd felt a tremor of both wonder and fear at what the letter's contents might reveal, for better or worse. Would Mr. Jamison reveal something of the man he was, the hopes he had? Or would it be no more than a formal invitation, from one stranger to another?

> *Dear Madam, How strange it is to address a letter to a woman whose name I do not know, and yet might become my wife! I confess, I have spent an hour or more staring down at this page and not knowing at all what to write. Should I tell you my age, which is thirty, or that I have brown hair and blue eyes? My nose is snub though; will that alarm you? Is it indelicate to mention any particulars at all? I do not know, but I apologize in advance.*

Isobel lowered the letter for a moment, her heart beating wildly. He'd said very little—and she was not particularly fond of snub noses!—yet already he had given her an insight into his character that she had craved. The wry tone, the laughing humor she sensed in his words, the pleasing hesitations… She looked down at the letter and began to read once more.

I could tell you that I hail from Philadelphia, which perhaps you already know, or that I studied Divinity at Yale. Perhaps you would like to hear of my three sisters, two older, one younger, who all call me Georgie, a name I admit I loathe and yet also secretly adore. Does that make me fickle? I fear I am not furthering my cause at all with these ruminations!

Isobel laughed out loud and continued to read, thrilling to every gently self-deprecating word. She could not help but feel he sounded like someone she would like, someone she would laugh with… *someone she could love.*

She continued to read about his childhood, his family, his faith in God as well as the desire to serve that had led him first to India, and then on to Burma.

I am well aware that whoever you are, and what hopes or dreams might reside in your heart, I am daring to ask a great deal of you before we have even met, never mind wed. To travel so far, on such a perilous journey, with so much unknown at its end… my own courage would flag, if not fail completely, at such a thought. And yet I hope, if you read my letter and it stirs you at all, that you might consider it. If you long to labor with another, serving God and working to do good in a world that is often hard and harsh, in a land that can be both beautiful and fierce, then I hope and pray you will consider my letter—and my suit—with both sober and joyful consideration. I await your reply, and perhaps even to welcome you one day to this land I've come to love as my own. Yours faithfully, George Jamison

Slowly Isobel lowered the letter, her fingers near to trembling from the emotion she'd felt while reading his words. It was, she realized, a very nearly perfect letter. She did not think she could have asked for better or for more. It blew all her reservations away as so much useless chaff. Here was a gentleman she could marry, she could love, surely. What did she have to fear?

Even so, her certainty was tested when she'd informed her family that she had accepted a proposal and was leaving in less than a week.

"What…!" Her mother had stared at her in complete shock, one hand pressed against her bosom. "But you do not even know the man."

"I know enough. He wrote a letter—"

"One letter!"

And yet what a letter it had been! Isobel was not willing to share the tender missive, written before Mr. Jamison even knew her, and yet still seeming as if he'd been addressing her directly. Already it felt too intimate to share.

"It is enough, Mother. My mind is quite decided."

"But to go so far away… Burma… I have not even heard of the place!"

Isobel smiled faintly. "It is where Mr. Judson has been serving," she said. It seemed eminently providential, that she would be travelling to the place that had started her on this journey.

"But what sort of place is it?" her mother asked. "Is it… is it…"

"It is different, of course," Isobel answered, her tone firm. "How different, I do not know. But Mr. Jamison spoke very highly, very warmly of it and its people." Though inwardly she quailed at the thought of all the changes and challenges ahead, she felt as if she already shared the enthusiasm that had been so apparent in Mr. Jamison's letter.

Margaret, thankfully, was thrilled for her, and even her father seemed pleased, if a bit sad to have her going so far, perhaps never to see her again.

The thought made her stomach clench with fear and grief, even as she held onto her excitement. Was she mad, to travel so far, to risk so much, all on the flimsy promise of a single letter? She would discover soon enough.

"Isobel?" Her mother appeared in the doorway, several starched handkerchiefs, embroidered with lace, in her hands. "I thought you could use a few more handkerchiefs. I did the lace myself."

"Oh, Mother." Isobel took them with a watery smile. "Thank you."

"You're packed, then?" her mother asked, glancing at Isobel's trunk with something close to apprehension.

Isobel nodded. "Yes… I only have to wait now, I suppose."

"Cook has made all of your favorite dishes for your farewell supper," her mother said, her smile as watery as Isobel's. "Pigeon pie and Washington cake."

Isobel smiled, remembering how just a few short months ago she'd been so tired of the staid, predictable suppers Cook put on. Tired of everything about her life, and yet now she knew she would miss it all, almost more than she could bear.

"That's very kind of her," she said, her voice choking a little, and her mother took a step towards her.

"Dear Isobel, I know I was… harsh when you first suggested this plan. I thought it outlandish and dangerous, and I still do, but even so you go with my blessing, and my prayers. Please know that." Her mother blinked back tears and so did Isobel.

"Thank you, Mother," she said, and kissed her cheek.

Her mother drew a quick breath to compose herself, and then gave a brisk nod. "Now you must change your gown," she said. "Margaret and her niece will be here shortly, along with the Campbells." Her mother's mouth tightened at the mention of Ian and his wife; she had never quite forgiven Ian for marrying Caroline instead of Isobel. It had been Isobel who had insisted they be invited; she had a surprising desire to say a formal goodbye to

Ian, and even Caroline, knowing it was likely they might never see each other again. So many farewells to say… tears pricked her eyes at the thought, and she gave her mother a quick, steadying smile.

"I shall be ready shortly."

An hour later Isobel descended to the drawing room in a dress of pale pink satin, its wide neckline emphasized by the short, puffed sleeves reaching the elbow from the dropped shoulders. It was the kind of gown she was hardly ever likely to wear in Burma, and indeed she was not even bringing it. As she entered the drawing room, she smoothed her hand down the expensive material, savoring the sensation. While there would be some cause to wear a formal gown on the ship journey over, none would need to be as elegant as this, and once in Burma, her gowns would be made of muslin, which, Mr. Anderson had informed her, was more practical for the heat.

"My dear." Her father clasped her hands and kissed her cheek as she came into the room. His eyes were bright but he still smiled, and Isobel was grateful for it. "How lovely you look."

"Thank you, Father."

He squeezed her hands and stepped away as Margaret and Maggie came into the room.

"Isobel!" Margaret exclaimed, rushing over to embrace her. "I can scarcely believe this day has come, and so quickly!"

"Nor I," Isobel agreed shakily. Although she was still filled with excitement for the adventure ahead, she still felt a sweeping sense of loss and even grief at saying so many farewells. To think she might never see anyone in this room again…!

"Are you very excited?" Maggie asked shyly. She looked very becoming in a new gown of dark green silk, her lovely auburn hair in coils behind her ears, and for a second Isobel envied her—to be so young and pretty, to have so much ahead of her. Then she remembered that she had much ahead of her as well, and she smiled at Maggie.

"I am, indeed. Nervous, as well."

Ian and Caroline came in a few moments later, and Isobel greeted them both warmly, the reality of her departure making her feel benevolent, able to forget, or at least forgive, all past slights and wrongs.

"We have found a replacement for you at school," Margaret told her a little while later, when the first course was being served.

"Oh?" Isobel glanced at Caroline, who looked only politely interested. "Who might that be?"

"Maggie," Margaret replied with an approving nod towards her niece. "She is quite adept with children, and she is looking forward to teaching little ones. Are you not, Maggie?"

"I am," Maggie said, and ducked her head.

"I'm so pleased." Isobel had already said her farewells to her pupils, with some tears on both sides. Patrick Finnegan had come up to her after school had been dismissed, looking forlorn for the first time in Isobel's memory.

"Now you really won't be a thornback, Miss," he'd said. "But I'll miss you."

She hoped now that Maggie would enjoy her time teaching at the school; she knew she would look back on those years, tinged as they'd been with disappointment, in fond memory.

The rest of the meal passed in bittersweet enjoyment, with Isobel conscious that everything was the last. The evening was warm and after supper they retired to the drawing room to play music or cards, the windows open to the night air. Ian took a moment when Isobel was sorting through the pianoforte music to speak to her quietly.

"I seem to recall some time ago you were thinking of doing something others would consider madness."

Isobel let out a trembling little laugh, her emotions so very close to the surface. "Yes, I was."

Briefly Ian laid a hand on her sleeve. "I'm so happy for you, Isobel, truly. I wish you Godspeed on your journey, and true joy with Mr. Jamison. He is a fortunate man indeed."

A few years or even months ago, Isobel would have found the bitter pill in the midst of all that sweetness, the sting in the honey. She would have thought that if Ian considered Mr. Jamison so fortunate, why had he not fallen in love with her himself? Now, however, she simply smiled and murmured her thanks, more than willing to let the past be in the past. She had the future to think about, after all.

CHAPTER ELEVEN

The last young pupil had trickled out of the First School into the September sunshine, and Maggie moved around the room stacking primers and slates. She had been helping her aunt teach at the school since the beginning of the month, after a lovely August of seeing the sights of Boston, without an intimidating drawing room in sight. Maggie had enjoyed it greatly, but she realized she loved teaching more.

Over the course of the last month she'd seen the markets and museums of the city, and spent several pleasant afternoons in Boston's new public garden, sailing paper boats with Charlotte and picnicking among the flowers. She'd also plucked up her courage to dine with her uncle Ian and his wife Caroline in an actual restaurant, and a fancy one at that. The Tremont House Hotel was considered quite the best place to dine in Boston, and Maggie had been overwhelmed by the seven-course meal she'd shared with her relatives, yet relieved and encouraged by their pleasant company. Caroline had been full of warm, well-meaning advice, and had also regaled Maggie with stories of her childhood.

"I was really very spoiled," she told her with a tinkling laugh. "Quite impossibly so! But your mother must have told you so, since she knew me then."

"No, she didn't," Maggie said, taken aback at the thought that this elegant and friendly young woman might have been anything like spoiled.

"Oh, but I was! You shall have to ask when you return to Prince Edward Island. But of course, I hope that is not for some time yet."

So did Maggie. Although she still missed her family and wrote them every week, she was coming to love her time in Boston—especially now that she had started teaching. Admittedly, on her first day she'd been a mass of nerves, practically skulking in the corner while Margaret had taken all the pupils in hand. Margaret had taken pity on her, and assigned her the youngest children, to help them with their letters, a task Maggie could certainly manage.

Now, two weeks on, Maggie had grown in confidence and was helping older pupils as well, with both their letters and sums. Yesterday she'd even taught a lesson on geography, unrolling the large map Margaret had brought from Henry's study to trace his journey to China, and Isobel's to Burma, for the children. They had marveled at the great distances across the sea, even though many of them had made a similar journey, coming from Ireland. It was different, Maggie knew, to see it on a map.

"All the way to China," one little freckled boy had said, shaking his head in wonder. "And he'll come back?"

"I certainly hope so," Margaret had answered briskly as she rolled up the map. Maggie knew she'd had one letter from Henry when he'd put in at Trinidad, but that had been some time ago. According to her aunt's reckoning, he should have reached China by now, but they hadn't had any further word, which Margaret told her was expected. Still, Maggie knew the waiting was hard.

She put the primers and slates on the shelf while her aunt tidied the desks and chairs.

"Another good day," she said with a smile for Maggie. "You really do have a way with the children."

"Thank you, Aunt Margaret."

"Perhaps soon you can take the main lessons?" Margaret raised her eyebrows. "From the front?

"Oh…" Maggie was both pleased and alarmed by the idea. "Do you really think so?"

They were just about to leave when the door to the schoolhouse opened, sending a shaft of late afternoon sunlight across the wooden floor, and then the shadow of a man. Maggie tensed, and even Margaret stilled, her expression suddenly alert. They had never actually encountered any danger while teaching at the school, but at that moment Maggie was acutely conscious of the fact that the school was on the fringe of Boston's notorious Murder District and guarded by Henry's man, John Caber, during the day, who was still surely outside of the school, and had allowed this man to enter. Maggie relaxed, and so did her aunt.

"May I help you?" she asked, and the man stepped forward so Maggie was able to see that he was only a little older than she was, perhaps eighteen or twenty. He wore the homespun shirt and trousers of a recent immigrant, and twisted his worn cap in his hands. "This is the school?" he asked, his accent distinctly Irish.

"It is, indeed," Margaret answered with a smile.

"And you teach reading and writing and things? To anyone who wants it?"

"We do, Mr.—?" Margaret raised her eyebrows inquiringly.

"Flanagan, Seamus Flanagan."

"And on whose behalf are you inquiring about an education, Mr. Flanagan?"

He blinked, and Maggie imagined he was trying to untangle her aunt's fancy words. Aunt Margaret did have a rather eloquent, if sometimes confusing, turn of phrase.

"My own, ma'am."

"I see." Margaret paused for a moment, a look of sympathy on her face as her gaze took in the cap in his hands, his worn and patched-over boots. "That is very admirable, of course." Another pause while both Maggie and the newcomer waited. "May I ask how old are you, Mr. Flanagan?" Margaret finally asked.

Maggie saw a blush stain his cheeks, but he kept his chin lifted, his gaze steady. "Eighteen, ma'am."

Margaret nodded, her lips pursing even as sympathy flashed again in her eyes. "I appreciate and admire your desire to learn, but our oldest student now is only ten years old."

"I heard you took on some older ones," Seamus Flanagan said hesitantly. "If they wanted to learn."

"Indeed we used to, when the school first started. I wish there to be no impediment to anyone who desires to improve themselves. But we have had so many children come to our doors, that it proved impossible to continue."

"I'd be quiet. I could sit in the back…"

"I'm sorry." Margaret's voice was compassionate but firm. "But surely you have some gainful employment, Mr. Flanagan? The Seamen's Bethel does classes in the evenings—"

"I work nights, as a watchman by the harbor."

"You are quite young for such a position of responsibility."

"My uncle manages one of the warehouses," Seamus replied with dignity. "He hired me. And since my days are my own, I wanted to get some education. Learn how to read." He nodded towards Maggie, although his gaze remained steady on her aunt. "Is this young lady not a pupil here?"

"She is a teacher," Margaret answered, and for the first time Maggie heard a surprising coolness in her aunt's tone.

"But Aunt Margaret," Maggie interjected impulsively before she could think better of it, "surely we have room. Declan left last week, after all, to work in a—"

"I don't think so, Maggie." Margaret gave her a quelling look that caused Maggie to blush.

"But you have the room?" Seamus asked slowly. His tone was polite but Maggie saw a spark of challenge in his eyes.

Margaret's mouth thinned. "We might have the room, but I am reluctant to admit so old a pupil as yourself."

Seamus's gaze didn't waver. "And why might that be, ma'am?"

"It could be disruptive to the classroom."

"Are you saying I'll cause a problem?"

"You might not mean to—"

"I just want to learn, ma'am. I thought that's what this school was about."

Margaret hesitated, her sympathy warring with some reserve Maggie didn't understand. "Very well," Margaret relented. "I will consider the matter. Why don't you return tomorrow? I'll have an answer for you then."

"Thank you, Miss."

Margaret nodded, still looking torn as Seamus turned and left, the door creaking shut behind him. Margaret turned to Maggie with a sigh.

"I appreciate your desire to help, dear, but it is best if we do not contradict each other in front of a stranger."

Maggie blinked, hurt and embarrassed by the slight censure in her aunt's tone. "I'm sorry, Aunt Margaret. I didn't see any harm."

"I know you didn't, and indeed there might not be." Margaret sighed again. "I am reluctant to turn anyone away from our doors, but we discovered quite early on how disruptive having grown men and women in the classroom could be. It is fortunate the Seaman's Bethel offers classes to such as—"

"But Mr. Flanagan can't attend those," Maggie pointed out as reasonably as she could. "And he seems quiet and polite enough." She tilted her chin, willing to be as fiery as her aunt in this matter. "I don't see why we have to turn him away. He wants to learn."

"And am I to accept every young man such as Mr. Flanagan who comes to our door?" Margaret asked, caught between amusement and exasperation.

"No—just this one. It isn't as if all sorts of men and women are knocking down the door, after all."

Margaret stared at her for a moment before sighing and reaching for her cloak. "I will think on it."

"What is your objection?" Maggie asked boldly. "Really?"

For a second Margaret looked annoyed at Maggie's presumption, and then her face softened and she looked as she always did, warm and approachable. "In truth, Maggie, I don't completely know. Experience, in part. When your aunt Eleanor and I first started this school, we had a day set aside for men and women who wanted to learn. It was mostly women, and the men who did come here were… difficult." She sighed. "They didn't particularly like to learn from a woman, and sometimes they fought with each other. We decided to offer learning only to women and children, and then when the Seaman's Bethel offered classes…" She shrugged. "I am reluctant to enter back into that fray."

"But Mr. Flanagan is only one man, and he's only eighteen. Surely—"

"You seem to have taken a liking to Mr. Flanagan," Margaret observed tartly. Maggie shrugged. In truth there had been something honest and open in Seamus Flanagan's face, and it had, she acknowledged, been a handsome face at that.

"I suppose I sympathize with him," she said after a moment.

"But you know how to write and read, Maggie—"

"Yes, but I've lived my whole life on a little farm, and my parents were born on a farm in Scotland, same as yours—and you yourself." Maggie's voice throbbed with sudden feeling, even as she inwardly quailed at her own daring. "You were all immigrants once, as fresh off a ship as Seamus Flanagan, if perhaps a little better off. There's not much difference between any of us, not really." She realized as she said the words how much she believed them.

"That's true." Margaret was quiet for a moment, her gaze distant. "I would hate to think I've let my years in Boston change me," she said slowly before turning to Maggie with a smile. "In truth, Maggie, you remind me a bit of myself, when I was your age! So full of righteous fire. I pray I have not let mine dim."

"Then…"

"When Mr. Flanagan returns tomorrow, I will tell him he can attend the school, as a trial, for one week. I believe that is fair?"

"Yes, Aunt Margaret," Maggie said, now as meek as a church mouse. She was pleased her aunt had agreed, but also embarrassed that she'd been so bold as to challenge her in such a way. Even now, after being with Margaret for several months, she still felt intimidated by her elegance and poise. "That is fair indeed."

"Good." Margaret smiled and briefly touched her cheek. "I am glad you are here, my dear. We all need to be challenged."

"I didn't mean to—"

"No, no, I truly am glad. Complacency is the enemy of progress, and may it never be said of me that I have turned into a snob! Now we should return home. Charlotte will be eager to see us both, I'm sure."

*

The Bulfinch Operating Theatre was buzzing with surgeons, medical students, newspaper men and more than a few curious gawkers. The mood was exuberant and, Ian feared, more than a little skeptical; from the corner of his eyes he saw a young medical student toss something at another. They were like schoolboys, rowdy and impatient. The operation had been delayed twice already, due to hospital politics, and now it was already September. The months of anticipation had made Ian feel both more determined and anxious, and, he feared, the crowd more cynical. It seemed almost as if they were hoping for the experiment to fail.

Ian stood to the side of the stage waiting for Horace Wells to be announced to come forward to demonstrate the first public use of ether as an anesthetic for a tooth extraction; it would be a simple operation for Wells, as an experienced dentist, and yet

Ian felt a deep-seated pang of uneasiness and even of fear at the prospect. Every eye would be trained on Wells as he performed the extraction… if it failed, it would be tomorrow's joke in the newspapers, or worse.

He studied Wells discreetly. Looking at him, he was forced to admit he was far from the purposeful man Ian had first met five years ago—his eyes were bloodshot, his gaze moving around wildly; his hair was unkempt, his frock coat stained, his cravat crooked. It pained Ian to see his colleague so transformed—and because of the very thing that united them.

In the months since he'd feared Wells had begun to take ether himself, Ian had not found it in himself to confront the man. They had only corresponded by letter, and to speak on so difficult and delicate a matter in written form hardly seemed possible or appropriate. And yet… it meant that they had come to this crucial moment without having said a word about Wells' capability.

Caroline's words echoed uncomfortably in Ian's mind. *If Mr. Wells cannot perform the operation, then you must do it.*

He'd considered the matter endlessly for the last few weeks, yet he had reached no satisfactory answer. He'd attempted to compose a letter to Wells in Hartford, but nothing he wrote seemed adequate. If Ian suggested he perform the operation, Wells would think he was trying to steal the glory for himself. And Wells, Ian acknowledged with a shaft of recrimination, might even be right. He'd worked on the experiments with ether for five years. He'd contributed just as much to the cause as Wells had, yet it would be Wells who would receive the adulation and praise if the operation succeeded.

And if it didn't?

It would be Ian, as a resident doctor of the Massachusetts General Hospital, who received the condemnation for allowing the procedure to go forward in the prestigious Bulfinch Operating Theatre. Either way, he suffered—and yet he told himself it didn't matter to him if

Wells received all the praise. The far more important thing was the acceptance of ether as an anesthetic by the medical community, the possibility of operations being carried out that were now nothing more than a distant dream. Conditions that were a death sentence could be treated, and in a far more humane way. How could he begrudge Wells anything, if all that came to pass?

Ian glanced at him again, saw Wells' hands tremble as he attempted to straighten his cravat. Ian's unease deepened to something close to panic. A man could not operate, or even extract a tooth, with shaky hands. Ian didn't know what was the matter with Wells, if his current condition was indeed the result of an addiction to ether or a matter of mere nerves, but he could see that the man was not in the proper frame of mind—or physical state. His mind made up, Ian approached him.

"Mr. Wells, are you sure you are all right?"

Wells glanced at him sharply, his eyes bright with suspicion. "Of course I am. Why should I not be?"

Ian tried to temper his words with a smile. "It is only… you look a bit unwell."

Wells' lip curled. "How now, Campbell? Are you attempting to dissuade me from performing the extraction at this late hour? Let me guess. You wish to perform the procedure yourself."

"I would do so if needed," Ian replied steadily, even as a flush touched his cheeks. "The most important thing, Wells, is for the operation to succeed, no matter who performs it. Surely we are in agreement on that?"

"It will succeed," Wells answered roughly. "I have done the same a hundred times before, which is more than I can say for you. I have been using ether on my patients for years, as you know—"

Frustration bubbled inside Ian. "And yet you do not appear in a state that is conducive to—"

"I am fine, man," Wells snapped. "Now leave it be. Mr. Warren is ascending the stage."

With his spirits sinking like a stone inside him, Ian watched as the Chief of Surgery introduced Wells to the crowd of spectators, and their rowdy chatter died to a hushed and expectant silence. The patient, a gentleman of about forty years old, was brought onto the stage, smiling rather dubiously, looking overwhelmed by all the attention.

Wells began to climb the short flight of stairs to the stage, and then he stumbled. Ian's heart caught in his throat, and he reached out to steady his colleague, one hand on the man's sleeve.

"Please, Horace," he whispered urgently. "Do not let pride stand in your way at this important hour. Permit me—"

Without looking at him, Wells jerked his arm away and ascended to the stage. Ian stepped back, concern and despair swamping him. Should he intervene? To do so now would create an inexcusable scene, and might be as damaging as total failure, if not even more so. Yet how he could allow the procedure to go forward, knowing the state Wells was in? He suddenly wished Caroline was here, even though women were not permitted in the operating theatre. They had been able to move past the tension that had risen between them over Riddell's money; now he longed for her serene smile, her steady advice. She would be able to find some way to keep Wells from performing the extraction…

Even as these thoughts raced through Ian's mind, the matter was out of his hands and he knew there was nothing more he could do. Wells had given a slight bow to the audience and was now placing the glass globe of ether over the man's face. When the patient's eyes fluttered, he began to extract the tooth.

Ian almost thought he was imagining the faint moan he heard, but the second one was loud enough for the first row of spectators to hear.

"He can feel it!" someone exclaimed.

"It doesn't work at all," another jeered, and the room erupted into howls and catcalls. Wells turned to the crowd, pliers in hand, his wild gaze moving over the derisive spectators.

"No…" he muttered, but his voice was lost amidst the shouts and jeers. Ian's stomach hollowed out with dread and disappointment as his gaze moved instinctively to Dr. Warren's. Standing on the other side of the stage, watching Wells stumble about with ill-concealed derision, Warren lifted his head to look straight at Ian.

"Humbug," he said flatly.

The experiment, Ian knew with a despairing certainty, had been a complete and utter failure.

CHAPTER TWELVE

Calcutta

Isobel's first sight of Calcutta was of low-lying buildings shrouded in an unfamiliar yellow haze. When she heard that they were entering the Hooghly River that led into the city, she went out on deck along with the other few passengers who had braved the four-month journey to India, including her chaperone, Katherine Daylesford, wife to another missionary in Midnapore. The humid air, so different from what she was accustomed to, felt like a heavy, wet blanket draped over her, the heat like nothing she'd ever felt before. She had been doing her best to become accustomed to it as they'd approached India, but it still felt strangely heavy and damp.

"There it is," Katherine said as the ship cut through the slug-gish water, passing an odd assortment of small brigs and skiffs crawling along the river.

For several hours, the ship had been passing what looked almost like English houses, with wide verandahs and lawns running straight down to the river. Isobel had been surprised by the number of people, even ladies in gowns like her own, who had come onto their verandahs to wave their handkerchiefs at the ship as it passed by. It had all looked strangely familiar, and not what she'd expected. Was all of India like this, no matter what she'd read in the books Henry had given her?

"No, no, this is just the English part," Mrs. Daylesford had explained when she asked. "It is called Garden Reach. Those who work for the East India Company live here." Her mouth tightened at the mention of that organization's name, revealing a dislike that, over the course of the ship journey, Isobel had come to understand. Mrs. Daylesford had told her that the East India Company, the "empire within an empire", had a domineering and bloody history that many missionaries despised. Moreover, they had only granted missionaries leave to enter the country in the last twenty years, as they'd believed their work might lead to social unrest and a loss in their mercantile profits.

"Of course they don't want the people they are attempting to subdue to have access to things like education," Mrs. Daylesford had said with some asperity. "Never mind actual hope."

The ship slid by the English houses, looking so unsettlingly grand, and on to the imposing Fort William, with its large verdant public square, and then to the city proper—a horizon of ramshackle buildings and pagodas intermingled with large stone structures such as one that Isobel noticed had been constructed to replicate an English country manor. She did not know what to make of any of it; it was all so disconcerting, the mix of the familiar and the strange, together seeming entirely incongruous.

"It is a beautiful city, is it not?" Katherine said, and slowly Isobel nodded. Yes, it was beautiful, but it was also so different from what she was used to, so different from what she'd even been expecting, because of course she had not known what to imagine at all.

In truth, everything about the journey had been strange and unsettling. She had never travelled on a ship before, despite her brother being a merchant sea captain. Her cabin had been tiny, with everything nailed to the floor, and she had been dreadfully seasick for nearly a month. She'd spent the first two weeks lying on her narrow bed, a pail by her head, utterly wretched. Katherine's sympathy and nursing, offering her weak tea and wet cloths for her head, had been welcome yet had also served to only make her more homesick. She had not even arrived in Calcutta and already she missed the familiar comforts of home quite desperately, even as she clung to the hope the letter from Mr. Jamison provided. She had convinced herself that once she met him all the strangeness would melt away.

Things had improved when she'd finally found her sea legs, and the dreadful *mal de mer* had abated. She'd strolled on the deck with Katherine, enjoyed the brisk salt air and felt her spirits lift a little. Then the ship had put into port at Malta and later Cairo, and she'd been fascinated by the many sights she'd never encountered before—buildings with flat roofs and boys in canoes who paddled to the ship and sold them baskets of sweet, delicious fruit she'd never seen before. It had felt like a grand adventure, and she'd looked forward to travelling on to India—and Mr. Jamison.

Now as she gazed at the city of Calcutta, she could not keep her old anxiety rising up again. It had been easy enough to buoy her spirits with thoughts of Mr. Jamison when she'd been in the middle of the ocean—but now? When meeting him was not a happy, hazy dream, but an imminent reality? She pressed one hand to her middle; the light muslin was already damp from sweat. Mrs. Daylesford had assured her she would become acclimatized to the heat, but she had not yet.

"Do you think Mr. Jamison will be at the harbor when we dock?" she asked Mrs. Daylesford, trying not to sound anxious. She'd been pestering the older lady with questions for much of the journey, longing for a glimpse into the life she had chosen for herself, and Mrs. Daylesford had been kindly patient with her answers, although they had availed Isobel little for the only question she really wanted answered was would Mr. Jamison be a good husband? *Would he love her?* Mrs. Daylesford had nothing to say on the matter, for she had never met the gentleman, having been in America for some years, settling her children into their education.

"One hopes, certainly," she said now, which did not comfort Isobel very much. Of course she *hoped*. "It is difficult to say. Any number of pressing matters might have kept him. It is a week's journey from Calcutta to Moulmein, after all. He might have been delayed, or called away." She patted Isobel's arm. "Do not fear, my dear. I am sure, when you do meet Mr. Jamison, he will be delighted to see you."

Isobel forced a smile, although she was not certain of such a thing at all. What if he thought her too old? Too severe? She knew how stiff she could seem when she was nervous. What if he did not find her pious enough? She feared even now that she did not possess the zeal of her fellow shipmates.

"Do not fear," Mrs. Daylesford said again. Isobel turned to look out at the seemingly chaotic city as it loomed ever closer, a jumble of people and buildings, stalls and huts and pagodas and palaces. It looked exciting and different and quite overwhelming. Somewhere amidst all that bustling humanity, was George Jamison waiting for her?

She knew she was to stay initially with missionaries in Serampore before marrying Mr. Jamison as quickly as possible and returning with him to Burma. She still held onto the hope that they might get to know each other first, that they might have the opportunity to conduct a courtship, no matter how strange or small.

But in all truth she knew it was more likely he would he wish to marry her right away, and secure her position as well as his own, a thought which brought equal terror and hope. Never mind if he did not like her, what if she did not like him? What would she do then?

The ship anchored some distance from a flight of steps leading right into the river—what Katherine Daylesford said was called a *ghat*—and a small boat came to escort the American passengers to the shore. Her chaperone seemed pleased to be back in Calcutta, and pointed out various landmarks as they were steered to shore, looking and acting more as if she were coming home than reaching a distant land. Isobel could barely pay any attention to any of it; all her concentration was focused on not being sick.

Once on land, Isobel felt dizzy both with nerves at meeting—or not meeting—Mr. Jamison, and the overwhelming nature of her surroundings. The clamor of bells, the shouts of those in a marketplace, the smell of sweat and sun and spice… all of it was entirely different from what she had ever known. Anxious as she was about Mr. Jamison, her sense of adventure flagged and she fought not to cover her ears.

"You shall get used to it, my dear," Katherine said in sympathy, linking her arm through Isobel's. "But I know it can seem quite overwhelming at first."

"Yes," Isobel agreed weakly. She was feeling faint, for the day was oppressively hot, and she could not see Mr. Jamison anywhere, which was perhaps just as well considering how near tears she felt. Perhaps it would be better to meet him later, when she had found her composure as well as her feet. She fanned her face as Katherine directed their bags into a wagon, and then led her towards the most bizarre conveyance she had ever seen—an enclosed wooden carriage hoisted on poles and carried by four Indians.

"We are to travel in that?" she exclaimed. "Carried on their backs?"

"It is a palankeen. It is how everyone travels here," Mrs. Daylesford replied. "You will get used to the jolting."

Isobel shot one of the bearers an uncertain, apologetic look as she clambered aboard. There did not seem to be something quite right about it, but no one else seemed to find it at all out of the ordinary.

"But where do you suppose Mr. Jamison is?" she asked, once they were seated quite comfortably inside the palankeen.

"He must have been waylaid, or perhaps he did not receive your letter?" Mrs. Daylesford suggested. "They will know in Serampore, surely."

"Oh, but…" Isobel drew back in dismay, for she had not thought of this particular eventuality. If George Jamison had not received her letter, then he did not know the first thing about her! She'd written such a long letter back to him, trying to capture something of her own personality as he had done with his lovely missive. She'd told him about the First School, and even hinted at her long ago disappointment with Ian Campbell, and described the books she'd read and the adventure she wanted to have. For him not to have read any of it, not to know even one thing about her, or even if she existed…! Why, she would appear suddenly without him even knowing he had a wife on the way, a woman who had replied to his summons. The thought was appalling.

"Do not concern yourself," Katherine said. "Mr. Jamison is no doubt waiting in Serampore. We'll go there now. If he is not there, then at least we shall have news of him. Do not worry, Miss Moore. I am quite sure things will soon be arranged to your satisfaction."

"Indeed, I hope so," Isobel said. It was strange to travel in such a conveyance; the jolting was not unpleasant but Isobel wished she could look out upon the city, and see where they were going, as well any number of sights she would be pleased to take in. When she'd attempted to open one of the latticed shutters, however, Mrs. Daylesford had advised her not to do so.

Half an hour later they came to a stop; Isobel peered between latticed shutters and saw they were in front of a neat Swiss-cottage-style abode on a quiet street with fenced-in gardens. It was, Mrs. Daylesford had informed her, a residential area for both Indians and foreigners, although too modest a neighborhood for the East India Company and its exalted employees.

"Let us hope Mr. Jamison is within," Mrs. Daylesford said with a smile, and Isobel swallowed dryly. Would she meet him at last? She had read his letter so many times during the sea voyage that the paper had worn to near transparency in places, and she had almost every kind, self-deprecating word memorized. She'd kept the letter on her person as often as she could, taking comfort in the feel of her hand closing around the paper. Now she might actually meet the man who had seemed as if he was writing to her, and only her, and yet in this moment she felt too awash with nerves even to leave the palankeen.

"Come, my dear," Katherine said, seeming to sense Isobel's inner turmoil. "The day has been exhausting for you. Come inside and have something cool to drink and rest upstairs. Then we shall see about Mr. Jamison."

Isobel nodded in grateful acceptance, strangely glad for a temporary reprieve. Although, she acknowledged as she headed up the little stone path to the cottage, if Mr. Jamison was in residence, she could hardly avoid him for very long. He might very well be waiting by the door.

Inside the house it was much cooler, and the missionary Joshua Marshman and his wife Hannah introduced themselves warmly to her; they had been in Serampore for some years and were working on a translation of the Bible into Bengali. Despite the friendliness of their greeting, Isobel sensed a hesitation from them that she did not understand. Was she not what they'd expected?

"Most likely you already know that Miss Moore has come to marry George Jamison," Katherine said as they all sat in the sitting room, sipping *nimbu pani*, a refreshing drink made from limes that was both tart and sweet, and like nothing Isobel had ever tasted before. "They have been introduced through the Board of Commissioners for Foreign Missions." Introduced was surely stretching the truth more than a bit, but Isobel did not correct her. Katherine smiled expectantly. "Has Mr. Jamison arrived yet from Burma to greet her?"

Joshua and Hannah exchanged uncertain looks, and Isobel felt her heart somersault in her chest. There again was the hesitation she'd sensed from them before, only more pronounced this time. She knew, immediately and sickeningly, that something had gone wrong. Had Mr. Jamison changed his mind? What if he'd married another somehow? Possibilities raced through Isobel's mind as her hands clenched in her lap. Why did they not say anything?

"He has not arrived," Joshua finally said, sounding strangely reluctant to impart even that information, and Isobel wondered if the missionary had already summed her up and found her wanting. Perhaps he did not think her a suitable candidate for Mr. Jamison's wife, never mind what the man himself thought. The thought made her face burn and her stomach roil.

After a pregnant pause, Isobel asked in an over bright voice, "How long a journey is it to Burma? Mrs. Daylesford said a week…"

"A week or more, at least, depending on the weather." Joshua Marshman hesitated, glancing at his wife again, who nodded her encouragement for him to continue, her lips set in a firm line, her eyes troubled. Isobel's nails dug into her palms as she waited for whatever they were going to say. "Miss Moore, I am sorry to be the bearer of such sad tidings, and after such a long journey. I cannot imagine your disappointment." Isobel stared at him in confusion, even as unwelcome realization began to dawn. "I am so very sorry to tell you that Mr. Jamison will not be coming at all," Joshua Marshman said, giving Isobel a look full of compassion and regret. "For he died two months ago, of a fever."

*

Summer had turned to autumn and autumn to winter as Maggie began to feel truly at home in Boston—and at the First School. The day after Seamus Flanagan had shown up in the schoolhouse, he'd appeared again, just as polite and quietly determined to get an education. Margaret had agreed he could attend, and the sight of the grin that split his face had made Maggie smile, as well. He'd caught her eye and immediately looked away, as had she, yet even so for a moment she'd felt strangely complicit with him, as if they shared a secret.

Ever since that first day, several months ago now, Seamus had acted with grave politeness, studying with determined diligence, and Margaret had had, by her own admission, no cause for concern. He didn't disrupt the classroom, as she had once feared, and he worked harder than any other pupil in the school. "Indeed, Mr. Flanagan has become our best pupil," Margaret had admitted with a laugh, yet Maggie still sensed that her aunt was uneasy about his presence in the little school room.

Maggie was pleased to have him at the school; she liked having the company of someone close to her age. As Seamus hadn't known how to read before he'd come, he'd joined her group of little ones learning their letters. He'd looked a little funny, his huge frame hunched over one of the small stools, but he'd been able to laugh at himself—and made the other children giggle—and he'd learned the alphabet in a single day. He'd moved on quickly through the primers, and now, several months later, could read as well as she did. She'd teased him once that if he continued apace he would be teaching the others rather than learning himself. He'd given her a grin that had made something fizz in her stomach and replied he would never make such a presumption, and surely she and her aunt were far better at the job.

Maggie had caught her aunt watching her and Seamus narrowly, and she'd turned away to hide her smile, unsure why she felt the need to, but knowing she did.

In December, little Charlotte came down with a cold and, worried for her daughter's health, Margaret told Maggie they might need to close the school so she could nurse Charlotte.

"I do not like to deprive other children of their education, of course, but I would hate for something to happen to Charlotte while I was away. It has been hard enough to leave her in the care of her nurse while I have been at school all these months."

Maggie nodded slowly, trying not to show the disappointment she felt at not being at the school for a week or more.

"Unless…" she began, her heart beginning to beat a bit harder. Margaret glanced at her, eyebrows raised, her brow furrowed over concern for her daughter.

"Unless?"

"I could teach, Aunt Margaret. I've seen you teach the older children times enough. I think I could do it on my own."

"On your own…" Margaret paused, her lips pursed, and Maggie had the odd feeling she was thinking not of the responsibility she might bear, but rather her being alone with Seamus. Of course, she would not really be alone with him. Henry's man Mr. Caber was always positioned outside the school, and there were plenty of other pupils there besides. Yet Maggie knew that although her aunt had never said anything, she was still not entirely comfortable with Seamus Flanagan's presence at the First School, and more and more she'd wondered if it was because of her.

Did her aunt think something—some sort of affection—might develop between the two of them? Just the thought of such a thing had Maggie's stomach fluttering, and not in an unpleasant way. Nothing remotely inappropriate had passed between them, of course, and nothing ever would.

And yet… seeing Seamus come through the door every morning, that little half-smile on his face, the way he gently teased the little ones, the serious, intent way he read a book or did a sum… all of it made Maggie yearn with a longing she was not yet ready to name.

"I suppose there is no harm in trying," Margaret told her slowly, making her hopes soar. "With Mr. Caber to watch over you. But if anything happens…"

"The only thing that might happen," Maggie answered with a smile, "is Patrick Finnegan will give me some cheek!"

Now, alone in the classroom waiting for the first pupils to arrive, with Margaret back at home tending to Charlotte, Maggie pressed one hand to her middle to stay the butterflies that were threatening to rise up. She'd spoken confidently to her aunt, but right now she was all too uncertain as to whether she could teach all the lessons. She'd barely had much schooling herself, self-taught by her parents and getting her knowledge from what few books they had. It was one thing to teach little ones to read, quite another to talk about history and science and math to pupils only four or five years younger than herself, if that.

And then of course there was Seamus. For some contrary reason Maggie began to blush when he arrived, ducking his head as he came through the door, his ready smile of welcome turning to a slight frown as he registered her aunt's absence.

"Where is Mrs. Moore? I hope she is well?" he asked her as the younger pupils settled themselves.

"My aunt is very well, indeed, but her young daughter has come down with a cold," Maggie explained. "It isn't too serious, but she wished to be on hand."

"Of course." His expression lightened and his mouth quirked in a teasing smile. "Are you our teacher then, Miss MacDougall?"

Maggie pretended to look officious, knowing she never could truly be so. "I am indeed, Mr. Flanagan. I hope you shall conduct yourself with all propriety today."

His smile widened, his eyes glimmering with humor. "I shall be sure to be on my best behavior."

"Good." They remained there, smiling rather foolishly at one another, until one of the younger pupils cried out when her plait was pulled, and Maggie hurried to set matters to right.

Throughout the day, Seamus's steady presence reassured her, his quick smile a balm. Several times, when Maggie was in a muddle, whether it was over a math problem she wasn't quite sure of the answer to, or a bit of rascally behavior by two young boys, Seamus helped her to deal with the matter with his own easy calm, and in doing so earned her deepest gratitude.

"It's five thousand three hundred and six, isn't it, Miss Mac-Dougall?" he said quietly, and in relief Maggie realized where she'd been about to go wrong with the sum.

"You are quite right, Mr. Flanagan," she said with a quick smile, and turned, blushing, back to the board.

He was attentive in other ways, too. Noticing the stove in the center of the room would run out of coal, he took it upon himself to make sure it was topped up, heading to the back shed to fill the scuttle without fuss or show. He also comforted one of the small girls when she fell and scraped her knee, and washed the cut with his own clean handkerchief dipped in the pail of water kept by the door for drinking.

His presence, Maggie realized, was a comfort to the younger pupils, steady and strong as he was, acting like an older brother or even a father. Aunt Margaret had been worried that Seamus Flanagan's place in the classroom would provide a distraction, but, Maggie realized, it was quite the opposite. He kept the pupils calm and focused, and he made her feel safer and stronger too.

Even so, by the end of the day Maggie was exhausted, and glad to see the last of the pupils trickle out the door. Seamus remained, looking far too big crammed into one of the desks meant for a much smaller child. Looking at him, Maggie couldn't keep from letting out a laugh. Seamus raised his eyebrows in inquiry.

"You should have a proper chair," Maggie explained. "That desk makes you look like a giant."

He smiled back, his eyes crinkling. "It would be better for my knees, I suppose."

She nodded, knowing she should look away, yet she was unable to keep herself from staring at him. With his blue eyes and dark, curly hair he was, she thought, not for the first time, a very handsome man. And he was, as her aunt had pointed out when he'd first asked to attend the school, most definitely a man. Maggie was never more aware of that than now, when he walked slowly towards her, and she could see the height of him, the breadth of his wide shoulders, the height of him topping her by half a foot at least.

"Miss MacDougall? I wonder if I might ask you something?"

"Of course." Maggie smiled in what she hoped was a friendly fashion. Her heart began to thud at the thought of what Seamus might ask her. She could not even think what it might be and yet a nameless hope still soared inside her.

"My sister Aisling is but eleven," Seamus explained. "She's had no schooling, but now that I'm coming here, she wishes to learn. She couldn't come every day, as she has chores at home and Mam needs her help with the little ones. But I wondered if she might come to the school when she can get away, and learn what she might?"

Maggie blinked, and then suppressed a treacherous, needling sense of disappointment. How had she let herself think he might ask anything else, anything actually *intimate*? She felt herself begin to blush at the presumption of her hopes, nameless and vague as they'd been. "Of course she is welcome whenever she is able," she said, managing a smile. "The First School does not turn away willing pupils."

"I think your aunt wanted to turn me away right enough," Seamus said without rancor, and Maggie gave a wry grimace as she acknowledged the truth of his observation.

"She had her reservations, I confess, but you have surely put them to rest most admirably."

"Do you think so?"

"Oh, yes, you have done so well here, Seamus," Maggie exclaimed, and some emotion she could not identify flickered across his face.

"That's the first time you've called me by my Christian name."

"Is it?" Maggie felt her cheeks heat even more. She was so unsettlingly conscious of Seamus's presence, his closeness. His hands were large and capable as he held his cap, twisting it just as he had on the first day. His eyes seemed very blue as he looked at her, and Maggie forced herself not to look away.

"May I call you Maggie?" he asked after a moment. "Not in the school room, of course, when you are the teacher. But…" He paused, and Maggie did not know if he was silently acknowledging the presumption of thinking he would have any other occasion to address her at all. And yet oh, how she hoped he would!

"I would be happy for you to do so. I am not much used to such formality, as it is."

Seamus's fingers tightened on his twisted cap as his blue gaze became more serious. "I hope your aunt won't mind such familiarity."

"Of course she won't," Maggie answered quickly, perhaps too quickly, for she could not suppress a flicker of doubt. Aunt Margaret had certainly not encouraged any friendship with Seamus Flanagan, for whatever reason, and yet why not? Seamus was kind and thoughtful, respectful and polite. There was no reason at all he should not have their acquaintance and yes, their friendship.

An idea suddenly sprung into Maggie's mind, one that was impulsive and even reckless, yet she felt determined to act upon it. If only her aunt spent some time with Seamus, if only she could put whatever nameless reservations to one side… *then what?*

Maggie did not even know what she wished to achieve with the proposal that was firing in her mind, and yet she continued on with it anyway.

"I have an idea," she told him. "Why don't you and your sister come to tea one afternoon? At my aunt's home?"

Seamus's eyes widened in obvious disbelief. Then he shook his head, and added with gentle wryness, "As pleased as I am for the invitation, I don't rightly know if that's a good idea, Maggie."

The sound of her name on his lips sent a thrill through her, and made her even more insistent. "Why ever not? You know my aunt emigrated from Scotland, just as you did from Ireland."

Seamus shrugged. "Wherever we came from doesn't matter so much. It's the difference in our stations now."

"Even so," Maggie said firmly, utterly determined now, come what may. "I insist."

His mouth quirked upwards again, making her heart skip a beat. "Do you now?"

"I do."

"I suppose I could bring Aisling along one day," he said after a moment. "She'd like to see a grand house sure enough. And if your aunt sends us both away with a flea in our ear, it's no more than we deserve."

"She won't," Maggie said heatedly. "I promise you, Seamus. She is a most accepting woman."

Seamus smiled and settled his cap on his head. "I'm not sure you can make such promises. But thank you kindly for the invitation, and no matter what happens, Maggie, I do appreciate your thinking of me and Aisling in that way." He paused, seeming to want to say more, but then simply ducked his head in farewell.

Maggie watched him leave the schoolhouse, and did not stir until Mr. Caber came to the door in his greatcoat, asking her if she was ready to return home.

CHAPTER THIRTEEN

Serampore, India

Isobel threw down the embroidery hoop she had been listlessly working on and stared despondently out the windows of the Marshmans' cottage, the shutters ajar to let in a bit of air during the hottest part of the day. The weather had been stifling as of late, the heat so sticky and damp that mold had grown on her embroidery overnight. Hannah Marshman had brushed it off and said such things were common and she would get used to it eventually.

And she would have, Isobel thought, of *course* she would have, if she had been wed and happy and arranging her own home instead of waiting out the days with no idea of what to do, grieving for a man she'd never even met.

After Joshua Marshman had told her Mr. Jamison had died of a fever, Isobel had sat frozen, a fixed look of stunned disbelief on her face as his sorrowful words washed over her.

"We only heard last week. It was very quick. These tropical fevers can come upon one so suddenly."

Isobel felt herself nodding, although she hardly had any experience of such an illness. Her mind felt oddly blank, as if she could not take in what she was hearing. George Jamison had been dead for two *months*. Where had she been then? Egypt, perhaps? Somewhere in the Indian Ocean? She'd had no idea he was in such grave danger, and of course he would have had no idea of her existence.

He'd never received her letter. Even on the fastest ship, the letter would have reached him only a few weeks ago, when he had already been in the grave for over a month! The thought was so appalling, Isobel could not even begin to grasp it, and so she simply stared.

"You are in shock," Hannah Marshman murmured. "It is understandable. Perhaps a rest...?"

Somehow Isobel managed to make a reply, she did not even know what, and Mrs. Daylesford helped her to a bedroom upstairs. She felt as if she were in some sort of trance as she peeled off her dress and lay down in nothing but her chemise, the gauzy mosquito netting that covered the bed blowing in the slight breeze as she tried to sleep.

At some point she woke; it was twilight, and the sky outside her window was the most incredibly vivid pink and orange, the colors so much brighter than she was used to. The blistering heat of midday had cooled slightly, and the air was still and drowsy. For a second, as she gazed at the spectacular sunset, she tormented herself with imagining that Mr. Jamison was downstairs; there would be a celebratory supper planned, a wedding to arrange. She pictured herself humming under her breath as she selected one of her best gowns.

But no, none of that was going to happen now. In fact, she realized dully, she had no idea *what* was going to happen, because how could she stay here in her current situation? She had no husband, no place, no purpose. And yet to board the next ship back to Boston, four months towards home and then nothing but more of the same—days teaching, evenings spent over a book or needlework, the occasional, interminable social engagement...

It had been ten days since she'd learned of Mr. Jamison's death, and Isobel was in as much of a despondent quandary as ever. Joshua Marshman had informed her at dinner last night that a ship was sailing to Boston in a week's time. He'd offered to book her passage on it, and Isobel had murmured something about needing to think.

Yet what, really, was there to think about? She could not remain in India; she was not even sure she wanted to remain here, alone as she was. The thought of sitting in her pretty bedroom at home on Beacon Hill, reading a book or enjoying a treat of marzipan or drinking chocolate—things she'd once taken for granted, and now all seemed to be the height of luxury and privilege—was tempting, but not nearly tempting enough. She did not want to go back to Boston.

Even so, she could not stay in Calcutta without a husband; Rufus Anderson had made that clear before she had left, and the Marshmans had intimated as much since her arrival. Yet to return to Boston both grief-stricken and made ridiculous… it was awful, *awful*. She could not bear to contemplate it. She wanted to find some purpose here, but what? Who? There was nothing. No one.

Groaning from the despair of it, Isobel sank back into her chair, her head in her hands.

"Miss Moore? My dear?" With a light knock Hannah Marshman opened the door to Isobel's bedroom and smiled tentatively. She had made some efforts to be friendly, Isobel knew, and Isobel felt helpless to respond in kind, as grief-stricken and bewildered as she felt. She acknowledged, with an uncomfortable pang of guilt, she had been a rather wretched, as well as enforced, houseguest since she had arrived.

Wishing to make more of an effort, she rose and ushered Hannah in. "Do come in, Mrs. Marshman. You have been so kind to house me here, and in such circumstances as these."

Hannah gave her a sympathetic glance as she came into the room. "It is no trouble, I assure you. I am only so sorry for the difficulty in which you now find yourself."

"You are really so very kind." Isobel sat down again, and Hannah perched on the edge of another chair, looking expectant, although for what reason, Isobel did not know. Was she going to ask about booking passage? Were they in such a hurry to have her gone?

"It must be a deep disappointment to you," Hannah ventured cautiously, "to find yourself without recourse so far from home."

Isobel nodded, the other woman's compassion making her feel again the full force of what she had lost. She could not truly grieve George Jamison —they had never met, so the person whom she was grieving was but a figment of her imagination, drawn from a letter—yet the heartache she felt was real. She grieved the possibility he'd offered her… the life she'd hoped to have, as both wife and mother, the love she'd been so eager to give to another.

"It is a disappointment, to be sure," she said, her voice choking a little. She drew a steadying breath, trying to compose herself.

"Have you considered," Hannah asked after a pause, "your possibilities?"

"I did not know they existed in the plural. It seems the singular one available to me is a return passage to Boston." Isobel turned to stare out the window, the watery sunlight filtering through the slats of the shutter, so Hannah wouldn't see the naked grief and despair on her face at such a prospect.

"Of course, that is the most obvious course," Hannah agreed. "But one, I fear, that does not bring you much joy…?"

"I do not wish to return particularly," Isobel forced herself to admit.

"Then I hope you might not find me too bold to suggest another possibility…?" Hannah's voice rose in query, but Isobel had no ready answer.

"Another?" she repeated blankly, turning back to look at her hostess. What other possibility could there be? She felt too cast down to feel even a flicker of hope.

"Indeed," Hannah answered, and the briskness of her voice made Isobel's brow furrow in bewilderment. "It is true you can no longer marry Mr. Jamison, God rest his soul. But is there any reason why you could not, perhaps, marry another gentleman?"

"Another…" Isobel stared at her in shock. She did not know how to answer; on the one hand, it seemed both cold-hearted and desperate to so quickly consider exchanging one betrothed for another; on the other, returning to Boston was surely worse. "I have not considered such a thing," she said at last. "I came to marry Mr. Jamison, and no other."

"Of course, of course," Hannah murmured, and Isobel ventured to ask.

"Is there—is there another missionary in need of a wife?" Her cheeks heated; what a question to find herself asking! She could not sound more desperate if she tried. Was she to be passed around like some sort of parcel?

"Not precisely," Hannah answered carefully. "There is a man, a widower, Mr. Casey, who works for the East India Company, but unlike many of his colleagues he is sympathetic to our cause."

Since staying with the Marshmans, Isobel had learned more about the oppressive presence of the East India Company, both for the people of India and the missionaries wishing to support them. She did not know how she felt about possibly marrying a man involved in that wicked-sounding enterprise, sympathetic though he might be.

"A widower," she repeated without inflection.

"Yes, with four children. Young ones, very well-behaved, of course, but they miss their dear mama. She died in childbirth, poor woman, and the youngest is only a few months old."

"I see," Isobel said faintly, for she was afraid she saw indeed. Four children…! This man, Mr. Casey, had to be as desperate as she was. But he was surely in need of a housekeeper and governess, not necessarily a wife, or at least the wife Isobel longed to be—a helpmeet, a friend and lover. She could not imagine taking four young souls, one of them no more than a newborn babe, into her care as soon as she'd said her vows. And what of the gentleman himself? She had no idea what he would be like, and yet already she felt sure he would not possess the wry grace and self-deprecating charm that George Jamison had in his one letter. None of this was what she'd ever expected or wanted.

"Do think on it, my dear," Hannah said quietly. "You would be doing such a noble service in offering yourself thus."

Which made her sound like some kind of terrible sacrifice. Was this why she'd come to India? For this unknown man and his family, to love and serve them as best as she could? Or would she be condemning herself to a life of hardship and thankless service? Once the vows were said, Isobel knew, there would be no going back. She would belong to her husband, and he would command both her days and her destiny for the rest of her life, wherever they went.

The thought was both alarming and awful—as alarming and awful as returning to Boston. Neither appealed in the least, and yet as Isobel looked at Hannah smiling so sympathetically, she knew she had at least to try. She could meet this gentleman, this Mr. Casey, and at least see if he were at all the sort of person she could consider vowing to honor and obey. *And if he wasn't…?*

That, she thought with an inward sigh, was a question for another day.

"I will certainly think on it," she told Hannah. "Thank you for the suggestion."

*

Boston

Margaret raised her gaze from the math lesson she was correcting, to let it fall with consideration on her young niece Maggie and the oldest pupil of the First School, Seamus Flanagan. Maggie was helping Seamus with the new primer he had started, her head bent rather close to his. Margaret watched as they exchanged smiling glances, and her brow furrowed.

She was fair enough to know she held a somewhat unreasonable suspicion of the strapping Mr. Flanagan, an eighteen-year-old who had chosen to spend his days learning alongside others far younger than he was. She looked upon him now, sat with his knees not even fitting under the desk he had been given. Maggie had suggested that perhaps it was time Seamus was given a proper chair, much like the one Margaret now sat in, behind the mahogany desk. Henry had given her the desk, inlaid with hand-tooled leather, as a gift when she'd founded the First School six years ago.

Before Margaret could tell Maggie that if Seamus Flanagan intended to remain a pupil of the First School, then he needed to act like a pupil in all particulars, the man himself—for indeed he was a man—kindly but firmly refused.

"I'm all right, Maggie," he'd said quietly, earning Margaret's grudging respect even as his words, so gruffly given, caused her a flare of alarm. Seamus Flanagan was addressing her niece by her Christian name, and doing so in a way that suggested he'd done it often enough.

What exactly was unfurling between her niece and this young Irishman? Margaret knew she could have no real objection to Seamus—he was kind, respectful, intelligent and hardworking. In every way he was admirable, and yet…

And yet Maggie was only sixteen. And Seamus was from an entirely different background than she was, no matter that they'd both come from immigrant families. Seamus, should this connection ever become something more serious, could not offer Maggie anything but a life of drudgery and hardship. Margaret was all for social reform, and had worked tirelessly towards that end for many years, but even she knew there were limits she had to accede to—and forming an attachment to a poor Irish immigrant fresh off the boat was definitely one of them.

If only she hadn't stayed away from the school when Charlotte had been ill. If she had been more diligent, more vigilant, she surely wouldn't be in the predicament she now found herself—desperately afraid that her impressionable young niece was developing an attachment for the handsome and wholly inappropriate Seamus Flanagan.

Margaret knew her niece would not listen to any warnings. Ever since Seamus had entered the First School, respectfully asking to learn, Maggie had been unreasonably defensive of him. When his sister Aisling had joined the happy group of pupils a week ago, Maggie had welcomed her effusively, shooting Margaret several challenging looks that she had resolutely ignored. In truth, Margaret was delighted to welcome the shy, well-behaved Aisling Flanagan, who at ten years old was a perfectly suitable pupil for the school. It was Seamus, with his deep voice and workman's hands and broad shoulders, that she still did not like seeing in her school, as unfair as she knew that sentiment might seem. Still, she decided as she saw Maggie give Seamus another teasing smile, she needed to address the matter directly.

That afternoon, she asked Seamus to stay behind to discuss his arithmetic, and sent Maggie to wait outside with John Caber.

Seamus stood in front of her teacher's desk, his cap in his hands, his gaze disconcertingly steady, almost knowing.

"Your ability in mathematics, Mr. Flanagan, is perfectly acceptable. In fact, you have an admirable grasp of all the particulars, and I daresay you are close to being able to teach the rest of the class yourself."

Seamus's face remained carefully bland. "Thank you kindly, Mrs. Moore. That is very good to hear."

"That said, I kept you back today not to discuss your mathematical ability, but my niece Miss MacDougall, and your connection to her."

If anything, Seamus's expression went even blander. Margaret had no idea what the man was thinking, which was all the more disconcerting. She wanted to be in control of the conversation, and she feared she wasn't. "What about your niece do you care to discuss with me, ma'am?" he asked evenly, his voice a low rumble.

Margaret was further disconcerted to hear how well he spoke; he had learned much in the last few months he had been attending the school. "It's clear she is developing an affection for you, Mr. Flanagan. An affection I am afraid I cannot countenance, and I hope you understand why."

Color touched Seamus's face but he did not avert his gaze. "I've done nothing to encourage such feelings."

"I don't doubt it," Margaret agreed. "However, my niece is young and impressionable and has come to Boston with ideas of adventure and romance, as any young girl might do. The very fact that you're in this school is reason enough for her to lose her head entirely, which I fear she has already begun to do."

Seamus stared at her for a moment. Once again, Margaret wished she knew what he was thinking. It was rare she found herself flummoxed. "I assure you, I won't do anything to make it worse." His brogue had thickened, and bizarrely that made Margaret feel satisfied. She felt a flicker of shame for her own seeming snobbery—she, the social reformer! She had been accused of being a crusader and yet now she felt as snippily sanctimonious as the worst of Boston's stodgy social circle.

"See that you don't," she said briskly, and she handed him back his math book. "Otherwise I am afraid I do not see how you will be able to continue at this school."

Seamus nodded slowly as he took the book, holding Margaret's gaze for a moment longer than she would have liked. He had not been forward, rather knowing, and she felt herself flush as again her own snobbishness assailed her. Who was she, an immigrant herself as Maggie had said, to discourage a young man who possessed both kindness and ambition? Who was she to meddle in another person's life when she, at only a year older than Maggie, had fiercely longed and fought for her own independence?

She wished suddenly that she could have spoken to Henry about this; he would have given her sensible advice, tempered her own often wayward emotions, helped her to laugh at herself and the situation. Unaccustomed tears pricked Margaret's eyes as, for a moment, she was swamped with loneliness. It had been nearly eight months since Henry had left Boston; it was nearly Christmas, and Charlotte had asked if Papa was bringing her a present. With a lump in her throat, Margaret had told her that he wasn't able to quite yet.

She'd received only one letter from him in all that time, and although she knew better than to expect letters to reach her, it still filled her with fear. He could have been lost at sea months ago and she wouldn't know. She might never know.

With an impatient sigh for her own maudlin thoughts, Margaret rose from behind her desk and reached for her cloak. Maggie was waiting anxiously by the door as she came out, locking it behind her; her niece fell into step with her, with John Caber following behind.

"What did you wish to speak to Seamus about?" she asked as they walked towards the carriage.

"His arithmetic. It is coming along nicely."

Maggie shot her a deeply suspicious look and Margaret did her best to keep her expression as bland as Seamus's had been a few moments ago. "Why did you ask me to leave, then?"

"It was a private conversation, Maggie. Now pray do not vex me with any more questions!" Knowing she sounded peevish and unable to help it, Margaret swept into the carriage. *Oh Henry*, she thought. I miss you. *When will I receive a letter from you? When will I know where you are?*

*

Ever since the public failure of the ether experiment, over three months ago now, Ian had been existing in a wretched fog of humiliation and even grief, for the failed operation felt like the death of all of his dreams. He had been working with Horace Wells for all those years, even as his superiors at the Massachusetts General Hospital ridiculed and insulted him. Now, they had just cause to do so, for Horace Wells had made a fool of them both, as well as the whole idea of using ether or any substance as an anesthetic. No one, Ian thought, would consider it again for years.

After he had been practically booed off the operating theatre stage, Wells had pushed past him and stormed out of the room in a rage. Ian had not tried to stop him—what was there to say? Wells had failed and Ian had not been courageous enough to force him to step aside. He had known, before Wells had ascended the stage, that he was unfit to perform the operation. His hands had been shaking! But Wells had been belligerent, and Ian hadn't insisted, and now… now he had no idea if they would ever chance upon such an opportunity again.

When he had returned home that evening, Caroline was waiting in the front hall, looking pretty and fresh in a pale pink gown, her face bright with expectant hope and suffused with love.

"Ian!" She walked towards him, her face wreathed in smiles, hands outstretched towards him. "Tell me how the operation went, do," she implored. "I haven't been able to sit still for a moment, I've been in such a state about it!"

"Have you?" Ian replied rather sourly, knowing he was being unfair. "Well, I'll tell you how it went then. A complete and utter failure."

Caroline had looked at him in amazement, her smile sliding off her face. Ian had turned away, divesting himself of his coat and hat, not wanting to meet his wife's gaze, feeling only the need to lament, to lash out. "Humbug," Warren had told him again, when Ian had been about to leave the theatre. "A complete and utter humbug, as I knew it would be!" The man had sounded sorry rather than smug, which somehow made it worse. No one had considered his research seriously at all.

"Oh my dear," Caroline murmured. "I am so very sorry. Come into the parlor and I'll have some supper brought to you. Then you must tell me all about it."

That was the last thing he wanted to do; it was already several hours past their usual suppertime, and Ian hadn't had a good reason to stay away for so long. He simply hadn't wanted to face Caroline and the admission of his own failure, much less describe it in all its grim detail.

"Thank you," he muttered rather ungraciously, and he followed her into the parlor. He sat down, and, unable to keep himself from it, put his head in his hands.

Caroline moved to him and took his hands in hers, perching on the side of his chair. "I suppose it was Wells?" she asked gently. "He needed a bit of courage to perform the operation? And so he partook of that terrible substance?"

"That terrible substance," Ian reminded her shortly, "is what we hope will be used in countless operations, saving, God willing, many lives."

"Ian, of course I know that, but—"

"Oh, never mind." He pulled his hands from hers as he sat back in his chair and raked a hand through his hair, not wanting to see how hurt he knew she must look. He was angry and disappointed and bitter, but none of it was directed towards Caroline. And what kind of sorry excuse for a man took out his professional disappointments on his wife?

With a sigh, he dropped his hand and closed his eyes. "I'm sorry, Caroline. You are perfectly right, of course. I suspect that Wells was under the influence of ether when he performed the operation. I tried to dissuade him from going ahead, but he would hear none of it, and the truth is, I was not strong enough to convince him."

"I'm so sorry, Ian."

"You realize you are now married to the laughing stock of Massachusetts General Hospital?" he asked as he opened his eyes to give her a flat look. "You should have heard the uproar in the theatre when everyone realized Wells had failed. The medical students were laughing like it was the most amusing joke they'd ever heard." He heard bitterness sharpen his words, felt it twist his mouth. The memory still stung terribly, that awful, mocking laughter echoing in his ears. He thought it would for a long time.

"It is Wells who failed, not you," Caroline replied staunchly. "Another opportunity will arise—"

"Not at Massachusetts," Ian cut her off. "No one will forget that failure. It shall follow me all of my days." And perhaps cost him his position, or at least the prospect of advancement.

"One forgets failure as soon as one encounters success," Caroline countered. "You believe in the possibility of ether, Ian. You have seen it work in other situations. You will persevere, and that is what is important."

Ian said nothing. He felt too downcast to be encouraged by Caroline's words; they only irritated him, and made him feel like a child who had failed at his lessons, which he knew was unfair. She was trying her best, which heaven knew was more than he was doing.

Caroline drew a breath and Ian tensed, knowing instinctively what was coming next. "Ian, it seems clear that Wells is unfit to continue your experiments," she said in a rush. "But there is no reason why you should not do so. I know you won't want to hear of it, but if you had your own source of funding, instead of relying on Wells—"

"Your uncle's money, I suppose?" He sounded tired rather than cold; he simply didn't think he had it in him to have this argument again.

Caroline met his gaze directly. "*My* money. Why won't you use it, Ian? It is now yours by right—"

"I have told you, it is tainted by Riddell's thievery—"

"Then am I tainted as well?" Caroline demanded, her voice shaking. "For I am related to Sir James Riddell by blood. I know full well what he did, Ian, taking your family's land—"

"*Stealing* it—"

"But it is my money now and it can be used for good. Don't you see how using this money would redeem the past rather than have us remain in it? Why must you be so stubborn, so unyielding?"

"*I* am stubborn?" Ian fired back, the disappointments of the day doing nothing to help him temper his voice. "And yet you are the one who insists on continuing to offer something I have refused again and again! Why will you not let the matter go, Caroline, for both our sakes? For it is truly a thorn in my side, and one that makes this marriage far from the comfort that I would wish it to be!" He glared at her, for once not caring at the hurt he saw in her eyes, making her face crumple. He knew his words had been harsh, and yet he could not regret them. "Please, understand my position. I cannot accept Riddell money. I will not. It is not mere pride, but honor. If you take that away from me, then I will no longer be the man you married. The man you fell in love with."

Caroline gazed at him for a moment, her expression evening out into an icy calm. She rose, gathering her skirts around her. "Then you are acting like a hypocrite," she said quietly. "For you take the money quick enough when it pays for fripperies or fuel or whatever else we have used it for. But as for your precious ether experiments—that must come from your own pocket."

"You wouldn't understand."

"If I don't understand," Caroline said as she walked from the room, "it is because you do not wish me to." She turned at the door to face him, her eyes flashing. "But I believe I understand all too well, Ian. So be it. I will not offer again."

She had left with a rustling of her skirts, and Ian sank back into his chair, his hands now gripping their arms. He *was* a hypocrite, a stupid, prideful one, and yet he did not know if he could act differently. His experiments with ether had given him a sense of self-worth that had just been swept away in light of Wells' failure. Accepting Riddell's money would simply be too much injury to bear.

Three months later, as Christmas neared and the weather became bitter and cold, Ian felt it all no less than the day of the experiment and the confrontation with Caroline. For three months they had both retreated into cool silence, being polite with each other and no more. It was untenable, unbearable, and yet he did not know how to change it and neither, it seemed, did Caroline.

More than once, as they'd sat in their parlor in the evening, involved in their own pursuits, the fire crackling merrily, Ian had wanted to say something, anything. Read a bit out of the newspaper to her, make a joke, reach for her hand. Somehow he had been unable to do any of it. He watched Caroline sew or read her book or write a letter, her blonde head bent, her expression hidden from him, and felt as helpless as a babe.

Now, as he walked back home from the hospital just a week before Christmas, Ian was determined to say something to her. It was unconscionable for the festive season to pass with them both frozen in this awful silence! He would be man enough to speak first, to ask for forgiveness.

Yet when he arrived at home, he discovered Caroline was out; she had gone to visit Margaret Moore, and their maid told him she would not be back for supper. It felt like a snub, but Ian tried not to make it so. He rifled through the day's post, somewhat cast down at the thought of a plate of cold mutton by himself for supper, when he saw his address written in an untidy scrawl.

He stared down at the letter, an uneasy awareness filling him for already he thought he knew who the letter was from. Quickly he broke the seal and scanned the contents—an incoherent ramble of accusation and anger, veiled threat and deep bitterness. It was unsigned, but Ian knew who it had to be from—Horace Wells.

CHAPTER FOURTEEN

Serampore, India

Isobel stared at the looking glass, its wavy surface speckled with the mold she'd grown used to just as Hannah Marshman had said, making it difficult to see her reflection. She'd arranged her hair in coils behind her ears, with curls at each temple, having kept it twisted in rags the night before. She'd also brushed her best dress, and now she smoothed down the skirt of light muslin, nerves making her palms damp and her heart flutter.

Tonight, she would be attending a party with the Marshmans—and she would meet Mr. Casey, the widower who was interested in marrying her. Briefly, Isobel closed her eyes and tried to summon strength for the evening ahead. She had no idea what Mr. Casey would be like, but she nurtured a small, frail hope that he might at least be kind, and that they might find a connection that could perhaps turn into something more, no matter how tenuous. She no longer allowed herself to nurture the dreams she'd once had for Mr. Jamison—whose letter she still read nearly every day—but she hoped some small amount of happiness might be allotted to her.

As for marriage…

She swallowed hard and turned away from the looking glass.

"Are you ready?" Hannah appeared in the doorway of Isobel's room, smiling in admiration at her dress and hair. "Don't you look handsome, Isobel! Is that what the fashions are these days?"

she asked, gesturing to the sleeves of Isobel's dress, which were cinched to the elbows before flaring out. She laughed ruefully at her own more modest and worn gown. "I'm afraid I wouldn't know."

"Fashions are always changing, aren't they," Isobel murmured, wondering if wearing the latest fashion in Calcutta was a mistake. If no one knew what was currently in fashion, it might look strange. Or Mr. Casey might think her shallow, only interested in fashion and fripperies. She felt as if she could do nothing right, and it made her head ache with the uncertainty of it all.

"The palankeen is waiting," Hannah said. "Shall we?"

The night was dark and sultry as Isobel stepped out into the evening, the stars no more than a bright haze in the night sky. The inside of the palankeen was stifling and as she arranged her skirts around her, she wondered out loud, "Do you suppose, in time, I will get used to the heat?" She was wearing her lightest dress, but she still felt overheated, perspiration prickling under her arms and on the back of her neck.

"Yes, in time," Hannah allowed. "I remember how humid and sticky I found it at the beginning! But now I warrant that America would feel far too cold for me now. And snow! I don't miss that in the least." She fanned herself with a small laugh. "But it is warm in here, I grant you that."

"Indeed," Joshua agreed with a smile. "I don't think there's a person alive who doesn't find it hot inside one of these contraptions!"

They didn't talk much after that for the duration of the journey to Garden Reach, where most of the British society, especially those employed by the East India Company, resided. As the palankeen came to a stop and Isobel gingerly climbed outside, she wondered who—and what—awaited her inside. It had been so long since she'd been in society, and she feared she would stand out even more as an unmarried woman alone in this country, never mind the doubts and worries she had about meeting Mr. Casey.

Hannah joined her as they walked up the house's wide veran-dah, the lights within gleaming through the shutters. "I confess, I am nervous as well," she whispered. "I have not been to a single such event since arriving in Calcutta. Mr. Marshman and I are only here at Mr. Casey's invitation."

"You haven't missed such entertainments, have you, my dear?" Joshua asked as he joined them on the walk, and Hannah gave him a quick, loving glance.

"Not in the least. Indeed, I am almost dreading the occasion, but I trust it will have its own amusements."

Isobel was dreading it too. She felt her palms go damp inside her gloves, and knew it was from nerves rather than heat. What would Mr. Casey be like?

As she came inside the grand foyer, she was handed a glass of champagne—an indulgence she hadn't had in ages. The crisp, cool taste of it on her tongue was delicious but also strange. Looking around the crowded reception rooms of the great house, she realized she had not missed such grand social occasions in the least. The music, the dancing, the champagne, the gossip. The evening had not even begun and it already all felt flat.

"I shall look for Mr. Casey," Hannah murmured. "Unless you wish to delay…?"

"No," Isobel said quickly. She would rather know what manner of man he was than not. "I see no cause to delay."

Hannah nodded her sympathetic approval, before turning to look around the room. "I have not met the gentleman myself," she murmured, "but Mr. Marshman has…"

"Here he is," said Joshua, and both women turned to see a red-faced man with rather overwhelming side whiskers and a too-tight waistcoat bearing down on them with an expression close to a scowl. Hannah's eyes widened in surprise and Isobel's stomach dropped.

Please, she thought desperately, *let this not be Mr. Casey.*

But she already knew, with a terrible sinking sensation, that it was.

"Miss Moore?" he said, his voice near a bark, and Isobel nodded. He stuck out a hand which Isobel took after a pause; it was custom for a woman to offer her hand first, but Mr. Casey did not seem aware of such niceties, or at least willing to observe them. He shook it before dropping it like a dead thing. Isobel glanced at Hannah, who was looking decidedly alarmed by the exchange.

"Come, Mr. Marshman," she said. "Let us give them a modicum of privacy."

It felt like the last thing Isobel wanted in that moment, yet she already knew she would not want this conversation to be overheard by a single living soul.

"Pray, let me introduce myself," her companion said, once they were alone, guests moving all about them. "My name is James Casey. I am pleased to meet you."

"Likewise, sir."

He gave her a brief, up and down look that made Isobel blush. "You know why I am making your acquaintance?"

"I believe so," she whispered, a flush rising from her throat all the way to the tips of her ears. "I am sorry for the recent loss of your wife."

"It was a blow to me, to be sure. She was a good woman. Quiet. Biddable." Were those the only qualities he cared about? Isobel felt quite faint. "You're older than I expected, but that's no bad thing," he said musingly. "I've got four children of my own to see placed. I don't particularly want any others."

"Indeed…" She could barely get the word out as he continued his awful assessment.

"Now the little one is but a few months old. I've got a wet nurse for him, but he needs a proper mother. Are you any good with children?"

"I have been a teacher, sir, and I believe I…" Isobel could not make herself continue. Why should she justify herself to this man? She would not sell herself as if she were a mare at market! "Perhaps we could speak of more seemly things first? I do not know you, and you do not know me." She swallowed dryly. "Which part of England are you from, Mr. Casey? I confess I have never been, although my brother has traveled—"

"I don't have time for a courtship," Mr. Casey interjected brusquely. He gave Isobel a rather knowing look. "And neither, I suspect, do you, Miss Moore."

Isobel drew herself up, her body stiff with affront. She already knew she would rather travel to Boston and back a dozen times than marry such an odious and unpleasant man as this. "I may not have time for a lengthy courtship, Mr. Casey," she replied stiffly, "but neither do I have time to be so thoroughly insulted. Your manners are woefully lacking! Good day." And without waiting for his reply, she stalked away, her whole body trembling as she realized what she'd done. She may have accused Mr. Casey of a certain lack of manners, but she had just been unforgivably rude—and yet, she realized, she didn't even care.

"That was a short interview," Hannah observed worriedly as she came to Isobel's side. "I fear the gentleman did not give a favorable impression."

"Indeed he did not!" Isobel tried to moderate her tone. "He was a complete and utter boor, and I told him as much myself."

"Isobel!" Hannah looked both sympathetic and scandalized by her words. "I know the man was… difficult, but you cannot say such things as that! Calcutta is a small community—"

"I'm sorry, Hannah," Isobel said, although she wasn't really. She was still shaking with fury at the indignities she had suffered during Mr. Casey's callous conversation. "But I could not countenance such rudeness," she continued. "I may be in dire straits, but I am not yet so desperate to tie myself to such an odious man!" She shuddered at the thought.

Hannah gave a reluctant sigh of agreement. "But then what shall you do? You know you cannot stay in India as a single woman. It is quite, quite impossible."

Any righteous indignation she'd been nurturing trickled away, replaced by cold reality. If she refused to marry James Casey, which she certainly did, she would have no choice but to return to Boston. Again, the thought was so wearying that Isobel felt her shoulders sag, her spirits plummet with a terrible rush. Why had she been so reckless? And yet she could not regret refusing Mr. Casey. A marriage to him was not to be considered.

"I do not yet know what I shall do," she told Hannah. "I will think on it some more—and pray, of course." In the distance Isobel heard the tinkling sound of a woman's laughter, and a servant nearby offered a tray of champagne to several guests. Music struck up and couples began a country dance. Suddenly Isobel felt reckless, almost wild—here she was at a party, all of twenty-nine years, and looking at the rest of her life had begun to feel like looking down the barrel of a gun. "For tonight, at least," she told Hannah, "I would like to enjoy myself." And defiantly she took another glass of champagne from the tray.

*

Boston

One evening in December, Maggie sat in her bedroom in her Aunt Margaret's house, the latest letter from her mother on her lap. She felt a surprising pang of homesickness for her family's farm on Prince Edward Island, with the red dirt road winding its way through the now bare birch trees, and the cheerful glint of the sea in the distance. She'd never thought she'd miss that poky place, yet in that moment, with the quiet elegance of her aunt's house stretching out all around her, Maggie found she missed it very much indeed.

Although if she were honest, Maggie knew, what she missed was the friendship she'd had with Seamus Flanagan. She'd noticed he'd started acting differently as of late; when she'd given him a friendly greeting, his own had been decidedly cool. There had been no gentle teasing, no moments of idle conversation, no special, secret smiles. Without his company, she had started to feel as she had at the beginning of her stay—no more than a country girl in the bustling city, whose plain ways and simple dreams could not be disguised by a few fancy dresses, no matter how much her well-meaning aunt tried.

Another bitter blow had occurred when Seamus had waited for her after school one day, when her aunt had not been able to accompany her to teach. Maggie's spirits had lifted to see him standing there, looking so serious and steady and strong, and she'd started forward with a smile.

"Seamus—"

"I'm afraid my sister and I won't be able to come to your aunt's house for tea as you'd suggested, Miss MacDougall," he said. They had not yet set a date for the afternoon, as Maggie had been unable to gather the courage to ask Margaret for permission, but she'd still hoped it might happen. Now she stared at him in wordless disappointment and shock. "We thank you kindly for the invitation, anyway." He started turning away before Maggie could so much as string two words together.

"Seamus!" she finally cried as he headed down the street, towards the docks and the tenements crowded with Irish families. The old warehouses that lined the harbor had been converted into shabby dwellings, with families crowded into the small, dark rooms. "Seamus," she called again, and recklessly she hurried after him, Mr. Caber making a protest, before she shouted back that she would only be a moment. Seamus kept walking, his shoulders hunched, his hands in his pockets, and Maggie reached for his arm, forcing him to still and then turn around.

"Why are you acting this way?" she cried. "And why are you calling me Miss MacDougall?" He stared at her with a stony expression and Maggie blinked back sudden tears. "I thought we were friends."

"This is the way it has to be, Mag— Miss MacDougall," he said resolutely, and shaking off her arm, he headed back down the street. Maggie watched him go, her mouth hanging open, trying not to cry as she stood in the middle of the pavement, an icy wind from the sea blowing straight through her.

"Miss MacDougall," Mr. Caber called, a note of alarmed disapproval in his voice, and slowly Maggie trudged back to her guard and keeper.

Now Maggie sighed as she stared out at the stark branches of the trees lining the street, the gray sky as blank as a slate above them. Aunt Margaret had promised all sorts of amusements during the Christmas season, but knowing that Seamus refused even to speak with her, Maggie couldn't look forward to any of it.

With a sigh, she folded her mother's letter back up and slid it between the pages of her Bible. She didn't know why Seamus had suddenly stopped being friendly to her, and she hadn't had a chance to talk to him again. He avoided her in the schoolroom, and hurried away as soon as lessons were finished. Now, just a week before Christmas, school had been stopped until January, and she would have no chance to speak with him or make him change his mind.

Something must have happened to make him this way, she knew, but she could not think what it was. She surely hadn't offended him… but what if he'd met someone else? An Irish girl he might marry, and who would not look kindly on his friendship with another young woman?

"Maggie?"

Maggie looked up to see her aunt, as lovely and elegant as always, standing in the doorway of her bedroom. Quickly she stood up and smoothed her crumpled skirts.

"Yes, Aunt?"

"You needn't be so formal with me, you know," Margaret said with a smile. "I've had the tea things brought to the sitting room. Would you care to join me?"

"Thank you very much, Aunt Margaret."

Her aunt rested a cool hand against her cheek as Maggie passed. "My dear," she murmured, "are you well? It's only that you've seemed a bit quiet lately. A bit downcast."

"I'm very well, thank you." Maggie didn't think her aunt wanted to hear about how she missed Seamus Flanagan's company. Margaret hadn't wanted him to attend the school in the first place, and although she had softened considerably since then, Maggie did not think her aunt had done a complete about face.

A sudden thought assailed Maggie, as sharp and pointed as an arrow. Could her aunt have said something to Seamus? Warned him against being too friendly with her? Was that why he kept away now? Surely her aunt Margaret wouldn't have done something so presumptuous, so coldhearted, especially considering her own somewhat scandalous romance with Uncle Henry. She'd only been seventeen when they'd met, and had not waited for her father's approval to agree to marry him. How could her aunt object to Maggie simply being friends with a man like Seamus, who was good and kind?

With a distracted smile Maggie followed her aunt downstairs, her mind still wrestling with this unwelcome possibility. Maggie only managed a few minutes of stilted conversation before Margaret put down her teacup and gazed at her with bemusement, her eyebrows raised.

"Maggie, you are clearly thinking of something else. I have asked you the same question three times now, about whether you would like to go to the Westons' Christmas party."

"I'm sorry." Maggie flushed and bit her lip. "I'm sure a Christmas party will be lovely."

"Yet you sound positively grim!" Margaret shook her head in bemused exasperation. "What I really wish to know is what is distracting you so this afternoon. Are you worried about something, my dear?"

Taking a deep breath, Maggie blurted, "Did you tell Seamus not to talk to me anymore?"

Margaret's mouth tightened. "Seamus, is it?" she remarked with a coolness in her tone, and took a sip of tea.

Maggie's hands clenched into fists at her sides. She'd always been hot-tempered, and the fact that her aunt hadn't denied her accusation nor even looked surprised made her assume the worst. "Yes, Seamus. He was—is—my friend, and yet now he is as good as refusing to speak to me."

"Maggie, I appreciate you have a certain camaraderie in the classroom, but girls of your age cannot be friends with men like Seamus, or any men at all, for that matter."

Maggie's temper flared. "What do you mean, like Seamus?" she demanded.

Margaret sighed and set her teacup aside. "Maggie, I can see your head has been turned by this young man, and I do understand that. You are new to this city, and your life thus far has been very quiet. Naturally you are looking for a little excitement—"

"That's not it at all, you know." Maggie spoke quietly even though she felt filled with a powerless rage which surprised her, aimed as it was at her aunt. "I don't like Seamus because he's different and *exciting*. I like him because he's familiar, because he's like me." She threw one hand out, gesturing to the elegant sitting room, the sashed windows with the view of Boston Common. "*This* is what is different, Aunt Margaret."

"The point is," Margaret returned rather sharply, "you should not like him at all. What would your mother, or your father for that matter, my own brother, say if they knew about your affection for an Irish immigrant fresh off the boat?"

Maggie's jaw nearly dropped at her aunt's blatant snobbery. "They'd be happy for me, I should think, if he were God-fearing and honest, which I know he is," she returned with heat. "They're simple people, same as me. And the same as Seamus. You're the one who is different, Aunt Margaret. You're the one who has changed." She took a deep breath. "You told me that you did not want to be accused of snobbery. Well, I accuse you now. There is absolutely nothing wrong with Seamus besides, perhaps, the fact that he's poor." Her eyes flashed as she met her aunt's troubled gaze. "And that doesn't bother me in the least."

"So you do care for him," Margaret said slowly, and Maggie was tempted to stamp her foot in frustration.

"And if I do? I am sixteen, nearly the age you were when you met Uncle Henry! Was that different, simply because he had money? For I'm quite sure my grandfather would not have approved you sneaking around, meeting him!"

"That is quite enough, Maggie!" Margaret's voice was thunderous as she glared at Maggie, and Maggie glared back. She'd never spoken so harshly to another person before, especially an elder whom she had always loved and respected, and yet she could not—would not—regret a single word she'd said.

For a few taut seconds the only sound in the room was both of their labored breathing. Then Margaret looked away first, her shoulders sagging as she let out a long, troubled sigh.

"How has it come to this," she said, almost to herself. "To exchange such cross words with you! And," she added, managing a small, sad smile, "to be accused of snobbery!"

"I think it is justified, Aunt Margaret. I won't apologize."

"Then I suppose I must. Maggie, if I seem too harsh to you, it is only because I am concerned for your welfare. There is much I would change about this world, and this city, that I cannot, though I do my utmost to better it. Seamus Flanagan might be a good and kind man—"

"He is!"

"But he is also poor, with such limited prospects that I could hardly countenance any association beyond that of teacher and pupil, which I was reluctant to accede to in the first place! He will never better himself, no matter what his education—"

"Then, Aunt Margaret, why did you start the school?" Maggie burst out. "Why give those children an education if you don't expect them to use it?"

Margaret stared at her for a long moment, her eyebrows drawn together, her gaze troubled. "I suppose," she said slowly, "it is different when it concerns one's own family."

"So you believe in change only when it does not affect those you love?" Maggie couldn't keep a jagged note of hurt from her voice. It was all so *unfair*.

"No, of course not.' Margaret sighed impatiently. "I can see we are at cross purposes, Maggie. Regardless of Mr. Flanagan's prospects, I am quite sure your parents would not be pleased if I encouraged any romantic attachment of yours while you were in Boston. Can that not be the end of the matter?"

"I just wanted to be his friend," Maggie said quietly. Yet even as she said the words, she knew they weren't quite true. Some secret part of her had harbored romantic notions about Seamus, even if she hadn't dared to acknowledge them even to herself. Yet if Seamus refused even to speak with her… "What did you say to him?" she asked. "You must have said something."

Margaret pursed her lips, looking torn as well as a bit guilty. "I simply told him his future at the school was uncertain if he continued to befriend you—"

"How could you!" Maggie shook her head, blinking back the hot, angry tears that threatened to spill. "How could you threaten him in such a way?"

"I was not threatening!" Margaret leaned forward, beseeching now. "Surely you can see, Maggie, that it is not seemly for a man such as Mr. Flanagan to befriend you in such a situation! To act so familiar!"

"Did not Uncle Henry act towards you with a similar familiarity?" Maggie flung at her aunt. Margaret paled, and then to Maggie's horror, her eyes filled with tears. "Aunt Margaret…"

"I'm sorry, my dear." Margaret brushed at her eyes. "It is only that it has been nearly nine months since I have seen your uncle, and I've but one word from him, months ago now. I'm sure if he were here he'd be able to explain my sentiments more clearly."

"Or explain mine?" Maggie answered, gentling her tone.

Margaret sighed wearily. "Perhaps. I feel as if I can be sure of nothing anymore."

"Please don't forbid my friendship with Seamus," Maggie entreated quietly. "I am convinced there is nothing unseemly about it, truly, Aunt Margaret."

Margaret opened her mouth to answer but was stopped by the sound of the front door being flung open with enough force it seemed to take it off its hinges. Shocked, Margaret half-rose from her chair, and Maggie started forward, her heart beginning to thump in her chest. Then Margaret let out a little cry as a familiar voice called out.

"Margaret! Charlotte?"

It was Henry, home at last.

CHAPTER FIFTEEN

Serampore, India

She'd missed the sailing. Isobel hadn't meant to miss it, not precisely, and yet somehow in the ensuing drama of her confrontation with Mr. Casey—he'd complained to all and sundry about how unladylike she was, causing her hosts to feel both protective of her and alarmed at the gossip—Isobel had not arranged her passage back to Boston.

Joshua Marshman had been away, preaching in Midnapore, and Isobel had simply let the days slide by until the ship had sailed, and she realized rather dully that she was now stuck in Calcutta for another six weeks. The Marshmans would surely be tired of her long before then, if they weren't already. Hannah was both sympathetic to Isobel and scandalized by the scene she'd created at the ball, when she'd told Mr. Casey what she thought of him, in no uncertain terms.

"Isobel, my dear, I understand your dismay, of course. Indeed, Mr. Casey was not the sort of gentleman I'd hoped him to be! But even under such trying circumstances, a certain amount of discretion must be advised."

"I am sorry, Hannah," Isobel had said as humbly as she could. "I was overcome with emotion."

She did not feel overcome with emotion now. She felt flat, numb, as if she were frozen inside, as if she couldn't remember how to feel happy, or even sad. She felt nothing, and it was far too easy to lie on her bed and watch the breeze blow the netting, or spend hours in the rocking chair by the window, thinking of nothing at all.

There were, Isobel had discovered, no other eligible gentlemen in all of Calcutta in want of a wife—especially not now Mr. Casey had so maligned her character. She no longer had the hope of marriage, if she'd ever had it at all, and the days stuck in the Marshmans' spare room seemed like nothing more but waiting, even if she knew there was nothing more to wait for.

"There you are." Hannah swept into the sitting room, looking amazingly cool and lively. Isobel tried to feel a flicker of gratitude to this woman who had been so kind to her, but she could not summon it. She forced a tired smile as Hannah added, "I have a proposal for you!"

"Then it will be my only one," Isobel joked flatly, and Hannah placed a reassuring hand on Isobel's shoulder.

"There is more to life than marriage, Isobel, and as it will be some weeks before the next sailing, I thought you might make yourself useful here."

The implication, of course, being that she was a drain on the Marshmans' limited resources. "I'm sorry—" she began, and Hannah shook her head.

"You mistake my meaning. I mean for your own sake. It is not good for the soul to be idle and without any occupation It leads to brooding, and eventually to despair."

"I suppose," Isobel agreed, for if she felt anything, despair was the most likely choice.

"I have recalled that you spoke of teaching at a charity school back in Boston?"

"Yes…"

"We started a small girls' school here in Serampore a few years ago. You might have heard me mention it?"

"I believe so…"

"And since you will be with us for little while longer, I thought you might be able to help to teach the little ones. They are darling, and eager to learn, and since you have experience, it seemed most providential."

"Of—of course," Isobel stammered in her surprise as well as the uncomfortable realization that she had not made herself useful at all. She had not even thought of it. She had spent all her time thinking about herself, wallowing in grief and self-pity, and clearly that had been obvious to everyone. In that moment she felt her uselessness sorely.

"It will be good for you, I think," Hannah said quietly, and Isobel murmured her agreement. Certainly it would be a distraction, at least.

Yet as Isobel considered the matter later, she realized she was looking forward to teaching again. The long, lonely days of wallowing had been an indulgence she could not afford, and one she was more than ready to relinquish. She wanted to turn her mind to other matters, and teaching was one thing she knew how to do.

She started at the school the very next day. The girls' school in Serampore was about as different from the First School as could be, with its floor of packed earth and mud brick walls, the airless room buzzing with flies, yet the moment Isobel stepped across that humble threshold she felt a welcome rush of familiarity. This was a schoolroom, no matter the walls or the floors, and despite the strangeness, she felt at home for the first time in this country. At last she knew what to do. How to be.

The main teacher, Elizabeth Benton, was another missionary's wife, and was more than happy to have Isobel's help. Within minutes of her arrival, Isobel was settled on a rough wooden stool with a battered primer on her lap, and a cluster of rapt young girls gathered around her, excited to meet their new teacher. Although the language barrier prevented her from understanding or speaking very much, she felt a rush of affection for their obvious enthusiasm, their delight in learning. She began reading from the primer, and even though she knew she was only doing what she had done in Boston for many years and often found so wearying, now she felt her heart lift with joy.

Over the course of the morning, she managed to communicate to her young pupils with a mixture of words and miming, and they did the same, and sometimes the misunderstandings were so comical Isobel couldn't help but laugh until her sides ached, in a way she could not remember doing as of late, if ever. Her pupils giggled too, clearly delighted by her attempts, and Mrs. Benton smiled tolerantly at all their antics before Isobel took up the primer again.

"I fear my talent with charades is sorely lacking," she said with a smile, when the day had ended and the girls had gone home in the drowsy heat of a still afternoon. The sky was turning rose pink, and the world looked burnished with gold, the heat making the air seem to shimmer.

"It is good to hear them all laugh," Mrs. Benton said. "I fear they do not have much laughter in their lives. the plight of girls here is a difficult one, indeed." She sighed before turning to Isobel with a smile. "But it is clear, even without the language, that you have a natural ability with young ones! I hope, for the sake of the school, that you stay."

"Oh, but…" Isobel looked at her in unhappy confusion, for she had assumed Mrs. Benton knew of her situation, and the seeming impossibility of her being able to stay.

"I know what they say," Mrs. Benton said, lowering her voice although there was no one nearby to listen. "An unmarried woman alone in such a country…! But I myself think the thing can be done. After all, you have the patronage and protection of Mr. Marshman, and you are doing useful work—work only a woman can do. Why shouldn't you stay?"

Isobel stared at her in surprise, for in truth she had never considered such a notion—her choices, she thought, had been to marry or to leave. "I fear there are not many who agree with you," she said as she stacked the primers on top of the desk.

"Perhaps not, but things are changing. Slowly, to be sure, but changing all the same. Look at this school." Mrs. Benton swept an arm out to encompass the little, dirt-floored room. "This is the only school of its kind in the entire country—the only school for girls. At its inception there was some resistance, but it has come to be accepted by all and sundry now."

"And yet what will these girls do with their education?" Isobel asked. It was a question that had troubled her back in Boston; to give immigrants a chance of hope and yet knowing there might be no real opportunity at the end of it.

"They will do what they always do, the only recourse they have," Elizabeth answered with a smile. "Marry, bear children, work the land. But they shall be able to read books, and count their own animals, and be far more productive in their domestic sphere. That is a change I can be happy with. And who knows what one day any of us might accomplish?"

"Would I had your optimism," Isobel answered with a smile, and Mrs. Benton gave her a challenging look.

"It is available to anyone, my dear, I assure you."

The days which had been before so endless and empty began now to fly by. Isobel was busy in the school from right after breakfast until nearly dinnertime, when she came home to help Hannah with the evening meal and any chores around the house. She fell into bed every night tired but happier than she'd been since arriving in Calcutta, or even before that.

The deprivations that had tried her when she'd first arrived seemed minimal now, and nothing compared to the indignities her pupils endured, with so few material resources to hand. She wiped the mold from her looking glass each morning without a thought to the chore, and aired the pages of her books. She wore only two dresses, for the others she'd brought were too heavy for the heat, and she carried a fan with her wherever she went. Amazingly, against all expectation, she found she was adapting. A week passed, and then another, and another, and Isobel realized that what had once been strange now felt almost normal.

"I fear my time here must be limited," Isobel warned Mrs. Benton when she'd been at the school for nearly a month. Although she'd considered ways to stay in the country as a woman alone, she feared she was not strong enough for the task. Even with the support of the Marshmans, she did not think she would be able to stay in Serampore. There would be far too much disapproval from various quarters, and she could hardly expect the Marshmans to host her forever. She realized, for the first time, the thought of leaving—rather than merely returning to Boston—made her feel a pang of loss. She would miss India, if she were to go.

That very evening after she'd given Mrs. Benton her warning, Joshua Marshman asked again if he should book passage on the next ship to Boston, sailing the following week, and Isobel was startled to realize just how much time had passed.

"I suppose I shall have to go," she said slowly, parting with each word reluctantly. "I cannot remain here forever?" She glanced at them, not quite having meant it to be a question, and it was one they chose not to answer. Joshua was too kind-hearted to agree with her and too pragmatic to suggest otherwise, and Hannah would never disagree with her own husband.

Her friend gave her a sympathetic smile. "I shall miss you, Isobel," she said quietly. "I have enjoyed your company these last weeks."

Isobel just nodded, her throat too tight then for words. She would miss Hannah as well, and Elizabeth Benton, and all the dear pupils at the school, and even India itself. She had become used to life here, against all possibility and belief. She didn't want to go, yet she knew, no matter how optimistic Mrs. Benton wanted her to be, that in her current position, she could not stay. How cruel was Providence, she thought bitterly, to force her to leave India when she had finally become used to it, and found some happiness at last! And yet she could not rail at God, for she knew that even if she had to leave, she was still glad she'd come to Calcutta.

Even so, the day the ship sailed into Calcutta's harbor, Isobel felt her joy-lightened heart turn heavy; it was another step towards her return to Boston and the life she'd once known. Would she return to the First School, and finish out all her days as she'd begun them? She dreaded a return to the stifling familiarity of Boston and the strictures of society there. She wondered if she could carve a new life for herself—perhaps she could ask her parents if she might set up her own home. It was not as shocking a thing to do as it had been a generation or even a decade ago, and plenty of people in Boston were embracing more liberal norms—but even as she thought it, Isobel wasn't quite sure yet if she wanted to be one of them.

And what of her pupils here, of whom she'd become so fond? She'd even learned a few words and phrases of Bengali to help with communication, and they had learned English. She would miss them all. Yet even so, she could see no other way.

That evening, Joshua returned from the harborside, where he'd inquired about booking passage for Isobel, with a gentleman by his side.

"You will never guess who I found on the quayside, having docked in Calcutta on their way to Burma!"

Startled, Isobel realized she recognized the gentleman. It was Adoniram Judson, whom she'd heard speaking in Boston over a year ago now, and who had inspired her to consider the mission field for herself. He looked older and frailer now, his hair wispy but his eyes still bright with enthusiasm for his work. He was accompanied by his wife Sarah; their children had remained in Burma, under the care of a nurse.

Joshua made the introductions, and Isobel murmured her own greetings. She felt strangely shy in front of this great man and his wife, and self-conscious about her predicament, which took some explaining over supper.

"How tragic for Mr. Jamison to die so suddenly," Mr. Judson said with a sympathetic look for Isobel. He spoke in a hoarse whisper, for a long-standing pulmonary infection had robbed him of his voice. "He was a kind man, with a wry sense of humor. I enjoyed his company very much."

"I had but one letter from him," Isobel admitted quietly, "and yet I felt as if I'd received the measure of the man, and would have counted him a friend, had I known him."

Mr. Judson smiled faintly. "Yes, I believe you would have. We labored together for several years. But although it hurts to say it, so we must—as Providence wills." He glanced at his wife, who gave him a sympathetic smile; Isobel had since learned that her first husband had died in Burma a few years ago, as had Mr. Judson's first wife Ann. "Tell me, Miss Moore," he asked, "your own disappointments aside, how do you find India?"

"I found it quite difficult when I first arrived," Isobel confessed, compelled to be honest by the grave yet kindly attentiveness of the older man who had experienced so much, including prison and torture. "Everything felt so unfamiliar; I didn't think I would stop thinking things strange. And yet the days I've spent at the school here have been some of the happiest of my life." As she said the words, she realized with a pang of shock just how true they were—and how much she didn't want to leave. If a way could be found, any way at all…

Mr. Judson smiled. "Your honesty is refreshing."

"Indeed," Mrs. Judson added. "The difficulties of adapting cannot be underestimated."

Isobel let out a little, self-conscious laugh. "I must confess, I came to India with some vague notion of adventure which I realize now was quite silly of me. I have been suitably chastened in my chasing of such foolish things, I fear."

"And what will you do now?" Mr. Judson asked. "It seems such a pity to return all the way to America after such a long and arduous journey."

Isobel lifted her shoulders in a shrug. "I fear I have no choice. India holds little opportunity for a woman alone, as I am sure you must realize, having had so much experience in the mission field."

"Indeed, although I hope to welcome unmarried women to the mission field in time." Mr. Judson cocked his head, his gaze sweeping over her. "Of course, if you *were* married, there could be opportunities in abundance," he continued thoughtfully, and Isobel felt her cheeks heat. Mr. Judson, she thought, could not be aware of her disastrous interview with Mr. Casey.

"I am afraid, sir, such opportunities have not arisen here."

Mr. Judson nodded, unfazed. "Not in Calcutta, perhaps, but what of Burma?"

"Burma..." Isobel repeated, nonplussed. She had never considered travelling on from Serampore, not since she had heard of Mr. Jamison's death, and in truth now that she felt so settled there, she was reluctant to do so. "Are you... are you saying, sir, that there is another gentleman in Burma who wishes to wed?"

"Mr. Braeburn has been laboring with Mr. Jamison at our mission in Burma. He is, I am grieved to report, without a wife."

"Oh no, not Mr. Braeburn..." Hannah exclaimed, and then fell silent, looking shaken. Mrs. Judson gave her a sympathetic look.

"It was so quick, from what we have heard," she said quietly. "A matter of days."

"I didn't know..."

Isobel shook her head in confusion. "But I thought all missionaries were required to marry. Mr. Jamison was an exception, as he'd been here since before the rule was put in effect."

"Mr. Braeburn was married," Mr. Judson explained. "His wife was taken of a fever at the same time as Mr. Jamison. A letter giving me the sad news was waiting for us here."

"Poor Mr. Braeburn," Hannah said softly. "And poor Martha."

Isobel glanced at Hannah. She must have met this Mr. Braeburn when he'd come through Calcutta, along with his wife—Martha. She would have to ask about them both later. That is, if she was actually considering Mr. Judson's proposition. Did she really want to go through the whole exhausting cycle of hope and disappointment again? What if Mr. Braeburn did not find her pleasing? What if he did not wish to wed, having so recently lost a wife? And then there was the arduous travel to another, even more unknown place, and the need to settle once more. She did not know if she had it in her.

And yet...

"You must think on it, my dear," Mr. Judson said with a kindly smile. "It is, of course, an important decision, the most important decision of our earthly lives. But I assure you, I can attest to Mr. Braeburn's character. He is a kind man, full of humor and vigor, and will remain so, I trust, despite his recent loss."

"I shall think on it," Isobel promised, even as her mind whirled with the suddenness of this new possibility.

Later that night, after Mr. Judson had retired to bed, Hannah came up to her bedroom. "To think you have another opportunity!" she exclaimed with a smile as Isobel sat in front of the speckled looking glass, brushing out her hair.

"You know this Mr. Braeburn, do you not?" she asked.

Hannah perched on the edge of the bed, her brow furrowed. "Yes, he has come through Calcutta several times and stayed with us, along with his wife. He's a lovely man, Isobel, full of life and fun just as Mr. Judson said. He is always finding the humor in a situation, and he has quite the nicest laugh of anyone I've ever heard." She blushed and smiled as she said it. "It is a small thing, perhaps, and in truth I do not know him all that well, but I always liked him."

Despite the resounding accolades, Isobel heard a note of doubt in her friend's voice. "You sound unsure," she remarked, watching her friend in the mirror. Hannah had pleated her fingers together, and the furrow between her eyebrows had deepened.

"I am sure of Mr. Braeburn," she said after a moment. "He would make a good husband for any woman, I know. But…"

Isobel kept Hanna's troubled gaze in the mirror. "But…?"

"He loved his wife Martha very much. They adored each other, or so it seemed to me. You can just tell sometimes, can't you? They came out here having only been married a few months, and even after the trials of the ship passage, they seemed to hang on each other's every word."

"I see," Isobel said heavily. So if she married Mr. Braeburn, it would be as a second, poor choice. He might never learn to love her, and never mind whether she fell in love with him.

"They had a son, as well," Hannah continued quietly. "William. He died last year, when he was only a babe—a few weeks old. I know it grieved them both greatly."

"So much sorrow."

"Yes, but it's as much as any of us have had to bear." Hannah shrugged, smiling sadly. Isobel knew she had buried two little girls over her years in Serampore, and had no children living.

"I'm sorry, Hannah."

Hannah nodded her thanks, lifting her chin. "But as to Mr. Braeburn, you could certainly do far worse. He is, I am glad to say, no Mr. Casey!" They shared a complicit smile before Hannah continued, "He is a good man. An honorable man, and also a kind one. And you have gifts of your own, Isobel, that you have been using here in Serampore. Gifts you could use equally well in Burma. I do not believe there is yet a school for girls there. Think on that, as well."

Isobel nodded, touched by her friend's confidence in her abilities as well as inspired by that novel thought—to stay in Serampore, or move to Burma, not simply as the wife of a missionary, but a woman in her own right, with gifts and abilities to use for the betterment of the world, and to the glory of God. The possibility gave her a thrill that had nothing to do with marriage.

Even so… did she wish to tie herself to a man who would be grieving both his wife and child, a second and perhaps even unwanted choice? Could she do anything else?

Yes. You could return to Boston. Return to your old life and all its dull, familiar comforts, the humiliation of coming back alone.

"I don't know what to do," Isobel admitted, and Hannah smiled, rising from the bed to place a hand on Isobel's shoulder.

"Think on it," she advised. "And pray. That is all anyone can do."

CHAPTER SIXTEEN

Boston

Margaret watched Henry rise from his chair by the fire and pace their drawing room with restless, anxious energy. He had been home from his voyage for several weeks, and he had not settled to anything, which was giving her an increasing sense of unease and even alarm.

When he had come into the house that wintry afternoon, Margaret had rushed to him, laughing and crying as he caught her up in his arms and hugged her close.

"Henry! I had no idea, no word…!"

"I know, I am sorry for it. I did not have time."

'Not have time?" Margaret exclaimed, trying to keep the reproach from her voice. Now that he had returned, she was able to acknowledge the terrible extent of her fear for his life. "What was your need for such haste? I have been so worried, Henry. So worried."

His arms tightened around her. "I'm safe now."

"I thank God for it." Margaret hugged him back tightly before stepping away to introduce Maggie.

"How you've grown since I've last seen you!" Henry exclaimed. "I am glad you have been company for Margaret. But where is my Charlotte?"

"*Papa*!" Charlotte broke away from her nursery nurse to fling herself into her father's arms. Margaret watched, her heart and eyes both overflowing with thankfulness and joy. She had been so afraid this moment would never come.

Yet over the course of the next few weeks, as they celebrated a quiet Christmas at home, Margaret had tried to get Henry to tell her about his journey, but he had seemed remarkably unwilling to discuss it all.

"It was a fruitless journey, in terms of trade," he'd told her with a shake of his head. "We were caught in a storm in the South Pacific, and rescued by a Chinese junk."

"And they relieved you?" Margaret asked, one hand at her throat as she considered all the details Henry did not wish to give her—a storm, needing rescue, a confrontation with Chinese sailors who might think him dealing in the wretched opium, and be hostile.

"They did, in time."

"In time—"

"There is no need to speak of it now, Margaret," Henry said repressively. "I am home now."

And yet Margaret could not keep from feeling that once again he was keeping secrets from her, and she hated the thought. There could be no denying that he'd been preoccupied since he'd returned; even the joys of the Christmas season, and the present he'd brought for Charlotte of a ship in a bottle, had barely raised a smile on her husband's face.

"Henry," she said now, laying aside her embroidery. She'd never been very good at it, in any case, and her roses looked rather lopsided. It had been simply a way to keep her hands busy; school would not start again until next week. "Please tell me what is troubling you, for I know it is something. You have looked... *haunted* since your return." She used the word self-consciously, for it implied the kind of melodrama Margaret had never liked. Yet it was true, Henry had looked haunted. Tormented, even, and by what? She could not begin to fathom it; she was not sure she wanted to, and yet she longed for her husband to be honest with her.

Henry came to a stop by the long-sashed window that over-looked Boston's Back Bay. "It is better," he said after a moment, his back to her, "if you do not know."

Margaret's insides gave an unpleasant lurch. "That sounds rather alarming," she said as lightly as she could. "Surely it is not as bad as all that?"

"Worse."

"Henry—"

He shook his head. "I find myself in an uncommon dilemma. Condemned on one side, damned on the other." He turned to her with a sad, wry smile. "Forgive my language, my dear, but I know no other way to say it."

"Do not think of such things now, Henry!" Margaret rose from her chair and went to the window to join him, laying one hand on his arm, her stomach still churning. "What has happened? Is it to do with *The Charlotte Rose*—and the Chinese ship that rescued you?" She could think of nothing else that would torment him so. "Did something happen? There is so much you have not said. I have not wished to press, but I have been worried. So worried."

"I know you have. I am sorry to trouble you—"

"I wish to be troubled! Henry, our marriage is no marriage at all if you cannot tell me the sorrows and cares that grieve you so sorely. Please, for both our sakes, tell me what has happened. Condemned and damned? I shudder to think of it, but I still wish to know." Gently she took his hand in hers. "Please."

After a second's pause, his hand unbearably tense underneath her own light touch, Henry spoke. "Commissioner Zexu rescued me and ruined me in one breath," he confessed quietly. "He asks me to do the impossible—to betray…" He stopped, shaking his head, his face gray and haggard even as his blue eyes blazed with desperation. "And yet I cannot blame the man. I cannot blame him at all."

"Betray…" Margaret repeated, feeling the weight of the word as she spoke. "But how? And whom? Who is this Commissioner Zexu?"

"He is an imperial commissioner of the Chinese Empire," Henry explained. "Who was tasked with travelling to Canton and ridding the country of the odious opium trade."

"But you have nothing to do with opium!"

"No, although Zexu was not convinced of that at first. He thought I must have offloaded my cargo before the *Charlotte Rose* was found by one of his patrols."

"Patrols!" Margaret's stomach swooped at the thought of all Henry had endured—and hadn't told her. "But you convinced him otherwise?"

"Yes, but at a price. He was holding me and my crew in Kowloon."

"Imprisoned—"

"The conditions were fair enough," Henry allowed. "Although I grant you, Zexu is a hard and ruthless man. He has had to be. Recently he dumped twenty thousand chests of opium into the sea."

"I am glad—"

"It will start a war."

"Not with America—"

"No, with England, no doubt. Even so." He sighed heavily. "I have my part to play."

"*How?*"

"By giving him the names of those in Boston who trade in opium." He sighed. "I do not agree with the opium trade, not at all, but it tries me sorely to betray men I have done business with."

"You know such men?" she asked after a moment, surprised.

"I believe so. It is no great secret, even if it is not talked about." He gave her a rueful smile, his eyes still shadowed with worry. "There are several prominent men in the shipping business who have made no secret of their belief that trading in opium is no worse than trading in French wine. But to find proof and give it to Zexu…"

"Surely proof is easy to find, if it is an open secret?"

Temper flashed in Henry's eyes. "Margaret, the man is asking me to betray my countrymen!"

"And your countrymen are involved in something vile."

"So you would have me betray them?"

"You are not sending them to their deaths," Margaret pointed out as reasonably as she could. It seemed clear to her, although she could appreciate the strength of Henry's divided loyalties. "You are simply making sure they cease an illegal and unpleasant activity, one that is damaging an entire country." She had read in the papers about the effects of opium addiction. "If you simply need to tell Commissioner Zexu their names…"

"First I must find proof. He will not act without it." He shook his head wearily. "It is exactly the kind of sly subterfuge I hate, Margaret. I am an honest man, with honest dealings. To ferret out information and then pass it on, a *traitor*—"

"Henry, those men are the traitors!" Margaret exclaimed. "They shame their business and their country by smuggling the awful stuff in the first place. You have said the nation of China is being enslaved—then these men are like slave traders, and I know your strong feelings on that subject! If you keep it from happening, you will be doing a great service not just to the Chinese nation, but to ours."

Henry turned to her with a tired smile. "You are ever the reformer, my dear, but most would not agree with you. Indeed, one could argue that the hospitals, railroads and schools of this city have been built on the money made by opium. I know at least one merchant who is a great philanthropist."

"That does not justify the trade!"

"And," Henry added quietly, "I confess I do not wish to hand over my countrymen to a man who is more my enemy than not."

Margaret paused, frowning. "I can understand that, but then what is compelling you to this? Has Zexu threatened you in some way?"

Henry looked at her bleakly. "He has kept my entire crew imprisoned in Kowloon, along with the *Charlotte Rose*. I returned home on a British tea clipper."

Margaret let out a soft gasp. "Oh, Henry."

His mouth twisted grimly. "So you see, I am truly caught."

"Then you must find these men and name them."

"Naming them is not the problem. Finding evidence is. I can hardly go nosing about their private papers, looking for receipts of opium bought in Turkey, and smuggled offshore of Canton harbor. The idea is absurd, but Zexu insists on hard, written evidence—not mere hearsay. "

"No," Margaret answered thoughtfully, as an idea—reckless, wild, and yet eminently possible—formed in her mind. "You can't go nosing about people's papers… But perhaps I can."

Henry's jaw dropped before he snapped it shut and shook his head. "Absolutely not, Margaret. I could never put you in such danger, and I do not even know how you would do it."

"Danger?" She raised her eyebrows in challenge. "We are speaking of your colleagues, are we not? The men whose wives I have entertained in this very room?"

"Perhaps, but—"

"I am much better placed than you to discover something," Margaret persisted. Suddenly, something had lit up in her that had long dimmed. She'd once been radical—longing to be tutored against her father's wishes back in Scotland, starting a charity school for immigrants in Boston's notorious Murder District. Somehow, over the years, she'd become soft and complacent. A snob. Her niece had been right. Now was the time to fight for a cause, to ensure justice prevailed.

Henry shook his head, caught between admiration and alarm. "And if you were caught?"

She shrugged her shoulders. "I won't be."

"Margaret—"

"If I am caught, I will be embarrassed," she allowed. "And it will surely sever the friendship. We might be compromised socially."

"I might never trade in this city again! In fact, I am sure of it."

"But what is the alternative? To leave your entire crew in Kowloon, at the mercy of this commissioner? In any case, who would want to have it known that I was snooping? If there are secrets to be hidden, the person in question will wish to keep them so."

"Perhaps," Henry allowed grudgingly. "But it is a poor man who allows his wife to do his work for him."

"It is a humble and wise man," Margaret corrected swiftly. "Who are we talking about, Henry? The Maltons? The Thorndikes?" Two of the prominent shipping families in Boston were the first who had sprung to mind.

"Daniel Malton is a churchgoing man," Henry answered slowly. "And his wife is part of the American Temperance Society. I don't think he would be involved in such things."

"You must have thought of someone…"

Henry sighed before admitting reluctantly, "Thomas Perkins."

"Mr. Perkins!" Margaret drew back a little. He was one of the city's wealthiest men and a known philanthropist. He'd donated money to the First School, as well as helped with the founding of Massachusetts General Hospital. He'd also been a senator.

"His connection to the trade is well known," Henry said with a shrug. "He has an office in Turkey for the buying of opium. I do not know if I could find anything here, and I must confess, I quail to think of crossing such a powerful man."

"Is there anyone else?" Margaret asked after a moment.

"Captain Forbes."

"Him, as well?" Margaret could not hide her shock. "I have not heard a word—"

"Nor would you. Not that either man makes much secret of it. They have no sympathy for the Chinese, at any rate. But it is hardly fit discussion for ladies."

Margaret tutted impatiently. "Really, Henry—"

"So he would say himself, Margaret. Captain Forbes does not talk business in mixed company."

"If he makes no secret of it," she answered slowly, "then it should be easy enough to find incriminating evidence."

"Incriminating evidence!" Henry chuckled, the sound utterly without humor. "You sound like one of London's Bow Street Runners, my dear."

"And so shall I have to act as one!" The thought filled her with both purpose and terror. She had not done anything so reckless in so long, if ever, and yet she felt determined. She wanted to help Henry and his crew, and even Commissioner Zexu. She wanted to *do* something with her life. She crossed the room to take his hands. "If only Rupert were here. A U.S. Marshal would do nicely in this situation, I should think."

"Sadly he would not have much progress. The opium trade is still legal, you know, at least in this country. Many people partake of it, in syrups and such."

"Even so, it is against the law in China. What do you think of this man, Zexu?"

Henry rubbed his jaw, considering. "He is hard and unyielding, and I imagine quite ruthless. But he is also wise and, in his own way, fair—he wants to rid his country of opium, and I can certainly sympathize with that."

"As can I. I may have never seen the distant lands of China, but only last week Caroline Campbell was telling me of men addicted to ether in this country—a terrible thing."

"So it is."

"Then I shall do it."

Henry frowned, and Margaret knew he still didn't like the thought of her doing anything risky or dangerous—or what he saw as his own responsibility. "And if I forbid it?"

She gazed at him seriously, for their marriage had never held such strictures before. "Would you?" she asked quietly, and he stared at her hard before his face broke into a tired smile.

"How could I? I married you for your spirit, Margaret, and that is not one of obedience, yet surely this a step too far, even for you."

"Obedience!" she tutted, smiling even though her insides felt liquid with fear at the thought of what she might do, and how she might be discovered. "It is surely overrated."

*

Prince Edward Island

Harriet stood on the porch of their farmhouse, the early spring wind still sharp with cold, and shaded her eyes against the sun. She could see Allan, no more than a speck in the distance, ploughing a field for an early crop of potatoes. George walked next to him, slighter and boyish still as he was yet to reach his teens. She could see the bulky shapes of their two workhorses plodding through the churned-up soil quite slowly, and wondered if it was the horses dictating the speed of the plough—or her husband.

"Anna?" she called into the house. Anna poked her head out of the door, her mouth stained with strawberry jam. "I thought you were feeding your brother," she said in exasperation and Anna, always merry, grinned.

"I was! But the oatcakes looked so good, Mam, and the jam's so tasty…"

"Our last jar until raspberrying time," Harriet reminded her with smiling exasperation. "But I suppose it was too much temptation for a lass to resist." Harriet came into the house, smiling at the sight of six-year-old Archie sitting at the table, his mouth as smeared as Anna's. He even had jam in his flame-colored hair. Quickly Harriet took a tin pail and cup from the hook by the door. "You watch your brother now," she said as she wrapped several of the fresh oatcakes in muslin and put them in the pocket of her apron. "I'm going to take something out to your father and brother."

"I can do it, Mam," Anna offered, but Harriet shook her head. She knew how her youngest daughter liked to dally, and she had an urge to see Allan for herself, feel his arms around her, the rough cloth of his shirt pressed against her cheek.

"You stay here, and clean the jam out of your brother's hair! I'll be back soon enough."

Hauling the bucket, she stepped out into the bright sunshine of a March morning, the river glinting diamond-bright in the distance. The distinctive red soil of the island was churned to rust-colored mud as Harriet walked the worn path towards Allan and George's plodding figures.

It had been a mild winter, but Allan had seemed to feel the cold more than usual. He never complained, but Harriet had noticed how he'd wince as he rose from a chair, or rub his chest after hauling wood. He was only in his mid-forties, but the farming life was a hard one, especially in this harsh land. Anxiety ate away at her sense of peace now as she came towards him. Surely she was worrying over nothing? Allan was a hale and hearty man, if getting older, just as she was.

There was more gray than brown in his hair now, she realized with a pang, and more lines on his face—although she knew she could say the same. The auburn hair she'd once been so proud of now had streaks of white running through it. Allan's shoulders were still broad and strong, but a bit more rounded than they had been a few years ago. Forty-six last December, and he looked every year of it and more, as did she. She was no fair flower anymore, if she ever had been.

Allan turned as he heard her approach, a smile creasing his tired face. "Harriet! You're a sight for sore eyes. I thought you'd send Anna with the water."

"I had a hankering to see you for myself," she said, and set down the pail. Allan called the horses to a halt and wiped his brow.

"It's warm out here, even though it's only March. A cup of cold water will be welcome, won't it, lad?"

George nodded his agreement and Harriet handed them both tin cups of water and watched as they drank it all. George was only thirteen, young for the work, although strong. She worried for him too, although he rarely complained. "Perhaps you should hire another boy to help with these fields," she suggested, keeping her voice light. She knew how Allan resisted the idea that he was getting older and needed help. In truth, she resisted it herself; he was still a man in the prime of his life—or so she prayed.

"I've got George," Allan answered, clapping a hand on his son's shoulder.

"Even so—"

"It's a sad day," Allan cut her off, an edge to his voice, "when my wife doubts whether I can manage my own holding."

Harriet bit her lip and glanced at George who was frowning at the tension that suddenly seemed to crackle in the fresh air of a spring afternoon. "Such a day came to your father—"

"He was a man in his seventies! God above, I'm still well able, Harriet. Do you doubt me?"

"Of course you are able," Harriet said quickly. "I wasn't suggesting otherwise, Allan, but why not have a little help? If you can afford it—"

"I'm fine here with George," Allan said, and his tone held a grim finality. Harriet knew better than to press the matter.

"Have another drink," she said, and refilled both of their cups. Allan accepted it, taking off his hat and sitting on the ground, his forearms braced on his knees.

"It's a good life we have here, isn't it, *cridhe*?" he said, using the Gaelic endearment Harriet hadn't heard in a long while. He squinted his eyes against the sunlight as he surveyed the green fields rolling to the blue sky, fleecy white clouds scudding across, the sun warm but the air still possessing a chill.

"It's a wonderful life," Harriet said firmly. "The best I could have ever hoped for."

"It has been good," Allan agreed, his gaze still on the horizon. "We've been blessed, you and I, Harriet, even though we've had our fair share of sorrows."

"We have." She thought of Allan's brother, dead now nearly twenty years, and their own firstborn son, who had died of a fever nearly as long ago. "I'm thankful," she said simply, and Allan turned to smile at her.

"As am I. But this field won't plough itself." He handed her the cup and rose to his feet, staggering slightly as he straightened.

"Allan—" Instinctively Harriet reached for him, grabbing his arm and he clutched at her to right himself before shrugging her off. "Perhaps you should rest—"

"Rest midway, when there's work to be done?" He jammed his hat back on his head and turned towards the plough. "It was a moment's dizziness, that's all, caused by the sun. We'll see you at supper."

Nodding, knowing better than to say anything more, Harriet hoisted the water pail once more. If she had come out here to allay her fears about Allan, Harriet knew, she'd failed.

Back at the house, Anna had cleaned Archie's face and tidied up the jam and oatcakes from the table. Harriet watched her two young children with a deep throb of love. How blessed she'd been, with a full house and heart. She missed Maggie more than ever, longing for her oldest daughter to be by her side. Henry had returned from China in January, but Maggie had written asking to stay until the end of the school year, a prospect which had filled Harriet with both disappointment and fear. Was it the school that was keeping her daughter in Boston—or something else? Someone else?

Maggie had not mentioned anyone, but there had been a liveliness to her recounting some stories of her time teaching that had made Harriet think there was a man involved. Didn't she remember the spring in her step, the feeling of having a lovely secret? But if Maggie had fallen in love in Boston, she might never return to the island, a thought Harriet could not bear to entertain for a moment, even as she continued to dwell on it.

"Mama, shall I do the darning?" Anna asked, and Harriet reached for her eight-year-old daughter, surprising her by drawing her into her arms.

"Not yet, *cridhe*. Not yet."

Anna drew back to look anxiously into Harriet's face. "Is everything all right?"

"Yes—fine. Fine." Harriet smiled, determined to banish her fears for Allan. "I'm missing Maggie, is all, and I'm thankful for you."

Anna smiled shyly. "As I am for you, Mama. But Maggie will come back, won't she? She said she would in June."

"Yes, I know." Harriet nodded, doing her best to keep her smile. "I'm just having a foolish moment, that's all. Let's get on with the darning, shall we?"

CHAPTER SEVENTEEN

Moulmein, Burma, 1839

They had been travelling up the Salween River for nearly a week, the air hot and damp and thick, the terrain on either side of the narrow river too rugged for any roads or paths. Isobel felt as if she were travelling to the edge of the world, or perhaps into the heart of it. There was no Garden Reach here, no pretense of British domesticity, like the sugar dusting on a sweet. It felt both stranger and yet more real, and despite the challenging conditions of the flat-bottomed barge that moved slowly through the yellow waters of the Salween, Isobel still felt an unquenchable excitement, a thirst for living she'd never experienced before… and was so different from the vague dread that had assailed her as she'd taken a similar journey up the Hooghly over three months ago now, with hope in her heart for a wedding to George Jamison.

After her conversation with Hannah, she had done as her friend had suggested, and both thought and prayed about her decision to travel to Burma. It shamed her more than a little to realize how little she'd prayed about her earlier decisions to put her name on the list and travel to India. Each time she'd simply acted, always out of a desperation to escape the narrow confines of her life. Now she sought true guidance, thinking not only of herself but of the man whom she might bind herself to. Would she—could she—be a good wife to him? Could she comfort him in his sorrow, help him with his work? Could she be the helpmeet he would both desire and need? They were questions, she realized, she'd never truly asked herself before. When she'd been travelling to meet George Jamison, she'd been thinking mostly of herself. Whether she'd please him, and if he would make her happy.

Over the course of the last few months, while Mr. Judson had stayed in Serampore, his wife going ahead to Burma to be with her children, Isobel had examined her own life and searched her own heart. She'd seen how the restless dissatisfaction she'd so often felt had its origin not in her circumstances, but in herself. It had been a humbling but necessary realization, and one she'd needed to have. She could leave Serampore and travel to Burma for this fresh start, but only if she herself changed. And she believed she had.

Now travelling up another river to meet another missionary, another gentleman—possibly, if God so willed—to marry, she felt so different. So much more at peace.

"What do you think to Burma then, Miss Moore?" Mr. Judson came to stand by the rail of the boat, his gaze on the near shore. It was dense with tropical vegetation brushing the water—pomelo trees, she had discovered, when last night a young boy had brought a basket of the delicious, sweet, green fruit to the boat and they'd all gorged themselves on it.

"I have not yet formed a true opinion," Isobel answered with a small smile. "Although on first glance it appears to be an even wilder place than India."

"Indeed it is," Judson said somberly. "But truly, I have been honored to have served here, Miss Moore. Honored."

"Even though you were imprisoned?" Isobel asked, wanting to hear his answer. She knew Mr. Judson had experienced many difficulties and hardships, yet his gentleness and enthusiasm remained.

"My time here has not been without its challenges," he acknowledged with a small smile. "Yet even those have served a purpose. I do not regret any of it, Miss More, of that I am sure."

Isobel heard a slightly melancholy note in the older man's voice, and she answered with deliberate lightness, "And you shall continue to serve here for many years, I am sure."

Judson shook his head. "We shall see what the Lord wills, but I am not a young man." He held up one hand to staunch her protest; he was nearing fifty, she knew. "Life in a place such as this is difficult, Miss Moore. It is short. It is good for you to know that before you agree to any marriage. I've seen many men, women, and unfortunate children die in these lands, from one tropical fever or another. It is as the Lord wills, but you must be aware of the dangers."

"Yes…" Isobel answered slowly, some of her excitement dimming in the face of such hard truths and Mr. Judson's rather grim countenance. Of course, he was telling her no more than she'd already heard and seen for herself—Mr. Braeburn's wife and child had both died, as had Mr. Judson's wife, three children, and Hannah and Joshua Marshman's two daughters. The list of losses was long. This was a place where hardship and grief were not merely acquaintances, but lifelong companions. Yet she'd come this far already, knowing all that and more, so perhaps she was stronger than she thought.

Mr. Judson's features softened suddenly, a smile deepening the lines that bracketed his mouth. "I am not attempting to alarm you, Miss Moore, though I recognize it might seem to the contrary. I only want you to be prepared. So many who come out here are not."

Isobel wondered who he was thinking of—Mr. Braeburn? His wife? Hannah had told her of a young missionary couple who had returned home after less than a year, wild with grief at the loss of their child. "I don't know if one can ever truly prepare for a life such as this," she said after a moment.

"Perhaps not. We must simply hold onto our faith."

Isobel only nodded, for even now her faith felt a rather slippery thing, hardly the anchor it was for a man like Adoniram

Judson—or perhaps even Mr. Braeburn... which made coming all this way to live in such harsh conditions for a man she knew not at all seem foolhardy to the extreme, and yet one she still clung to. In any case, it was far too late for doubts.

"Miss Moore, it has been on my conscience that I might have been seeming to force your hand," Mr. Judson said, his gaze on the sluggish river. "You do not have to marry Mr. Braeburn if you don't suit."

"I could not stay in Burma otherwise," Isobel reminded him.

"Could you not?"

Surprise had her turning to the older man, her jaw dropping in a most inelegant manner before she thought to snap it shut. "An unwed woman—surely not, Mr. Judson? From all I have heard..."

"The marriage policy has been under review for some time, Miss Moore. There are several women, unmarried women, who have a strong calling to this mission field. Should one insist they marry in order to meet this calling? I think not."

"But—"

"Of course, it is better for missionaries to be wed. It is a lonely occupation, filled with danger and discouragement as well as grief and loss. To have a helpmate and confidant amid trials is welcome, perhaps essential, at least in some cases."

"I had no idea that it could even be thought of," Isobel murmured. Mrs. Benton had had her hopes, but Isobel had assumed that was all they were. To think she might stay in Burma—or return to Serampore—without linking herself to a man!

"I tell you now," Mr. Judson resumed after a moment, seeming to have read her thoughts, "in case you and Mr. Braeburn do not suit at all, and yet you still feel a calling to the work here in Burma. However..." He turned to face her, his expression both shrewd and kind. "One should only consider remaining in the mission field if it is one's deepest desire as well as God's will. It is not the life for a last resort." Isobel blushed at this astute remark and he smiled, his voice gentling. "I think, perhaps, dear Miss Moore, you feel your calling is not to missions, but to marriage, and yet it could be to both." The boat came slowly around a bend in the river, and Mr. Judson turned, nodding towards the horizon where suddenly she noticed a huddle of rickety wooden buildings, along with the impressive, tiered roofs of the zayats. "Look," he said, his voice rising in excitement. "We are almost at Moulmein."

*

Boston

"Care for a meal up at the Oyster House?"

Ian glanced up from his untidy desk where he'd been scrawling a few last notes on one of his patients. His colleague, Peter Smythe, sandy-haired and smiling, stood in the doorway. Outside it was already dark and the hospital was emptying out—at least of doctors and visitors. The patients still lay in their beds, many of them waiting to die, for often the only reason one came to the Massachusetts General Hospital was because options—and hope—had run out.

"I'd be glad to," he said and put his pen and ink away. Going to the Oyster House was a far more appealing prospect than returning to his house and Caroline's stony silence.

A silence, Ian knew, that was more in his own mind than in reality. On the surface Caroline had been nothing but patient and loving these last few months since the failed operation. She'd never mentioned her inheritance again, and had arranged all the household matters with the quiet competence she'd developed in six years of marriage.

Still Ian felt the guilt of his refusal to use her uncle's money to fund his research. He was a hypocrite, just as Caroline had said, to refuse it, and his stubbornness had hurt his wife. He had insulted and betrayed her by clinging to his pride, and yet even now he knew he could not help it. His hatred of Riddell was too deeply ingrained; it had been branded onto his soul for almost twenty years.

Gathering his hat and coat, he headed out into the chilly March night with Peter Smythe at his side. They chatted inconsequentially about hospital matters as they walked towards the Union Oyster House, and it wasn't until they had a dozen oysters each in front of them that Ian realized the real reason Smythe had invited him out.

"It's a good business you're finished with that ether nonsense," he said, and Ian stilled.

"I wouldn't say finished," he answered carefully. "One failed experiment hardly ends the matter." Even though he knew he had said as much to Caroline, and the rambling, disjointed letter from Horace Wells had hardly endeared him to the man, or given him a desire to continue their collaboration. Since he'd received it several months ago, he'd done his best to put it out of his mind. Wells might have seemed rather unhinged in his letter, but he was also far away in Hartford. "Scientific progress would not exist under such strictures," he told Smythe, trying to keep his voice light.

Smythe prodded one of his oysters rather doubtfully. "I suppose that is true, and I certainly have no word to say against experimentation on principle, or even of ether. We've all had our frolics with the stuff, haven't we?"

Ian shrugged; he had not partaken in such reckless frivolity, but he knew many medical students had.

"Even so, it seems a dodgy business, Campbell, don't you think?" Smythe paused, looking unhappy. "That Wells fellow... he's a loose cannon if I ever saw one. I won't say a word against using ether as you do, because what do I know of such things? But I'd stay away from Wells if I were you."

"Why are you giving me such a warning?" Ian asked rather sharply, thinking once more of that unfortunate letter. "Do you know of something he has done?"

Smythe shrugged uncomfortably. "I thought I saw him outside of the hospital a few times in the last month. A gentleman who looked like him, at any rate. He was wandering about, muttering under his breath, looking half out of his mind. Quite a nasty character, if you ask me. You don't want to be associated with someone like that."

"Quite," Ian murmured, his stomach clenching at the thought. Horace Wells, back in Boston? Why? The failed experiment had obviously affected him badly—but had it sent him over the edge into true madness and addiction?

"Now, what do you think of Warren's latest record?" Smythe asked cheerfully, clearly feeling that his duty to warn Ian had been dispatched. "Removed a tumor in forty-two seconds at last count."

"And the patient bled to death, while writhing in agony," Ian replied shortly. "Hardly a success."

"There's nothing we can do about that," Smythe answered with a shrug, and Ian did not bother to reply. He had had the argument too many times before. Pain was a necessity of surgery; there was nothing to be done about it.

Fortunately Smythe steered the conversation onto more temperate matters, but Ian still felt disgruntled as he left the Oyster House an hour later, half-dreading returning to Caroline and the coolness he felt from her, even under the smile. How had this become such an impasse for them both? Why could they not circumvent it?

Guilt niggled at him, along with dread, as he realized Caroline would be waiting, perhaps worried, since he'd sent no message. She wouldn't rebuke him, though, and that only added to his guilt. She would be long-suffering, and he would be the cad. Again. He did not know how to solve the matter, and make up with his wife—save doing that which he knew he could not, accepting Riddell's money.

"There you are, Campbell."

A few steps from his own front door Ian faltered, blinking in the gloom. "Wells?" he asked uncertainly, registering the man's stained clothing and wild hair, more noticeable than ever before. "You don't look well, man."

"Don't I?" Wells let out a wild laugh. "And I wonder who is to blame for my fall in fortunes, Campbell!" He came towards him, his hands balled into fists at his side.

Ian stepped back, conscious now of a very real danger. "Speak sense, Horace," he said urgently. "There need be no blame. The experiment failed, but we can try again—" Even if he had no intention of doing so, at least not with Wells.

"But I blame you," Wells answered as he took another menacing step towards Ian. "Suggesting I wasn't fit to perform the surgery! Doubting me every step of the way. Is it any wonder I failed? What man wouldn't, under such circumstances?"

"What's done is done," Ian answered evenly. He gauged the distance between him and Wells, wondering if he could somehow subdue him and get to his door. He was not a fighting man, and the thought of two doctors brawling in the street made him wince. If anyone saw, it could be the ruination of his career. He'd barely managed to salvage it after the last disaster. "Come inside, Wells," he said after a moment. "My house is right here. Come inside, and we'll talk about these matters. I never wished you to fail, or even cast doubt on your abilities." Although he did not relish the idea of bringing Wells, unstable as he was, into his house where Caroline waited, he saw no other way to placate the man.

"I know where your house is, Campbell," Wells answered. "I've been waiting here half the night for you." All Ian saw was the glint of moonlight on metal as Wells came towards him, one arm raised in a menacing arc.

"Horace—" he began, and then felt a searing pain in his chest. With one hand still stretched out to appeal to his one-time friend, he fell to the ground, the world around him fading to a pinpoint, and then to nothing.

*

Maggie kept her head lowered as she walked down the refuse-covered street, the brisk March air ruffling her skirts. A sailor stumbled by her, and she drew away quickly. She had never gone so far into Boston's notorious Murder District.

Her Aunt Margaret and Uncle Henry didn't even know she was here. After they had returned home from church, Maggie had pleaded a headache and gone to her bedroom. When her aunt and uncle had retired to the drawing room, she'd snuck downstairs and out the front door without even one of the servants noticing. She was determined to find Seamus.

It had been three months since her uncle had returned and Maggie had had the argument with her aunt over her friendship with Seamus, three long months that had become more and more trying. She had not spoken to her aunt about the matter, and Margaret had not made any remarks, either. Since Uncle Henry's return, her aunt had seemed preoccupied indeed, sometimes almost seeming to forget Maggie's presence entirely. She'd stopped coming with Maggie to the school house every day, instead joining her once a week, if that. When Maggie had asked why, Margaret had simply shrugged.

"You have the matter well in hand."

Even without her aunt there, Seamus had done his best to avoid her, making her feel even more miserable. Every attempt at conversation was rebuffed, and then, a week ago, he'd stopped coming altogether. When Maggie had worked up the courage to ask Aisling about her brother's whereabouts, the little girl had wrinkled her nose, nonplussed.

"He said he's had enough schooling."

Enough schooling…! And not even a goodbye for her? Maggie was hurt, perhaps more, she acknowledged, than she should be.

Seamus's absence at the school had made her determined to find him another way—and it had brought her here, a woman alone in Boston's most dangerous neighborhood, looking for a man she wasn't even sure wanted to see her.

She didn't have much of a plan beyond finding Seamus, and she realized it wasn't a very good plan to begin with. She didn't know where he lived, only that his family shared a house in the shanties by the harbor where the city's newest Irish immigrants generally ended up. She might not find him at all; the neighborhood was a rabbit's warren of narrow streets and derelict buildings. And even if she found him? Somehow, she would convince him to start talking to her again. To come back to school. That, Maggie thought nervously, at the very least.

A woman hurried by, her head lowered, and quickly Maggie stepped towards her. "Excuse me, but do you know where the Flanagans live?"

"The Flanagans?" The woman shook her head, not even meeting Maggie's gaze. She watched the woman hurry down the street and waited for someone else to pass by—someone she felt comfortable asking, at any rate.

Twenty minutes later she was shivering in the chilly spring breeze and trying to ignore the curious and sometimes hostile glances her presence in this part of Boston caused. She might have told her Aunt Margaret that she and Seamus were alike, but people here clearly saw her as a stranger, and a well-to-do one at that. She'd worn her plainest dress to come here, but even it was far finer than anything anyone else was wearing.

She asked six different people where the Flanagans lived, and nobody knew. Most hadn't even answered. The closest she'd come to success was when a tall, beaky woman asked her which Flanagans she meant, but then said she'd never heard of a Seamus.

Dispirited, Maggie wondered if she should turn back for home. What if her aunt and uncle missed her? They might be beside themselves with worry. She could be in the greatest trouble she'd ever known… which made it even more imperative that she succeeded in this foolhardy mission, and found Seamus.

She stood there on the street, people hurrying past her, wondering what in heaven's name she could do—when suddenly, there striding purposefully towards her, she saw the most wonderfully familiar, brawny figure.

"*Seamus!*" He didn't hear her at first, and so she had to call again. He looked up, squinting his eyes against the sun, and then he caught sight of her, and a lovely smile broke over his face, and was quickly replaced with a frown.

"Maggie!" He came towards her and took her by the arm, steering her off the street into the shelter of a doorway. "What in the name of all that's holy are you doing here? This is no place for a girl like you."

"A girl like me?" Maggie let out a laugh that was half-wild. She felt overwhelmed by what she had done, and the fact that she'd finally found him. "Seamus, you have no idea about a girl like me. It's my aunt who lives in a Back Bay mansion, not me. I'm happiest on a farm."

He just shook his head, his expression turning all the grimmer. "This is no farm, and I shouldn't even be talking to you."

"My aunt told me what she said to you back in December," Maggie said, her voice trembling. "And it's so unfair." She bit her lip, struggling against sudden tears. "She shouldn't have done it."

Seamus didn't quite look her in the eye as he answered roughly, "Maybe not, but the truth is, she was right, Maggie. I was acting too familiar with you, and I'm sorry for it. I never should have done so. It wasn't my place."

"Your place?" Maggie cried. "And what was your place?"

"As your pupil, with you as my teacher." Seamus folded his arms, his face settling into unfamiliar, unfriendly lines. Maggie stared at him in despair. What more could she say? She'd already been shockingly forward, coming this far to see him and talking to him in the street.

"But I thought we were friends," she said quietly, trying not to let her voice waver. Seamus shook his head.

"We can't be friends, Mag—Miss MacDougall."

"But why not?" she protested, and now her voice did waver. "I thought… I thought…" *I thought you liked me.* She could not say it, as much as she wanted to. What would Seamus think of her, if she said such a brazen thing?

For a moment Seamus' resolute expression softened, and Maggie's heart leapt. "I'm sorry," he said.

"But I don't understand. Our… friendship. It wasn't inappropriate." She blushed to say the words.

Seamus was silent for a long moment, regarding her unhappily. "Your aunt is a powerful woman," he said at last, and Maggie stared at him blankly.

"But you're not afraid of her, surely? She wouldn't… she wouldn't *do* anything, Seamus. In truth I think she's changed her mind about what she said before." That was more of a half-truth than a whole one, but her aunt had seemed to relent, at least a little, when they'd had cross words between them.

"I don't fit in that world, Maggie," Seamus said quietly. "I should have realized that when you invited Aisling and me to tea."

"But you didn't even go—"

"Because I can't! Do you think I know what cup to drink from, or what pretty manners to have? Do you think I'd fit in there, with these clothes and this mud on my boots?" He sounded almost angry as he gestured to his rough, workman's clothes and worn, mud-caked boots. "It's impossible."

"But that isn't my world, either," Maggie protested. "I'm a farm girl, Seamus! I grew up in a cabin with one great room and two bedrooms and that's all. Before I came to Boston, I had one good dress for Sundays." She was practically gabbling in her urgency to make him understand, but she could already tell he didn't. Wouldn't. Already he was shaking his head.

"It's not the same."

"Is that all you're going to say?" she asked despairingly.

Seamus nodded, and Maggie stared at him in misery. Had she expected him to say anything else? She had risked so much and come all this way—and for what? Simply for Seamus to tell her what she already knew he'd say. And yet… she couldn't leave it like this. Not when this might be her only to chance to speak to Seamus… to *know*…

"Seamus," she asked in a low voice, "even if you can't talk to me… even if you won't return to school or be my friend… tell me, please tell me the truth, do you care for me? At all?" Her voice trembled and she kept his frowning, unhappy gaze with effort, embarrassed as she was by her own desperate brazenness. What a forward thing to have asked! And yet she wouldn't take back the words even if she could. She needed to know.

Seamus gazed down at her, his eyes stormy with conflicting emotion. Tenderness, which gave her hope, and torment, which made her heart twist inside her.

"Yes," he said quietly. "Yes, heaven help me, but I do."

"Then why…" She shook her head. "It doesn't matter why. You came to this new world for better opportunities, Seamus. For every man to be able to be master of himself, to go as far as he may. My family did the same! My father wanted his own farm, my grandfather as well. We're not so different, you or I, we're just from different places. If you care for me, if you truly care for me, please don't let us leave it like this." She reached out one hand to grasp his own. He tried to pull away but she held on, and then with something close to a groan, he laced his fingers with hers.

"Maggie…"

"You care for me. I care for you."

"Does your aunt even know you're here?"

"Does it matter?"

She took a step towards him and he reached for her shoulders to set her away from him, but in that moment of push and pull, with Maggie tilting her chin so she looked deep into his eyes, he drew her towards him instead.

"Maggie…" he said softly, and then, with her heart fluttering in her chest like a wonderful, wild thing, he kissed her.

CHAPTER EIGHTEEN

Ian blinked slowly in the dim light, every muscle in his body aching unbearably. He took a breath and felt a sharp, stabbing pain in his chest. He tried to raise his hand to examine where he was hurt, but the effort cost him too much and his arm fell uselessly back to the pillow.

"Ian, Ian… thank heaven you're finally awake."

He blinked again and Caroline came into focus, her face pale, her eyes anxious. He turned his head and saw he was in his own bedroom, the curtains drawn against the weak morning sunlight. He could see twists of paper that held medicine powders on the table by the bed, and fresh linen bandages folded on a chair. Judging by all this, he had been bed-ridden and unconscious for some time.

"What… what happened?" His voice sounded croaky and hoarse. His mind was a blur of jumbled, half-remembered moments.

Caroline bit her lip. "Do you not recall?"

"No… wait." He closed his eyes, the memories slowly gaining clarity and focus. He'd been walking home from the hospital, no, from the Oyster House where he had shared a meal with Peter Smythe. Smythe had warned him about proceeding with the ether experiments, about Horace Wells. He'd said he was loitering outside the hospital, and then… and then, right outside his own front door, he'd come across the man, looking almost ill, or even mad, because he'd had a knife—Ian had seen it flash in the moonlight before the world had gone dark.

He opened his eyes and stared at Caroline. "Did Horace Wells attack me?"

She nodded unhappily. "I saw it from the window. I was looking for you, since you were so late, and I saw the two of you talking, and then he raised the knife in his hand—" She drew in a ragged breath, her eyes shadowed with memory, a tear slipping down her cheek which she dashed away. "Oh Ian, I've never been so afraid! I ran outside at once—"

"You shouldn't have. He could have harmed you." He struggled, uselessly, to raise himself in his bed. "He didn't, did he? God help him if he did—"

"No, he did not. He was raving, Ian, and half out of his mind. After he attacked you, he…" She swallowed hard. "He turned the knife on himself."

"God have mercy on his soul." Ian shook his head, too dazed to fully comprehend the extent of the evening's horror. "Is he—is he dead, then?"

"No, at least he wasn't right then, but there was so much blood. It all caused a great commotion. The neighbors came out, and someone fetched one of the police." The Police Department had just formed last year, and the sight of the officers on patrol of the city streets still surprised some people, a change from the watchmen who had patrolled the city before.

"And they came?" Ian asked. He knew their headquarters were on School Street, not very close.

"Yes, they did. They took Mr. Wells away."

"To hospital?"

"I don't know. I told the police what I had seen. They said they would arrest him."

Ian grimaced, pain shooting through him as he tried to settle himself more comfortably against the pillows. "I hate for you to have witnessed such a scene. And you might have been in very grave danger yourself, Caroline. I couldn't bear to think of you hurt or worse—"

"And I couldn't bear to see you hurt or worse," Caroline returned. "Ian, I thought he'd killed you!" Her eyes turned glassy with tears and she blinked rapidly, her voice choking. "I thought you were dead. I truly did."

Ian managed a small smile even though his whole body ached abominably, and his chest where Wells had stabbed him still throbbed with a red-hot pain. "It will take more than a single stab wound to finish me off, I daresay. You're stuck with me, for now at least."

"And happily so." She touched his hand lightly, as if afraid to hurt him, and drew a shuddering breath. "Ian, this whole business has made me realize how wrong it's been of me to try and force you to take Uncle James's money, and how childish I've been in holding it against you, and letting it come between us. This tension between us has gone on for so long, and I want to have an end to it. I hate to think I might have lost you when we still had ill feeling towards one another."

Ian could see how sincere and anxious Caroline looked, her face pinched, her teeth sunk into her lower lip, and he struggled to respond. He could not bear to think of his ether research now, or her uncle's money, and yet even in his pain-clouded state he recognized the truth of her words… and knew he had been distant from his wife for far too long. It was as much his fault as hers, if not more so. He'd been stupidly, uselessly stubborn, and for what? For some remnant of schoolboy pride he still felt over the loss of Achlic Farm twenty years ago.

With effort, he reached for her hand and grasped it loosely. "If anyone has been childish, Caroline, it is I, for holding a grudge for nigh on twenty years, and then taking it out on the one person I hold more dearly than any other, the one person who has championed me again and again. What a fool I've been. A stupid, stubborn fool." He drew a breath, the movement making his chest throb once more. "I'm sorry for letting the past diminish our present, and even our future, which is so precious to me. I will not let this come between us again, not in the least. If you wish to support my—"

Caroline shook her head and gently squeezed his hand. "We needn't talk about all that now. I just want you to get well."

Ian nodded, fatigue crashing over him once more. "I will," he promised, even as he closed his eyes. "I still have work to do here." And then, with Caroline still by his side, sleep claimed him.

*

Moulmein, Burma

Isobel had spent three days in Moulmein, and so far they had been the most awkward days of her life. She'd come to Burma full of hope and determination, determined to start a fresh chapter of her life in this strange yet beautiful place, but that sense of purpose was flagging now.

It wasn't the strangeness of the city, which indeed was different even from India, but rather the strangeness she felt in herself and her position.

All the cautious optimism and shy hope she'd felt while on the flat-bottomed boat with Adoniram Judson and his family had leaked right out of her as she'd stepped ashore in Moulmein's crowded harbor and seen Mr. Braeburn jerk back in surprise. She knew Mr. Judson had written to him from Serampore to inform him of her existence, but clearly the reality of her was a surprise—and, it seemed, not a particularly welcome one at that. Isobel had tried not to show her hurt as Mr. Judson had made their introductions.

"Pleased to meet you, I'm sure," he'd said, not meeting her eye, and Isobel had ended up looking anywhere but at him. Moulmein was a busy, bustling city, the headquarters of British Burma, with a plethora of government offices, churches, and English-looking buildings, as well as a massive prison. There was a neighborhood for the British residents known as Little England, but the mission was in a more modest Burmese neighborhood.

"Most of the British here own rubber plantations," Mr. Judson explained as they took a palankeen back to the mission. Mr. Braeburn was seated on the opposite side to Isobel, gazing at the curtained window as if he could see the view of the city, and acting as if Isobel were not there at all.

Hurt at his obvious slight of her burned, even as she supposed she could hardly blame him. She was being foisted on him, a man still in mourning, when he hadn't even indicated that he wished to marry again. And if he didn't marry her, she had no real place here, no matter what Mr. Judson said about single women as missionaries. She was no pioneer, and she did not wish to be the first single female missionary, especially in such uncomfortable circumstances as these, laboring alongside a man who had refused her.

Yet what, really, were her options? She was no longer in Calcutta, which at least had regular ships to America. Burma had none; to return home now would be much more difficult. She could not travel alone, and no one was travelling back to India for months yet, if not a year.

She was stuck, whether she liked it or not—and whether Mr. Braeburn liked it or not. In the three days since that first awkward introduction, their interactions seemed to be but murmured greetings when they crossed paths in Mr. Judson's household—she shied away from him, and he seemed content to do the same. Isobel spent most of the time in the kitchen quarters with the Burmese housekeeper, a smiling woman who knew a little English and taught her a little Burmese. Sarah Judson had made her welcome, but she was busy with her young children, and while Isobel had spent time with them, she did not wish to encroach on their time together.

All of it begged the question, she thought as she gazed out at the magnificent Moulmein pagoda, standing on a ridge and surrounded by no less than thirty-four temples, just what she was doing here.

She did her best to fight a wave of homesickness that threatened to sweep over her with tidal force, of the kind she hadn't felt since she'd first learned George Jamison had died. She had considered speaking to Mr. Judson about starting a school for girls, but she could not bring herself to when her circumstances were so unclear. She'd come so far, and for so long, and yet she felt as adrift and purposeless as ever.

The newfound faith that she'd begun to feel was also flagging. The Judsons were as kind and welcoming as ever, but she was honest enough to admit she did not share his zeal for missionary work. She'd had moments of conviction, she knew, and she'd believed Providence had directed her to come to Burma, but beyond that… she did not know what she believed. She feared she did not possess the kind of unmitigated conviction and enthusiasm that Mr. Judson, or for that matter Mr. Braeburn, felt, and if that were the case, why on earth would Mr. Braeburn wish to marry her?

Obviously, she thought now, he didn't.

And while Mr. Judson had suggested she might remain in Burma to help them with their work, Isobel wondered at such a possibility. How could she stay here, a hanger-on yet again? Working with Mr. Braeburn nearly shoulder to shoulder, when he so obviously did not wish to marry her? She was trapped, at least until the next sailing, and that felt like an endless amount of time.

Sighing, she leaned her head against the bedpost, one hand wrapped around it as she fought useless tears.

"Dear Isobel." The door had opened without her having heard the noise, and Isobel opened her eyes and straightened, a flush spreading to her face. Sarah Judson smiled at her in sympathy. "I am sorry to see you looking so desolate."

"I am sorry for you to have caught me in such a moment of self-pity," Isobel answered with a blush. "Truly I am grateful to you, and your most generous hospitality. You have been kindness itself."

"But it is a strange season for you, is it not?" Sarah said, coming with easy familiarity to sit beside Isobel on the bed and put one arm around her. Isobel stiffened under the surprising embrace but then found herself relaxing into it, and even craving that essential human touch she'd missed for so long. "We must see you properly settled," Sarah said.

"I'm not sure how," she said, her voice choking just a little. She fought the urge to bury her head in Sarah's shoulder like a child would with its mother.

"I think," Sarah answered, a faint thread of humor in her voice, "I can think of a way."

"What do you mean—"

"I see two unhappy, uncertain souls who are circling around another without a word," she said with faint, gentle reproof. "And that is no way to conduct a courtship."

"There is no courtship as far as I can see," Isobel forced out.

"You know, I think," Sarah answered after a moment, "that I was wed to another missionary, Mr. Boardman, here for many years? Mr. Judson and Mr. Boardman labored together, as did I with his wife, Ann."

"Yes, I had heard something of it…"

"When Mr. Judson and I both found ourselves widowed, it seemed both ordinary and unnatural for us to marry. Mr. Judson wished to offer me protection, and we both recognized the importance of having a partner in this difficult work. And, in truth, I did not wish to return to America. The love that blossomed between us came with time and effort, as it often does. Marriages are not romances, even if that element comes eventually. They are based on vows, not feelings."

"I fear Mr. Braeburn does not wish to make such a vow," Isobel managed, even though to admit so much felt humiliating.

"We shall see about that."

That very evening Sarah Judson managed it. Isobel had helped clear away the evening meal when Mr. Braeburn appeared in the doorway of the kitchen.

"Miss Moore? If I may have a word?"

Isobel's heart lurched inside her chest. Both the Marshmans and the Judsons had assured her he was a man of humor and kindness, but she'd yet to see either attribute in person and right now he sounded unaccountably grim.

"Of course." She did not add, but certainly thought, that he had not said so much as a word to her through the meal they'd just shared, or the days past, so she did not know why he would desire one now.

They both repaired to the sitting room, its wooden shutters closed against the dark night. Isobel felt perspiration prickle along her shoulder blades not from heat but rather from nerves. She had no idea what Mr. Braeburn was going to say to her. Was he going to reject her directly? It seemed likely, judging from the seriousness of his expression, and in that moment she decided if he did, she would leave Burma on the next sailing, whenever it was. She would leave India, as well; she would return to Boston where things were at least known and comfortable, in their own way. This whole journey, from beginning to end, had been madness. Utter madness.

She laced her hand across her middle and attempted a smile, cool though it was. "You wished to speak to me, Mr. Braeburn?"

"I did." He gazed at her solemnly for a moment, and Isobel struggled to keep looking composed. He was a handsome man, with dark brown hair and eyes, his skin tanned from several years in the tropical sun, deep crow's feet by his eyes although he was only a few years over thirty. His shoulders were broad underneath his plain frock coat, and he topped her by six inches at least. As pleasing as all that might have been, his expression bordered on grim, and Isobel quailed beneath it. "I confess," he continued, "that I am hesitant to do so when you look like you would like to take me to task." His mouth quirked in the tiniest smile that made Isobel feel as if her world was, for a brief moment, upended.

Could she trust that smile, the way she'd trusted Mr. Jamison's letter? She felt too battered and weary to do so, to see stars in a sky that was nothing but dark. "I have no desire to take you to task, Mr. Braeburn. In fact, I do not know you, and I am well aware you do not know me."

"As am I," he returned. "That, indeed, is the nettle we have both needed to grasp, Miss Moore."

"Indeed." Isobel looked away, discomfited. Despite what everyone had told her of this man, she had not expected such wry honesty.

"But perhaps," he continued quietly, "I should be taken to task, for ignoring you quite cruelly these last few days. In truth, it was because I did not know what to say to you, and I feared saying something that would cause offense or pain."

So he was rejecting her, then. She was not surprised, yet she was still hurt. Isobel lifted her chin. "I would rather you had caused it, than leave me in such uncertainty."

Mr. Braeburn inclined his head in sorrowful acknowledgement. "Then I must ask your forgiveness."

"You shall have it, but I still do not know to which purpose you called me here." She wanted him to say it plainly, Isobel realized, no matter how much it hurt. She deserved that much. "I trust you have some notion of Mr. Judson's proposal?"

He arched an eyebrow. "It should be my proposal, by rights," he said, his tone light and perhaps even teasing. Isobel stared at him in unhappy confusion.

"But it is not a proposal you wish or indeed intend to make."

"That is not so."

"I... I don't understand. I thought the idea did not please you." She knew her face must be crimson, and she had to hide her trembling hands in the muslin folds of her skirt.

Mr. Braeburn was silent for a moment, his teasing expression turning pensive. "I do not yet know if it pleases me, or if it pleases you, for that matter," he said finally. "But pray let us be seated and at least begin to determine if that might be the case."

Isobel glanced at him warily. Was she now to be put to the test in such an unromantic fashion? Mrs. Judson had told her marriages were not romances, but even so she had not expected such plain speaking as this. "There are things you wish to know...?" she asked tentatively once she had seated herself on the horsehair loveseat, with him sitting opposite her.

"There are many things I wish to know. And I imagine there are many things you wish to know about me, if we are indeed to consider marriage." He sat back, giving her another wry smile that Isobel realized, despite her propensity to caution, she was beginning to like. "I confess, I would like to be married again. It can be a lonely life here, and companionship of the gentler kind can be a great comfort."

Isobel stared down at her lap. "I'm sure," she murmured.

"But if we wouldn't suit each other, then there is no point to consider it, as I expect you'll agree. You surely have not travelled all the way to Burma to be so disappointed."

Was he trying to let her down easily, Isobel wondered? She glanced up quickly. "Mr. Braeburn, I am to turn thirty soon and as yet am unwed. *That* is my disappointment."

"And I confess it is quite a surprise to me," he answered with a smile. "I would have imagined you had all sorts of suitors."

"Alas, no," she replied shortly.

"I also imagine that a woman such as yourself would prefer not to be wed to a man who does not suit you."

Isobel stiffened. "A woman such as me?"

"Handsome, intelligent, well-bred..." He spread his hands. "Surely you wish to be discerning."

His words warmed her, even if his assumption was mostly wrong. "Indeed, there was a gentleman in Calcutta that I did not care for," she said, surprised to enjoy the unexpected feeling of recklessness. "But then I believe he wished for a housekeeper and governess rather than a wife."

"Ah." There was a wealth of understanding in his voice that made Isobel smile faintly. "Well, I assure you, I do not have such expectations."

"What are your expectations?" she asked baldly.

Jack cleared his throat, and Isobel saw that now he was blushing as well. They were quite a pair, it seemed. "I confess, I do not have very many. I desire a wife who is a helpmeet and a friend, and all I would ask, Miss Moore, is that we attempt to get to know one another, spend time in each other's company, before we decide on a course of action."

Isobel clenched her hands in her lap. "That seems reasonable," she said carefully. "But as I have said before, I am not young, Mr. Braeburn. My time is precious to me, especially if I... if I wish to enjoy marriage in all its wholesome benefits, such as motherhood." She surprised herself at making such a bold admission, but he took it in his stride.

"That is a fair point," he said, and settled more comfortably in his chair. "Then we will waste no time in preliminaries. Let us get to know one another immediately! You hail from Boston, I heard? Tell me about your life there. What did you do with your time?"

"I—" Isobel stopped, at a loss. How could she begin to describe herself?

"Mr. Judson said you were well read," he offered helpfully. "And that you started a school?"

"I didn't start it," she said quickly. "I only helped—"

"Tell me of it," he said, settling back to listen.

Isobel stared at him, finding it hard to believe he wanted to know. But then she saw how his eyes crinkled up at the corners, and that they were bright with interest and kindness. She did not know this man, but already she felt as if she might come to like him. Love him even, for as Mrs. Judson had said, marriage was founded on a vow. Love could come with time—and effort. A new hope kindling in her heart, she began to speak. "I taught at the First School for five years," she said slowly. "And I confess I began simply because I was bored and disappointed with my life."

"Disappointed?"

Isobel hesitated, wondering how much to impart. Then she decided that he deserved her full honesty if they were to decide whether they suited one another. She would ask for the same. "There was a gentleman," she said carefully, "a friend of my family who had escorted me to various events. I am afraid I read far too much into his intentions, and expected a proposal when none was forthcoming."

He frowned. "And he was not aware of this?"

"Not until it was too late. As it happened, he loved another. But he was a gentleman, and he offered to marry me anyway. I refused."

Jack smiled and nodded. "As I would have expected."

"How?" Isobel challenged. "You don't even know me."

"I know you must possess strength and determination, to travel from Boston to Burma. Not a small feat, Miss Moore. Not a small feat at all."

"Perhaps not, but I have struggled with the strangeness of things," Isobel confessed. "And the Marshmans could tell you how disconsolate I was when I arrived—I sat in my room for weeks."

"Are you trying to put me off, Miss Moore?" Jack teased and she blushed and shook her head.

"No, I only mean to be honest. You deserve that much, as do I, I hope." She paused and then added, "In truth, I do not know if—if I possess the conviction that you and the Judsons do. The Marshmans, as well. There have been times when I have felt positively beleaguered by doubt." She lowered her gaze, afraid to see censure in his own at such an admission.

"Then you are no different from me," Jack said quietly. "I have had my fair share of doubts, Miss Moore. It is difficult not to."

"And your fair share of grief, it would seem," she added, daring to look up at him again. She saw only compassion in his gaze.

"One begets the other, I fear." He smiled at her sadly. "But let us talk of happier things. You taught in Serampore for a little while?"

"Yes, but who told you?"

"Mr. Judson brought a letter from Mrs. Marshman, recommending you to me."

"*Oh.*" Isobel didn't know whether to be pleased or mortified by this. What had Hannah said of her?

"She did an admirable job," Jack continued quietly, and Isobel could not think of a thing to say. "An admirable job, indeed."

Isobel bit her lip. "Then I fear she might have been too kind."

"I must disagree. I fear you have had many disappointments in life, Miss Moore, as have I. But I hope, in time, that I may not be added as one more."

A thrill went through Isobel at his words. Could this be what—who—she'd been looking for at last? "I pray for the same to you, Mr. Braeburn," she said, and for a few moments they simply sat in silence, smiling at one another.

CHAPTER NINETEEN

Boston

It had been several weeks since Maggie and Seamus had first kissed right there on the street in Boston's Murder District, weeks of waiting and wondering, fearing that Seamus regretted their sole indiscretion. He had, thankfully, returned to school, and occasionally Maggie found a reason to speak to him there, or to steal a moment with him when he stepped outside the building to refill the water pail or coal scuttle, yet during these hasty conversations he seemed reluctant to linger, and he never spoke of that kiss in the street.

Even so, Maggie knew she loved him. And despite his obvious reticence at being with her, she believed he might love her back. At least, she hoped he did.

They had not been alone together long enough to have a conversation about it, or any possible future they might share. Maggie was afraid to ask; she knew Seamus didn't like disobeying her aunt, or perhaps even all of society, for she knew he still felt the difference in their stations even if she did not. But if those could be overcome… Maggie hardly dared to hope, and yet she did not think she could take much more uncertainty. She loved him, with a woman's heart, and she longed to know how he felt about her.

Now that the school year would be ending soon, her parents would expect her to return to Prince Edward Island in the summer, to help with the busiest time of year. She had already been gone so long, and there were days she missed the island with all its familiar ways as well as her family. Yet how could she leave Seamus?

An opportunity to talk to him came unexpectedly, when Maggie came down to the dining room one morning for breakfast to find her aunt dressed for visiting rather than wearing one of the plain, serviceable gowns she chose for her work at the school.

"I'm afraid you'll have to teach alone today again, Maggie," she said briskly. "I have an invitation to tea with Mrs. Forbes that I wish to accept."

"I see," Maggie said. Her aunt had been spending less time at the school, but she had still been teaching several times a week at least, and she had never stayed away from the school simply to accept a social invitation. Still, she was hardly going to question it, not when it might provide her with a better opportunity to speak with Seamus. She decided that today she would force the issue, come what may.

"I trust," Margaret continued, "that you will have no difficulty? You have done well these last few months, on the days I have not been able to be with you."

"Thank you, Aunt Margaret," Maggie answered. "I am sure I shall be fine today."

Maggie's heart seemed to be beating double-time as she entered the First School that morning. She busied herself with starting a fire in the coal stove and setting out primers and slates, all the while keeping an eye out for Seamus. He usually came early, if he came at all.

Although he'd returned to school, he didn't come every day, often needing to work or help with his family. She prayed today would not be one of those days. If he didn't come to school, she would not be able to tell him… *what?*

She paused, a primer clutched to her chest, as she considered just what she intended to say to Seamus. Could she be so bold, so utterly *brazen* as to tell him she loved him? Ladies never declared themselves first, but she feared Seamus wouldn't, because of the reservations he already had. She would have to be the one to speak first, even if it appeared shameless. Her heart thudded harder at the thought. And what if he rejected her because of her boldness? *Then* she would feel shame… as well as a terrible heartbreak.

She had no more time to think on it for the first pupils were arriving and she was soon busy with settling the young ones to begin their lessons.

She had just instructed the youngest group to open their primers when the door to the school creaked open, and Maggie looked up to see Seamus coming in, his cap jammed low on his head. He slid into his seat, lifting his gaze to meet hers for one quick look that still made Maggie tremble. She would tell him she loved him, she vowed. She could not live with this uncertainty any longer, and who knew when she might have another opportunity? Seamus seemed determined not to give her one.

Yet the hours passed, and such an opportunity did not arrive. Maggie was kept busy with all the other pupils, and during the lunch hour Seamus left for home before she could so much as bid him a greeting.

"Where has Seamus gone?" she asked his sister Aisling, deliberately keeping her voice light.

"Mam's been a bit poorly," Aisling answered. "Seamus said he'd check on her, make sure she had a bit to eat. He'll be back for lessons, I think."

"Oh, I'm sorry to hear she's ill," Maggie answered sincerely, even as she felt a rush of relief that he would return. "I hope she fares better soon."

"It's her chest," Aisling explained. "Always has been."

Seamus returned, his expression shuttered and grim, and still the hours passed after lunchtime with not a single word spoken between them, or an opportunity for any further conversation.

Finally, Maggie lit on a solution. The fire in the coal stove had burned low and the scuttle was nearly empty. The coal shed was in the small yard behind the school, and Margaret usually asked one of the older boys to fill it when needed when Seamus was not present. Today she would ask Seamus.

"I'll just unlock the door for you," she said, and instructed Lizzie, one of the older girls, to watch over the classroom while she was gone.

Seamus didn't speak to her as she led him out to the tiny yard behind the schoolhouse. Although it was April the air still held a damp chill and Maggie tried not to shiver as she summoned the strength to begin.

"I've been wanting to speak with you," she said as she fumbled with the key in the lock. "And I fear this might be my only opportunity. At times it has seemed as if you're avoiding me, Seamus."

"It seemed best," he answered in a low voice, his tone terribly final.

"It doesn't seem best to me," she answered, and with the key left in the lock she turned to face him. "Seamus, the last time we spoke, you told me you cared about me." She paused, waiting for him to confirm it, but he said nothing. Quailing under his forbidding gaze, Maggie continued, "I—I care about you."

"You shouldn't."

"Don't say that!" she implored. "You keep thinking I'm some sort of grand lady, but I'm not. I'm just like you." Seamus shook his head, and frustration made Maggie want to stamp her foot or worse, cry. She swallowed hard and lifted her chin.

"You told me you cared about me. You kissed me!"

"I shouldn't have—"

"Do you have any feelings for me at all?" she demanded. "Or have you rooted them all out?"

Seamus glanced away, and the moment stretched on. "I haven't," he answered at last, his voice so low Maggie strained to hear it. "But I have tried."

"Then stop trying!" Desperation making her bold, Maggie reached up to put her hands on his broad shoulders. "I love you," she said, her voice trembling. "And I even dare to think you love me back, no matter how hard you fight against it."

Seamus closed his eyes, clearly battling against his emotion. Against her. "Maggie—"

"My aunt doesn't matter," Maggie continued rapidly. "Boston doesn't matter! I'll be going back to Prince Edward Island, to a simple farming life—that's who I really am! Why can't you see that?"

Seamus opened his eyes. "And if you're going back, then what future is there for us? My family is here in Boston, Maggie. My livelihood."

Maggie bit her lip. Could she be so bold...? Yet what did she have to lose, having said so much already? "There could be a future," she said, her voice a whisper, "if you made it so. If you... declared yourself." Her cheeks were scarlet with mortification and she stared down at her feet. Had she actually asked him to propose? What woman did such a thing? Seamus did not reply, and she felt grief add its terrible weight to her humiliation. Even so, she could not stop herself now. "You could speak to my aunt," she whispered, still unable to look at him. "If you were of a mind to." Still Seamus said nothing, and Maggie risked a glance upwards. His expression was stony, and yet she saw a conflicted torment in his eyes. "Seamus..."

"You should get back," he cut her off gruffly. "Or the whole classroom will be in a state, to be sure."

She nodded, swallowing past the hot lump that lodged in her throat as she fought off the tears. So that was that, then. He didn't love her, not enough anyway. She'd made a complete fool of herself, and for nothing.

"Maggie…" His voice stopped her at the door, her back to him. "I'll… I'll think on it," he said roughly, and then cleared his throat. "I… I…" Another pause, endless and aching. "I do love you," he said at last, and Maggie whirled around.

"You *do*—"

"Get back in there." Seamus waved towards the school. "I can't say more now. I daren't."

And yet, Maggie thought, her heart singing, he'd said enough.

*

Boston

Margaret swept into the Forbes's Beacon Hill mansion with an airy smile and a thundering heart. She had been waiting for the right moment to approach one of the wives of the merchants who dealt in opium, and meanwhile months had passed with Henry's crew still in Kowloon.

"I cannot force an acquaintance," she'd told Henry. "Or they will be suspicious. I have known Mrs. Forbes, but not very well. I must further our friendship and then wait for an invitation."

It had taken painstaking months of seeking Rose Forbes out at every social occasion she could; contriving to run into her while at the modiste's or the glovemaker, forcing conversations that she would not have bothered with before, all to get Mrs. Forbes to invite her into her home. It had meant neglecting the school, and even her own niece, which Margaret could not help but feel guilty about. She feared Maggie was furthering an acquaintance of her own, and when she'd spoken to Henry of it, he'd frowned and then shrugged, his feelings on the matter as ambivalent as her own.

"I admit, I would have preferred her to set her affections on a man with more prospects, but you know as well as I do, my love, that we cannot choose the direction of our hearts."

"And what am I to say to Harriet and Allan?" Margaret asked. "They entrusted me with their daughter's care and protection—"

"And Maggie is in no danger," Henry pointed out gently. "She is sixteen, almost seventeen, about the same age as you were when we met. And perhaps nothing has happened yet."

"Perhaps," Margaret allowed, although she doubted it.

She could not think on Maggie now, however; she needed all her wits about her for the forthcoming interview.

"I am so glad you accepted my invitation," Rose Forbes said as Margaret came into the spacious drawing room, decorated in the latest American Empire style, with plenty of gilt and rope-twist carving.

"As am I," Margaret assured her. They exchanged pleasantries as she removed her mantlet and bonnet and handed them to the waiting maid. "I'm so pleased to have seen you at the musicale last week," she continued. "We must catch up on our news."

Rose smiled and gestured to the maid to bring tea. "Indeed. Captain Forbes mentioned that Mr. Moore has returned recently from China?"

"Yes, several months ago."

"And I trust he had a safe journey?"

Margaret thought of the storm that had shattered the *Charlotte Rose's* mast, and then of his crew captive in Kowloon. "I am thankful he has returned home," she said simply. "Although sadly his ship the *Charlotte Rose* did not."

"Such a pity," Rose murmured. "Captain Forbes, you know, has not sailed to China since last year. It is so dangerous these days."

Margaret nodded. Henry had already told her that Forbes did not currently trade with China, having delayed his smuggling until the Opium War was resolved. Yet he might already be making plans to trade again, especially if the war's end resulted in the traders' favor. Yet would she find proof of such a thing, if she managed to get into his study? And how would she contrive to do such a thing in the first place? It had seemed a sensible plan when she'd suggested it to Henry, but now Margaret could not help but think it verged on lunacy. What excuse could she possibly make to leave this pleasant room and go creeping about the house?

Her mind raced even as she accepted a cup of tea and sipped it carefully. She wished she had thought of some decisive plan before arriving, but nothing had come to mind. She'd hoped something might occur to her once she'd seen the Forbes's house, but her mind remained blank as she listened to Rose's desultory comments on the upcoming season and made her own mindless replies, all the while desperately trying to think of a way to excuse herself.

A half hour passed, and Margaret knew that Rose would expect her to take her leave soon. Extending her stay much beyond that would be seen as both rude and out of character, and therefore suspicious. Yet she still had not thought of a way to get into Robert Forbes's study.

A gentle commotion was heard outside, and then the maid admitted Elizabeth Malton, a mutual acquaintance of theirs, into the drawing room.

"Elizabeth!" Rose stood gracefully. "How lovely to see you."

The maid took Elizabeth's outer things and left the room, and Rose poured more tea. Margaret saw—and took—her only chance.

"I must not stay any longer," she said, trying to keep her voice bright and airy even though she feared it trembled. "But you must not disturb yourselves, with Mrs. Malton having only just arrived. Don't bother to summon the maid, Rose. I can surely see myself out." With a quick, charming smile to emphasize her point, Margaret turned towards the door before Rose could insist otherwise, as she would undoubtedly do as a gracious hostess.

She barely heard the other women's surprised farewells over the hard thudding of her own heart. The entry hall of the mansion was empty and silent, save for the murmur of voices from the room she had just left, closing the door behind her.

Several other doors led off the hall, but Margaret had no idea which one might be Robert Forbes' study and she knew she could not afford any margin of error. What if she opened a door to a room that was occupied? She would have absolutely no excuse.

Taking a deep breath, she crossed the hall and turned the brass handle of one of the doors. It opened with a tiny squeak, making Margaret's blood race. A maid might come by at any moment and ask her what she was doing. She peeked in, and saw what looked like a small morning room. Quickly she closed the door and tried the one on the other side.

It opened into a room with rich, crimson drapes and a large walnut desk scattered with papers, a room that could only be Captain Forbes' study. Margaret breathed a sigh of relief and slipped in, quietly closing the door behind her, hardly daring to believe she was creeping about in such a way.

She tiptoed quickly to the desk and began to examine the papers lying on top of it, trying not to disturb them. She had assured Henry that if she were caught in such a position as this, she would merely be embarrassed, but as Margaret picked up one paper and scanned it before turning to another, she knew she was taking a greater risk than that. She would be utterly ruined socially, and perhaps even worse, especially if Robert Forbes were involved in anything of a private or possibly illegal nature. Was she in actual physical danger? She did not know.

Of course, the opium trade was not illegal in this country, she reminded herself. Men engaged in it proudly enough, and some had even published pamphlets extolling the benefits of the drug as well as the trade. Yet Zexu wanted names and no matter how many pamphlets were printed in this country, Margaret doubted such men wished the High Commissioner to know them personally, or the movements of their ships and their cargo.

She reached for another sheet, saw this letter was from Russell & Company, one of America's great trading houses in

Canton. Robert Forbes, she saw, was intending to take over its leadership.

> With her breath held, Margaret read the rest of the letter. *As respects Opium I must take all the blame in going as far as we have… I am mortified that the quantity that will go out in the spring so far surpasses your wishes, and considering the danger we find ourselves in.*

He had, she saw, placed an order for one hundred and fifty thousand pounds of opium, to be smuggled into Canton. Surely this was enough proof? Her hands trembling, she folded the paper, intending to slip it into her reticule. Then she heard male voices outside the door, and she tensed, frozen behind the desk as she watched the door handle inexorably turn.

*

Moulmein, Burma

It had been a courtship like no other, although Isobel hardly knew whether to name it as such. Not, she acknowledged, that she'd ever truly been courted. Her friendship with Ian Campbell, poignant as it had been, could not be counted as such. And yet over the last few weeks, as she had come to know Mr. Braeburn—he had asked her, when they were alone, to call him Jack—a courtship it had been, both strange and sweet.

Their conversations had sometimes been stilted, sometimes full of laughter, as they'd navigated this bizarre turn of events that found them contemplating marriage without even knowing the other person at all. Jack had asked her to quiz him on all matter of things, and Isobel had taken him at his word, firing questions at him about his home, his family, his childhood, along with his interests, his thoughts, his dreams. The Judsons had left them alone in their sitting room on many occasions, smiling faintly but saying nothing.

At first Isobel had worried how they would fill that endless hour, yet soon enough she found the minutes flying by, and that one short turn of the clock's hands became the highlight of her day. John was sober-minded when it came to missions, but he had a wry sense of humor and a lightness of speaking that warmed Isobel's long-frozen heart.

And yet she did not fear he was shallow or capricious, for he'd talked honestly and painfully of his dead wife, and how much he had loved her.

"And yet," Isobel had been emboldened to ask one evening, as the cicadas chirruped outside and a bird gave its mournful evening cry, "you believe you could... love again?" She blushed beet-red at the impudence of the question, but Jack's expression only became thoughtful as he cocked his head to one side and considered the question.

"I believe I could," he finally said quietly, his gaze meeting hers with unflinching implication, and Isobel thrilled to the words.

The last few weeks had held more activity than courting; Mrs. Judson had quizzed Isobel on the school in Serampore, and, heartened by what she had heard, had wasted no time in beginning a school for girls, right in the sitting room of the Judsons' house. They had no primers or slates, and the four little girls who attended on that first day spoke not a word of English. Sarah Judson spoke competent Burmese, and Isobel was learning more every day. Mr. Judson was quite insistent that all who served as missionaries must learn the language; he himself had spent the first eight months of his time there, studying Burmese for twelve hours a day.

Soon Isobel was enjoying her morning spent teaching as much as she was that sweet hour with Jack. A month had slid by without her even realizing.

"You seem content," Sarah remarked one day, when the girls had filed out of the school and they were tidying up the sitting room.

"I am," Isobel agreed with a smile. She had recaptured that sense of settledness in herself that she'd experienced so briefly in Serampore, and she was glad.

"And you are… hopeful?" Sarah queried with a small smile, and Isobel blushed and ducked her head.

"I am," she said again, hardly daring to confess such fragile, unspoken hopes, for she had been disappointed time and again in the past. What if her friendship with Jack came to nothing? Hope, she thought, was a dangerous emotion, lifting one's spirits only to send them crashing down again.

"And I believe you have reason to be," Sarah returned, smiling more widely, and Isobel's hope-filled heart fluttered in her breast.

"You do?"

"I can say nothing more now," she warned her. "But I believe it is only a matter of time."

Isobel turned away, feeling an instinctive need to hide the naked yearning she knew must be plain on her face. She hoped Sarah was right. Even now she hardly dared to believe her friend's words. Could this be the time she found happiness—and even love—at last?

*

Prince Edward Island

Harriet tapped her foot to the rhythm of the fiddle being played in one corner of the Andersons' swept barnyard. The Scottish community was having a ceilidh in celebration of spring, and nearly everyone had come along to join in the merriment.

Harriet's heart was light as she looked around at her neighbors and friends; Allan was talking with a few other farmers, and he looked hale and full of health, the husband she remembered rather than the pale, drawn man he'd been through the winter. Perhaps he'd just been tired, she thought with a ripple of relief. Winters did take their toll in such a harsh country, with the endless cold and snow. Now it was finally warm, the spring air almost balmy.

Harriet watched Anna and Archie cavort around the dancing couples with a smile. Her children were like little lambs, gamboling about, grateful to be released from winter's clutches. With a pang, she imagined how Maggie would enjoy an occasion such as this. There were surely a few farmers' sons who might have had their eye on her for a partner, and Harriet knew her daughter would have enjoyed the attention as well as kicking up her heels. Harriet suppressed a sigh. She missed her daughter, her ready smile and easy companionship that made the long days of chores and cooking fly faster.

She'd be home soon, she consoled herself, now that Henry had returned from China and the school year was almost over. Harriet had already written the letter asking for Maggie's return in June; all that remained was for Allan to arrange the passage.

"Care for a dance?" Allan had left the group of men he'd been chatting with and now stood in front of Harriet, his dear, weathered face creased into a smile she knew so well and loved even more.

"I certainly would, Allan MacDougall," Harriet replied with a teasing smile. "In truth I was wondering when you would ask."

"After nearly twenty years of marriage, I didn't think you'd have to wait for me to ask," Allan replied as he took her arm. "But here I am, asking. May I have a dance with my lovely young wife?"

"I don't know about the young part," Harriet answered with a laugh. "But yes, you may."

Her heart felt buoyant with happiness as Allan took her in his arms and they joined the happy group sweeping about the barnyard in a waltz, dust swirling in the air.

"You look as bonny as you did when I first asked you to wait for me," Allan assured her as they danced among the other couples. "Back at Duart Castle, all those years ago."

Harriet laughed and shook her head. "Away with you. I know there's more gray than red in my hair now."

"When I look at you, I still see that young woman willing to stand faith for me," Allan answered in a low voice, and Harriet could not answer, her heart brimming with both happiness and a bittersweet sorrow. The years had been both hard and kind; they'd endured much, but they'd endured it together. Allan, she knew, had never been one for flattery or easy compliments, and she hadn't minded. She'd always liked his plain speaking, yet now she heard a heartfelt sincerity in his voice that left her quite speechless.

"I shall stand faith for you as long as I live, Allan MacDougall," Harriet said when she finally trusted herself to speak. "Wherever we are."

As he whirled her around the yard, Harriet's mind drifted through the years that had brought them here. She and Allan had always been childhood friends back on her home island of Mull, but when Allan's family had emigrated to the New Scotland, Upper Canada, Harriet's faith in both Allan and God had been sorely tested.

Years had passed before she'd received a letter from him; it had been the machinations of others rather than the fickleness of Allan's heart that had caused Harriet to suffer that silence, and her heart had, in its pain, nearly gone its own wayward path. She'd almost married another, and thanked heaven daily that she hadn't gone so far as to say the vows.

When she and Allan had finally found each other in a lonely cabin near Red River, out west, she'd known God had always meant them to be together. And together they were and would be for as many years as God saw fit to grant them.

The fiddle ended its merry song and with consternation Harriet saw Allan put a hand to his chest. His face was flushed, his eyes bright, and he rubbed his chest with a wry smile.

"No matter how I might wish it otherwise, I'm not the young man I once was, even if you still look the same. Truth be told, I'm as breathless as if I'd been pitching hay all afternoon."

Harriet tried to quell the sudden churning of fear she felt in her belly at how flushed he looked, his breathing raggedy. And only moments ago she'd been resting sweetly in the knowledge that her husband seemed hale again. She slipped her arm through his as they left the cleared yard.

"Come have a cup of cider with me," she told Allan. "I would fain sit down myself."

Allan nodded, and didn't even protest when Harriet led him to a wooden bench and went to fetch their cups of cider herself. *He's just a bit out of breath, that's all*, she told herself as she dipped the ladle into the cauldron of steaming apple cider, fragrant with cinnamon. *And neither of us is getting any younger, no matter what foolish flattery Allan might tell me.*

She had just turned around, two tin cups in her hands, to return to Allan when a sudden cry rent the air and stopped the lively chatter all through the yard. Harriet felt her heart lurch right into her throat, and the hot cider spilled over her hands as she started forward.

A space had cleared around the bench where Allan had been sitting, except he wasn't seated there now. As Harriet hurried forward her heart seemed to stop beating altogether.

Allan had collapsed and was lying unconscious on the ground.

CHAPTER TWENTY

Boston

"One moment, Malton."

From behind the heavy damask drapes she'd bolted behind when she'd seen the door handle turning, Margaret could hear Robert Forbes moving around his study. She stared at the letter clenched in her trembling hands, and willed her legs not to shake. If she were discovered now, there could be absolutely no excuse whatsoever, not even the flimsiest pretext! She was hiding behind the drapes, a letter in her hand, as condemned as she could possibly be in such a situation.

But if Forbes found her here, she would be ruined; Henry's business could very well be ruined as well. They might have to leave Boston altogether. She had risked everything she held dear, and for what? A piece of paper whose value was not certain? It seemed absurd that she had attempted such folly, that she had thought herself capable of it. She'd wanted to be an ardent reformer again, and to help the husband whose strain and worry had made her ache, but to come to this…! At least she'd had time to hide behind the drapes before the door to the study had opened.

Robert Forbes continued to shuffle the papers on his desk and Margaret heard another person enter the room; Mr. Malton, Elizabeth's husband, she supposed. No wonder the woman had called on Rose Forbes! She had been foolish not to realize.

What if the men stayed in the study to discuss their business? She might be stuck here for hours, and how on earth would she extricate herself without notice when—or if—the time finally came? Feeling sick with nerves, she closed her eyes and pressed back against the wall, fighting a most unwise urge to laugh wildly in her near-hysteria.

The men spoke for a few minutes about various business matters, although Margaret could barely take in what they were saying. Her legs felt like water and her heart was pounding so hard it hurt to breathe. She tried to take quiet, shallow breaths, afraid some small movement or sound might alert the men to her presence, and then what?

Then she heard the chair creak as Robert Forbes stood up—or sat down?—and finally, finally the door opened and closed again with a decisive click. Was she alone, or was it just Malton who had left? Margaret waited, holding her breath, yet the room remained utterly silent. Finally she dared to peek around the edge of the curtains, and saw, to her great relief, that the study was empty, save herself. She let out a rush of breath as she sagged against the wall. The study was blessedly silent.

Still, she counted to a hundred before she dared move from behind the drapes, just in case one of them returned. Her fingers trembling, her hands clammy, she folded the letter from Russell & Company and forced it into the small confines of her reticule. Then, her heart still pounding, she went to the door.

The wood-paneled door was thick and muffled any sound from the entrance hall. Margaret knew she was taking a great risk in opening it even a crack; if anyone, maid or mistress, was out there, it would be impossible to explain her presence. She'd excused herself some time ago—she did not even know how long. Half an hour? An hour? In any case her presence would be inexcusable.

She pressed her ear against the door and heard only the muffled ticking of the grandfather clock. No creak of floorboards, no murmur of voices. Holding her breath, she opened the door a tiny crack—and saw no one. She forced herself to open it further, and when with relief she saw the silent emptiness of the hall, she slipped out and made for the front door. Her legs felt hollow and weak and she prayed they could carry her the last few steps to safety. She grabbed her cloak and bonnet from the stand and had just turned the handle when she heard the doors to the drawing room open, and Elizabeth Malton's carrying voice. Almost wildly she wrenched open the door and slipped through it out into the blessed freedom of the street.

She knew she wasn't safe yet, though; she had not taken the carriage that morning, as she had not wanted its presence to alert Rose to her prolonged stay in the house. If Elizabeth Malton were to come out now, she would certainly remark on her presence. Her heart still thudding, Margaret walked as quickly as she could without attracting unseemly attention down the street, past townhouse after gracious townhouse until she was well on her way to the Back Bay and home.

It was only when she was safely ensconced in her own drawing room that her hands finally stopped their shaking and her heartbeat began to slow. She called for tea and sank into a chair, wobbly and weak-kneed with relief.

The door opened and she jerked upright, still far from calmed, then laughed self-consciously as she saw Henry come into the room.

"You look as if you have seen a ghost," he remarked. "Did I startle you?"

"My nerves are a bit strained," Margaret admitted. "But… I hope this might be of use to you." She pulled the folded letter from her reticule and handed it to him, her gaze eagerly scanning his face as he read it silently.

A frown settled between Henry's brows as he absorbed the contents of the letter. "Forbes is taking on Russell & Company?

That's been kept quiet… one hundred and fifty thousand pounds of opium! Good heavens." He lowered the letter to subject her to a penetrating stare. "But where did you get this, Margaret?"

"Is it any use?" she asked, deciding to ignore his question for now. "Will it appease Zexu?"

Henry's frown deepened. "You're avoiding my question. I told you I did not want you to put yourself in any danger—"

"And I told you I could help, if I deepened my friendship with Rose Forbes. You knew I was calling on her today."

"Yes, but I did not actually believe you would go snooping…! Is that what you did? For I doubt Mrs. Forbes handed you this letter as you took tea."

"Indeed she did not. I found it on Captain Forbes's desk."

"Margaret!" He shook his head, looking as if he wished to scold her for such foolhardiness, but then he broke into a smile instead. "You are a marvel," he said, and drew her up from the chair and into her arms. "And I pray this will appease Zexu. It is certainly more information than he had before, and it might be enough to release my crew."

"I pray it is, Henry."

"To think of you tiptoeing around Forbes' study!"

"It was but a matter of a moment," Margaret replied. She would not tell him of hiding behind the curtains, or Forbes and Malton coming in and almost catching her. Not yet, at any rate.

Henry drew her closer. "What would I do without you?" he murmured as he lowered his head for a kiss.

"Pray you never need find out," Margaret answered, and kissed him back.

*

"Resign?" Ian stared at the General Chief of Surgery in numb disbelief. He knew his reputation had suffered since the failed experiment in Bulfinch Theatre, but he had not been expecting this.

"You must see the sense of it," John Collins Warren answered. "Our hospital depends on several charitable benefactors. We cannot be seen to have the least thing to do with notoriety or scandal."

"But…" Ian licked his lips, his mind spinning. It had been three weeks since Horace Wells had attacked him outside his home, and his chest still ached where he'd been stabbed. Yet now his heart ached far worse, for the thought of leaving the hospital, his career ruined, filled him with both grief and shame. "Wells was deranged, sir. Quite out of his mind. He had nothing to do with me—"

"Nonsense, Campbell. He was your colleague. Have you not been haring off to Hartford to work with him at every opportunity?" Warren's eyebrows rose from behind his spectacles and Ian felt himself flush.

"We had a professional association, it is true, but that connection was severed when—"

"The connection was well known," Warren cut him off. "And so you can no longer be associated with this hospital." His superior spoke with an ominous tone of finality. "I will give you a reference. That is, I am afraid, as much as you can hope for, considering these unfortunate and unpleasant circumstances."

"But…"

"I'm sorry, Campbell. You had promise, to be sure. But it ends here. There is always private practice, after all."

A few minutes later, Ian stood out on Fruit Street in front of the iconic Bulfinch Theatre where Wells had performed his attempted surgery months ago now.

On that fated morning, Ian had been full of both hope and fear, yet still believing the best was yet to come. Needing to believe it—and now what did he have? He was without a position, a purpose, and he could not bear to return to his home at such an early hour and confess to Caroline the extent of his shame and ruin.

Over the course of his recovery, they'd drawn closer, but Ian nevertheless now chafed at the thought of revealing to her how low he had now fallen. The issue of whether he used her uncle's money for research had become moot, ridiculous—who would take him, a disgraced doctor without position, seriously? There would be no research now.

The spring morning was fine and balmy, the cherry blossoms bright pink puffballs framed by an achingly blue sky. Ian found himself wandering the streets of the city he had come to call home, the city he loved, recalling those first years as a fearful boy under Henry Moore's protection, and then as a young medical student full of daring and ambition—and finally a young man, swept away by Caroline Campbell's fresh beauty.

He ended up in Boston Common, remembering how cows had once grazed where society matrons now walked, their full skirts brushing beds of tulips. How changed the world was, and yet still it had not changed enough. Some things, he thought desolately, felt as if they would never change, for again he had failed, and fallen from grace, just as he had as a foolish boy. He was still as without resources or hope as he had been as the fifteen-year-old who gambled away his family's farm and future on a reckless act of what he'd thought had been manly authority.

He'd been a fool then, and he was a fool now. What hope did he have, what hope at all? Ian lowered his head, closing his eyes against the sense of despair that threatened to crash over him. What could he do now? Where could he go? He could see no way forward at all.

"Ian?"

Ian tensed, and then glanced up to see Caroline coming towards him, her face drawn in a frown of confusion. She looked lovely in her fashionable gown, her hair dressed in clusters of curls, her blue eyes wide with concern. "I just came out to take some air. What are you doing here? Aren't you meant to be at the hospital?"

"I…" Words failed him.

She held her gloved hands out to him, her expression now one of concern. "You look deathly pale. Are you ill? Is your wound bothering you?"

He almost wanted to say yes, to dissemble and pretend that his injury was all that concerned him now. Yet as she came towards him, her hands still outstretched, he remembered the look of tender concern and love on her face when she had confessed how afraid she'd been for his life—and how much she loved him.

No matter what he had lost, he still had that, and surely Caroline's love was the most precious thing he had ever possessed. He treasured it now, and he knew he did not want to hurt her by such pointless deception.

"Caroline…" He grasped her hands. "I've been asked—forced—to resign my position."

Her fingers slackened on his and she stared at him in surprised bewilderment. "Resign? But why?"

"Because of the business with Wells. Warren doesn't want any scandal brought to the hospital's doorstep, and I suppose I can understand that. The attack was in the newspapers, after all."

"But Wells was the one who attacked you!" Caroline exclaimed. "You were innocent of any—"

"He wouldn't have attacked me if he had not known me," Ian felt compelled to point out. He could hardly credit he was defending Warren's position, yet even in his disappointment and shame he recognized the truth of it. "I worked with him, Caroline. For years."

"And he was clearly mad," she answered stoutly. She shook her head as she squeezed his hands. "There is no justice in this world, if you are to be punished for his crime."

"There is some, I hope, even if I cannot find it in this moment."

"But it is so unfair!" Ian almost smiled at how outraged his wife was on his behalf. "I shall surely write a letter of complaint." Her expression softened as she looked at him. "I am sorry. I know how you love your work."

"I am sorry for you," he answered rather grimly. "You are the wife of a man without position or resource."

"Without resource?" Her mouth curved in a surprising smile. "Do you really think so little of yourself? As for position... surely that is only temporary. You are a man of immense talent and ability!"

"Yet with a scandalous past, at least in this city." He let go of her hands to spread them uselessly. "Boston is closed to me, of that I am sure."

He expected her to blanch upon hearing such news at the very least, but she simply shrugged. "There are other cities."

"I do not know how far the talk and rumor might have spread..."

"You are not a man to be stopped by such challenges, Ian," Caroline said gently, and reached for his hands again. "But I do not believe you would be happiest chasing opportunities in Philadelphia or New York, or indeed some other city in this country."

He let her clasp his hands again as he searched her face, trying to understand her meaning. "What are you saying? Where can I go?"

She smiled with poignant and tender affection. "For almost twenty years you've been dogged—no, indeed tormented—by the past and the mistakes you feel you made then. Would not now, perhaps, be the time to finally set them to rights?"

He stared at her in bewilderment. "I do not know how I would even begin to do such a thing."

"I do," Caroline answered and drew closer to embrace him, even thought they were here for all to see in Boston Common.

"Caroline...?"

"Return," she whispered as she put her arms around him. "Let us return to Achlic."

*

Moulmein, Burma

It had become their custom for Jack and Isobel to take the hour after the evening meal to chat together in the little front parlor, and the Judsons discreetly left them alone for that sweet time. Today, however, a month after she had arrived in Moulmein, Jack asked her to accompany him on a stroll through the neighborhood. It was the first time Isobel had been so alone with him, without the Judsons nearby acting as chaperones.

The air was sultry as she stepped out into a hazy afternoon with Jack by her side. She tried to armor herself with an air of insouciance, but Isobel knew she had never been one for affecting airs and she felt a pulse of relief when John smiled ruefully at her and said, "I confess, I am a bit nervous."

"As am I," Isobel answered. "Although I don't know why." In truth she hoped she did, after Sarah Judson had given her cause to hope, even to believe. Still, now that the moment seemed to have come, Isobel hardly dared to believe in it.

He took her elbow as he guided her along the dusty street. "We've been courting, for want of another term, for nearly a month now. I am conscious, Miss Moore, of your timely concerns."

Her age, Isobel thought, glancing away. A Burmese man was herding a donkey along, switching its tail as flies buzzed around it. "Yes…" she murmured, moistening her lips, for despite the humidity her mouth suddenly felt remarkably dry.

"Not," John continued, "that they are my concerns. But I hope I am sensitive to your own needs in this matter, as in all others."

"I'm sure you are." They walked towards the mission's zayat that Adoniram Judson had built with his own hands, a place for the Burmese to meet in surroundings they found both familiar and comfortable. Isobel was barely conscious of what she was saying; words were coming out of her mouth but her brain seemed to be filled with a sudden, loud buzzing, and her senses were overwhelmed by a heightened awareness of Jack walking so solidly next to her, the serviceable cloth of his frock coat stretching across his shoulders, the dark hair curling behind his ears and on his neck.

He didn't speak for a moment, simply guided her through the busy press of donkeys and pushcarts, a ragtag group of children following their wake. "I wonder, Miss Moore," he finally inquired, "if you could see yourself in a place such as this for what might be the rest of your life?"

"A place such as this?" Isobel repeated. She pulled the hem of her skirt away from a muddy puddle, her mind still buzzing. She wished she could *think*, but she seemed only able to murmur meaningless pleasantries.

"In Burma, and indeed Moulmein, and… with me." He paused, glancing at her in bemused concern, for Isobel was simply staring blindly back at him. "I do not know what the Lord holds for my future, of course, but I have felt called to serve here for as long as He allows me to do so."

"I know that well," Isobel murmured. Jack had made no secret of his devotion to the work in this country, and she knew she herself was coming to share it.

"And so, I wonder," he resumed, stopping to clear his throat, "if you could see yourself in a similar place, living your years out here, enjoying the work you have done with the school, and more such endeavors, as the Lord wills? I know you did not come to Burma with the missionary calling that I experienced, so I am asking to make sure you are in full understanding and acceptance."

"It is true I did not come here with such a calling," Isobel answered slowly. Her mind still buzzed, even as a clearer picture of what Jack was asking was emerging from her confusion and nervousness. If she married him, she would stay in Burma, perhaps forever. She would never see her family again, or at least no more than once or twice in her lifetime. As for children... the Judsons had buried three children already, the Marshmans two, and Jack himself one. Would her own children, if she were so blessed, share such a terrible fate? Could she endure it?

She'd considered such things before, but it had been in a distant, unreal way, no more than a remote possibility, with marriage to a man she hadn't even met, a hazy and unknown figure. Now it was very real and present. And now that she knew Jack and loved him, she saw more clearly what marriage to him would entail, in all its dangers and hardships.

To live and die among a people she did not yet truly know, to combat the heat, the disease, the mosquitoes even... to sacrifice all she had known and risk everything she stood to gain, to perhaps bury her children or her husband, to risk any number of fevers or illnesses...

For the first time Isobel truly wondered if she possessed the stamina and courage to live such a life, and that to the glory of God. The comforts of Boston, as much as she'd once despised them, still held out their lingering temptations.

"Isobel?" Jack asked gently. He looked sad, as if he sensed the nature of her thoughts, as if he thought she would refuse him.

They had come to stand in front of the Judsons' zayat, with its bamboo walls and thatched roof, a place liked by the Burmese and missionaries both—a place where minds and hearts both met, as theirs could, in time.... and even now. Isobel gave him a rather shaky smile.

"You are right to ask me," she said quietly. "It is a fearsome thing to consider."

"Indeed, I know it full well, and it is not a decision to be made lightly."

"And despite having travelled this far, and that being no easy feat," Isobel continued, "I realize I had not considered the matter as properly as I should have."

Jack nodded, his gaze still full of apprehension. "Such a thing is, of course, understandable."

"You are very wise, to make it all so clear to me." She pressed her hands together, willing herself on. "And I confess my heart trembles at the thought of what might lie ahead, what suffering and hardship and even what unfamiliarity I may encounter. I am a stranger here, more than you are certainly, and perhaps more than you ever were or felt."

"You could learn," John said quietly, "if you desire it. But only if you do desire such an outcome."

Isobel gazed into his now-familiar face, his eyes dark but still glinting with that wry humor she knew she had come to love. She smiled, her heart pounding and yet also feeling wonderfully full.

"I could learn," she agreed, "and I will. That is, if… if you are asking me to. If you wish me to stay in Burma… with you."

"I do wish it," John said and to Isobel's surprised delight he sank to one knee as he clasped her hands in his. "Isobel Moore, I have come to know you and love you. Will you do me the greatest honor and pleasure of becoming my wife?"

Isobel blinked back tears as she urged him to his feet. "Yes," she said, her voice choked with happiness. "Yes, I will."

CHAPTER TWENTY-ONE

Boston

Maggie stood by the kitchen door of her aunt's townhouse, her heart beating hard, her fists clenched in both anticipation and fear. Seamus had agreed to meet her here, so that he could finally speak to her aunt and uncle about his intentions.

His intentions! Maggie hugged those wonderful words to herself, and did a little twirl on her tiptoes. Despite her nerves, she looked forward to this interview with an almost wild excitement. After Seamus's confession of love, so reluctantly made because of his sense of both place and propriety, he had, quite wonderfully, asked her to marry him. Subject, of course, to her aunt and uncle's approval, as well as that of her own parents, both which Maggie hoped would come with speed.

She refused to entertain any doubts about rejection. They had come this far… he had admitted he loved her! He wanted to marry her. Surely her aunt wouldn't fight against that?

"Maggie." Seamus appeared by the gate that led to the street and Maggie flew to him.

"You came!"

The smile he gave her was crooked, his eyes filled with both determination and uncertainty. "Did you think I wouldn't?"

"No, I knew you would," Maggie answered. "I just couldn't bear waiting. My Aunt Margaret and Uncle Henry are inside, in the drawing room."

"My boots are muddy," Seamus said, twisting his cap in his hands, and Maggie just laughed.

"Seamus! You can hardly conduct the kind of conversation you're to have in the yard here. Wipe your boots by the door, if you're so worried."

"I am worried," he said in a low voice. "You know that. I don't feel—"

"I know what you don't feel," Maggie interjected as gently as she could. "But I also know what you do. You do love me?"

"You know that I do."

"Then that is all that matters."

With a sigh and a smile Seamus drew her to him. "I pray it is so," he murmured before brushing a kiss across her forehead. "I pray it is so."

The cook and two kitchen maids were stunned into silence as Maggie led Seamus across the room and to the hall that led to the front rooms of the house. She gave them all challenging looks, daring them to say a word, and none of them did. The drawing room door was slightly ajar, but she knocked anyway, her heart starting up its relentless hammering.

"Aunt Margaret? Uncle Henry? May I—may we speak with you?"

There was a short silence, and then a rustle of paper. Margaret herself came to the door and opened it, her face tense and pale even before she caught sight of Seamus.

"Of course—" She drew herself up short, her eyes widening. "Mr. Flanagan."

Seamus bobbed his head in answer. "Good day, Mrs. Moore."

"I cannot begin to wonder what you might be doing here," Margaret said, and she sounded resigned rather than angry. "But I suppose I could hazard a guess. Come in, both of you."

Maggie came into the well-appointed room, followed by Seamus. Both her aunt and uncle looked unhappy and anxious, and Seamus hadn't even spoken yet. She supposed, as her aunt had said, his presence here was easily explained, and her hopes began to falter. Surely they could have no objection now...

"I've come to speak of your niece," Seamus began, and in his nervousness his Irish brogue was more pronounced than ever. "And my intentions towards her."

"I was not aware that you were sufficiently acquainted with my niece to have any intentions towards her whatsoever," Margaret remarked rather coolly, and Henry put one hand on her shoulder.

"Margaret, peace. Let's hear what the lad has to say, although I daresay we both know what it is."

Margaret turned to Maggie, her lips pursed. "Have you been deceiving me, Maggie?" She glanced at Seamus. "And you, Mr. Flanagan? You know what I asked—"

"Just as you know it wasn't your place to ask it," Maggie fired back before she could help herself. "And you said as much to me months ago. Please, Aunt Margaret. Listen to what he has to say."

Margaret let out a sigh as she waved a hand towards Seamus. "If I am concerned, it is for your sake. Both your sakes. You cannot know..."

"I do know," Seamus replied, "well enough. I'm not the sort of man you'd wish for your niece—poor, humble, barely educated. I know that, Mrs. Moore, I assure you."

Margaret blushed at this plain speaking. "Mr. Flanagan, I admire your honesty as well as your kindness and dignity. I always have. But yes, I would wish my niece to have better prospects than those you offer."

"But it is not your place to refuse him," Henry reminded her gently. "It is Harriet's—and Allan's."

"Allan," Margaret said softly, and shook her head.

Maggie stared at them both in confusion. She felt there was something they were not saying, yet she could not imagine what it was. "So you will listen to Seamus?" she asked.

Margaret nodded.

"I promise you," Seamus began, his voice a low rumble, "I have done nothing improper. My intentions towards Maggie are honorable. I wish to make her my wife."

Margaret stared at them both, her expression inscrutable, her face pale. Maggie felt a stirring of unease at the almost desolate look on her aunt's face.

"I'm pleased to hear of your intentions, Mr. Flanagan," Henry said into the awkward silence that had descended upon the room. "For it is certain we could use some good news about now."

"Henry—" Margaret turned away, her hands pressed to her face. "Don't tell her now, not like this…"

Maggie's fragile bubble of happiness at her uncle's words seemed to burst right then and there. She stared between the two of them in confusion. "Tell me—?"

"I'm so sorry, Maggie," Henry said gently. "Especially in light of your own happy news." He glanced at Seamus. "I believe you, Mr. Flanagan, in what you say of your intentions. It is, of course, up to Maggie's father to agree to your suit." He turned back to Maggie, his expression so very grave as she stared at him in rising fear.

"Uncle Henry… what is it you have not told me?"

"It's your father, Maggie," her uncle explained, his eyes shadowed with sorrow. "We've just received a letter from your mother this very afternoon, and I'm afraid it isn't good news. He'd had some kind of trouble with his heart, and the doctor… the doctor says his chances aren't good."

Maggie stared at him in confusion, unable to absorb what he was telling her. *His chances.* The words rattled around in her brain, unable to find any purchase.

"No…"

"I'll arrange your passage to Charlottetown immediately," Henry said. "You can leave tomorrow morning if you like."

"No," Maggie said again. She could not seem to think of another word. "No. He's still young…" She felt Seamus's hand on her shoulder, and she covered it with her own, needing his strength. "How long has it been already?" she asked, scrambling to make sense of it all. A numb shock was giving way to a far deeper sorrow—and fear. "What if he's already…" She could not bring herself to say it.

"Your mother's letter was written only four days ago," Margaret interjected. "The mail travels so quickly now, thank heaven. There's still time, Maggie. There must be."

And yet Maggie knew, as they all did, that her aunt could promise no such thing.

The afternoon seemed to pass in a blur of motion and yet also with a strange, numbing stillness. Henry left to arrange her passage; Seamus embraced her and told her he would write. Maggie couldn't bear to see him go. When would they see each other again? She prayed it would be soon.

Margaret would come with her to Charlottetown, for she longed to see her brother, too. Maggie began to pack, staring at the lovely new dresses her aunt had had made for her nearly a year ago, feeling as if they belonged to another life. Another woman.

"Dear Maggie." Margaret stood in the doorway of her room, her face filled with sorrow. "I am so sorry for your heartache now."

"And yours," Maggie returned a bit woodenly.

"I love my brother," Margaret agreed quietly. "Perhaps… perhaps your mother was overcautious…"

Maggie shook her head. Her mother would not have written so if she had not believed it to be the case. Her father was dying.

Still, she held onto her aunt's faint hope and she wondered at her father's chances as they sailed northward. She was not travelling alone; not just Margaret but Henry and little Charlotte had all come with her, as had Ian, her mother's brother, and his wife Caroline. And unexpectedly, wonderfully, Seamus had booked his own passage on the same ship, turning up at the dock with a crooked smile and sorrow in his eyes.

"If this is my only opportunity to ask your father for your hand, then I'll take it," he said, and tears filled Maggie's eyes at both the love shining in his eyes and the realization that if this were his only chance... her father really might be going to die.

Standing at the rail as the ship sailed into Charlottetown's familiar harbor, Maggie was assailed with memories of her father, all of them achingly poignant. The way he called her Maggie girl, the craggy seams of his face splitting into a wide smile, the way he silently considered a question before making his own measured answer. She had chafed occasionally against what she'd seen as his stolid, plodding ways on the farm, but she'd trusted him completely. Loved him utterly. The thought of a world where he wasn't patiently tending to his tasks seemed a terrible—and terrifying—thing.

Seamus joined her at the rail. He had kept his distance from her on this short passage, sensing her need to be with her family, although in truth she'd spoken little to anyone. But now she wanted him, and she reached for his hand as Charlottetown's familiar line of buildings, from the military fort to the lighthouse, came into view.

"'Tis a beautiful place," he said quietly, and Maggie swallowed past the thickness in her throat.

"Yes," she said softly, remembering how just last year she had wanted to escape this place. "It is." It was, she realized, home... in a way Boston never could be.

It was nearing evening by the time they drove up to the Mac-Dougalls' homestead in a hired wagon. The island was alive with spring; the horses' hooves churned up red dust and verdant fields rolled to the cloudless horizon, the sparkle of the sea visible as no more than a glimmer where violet sky met rolling, green land.

The house seemed uncommonly quiet and even empty as the wagon rolled into the yard. Maggie scrambled down from the board, barely aware of the others behind her.

"Mama? Pa?" She hurried up the weathered steps and flung open the door, her heart beating painfully hard. Blinking in the interior gloom, she took a step into the front room, which was uncharacteristically empty. Where were George, Anna, and Archie?

"Ah, Maggie, *cridhe*. I knew you'd come." Her mother came from the main bedroom, her hair falling from its pins, her face drawn and haggard even as she smiled and opened her arms to her daughter.

"Is he—is it too late?" Maggie whispered as her mother enfolded her in a tight embrace.

"No, *cridhe*. Not too late. Your father is still with us but—" Harriet's voice broke and she drew a shuddering breath. "God help us, it won't be long. I know that. The children have gone to stay with the Dunmores for a little while, but they will be back soon, to say their goodbyes."

"Oh, Mama." Maggie pressed her hot face against her mother's shoulder, tears seeping from under her lids. "I shouldn't have gone to Boston. If I'd been here, I could have helped—"

"Nonsense, child. There is nothing you nor I nor anyone could have done. It was God's will, and your father has had a good life. A very good life." She drew a little away from her, her smile sorrowful, the weight of the world on her shoulders and reflected in her eyes. "Now, Maggie, will you have tears when you greet your father? He wants to see you smile, and remember you happy."

"Oh, Mama—" Her voice choked, Maggie held her hands up to her tear-streaked face and wiped her cheeks. "I'll try."

"Good girl." Harriet went to greet the others and, drawing a deep breath, Maggie turned to the bedroom where she knew her father lay.

The first sight of him made her still right there in the doorway, realization pouring through her afresh. Her father looked like a shadow of the man he'd once been, the man she remembered as vibrant and so very alive. His hair had become lank, his face gaunt and pale against the pillow. His eyelids fluttered as Maggie approached and although he couldn't speak, he lifted one hand feebly to bid her greeting.

"Pa," Maggie whispered, and came to sit by his bed. She reached for his hand and gently pressed it against her cheek. "It's Maggie, Pa. I've come home."

He nodded, the smallest gesture seeming to take all his effort, and Maggie felt his fingers stir against her face. "It's so good to see you again, Pa. I've missed you, you know, so much. I thought I'd love Boston, but I discovered I'm more of a farm girl than I thought, or perhaps even wished to be." She let out a trembling laugh and her father's worn face creased into a lopsided smile, his eyes bright despite his weakness. "But I did find a different kind of love… one I never expected to find." She heard the door creak open behind her and knew instinctively it was Seamus who had come to find her—and her father. "I've found a man, Pa. A good, good man, a man I know you'd like and respect. And he wants to marry me."

Allan tried to lift his head, and Seamus stepped forward. "I do, sir. I love your daughter very much and I look forward to taking care of her for the rest of my life, with your permission." Seamus hesitated, but when he spoke his voice was strong and firm. "Will you allow me to marry your daughter, sir?"

Maggie gazed at her father, his smile fading as his gaze moved from her to Seamus. She knew he was, just as she was, thinking how different he wanted this to be, how different it should have been. She could imagine Seamus and Allan striding through the fields, heads bowed underneath a summer sun, two men both in the prime of their lives. Her father, after all, was only in his forties.

Slowly, once again with agonizing effort, her father nodded. Then he smiled and lifted one hand a few scant inches from the counterpane to beckon Seamus forward.

With one hand still clasped against Maggie's cheek, Allan placed the other over Seamus's hand—and tears spilled freely down Maggie's face.

*

Moulmein, Burma

It was a wedding to remember—vows said in the sitting room of the Judsons' house, and a celebration for missionaries and Burmese alike in the zayat Adoniram had built. Everyone's faces were wreathed in smiles, and none more so than Isobel's herself, her hand clasped in Jack's, her heart so wonderfully full.

At last, at last, she kept thinking. At last, and forever.

"I am so pleased for you, my dear," Adoniram said when they found a quiet moment amidst the festivities. "So pleased for you both, for I can see plainly that what might have begun as convenience has ended as affection and even love. How gracious and good our Father is, to bless us twice over." His worn face creased into a smile.

"Indeed, I agree with you, sir," Isobel answered with a smile. Now that she knew and loved Jack, she could see that what she'd felt for Ian Campbell—and even George Jamison—had been mere shadows compared to what she felt for her husband, a man who loved her with both his heart and his strength.

Some weeks ago she'd written her family to tell them her happy news, and with it she felt as if she'd severed some faint tie that had been binding her all these months to Boston, and the life she'd known there. She would not be going back. The ship's sailing that had always, in its own way, beckoned, did so no longer. She had cast her lot in Burma—with Jack, and she was glad.

With a smile Adoniram melted away as Jack came towards them. "Happy, Mrs. Braeburn?" he asked, and Isobel thrilled to her new name.

"Yes," she said, and took his hand. "Very happy, indeed."

*

Prince Edward Island

Harriet sat by the bed, her hand resting lightly over Allan's, her body aching with weariness, her heart with sorrow. Maggie and the others had arrived two short days ago, and already Harriet sensed this might be her husband's last.

She gazed down at his dear face, her heart knowing every line and crease. She wanted to imprint this moment, this memory, on her mind forever, to be able to recall when Allan was still alive, and loved her. And yet there were so many other memories to recall and treasure—when he'd asked her to wait for him, by Duart Castle. How angry and hopeless she'd felt at his leaving, and yet back then they'd still had their whole lives in front of them. She would trade places with that fiery girl now, and live it all over again if she could. If only they could…

"Harriet…" The rasp of Allan's voice had shock jolting through her. She'd thought him past speech, past knowing she was there.

"Allan, oh, Allan."

"It's the end for me, *mo leannan*. Heaven feels very near."

A tear slipped down her cheek as she gazed at him, the faintest of smiles curving his mouth. "Heaven will be a better place for you being there," she managed, although it took all her strength not to break down into sobs.

"Aye, and I'll be waiting for you there." He reached for her hand, and she clung to his, pain-wasted one.

"Allan…"

"We've had a good life, Harriet, my love. I… I never regretted any of it." His voice came in shudders and gasps as he struggled to say what was on his heart. "Never wanted any other."

"Nor I, not ever," Harriet vowed.

"It was a lot I asked of you… all those years ago. To wait… how angry you were with me!" He chuckled, a dry, rasping sound.

"I shouldn't have been angry, Allan. I was glad to wait. Honored..."

"Ah, lass," Allan said with a chuckle, "you should have hit me over the head with your saucepan. What a... what a proud young fool I was."

"A fool I loved, then," Harriet returned fiercely.

"As I loved you, and always will." He smiled and squeezed her hand, a pressure Harriet could only just feel. "Never doubt that. Never forget it."

"I won't."

"The farm..."

"Seamus and Maggie are going to work it, along with George." Harriet told him. "Never you worry about that."

"Good." Allan nodded, sagging back against the pillows as his eyes fluttered close. "That is good." Harriet watched him, sensing his strength draining away from him even in this moment. How she loved him! How she would always love him, from that moment at Duart, to when they'd been reunited so turbulently in Red River, to this. This painful yet beautiful reckoning that every soul had to face. "I am a blessed man," Allan said softly as his fingers slackened on hers. "A blessed man indeed."

His hand fell from hers and as Harriet watched him with all the love she'd always felt in her eyes, her beloved Allan slipped gently from this world into the next.

*

Isle of Mull, Scotland

Dawn broke over the horizon, the placid surface of the sea shimmering with golden light. From the highest point on the property Ian could see the stretch of smooth sea, and in the distance the dark mound of Lady's Rock by Duart Castle.

The wind ruffled his hair and the late summer sun was warm on his face. He'd woken early, too restless and eager to wait until a decent hour to explore the land he had once called his own.

And it was still his own… even if he could hardly believe it. Achlic Farm was his again.

So much had happened in the last few months, not only for him, but for his whole family. Soon after arriving on Mull, he heard the tragic news that soon after the family had been reunited, Allan MacDougall had died with his wife Harriet by his side. Maggie and Seamus had married and settled there on Prince Edward Island, with Seamus taking over the farm, helped ably by George. Harriet stayed on with her children, glad, Ian suspected, of the company and support.

Henry had returned to China, and although there had been no word yet, Margaret seemed confident of his return, along with his crew, on the *Charlotte Rose*. She continued to teach at the First School, with ambitious plans to expand its classes and increase its teachers. Dear Isobel had married a missionary in Burma of all places, and from all Ian had heard from others, was very happy there.

Ian had also had news from his own sister Eleanor, who was now in Tennessee with her husband Rupert, Margaret's brother and a U.S. Marshal, en route to the Indian Territories out west, with two children living, and another expected.

Ian shook his head in wonder at the thought of his family scattered about the globe like chess pieces on an ever-increasing board. Yet, God willing, everyone had found a place, a purpose… a hope. Even him.

"Ian?" Caroline's voice was soft behind him and Ian turned to see her smiling at him as she ascended the hill, one hand resting protectively on the barely-there swell of her bump. She had told him on the ship to Tobermory that she was expecting their first child at last. "When I woke, you were gone. I thought you must be out here."

Ian smiled. "I'm here, love." He held out his hand, lacing his fingers with his wife's as they both surveyed the land they both loved.

The land Ian had once lost in his folly, his once again, through marriage to Caroline. Although she had inherited Achlic Farm upon her uncle's death, it had been rented to a tenant and Ian had never truly considered it his... not until now, when he finally felt the burden of guilt and grief fall from him and he knew he was free from the folly and sin of the past. Free to pursue a future with a wife he loved.

Ian knew he was no farmer, and he had no intention of attempting it now. He and Caroline had already discussed leasing the land to tenants while they lived in the farmhouse he'd been born and grown up in, and offered his medical services to the community. There had been no capably trained doctor on Mull, and Ian was proud to be the first one.

"It's been a long time, hasn't it?" Caroline said softly, and Ian nodded, his heart full to overflowing with gratitude and love. He could hardly believe he was here, *they* were here, with their future unfolding in front of them like a road of shining gold.

"Are you glad to be back?" Caroline asked.

"Yes, and thankful to you for suggesting we come here." He drew her to him and kissed her softly. "I had never considered it, even as the loss of it never seemed to leave my thoughts. But now we are here together, and I couldn't be happier." They both watched as the dawn light spread over and warmed the earth, and he was thankful that he, and everyone else in his family, had found their place. Their calling.

"Come," he said, and drew her away, down the hill. "Let's go home."

A LETTER FROM KATE

Thank you so much for reading *This Fragile Heart*, and I hope you enjoyed it. If you did, and want to keep up to date with all my latest historical as well as contemporary releases, just sign up at the following link. Your email address will never be shared and you can unsubscribe at any time.

www.bookouture.com/kate-hewitt

I began writing the first book in this trilogy, *The Heart Goes On*, because I was inspired by the letters between Allan MacDougall and Harriet Campbell that had been passed down through my family. By the time I came to write *This Fragile Heart*, I'd left my ancestors' story behind, and was fascinated by the things I'd discovered in my research of the time period in which the trilogy is set.

Of course, the question readers ask me the most is how much of the story is true, or based on fact. In the case of *This Fragile Heart*, much is based on fact, although I've had to alter a few details to fit my story.

As I discovered through my research, 1838–9 was a period of great change and turbulence in America's history. People were still recovering from the Panic of 1837, and the Opium War between England and China was just starting. Advances were being made in the fields of medicine and science. It was a very exciting time.

So what is fact and what is fiction? Horace Wells really did conduct an experiment with ether in the Bulfinch Dome and failed, although it took place in 1846 rather than 1839. The medical community initially doubted the use of ether as an anesthetic, and when the second experiment succeeded, John Collin Warren was quoted as saying "That is no humbug!" Wells later became addicted—although to chloroform, not ether—and was stabbed in the thigh by a prostitute, ending his life in prison.

Boston sea merchants did trade in opium and wrote pamphlets commending it. Commissioner Zexu is considered to be one of China's great moral leaders, and he did dump twenty thousand chests of opium into the sea, setting off the Opium War with England. Henry's part, however, is fictional.

Perhaps my favorite part of *This Fragile Heart* is Isobel's experience in Burma. After reading a biography of the missionary Adoniram Judson, I was eager to write about him. He was an amazing man, and his work in Burma during the often brutal time of colonialism is truly inspirational. He was a man in many ways not of his time, choosing to learn the Burmese language and wear traditional Burmese clothes rather than impose his own culture upon the people he served, as often happened during that turbulent era. The words of his speech in Boston are taken from a transcript, and he did indeed have a pulmonary infection which required a 'translator'. Regarding Isobel's story, a list of pious women who wished to marry missionaries did exist, and at the time of *This Fragile Heart* single women were not allowed to be missionaries, although this changed a few years later, thanks to Adoniram Judson. Joshua and Hannah Marshman were real people, and served as missionaries in Serampore at the time of the story. If you would like to read more of Adoniram Judson's amazing life, there are several informative biographies about him and his first wife Ann, who was also inspirational.

I hope you loved *This Fragile Heart* and if you did I would be very grateful if you could write a review. I'd love to hear what you think, and it makes such a difference helping new readers to discover one of my books for the first time.

I love hearing from my readers—you can get in touch on my Facebook page, through Goodreads or my website.

Happy Reading,
Kate

 katehewittauthor

www.kate-hewitt.com

ACKNOWLEDGMENTS

This Fragile Heart has gone through many versions, and I'm grateful for the help I've had in bringing it to its current form. I'm especially grateful to my mother, Margot Berry, who first told me about the MacDougalls when I was a little girl, and even took our whole family on a trip to Ardnamurchan to visit Mingarry Castle, then a ruin, now, amazingly, a hotel. She also passed on typewritten copies of the original letters between Harriet and Allan, and gave me a love of our family history. Thanks, Mom! I love you!

I also want to thank the Bookouture team who are all so amazing and generous with their time and expertise. Firstly, my lovely editor Isobel, who has always been so encouraging. Also my copyeditor Natasha Hodgson, whose careful insight helped me to see this manuscript through a twenty-first-century lens. Thank you also to Kim, Noelle, and Sarah, who are all so unfailingly wonderful with their marketing efforts, as well as Alex H, Alex C, Leodora, Peta, Radhika, and many others whose time and talents invested in this book I'm not even aware of! I wouldn't want to be with any other publisher, and I am grateful to all who work so hard on my, and my stories', behalf.

Lastly, thank you to all the readers who have loved the stories of the MacDougalls and Campbells over the years. I have written many, many books, and this series has always generated the most interest and affection, so I'm very grateful that readers have resonated with my ancestors' story almost as much as I have. I hope to write more about the MacDougalls, Campbells, and Moores one day, and discover where their adventure-filled lives take them!

CPSIA information can be obtained
at www.ICGtesting.com
Printed in the USA
BVHW032343010321
601410BV00025B/204